The woman could speak to him only via voice transmission, but Odo still felt quite certain that it was really her. It had been the sound of Kira's voice that had finally brought her identity back to him those few years ago.

"So, will you help me, Constable?"

"I don't know," he said. "I still don't understand why you've come to me."

"Because I trusted you once before, Odo, and I want to trust you now. I believe that ultimately—despite your position, I mean—you are on our side."

"I'm on nobody's side," Odo said firmly.

"If that's true, then why did you help me before? Why not just arrest me?"

"Because," he said, not immediately sure how to follow it up. "I . . . suppose I regarded you as an individual, in need of help. It wasn't your cause that provoked my sympathy—it was just . . . it was just . . ."

"What?"

"I don't know," Odo said. He really didn't know. It was true that he had helped her once, and it was therefore true that he had helped the Bajoran resistance movement once, too. But he'd been much less experienced then—he had been reacting to his immediate circumstances without thinking through the consequences.

"You're lying," the woman said. *"You knew the Cardassians were wrong then, and you know it now."*

"Do I?" Odo said, trying to sound threatening, but it fell flat.

"Yes, you do. You're not one of them, Odo. You're one of us."

STAR TREK®
TEROK NOR

DAWN OF THE EAGLES
2360–2369

S. D. Perry & Britta Dennison

Based upon STAR TREK
created by Gene Rodenberry,
and STAR TREK: DEEP SPACE NINE®
created by Rick Berman and Michael Piller

POCKET BOOKS

New York   London   Toronto   Sydney   Kendra Valley

Pocket Books
A Division of Simon & Schuster, Inc.
1230 Avenue of the Americas
New York, NY 10020

First Pocket Books paperback edition June 2008

POCKET and colophon are registered trademarks of Simon & Schuster, Inc.

For information about special discounts for bulk purchases, please contact Simon & Schuster Special Sales at 1-800-456-6798 or business@simonandschuster.com.

Cover art by John Picacio; cover design by Alan Dingman

Manufactured in the United States of America

10   9   8   7   6   5   4   3   2   1

ISBN-13: 978-1-5011-2179-1
ISBN-10:   1-5011-2179-0

For Britta, who works harder than me
—S. D. P.

For Lucy and Ruth
—B. D.

Acknowledgments

S. D. Perry would like to thank Paula Block and Marco Palmieri; James Swallow and all the *Trek* writers, past and present; her marvelous husband, two perfect kids, and the lovely ladies at the School of Autism who keep the faith. And again, thanks to Britta.

Britta Dennison wants to thank anyone and everyone who contributed to the *Star Trek* wiki sites, along with Marco Palmieri, Paula Block, James Swallow, and everyone who has contributed to the *Trek* universe. Thanks to my family, especially Thad. Thanks to S. D. Perry, who prevents me from friendlessness and joblessness, and to every teacher I've ever had, with the exception of my ninth-grade algebra teacher.

OCCUPATION YEAR THIRTY-THREE

✦   ✦   ✦

2360 (Terran Calendar)

Prologue

Opaka Sulan was silently watching the landscapers as they worked under the direction of Riszen Ketauna, an artist from a nearby village in the Kendra Valley. She stood at the edge of a covered porch, one of the more recent additions to the shrine, and looked out at the patch of land that had been cleared of brush, trying to envision the finished product as Ketauna had described it. She had no doubt that the gardens would be beautiful within a year or so. But while she appreciated Ketauna's hard work in planning the aesthetic of the grounds, she was concerned about the use of resources. She couldn't help but worry.

Ketauna called out orders and encouragement to those who surrounded him on the crumbly blackness of the newly tilled soil. Later, they would break for what amounted to a feast, soup made from *porli* fowl and *kava* root, fresh berries, iced *deka* tea. One of the workers had gifted the new shrine with a sizable coop, and there had been eggs and meat for weeks now. It was a sunny day, the land bright with it, and Opaka struggled with a sense of guilt that they should have so much when their world was so troubled. The Cardassians had only tightened their grip since the resistance had truly begun to fight; elsewhere, she knew, Bajorans were hungry, were suffering . . .

She closed her eyes for a moment, praying that she

would not take her own blessings for granted, that she would always be grateful for what she had. Besides, as Fasil was often quick to point out, they had to eat, too. Feeling guilt over that would feed no one.

She found Ketauna on the field. He was dressed in shabby and rough clothing like the volunteers around him. He had his back to Opaka as he bent to assist a woman who was planting a large rubberwood sapling. After a moment under Opaka's gaze, the artist cocked his head and then turned, as if he had felt Opaka looking at him. He shaded his eyes with his hands to block out the midday brilliance of B'hava'el.

"Your Eminence," he called up to her, waving. He started toward her, his expression as bright as the day. "I am pleased with the way the gardens are beginning to come together."

Opaka nodded to him, putting her hands together underneath her robes. "Yes, Ketauna, it's going to be lovely." She walked down the steps from the porch to speak to him, a friend of hers since long before she had been named kai—and one of those who had accompanied her when she had recovered the last Tear of the Prophets, that which was believed to be the lost Orb of Prophecy and Change, missing since the time of Kai Dava. The Orb was safely hidden now, looked after by the monks who presided over the shrine at Ashalla. Opaka visited Ashalla when she could, but she did not do as much traveling now as she might have liked; her health would not permit it. In the past six years, she had come to spend more and more time at this location, a place that remained hidden from the Cardassians' attention, nestled as it was in a remote location between two provincial boundaries.

Opaka was reluctant to commit herself to a single place, but she had to admit that she was not getting any younger; her aging body would not sustain the nomadic lifestyle to which she had been committed when she had first begun to preach. But there was no small measure of selfishness in her acquiescence to allow this place to be constructed, for if she remained here, she would be closer to her son, Fasil, a resistance fighter who lived in nearby Kendra. It was generally understood that this place, in addition to being home to Opaka, was a place of sanctuary for the freedom fighters of Kendra, Opaka Fasil among them.

Ketauna bowed slightly as they met. "I would offer no less to the shrine that will become home to the kai."

Opaka hesitated, and then smiled. "I agree that it is appropriate for the shrine to be a peaceful place, a place of respite and beauty," she said. "But . . . sometimes the extravagance seems a bit . . . brazen, considering its purpose . . ."

"Oh, but, Your Eminence," Ketauna exclaimed, "you know the workers have all volunteered their time. The resources we have used in the construction and adornment of the shrine—all have come from people who gave willingly. Your followers want this place to be the most beautiful shrine on Bajor, Your Eminence—as an offering to the Prophets who watch over us. It will belong to *all* of your followers, Opaka. To all of Bajor."

Your followers. She still never knew quite what to do with herself when she heard that. She nodded her concession instead. The shrine was nearly finished, and there was little reason to squabble over the particulars of it now.

I am not the potter, but the potter's clay, she thought randomly, watching Ketauna return to work. While she was grateful to the Prophets for Their many blessings, it was difficult at times to know that so many looked to her for guidance. She could only speak her heart, and hope that the men and women who listened to her would venerate the message rather than the messenger.

Ever since her vision, which had revealed to her the hidden Orb, there had been others. Of late, she'd had a recurring dream that had begun to intrude upon her waking time. A man's name had been spoken repeatedly by various shadowy figures in her visions, a name unknown to her. She had not yet asked anyone at the sanctuary if the name was one she should have been familiar with, trying to find it somewhere within the archives of her own memory, but there had been so many new people, so many names and faces since she'd left her home, each with their own stories . . .

Fasil joined her on the porch to watch the planting. Her son had come every few months since the beginning of the shrine's construction, sometimes for a day, sometimes longer. Opaka wished he would come to stay, but his allegiance to the cause kept him well occupied for most of the year.

Opaka slipped an arm around his waist. "What do you think of the progress Ketauna has made on the grounds?"

"The shrine will be a jewel in the wilderness," Fasil said. "As it should be."

Opaka gave him a squeeze, reluctantly letting him go. She wanted to enjoy their brief times together, but there was always an undercurrent of fear, that each visit might be their last. He did not share the details of his activities with her, but she overheard things, she listened to others talk of the resistance. The occupying forces' advantages often made the Bajoran resistance fighters seem to have a deliberate death wish—though Fasil's cell, along with a great many of the fighting Bajorans, continued to persist, and occasionally to triumph, year after year.

A third person came down the steps of the porch to join them: a ranjen who had come to live at the shrine shortly after the first structure was built here, over six years before. Her name was Stassen, and she was the daughter of one of Opaka's oldest friends and followers, a man named Shev.

"There is a traveler here, Your Eminence," Stassen said.

"A prylar. He has come on pilgrimage—all the way from Relliketh. He says he must see you."

"Relliketh!" Opaka exclaimed. "He has come a very long way." She considered. Most seekers did not know exactly where she could be found at any given time, and it was alarming to be told that someone had found her here already. Especially someone as far away as Relliketh.

"Did you ask him his name, Ranjen Stassen?" Opaka climbed the steps of the porch to enter the shrine with the young monk, and together they walked across the glossy stone floors, made of locally quarried burnished rock that had been polished mirror-smooth. Opaka could see a hazy reflection of herself, seeming to float beneath her feet as she walked. Fasil followed them not far behind, his gaunt, hollow-eyed reflection moving quicker and more cautiously than his mother's.

"His name is Bareil Antos," Stassen answered.

Opaka stopped walking for a moment to reflect on the name. Did it mean anything to her? She was fairly certain that she had never heard it, and yet it had a distant ring of familiarity. Was it connected to the name in her dreams?

"What else did he say?" she asked.

Ranjen Stassen spoke softly. "Would you like to speak with him yourself, Your Eminence?"

Opaka hesitated for a moment and then nodded, recognizing that Stassen knew her well.

"Mother," Fasil said, placing a warning hand on her shoulder, "Perhaps I should see him first. We cannot be too cautious regarding visitors . . ."

"I know, Fasil," Opaka replied, "but if this prylar knew where to find me . . . there is no sense in turning him away."

Opaka followed Stassen through the front gates of the sanctuary, her son protectively at her heels. The young prylar stood with his head slightly bowed, dressed in the saffron-colored robes of his order, his earring tilted forward with the inclination of his head. He raised his face to greet the kai, and a hesitant, nervously eager smile spread across his face when he saw her come through the gates.

"Your Eminence," he exclaimed, and took one of Opaka's hands to press his lips against her fingers.

"Please," Opaka told him, squeezing his hand reassuringly, "there is no need for such a demonstration. Tell me, Prylar Bareil, how is it that you have come to find this place?"

He bowed his head slightly once again. "I followed my own heart, Kai Opaka."

Opaka studied him, searching for dishonesty. "Do you mean to say that no one told you where to find this place, Prylar?"

Bareil looked a bit sheepish for a moment. "Well," he confessed, "I may have had a very little help . . . from the locals. I pestered many of them quite significantly—but only to confirm what I already knew was true."

Opaka smiled. "Is that right?" She could tell by his constitution that he was an honest man. There was no need to take his ear, examine his *pagh*. The sincerity of his youth and spirit were written plainly on his face. She nodded slightly to Stassen and Fasil, and they stepped back slightly. Not enough to give them real privacy, but an illusion of it.

Bareil seemed to study her in turn, his eyes alight. "You see, Your Eminence, I . . . knew that I must come to you . . . to be under your tutelage. . . . I . . . I have had a vision, Your Eminence." He bowed his head.

"A vision," Opaka said quietly. "Tell me about it, Prylar."

He continued, his words tumbling out with long-pent-up anticipation. "It told me that I must come to be in service to the kai during the time of the Emissary."

Opaka took a small step back. "What do you know of the Emissary, Prylar Bareil?" She herself had lately been reading many prophecies that concerned the Emissary, a few of which had become interwoven with items from her dreams, and she had shared her revelations with no one. A name had come to her lately, and she had begun to believe that it was somehow associated with the fabled Emissary of the Prophets, though whether the name—Kalem Apren— was the name of the Emissary himself, Opaka did not know.

"I—not much, your Eminence," the prylar said, looking somewhat embarrassed. "But . . . I was hoping that perhaps you could tell me the things that I wish to know."

Opaka opened the gate where Fasil had closed it behind them. "Yes," she said. "Perhaps I can . . . and perhaps there are some things that you will be able to tell me, as well, Prylar Bareil. Please, come inside."

Opaka could immediately sense hesitation in her son, but she touched his arm in an absent-minded gesture of reassurance, and went on speaking to the prylar. "I bid you welcome to the sanctuary of the kai." She gestured to the youth in the saffron robes, and he followed her through the gates.

"Tell me, Prylar Bareil," Opaka said as they entered the sanctuary, "have you ever heard of anyone named Kalem Apren?"

"Yes, I have," Bareil answered without hesitation. "He is one of the locals from the Kendra Valley that I spoke to when I was attempting to locate you."

"From the Kendra Valley," Opaka repeated, thinking to herself that he must be someone that she had already known before, in some capacity.

Fasil cut in. "Kalem Apren is an arbiter in the Kendra Valley," he told his mother. "He was a member of the Ministry, before the occupation—from Hedrikspool, originally. He is still well-respected among many in the region, and has taken up the mantle of informal governing."

Opaka was taken aback at her son's casual reply. It seemed Fasil had possessed the answer to her question all along . . . and suddenly, she was afraid. Sometimes, there were associations made, feelings that she'd learned not to deny in spite of the seeming implausibility of their connection. As they walked with the prylar whom she had just admitted to the sanctuary, observing him as he took in his new surroundings, she felt it strongly; the young man belonged here, she had no doubt of it, but something about his arrival, Fasil's awareness of the name that had settled into her thoughts . . .

She continued to walk and smile, but felt something inside of her closing, shuttering against the implications. Something had underscored her constant fears, lent them a credibility that went beyond the usual—that her only son might leave her soon, to walk with the Prophets.

1

Kalem Apren could have been perfectly content with his current lot in life. When he had been minister of Hedrik-spool Province, before the average Bajoran even knew that there was a Cardassian Union, there was always a part of him that resented the responsibility that came with his birthright. He had never been like Kubus Oak, who relished his power so comprehensively that it had devoured him, landed him straight into the lap of a traitorous alien presence. No, Kalem had never been one to clutch and grapple at the authority of his *D'jarra*; he had always thought himself more like Jas Holza that way, content to simply wield his title and let his adjutants do most of the actual governing.

How times have changed, he thought grimly as he wandered through the afternoon marketplace at Vekobet, in the central region of Kendra Province. Kalem had never particularly cared for Kendra, and had often wondered why the Prophets arranged it that he would be here on business when the Cardassians first showed their true colors. It had been a chaotic time, frightening, infuriating, terrifying. He had offered to help reorganize civilians in the aftermath, with Jaro Essa and some of the other Militiamen on the scene—those of the Bajoran homeguard who had not been killed or absorbed into the false Cardassian-sanctioned new government. And somehow, he had remained here for all these years. He was fairly certain now that he would die here, too, for his new wife was from Kendra, and she seemed to have no intention of leaving. What was there left for him in Hedrikspool anyway? Hedrikspool had lost more than half its population to the exodus, even before the soldiers had come; the government had effectively been taken over by Cardassian political "liaisons," with most of the older civilians falling in line and the younger running off to join the resistance or subsiding into apathy. Bajor didn't need politicians at the moment; it needed leaders.

So now that he lived out a simple life in Kendra Province, with a beautiful new wife and many friends, he could simply resign himself to having been plucked from that uncomfortable seat of responsibility and deposited here, to a time and place where a former politician's roles were much less complicated than before. He still had money and resources; though they had dwindled significantly, there was enough to keep him in relative comfort—relative to the suffering elsewhere on his world. He still had residual influence among the people here, as much for his role in quieting citizens in the aftermath of the first attacks as for his former minister's seat.

But he could not accept his lot in life. He would not. He recognized now how much he had taken his position for granted in the past—he could have done more, so much more to prevent his world's current circumstances. But there was nothing to be gained from regret; the only thing to do now was to plan the next step. Because, despite the pessimism of many, Kalem had to believe there would be a next step. It was the only thing that kept him moving.

People greeted him as he passed through the marketplace; a few even stopped to shake his hand. He met the eyes of a man about his own age, a man with a taut, malnourished visage and a pleading expression in his eyes.

Please, Minister, his expression read, *please assure me it's going to get better.* Kalem smiled at the man, saying nothing, but his expression telling him what he wanted to hear. *Just wait. Things will be different someday.* Did any of them truly believe it? Kalem knew they couldn't possibly—they simply repeated it to themselves to shut out the roaring insistence of defeat.

Passing through the marketplace, he found his way to the residence of Jaro Essa, who had been a major in Bajor's Militia before it had been disbanded. A great many were slaughtered in the early days of the Cardassian attacks, and the handful that were left put in a very quick surrender—much to the chagrin of those like Jaro, who had been in favor of a military coup since long before the Cardassians had announced their formal annexation. If only Kalem and the others would have supported his position! But there was that regret again. Nothing to achieve from it now. The Militia was a distant memory, as was any semblance of real Bajoran government; Kubus Oak and the others were a mere panel of Cardassian pawns.

Kalem represented one of dozens of former politicians and leaders who had sunk into informal law-keeping positions, men and women who had simply taken charge of things at the right time to have fallen into permanent ad hoc positions that seemed to carry lifelong terms, for who else would fill their shoes? There were no elections, no formal designations—only secret town meetings with the few Bajorans who weren't too despondent, who still saw the point in trying to maintain government at the provincial level. Time and again, the people of Kendra agreed that Kalem, Jaro, and a handful of other volunteers continued to do what they had always done—which was to prevent complete chaos from taking over in the wreckage of their cities.

He stepped to the door of a small adobe home, which opened to his knock.

"Hello, Major," Kalem said.

"Minister," Jaro replied. It was foolish, perhaps, that they kept to their old titles when they spoke to each other, but some shared grain of stubbornness would not allow either to acknowledge for a moment that it wasn't entirely appropriate to do so. Kalem entered the house, and Jaro shut the heavy wooden door behind him, first peering outside as if it would truly ensure they were safe from the prying of collaborators.

"I received the communiqué from Jas Holza," Kalem informed Jaro as the old militia leader gestured for him to sit in a cracked leather chair coated in a thin layer of dust. Jaro was a bachelor, too busy with his informal adjutant position to keep his home especially tidy.

Jaro was taken aback. "Already? I thought he wasn't due to contact us until—"

"A discrepancy with the calendar on Valo III. We still haven't adjusted it satisfactorily to coincide correctly with Bajor's. I suppose we've been too . . . *preoccupied* here to bother with such trivialities concerning the outlying colonies."

Jaro never bothered to acknowledge Kalem's acid sarcasm anymore. He sat down himself, in a chair nearly identical to Kalem's except that the seat was split open along lacy cracks, the stuffing coming out in tufts. Jaro's things had once been sturdy and expensive, but time took its toll. "What news did he have?"

Kalem frowned, feeling disgust as he related the information. "News we should have expected. Jas has managed to make himself out to be some kind of goodwill ambassador to the Federation. They have no idea what our real situation here is, and it doesn't sound as though Jas has any intention of clearing matters up for them. He's enjoying his status far too much to make waves."

Jaro nodded. "As I've been saying, Minister—we can't

rely on the Federation to help us. Perhaps it's better that we forge our plans without the consideration of fickle outsiders."

Kalem shook his head. "But if the Federation truly knew—if we could make it plain to them what the Cardassians' presence here has become . . ."

"They won't listen," Jaro said firmly. "It's possible that Jas did try to tell them, Apren, but there simply wasn't anything they could do to stop it—not within the realm of their own rigid code of sanctimonious laws. We must not pin our hopes on the Federation, or anyone else. There is only us."

Kalem resisted the urge to argue; it would get him nowhere—they had been over this many times. "What about Keeve Falor?"

Jaro sighed heavily. "What about him?" he said. "My own attempts to reach him have still been mostly unsuccessful, and you tell me that you have had a similar experience."

Kalem nodded in reluctant acknowledgment. Jas Holza was easy to reach, just as long as he wanted to be reached. He still had money, still had influence in alien trade partnerships. He still had a few warp vessels that he somehow managed to keep under the Cardassians' notice—the Union paid little attention to what went on in the Valo system, too far away to disrupt their own business ventures. But it was another matter for Keeve. Valo II had fallen into dire poverty—the people there were struggling just to stay alive, to maintain a few strained trade relationships. If it hadn't been for Jas Holza, probably the Valo II settlers would have perished decades ago. A reliable comm system was the least of Keeve Falor's worries.

"We should keep trying," Kalem said. "We should tell Jas to connect us. Bajor needs strong voices, strong leaders who will be ready to do what it takes when the time comes. Keeve is someone I know we can count on."

"*If* the time comes," Jaro said.

Kalem shook his head. "Major," he said, "we cannot think that way."

Jaro's mouth tightened. "You're right, of course, Minister," he said faintly, but Kalem could clearly detect the brittleness in his tone. They had discussed such things often, but still, the years passed and so little had changed.

It will change, though, Kalem told himself. *And we'll have to be ready.*

They talked over a few local matters—rationing their allotment of winter crops early this year, a minor boundary dispute between neighboring farms that they needed to resolve before the Cardassian "peacekeepers" got involved. After a time, Kalem rose to go, shaking the old Militia officer's hand as he left, considering the wisdom of his own dogged optimism as he stepped out into the gathering twilight. Of course, his beliefs were not far removed from Jaro's, but he could not bring himself to speak them aloud, even if Jaro could. Even if everyone else on Bajor could. There *was* logic in making preparations to guide Bajor in the aftermath of a Cardassian withdrawal, and even if he didn't quite believe that the Union would ever leave them, Kalem would keep moving, keep working to have everything ready. To stop, to hold still, was to welcome defeat.

The services at the would-be shrine had concluded some time ago, but Astraea remained behind, as she always did—sometimes to speak to individual followers about their concerns, but just as often for her own contemplations.

She had fashioned a small chamber in the cellar of this old storehouse, in the heart of Lakarian City, to be a sort of office for herself. As the guide of her faith, she needed a place where she could counsel her followers, though it had been difficult for her to accept the authority of guide from the very beginning. She had known almost nothing of the Way when she had taken on this persona, the name Astraea and everything that went with it.

The Oralian Way performed their rites now in secret, the once great faith having been reduced to the indignity of meeting in basements and back alleys, forced to communicate in codes and over scrambled contact lines as though they were common criminals. Anyone who could be associated with the Oralian Way in any capacity was immediately categorized as a wanted fugitive. Their crimes were no more serious than peaceful congregation, but Central Command had managed to paint the Oralians as dangerous dissenters whose ideals sought to destroy the very fiber of the Cardassian Union—and of course, no member of the military had any inkling of what those ideals truly were. They remembered only the threats of civil wars, and the angry public demonstrations of yesteryear, all conflicts that had been borne of misunderstanding. Modern Cardassians did not care to attribute their people's achievements to anything beyond perseverance, hard work, and superiority. But Astraea and her followers believed it was not so simple as that, and for that belief, they were pariahs.

Alone in her chamber, seated at a desk before a small computer, her monitor chimed to indicate an incoming communiqué. She started at the sound; she had not been expecting to receive a transmission so late. The followers of her faith generally came to her in person if they had a query or concern, and there were very few of those who even knew her transmission code. She knew where the call was coming from with near certainty, but still her eyes lit up with anticipation when she confirmed that the message had indeed come from Terok Nor.

The call was scrambled, as it always was, and necessitated a code to access; but once the correct sequence was tapped in, the blank density of her screen broke with a horizontal snapping of blue light that settled into the image of her most cherished friend.

The soldier's black hair was pushed back over a wide forehead that housed a pair of deeply scrutinizing eyes. His gaze flicked up and instantly softened as her countenance appeared on the screen in his office, far away on the space station that orbited Bajor.

"Astraea," he said, the timbre of his voice almost turning it into a pet name—but the name carried much more weight than just this man's affection.

"Is it safe to speak my name, Glinn Sa'kat?" she asked him, though she instantly regretted the question—he would not have spoken it aloud if it was not safe.

"I have full control over who reviews these transmissions," he assured her.

"Even over the Order?"

His lips thinned in demonstrative impatience. *"I have told you, we have nothing to fear from the Obsidian Order."*

She shook her head. "I know you think I'm being foolish, but lately I've had these feelings that I can't shake . . ."

He leaned closer to his transmission cam. *"Feelings?"* he repeated. *"Do you mean . . . like those you had before?"*

A vision, he meant. Astraea shook her head; she was not talking about the kinds of feelings she'd had just after she'd come in contact with the Bajoran artifact at the Ministry of Science. The Orb. In those days, she had still been the Cardassian scientist who bore the name Miras Vara, but that name—that identity—was no more. Miras Vara had disappeared from the Union, from her family, from her job at the ministry. She had become the Guide for the Oralian Way, and had taken on the name used by her forebears as much a title as a designation.

The guide was supposed to be a vessel for Oralius, the noncorporeal being who was said to have dictated the tenets of the faith both in ancient and modern times, before the faith was forced to go underground. Astraea did not know if Cardassian officials were familiar with the title, but she thought it best not to take any chances. It was a well-known secret that the Oralians of past generations had been systematically exterminated by Central Command. The Way was still popularly perceived as a threat to modern Cardassian sensibilities, but Astraea knew better. She believed that the Way would be essential in rebuilding Cardassian civilization someday, for she had foreseen it—she could still see it, and often did, in her dreams. The near-total destruction of Cardassia Prime.

"Not a vision," she told him. "At least, not about the Order."

The soldier nodded, looked grave for a moment. *"The Order can't decipher the encryption that I have used. Our friend has assured me of that."*

She knew that he was sure of his "friend's" loyalty, and she didn't doubt that there was at least one Obsidian Order shadow who walked the Way, whose allegiance to Oralius was greater than his allegiance to Enabran Tain, even though the aging head of the Obsidian Order inspired a fierce loyalty in many of his agents. Still, the Order troubled her—all Cardassians had a healthy respect for the Obsidian Order, and a person in Astraea's position would naturally fear them more than the average citizen.

"But you have seen something, then," the soldier deduced.

"Yes," she confirmed, thinking upon her recent dreams. "A Bajoran. A religious man. I don't know his name, but I have a picture of where he might be. It is not far from the place where I experienced my first visions of Bajor . . ."

"Kendra," the soldier said.

"As you say." Astraea knew nothing of Bajoran geography, only what she saw in her visions.

"What have you foreseen regarding this man?"

She paused, trying to put into words the things she had

sensed about the Bajoran. She was often frustrated by the cryptic "awarenesses" she experienced; even after years of working to cultivate the ability, her impressions were regularly less than enlightening. But then, the Way was a path, not a goal; Oralius taught that many truths were subjective. It was a lesson she continued to struggle with.

"Cardassia needs him. He will bring peace between the two worlds someday, though I don't know when it will happen." He seemed to be waiting for more, and she pursed her lips. "That is all," she told him. "I'm sorry."

The soldier nodded, patiently accepting the fragmentary nature of her prophecies. *"You must tell me if you see anything more."*

"Of course," she said. "Now. What do you have to tell me, Glinn Sa'kat?" It was clear from his expression that he had information. More often than not, his transmissions bore news that frightened her. While the two shared a mutual affection that sometimes seemed to border on intimate, at least for her, he did not call her without serious motive. Her pleasure at seeing him was always tarnished by what he had to say.

"Our friend tells me that the agent who has been assigned to seek out the Oralians has finally found the object that you hid at the Ministry of Science."

Astraea felt her heart sink. While she believed that the so-called Orb would remain silent for anyone who was unworthy, she also feared that whoever wielded it would undeniably have access to a great source of power, a means of controlling others who sought it. If the Obsidian Order took hold, the Orb would be impossible to recover.

"It will reveal nothing for them," she said with flickering certainty.

"Nothing . . . except perhaps your whereabouts," the soldier said softly. *"The object's shipping container had a digital log, a log that clearly recorded the identification numbers of all who came*

in contact with it during its stay at the Ministry of Science. Miras Vara was the last person known to have handled that object. The Order has not yet connected the item to us, but it is only a matter of time. Our friend has very emphatically suggested that you change your location."

Astraea took a moment to catch her breath. She had just begun to grow fond of the makeshift shrine where she was currently holding services, and leaving it behind would be an unwelcome upheaval. "Where should I go?" she asked him, without rhetoric.

"You must go to Cardassia City."

"But—"

"It is the only way. The best means to stay out of the sight of the Order is to be right under their nose. Our friend is going to arrange a place in the Torr sector where you will be safe."

"But the Walkers here . . ."

"It is the only way," he replied firmly, and then he stopped speaking as his comcuff signaled. *"I must go."*

"May you walk with Oralius," she said to him, but he had already signed off.

Dukat was agitated, going over the daily output reports in his office alone. There had been a significant drop in productivity in the last few years, and it was getting markedly worse with each service quartile. The reports in front of him painted a bleak picture of whether his tenure here was going to be regarded as a success or failure; he feared it had long been edging toward the latter, through no fault of his own.

He knew that back on his homeworld, many people were beginning to wag their tongues about diminishing resources in and around B'hava'el, the star system that was home to Bajor. But it wasn't for lack of resources that the output had begun to wane. It was because the civilian government had pressured Central Command into withholding funds for numerous ventures here, ventures begun and then abandoned when the stores of minerals were not immediately as abundant as they had been decades ago, at the annexation's very start. The Detapa Council had once been nothing but a figurehead, but they were steadily gaining power, thanks in part to the family of Kotan Pa'Dar, a political rival of Dukat's for many years now. Pa'Dar was the exarch of Tozhat, a Cardassian settlement on the surface of Bajor, and he made no secret of his opinion that the Bajoran "project," as he called it, should be retired. The prefect could not disagree more, and the reports he saw in front of him were clearly illustrative of why it would be an expensive mistake to think otherwise. Pa'Dar was a shortsighted fool.

His companel chimed. One of the duty officers in operations addressed him briskly. *"Gul Dukat, this is Gil Trakad."*

"What is it?"

"Reporting, sir—the delayed shipment of mining equipment has finally arrived."

Dukat sighed heavily. "Well! How very kind of the Valerians to finally bring us our merchandise! Inform the captain that I expect a formal explanation for the tardiness of this shipment."

The young gil hesitated. *"It was not the Valerians who delivered this cargo, sir. Their ship experienced a mechanical failure and was forced to make an emergency landing in the Solvok system."*

Dukat leaned back in his chair. "I see," he said. "So, who, exactly, has brought us our much-anticipated package, Gil?"

"It . . . it couldn't be helped, sir, the ship grounded on the Solvok moon, and there are a limited number of ships that run through that system, this time of year—"

Annoyed, Dukat switched on his holoframe to have a look at the security images that cycled along the docking ring and the cargo bays. What he saw instantly made his lip curl, for a familiar-looking ship had docked, and its crew was beginning to unload its cargo. The rust-colored vessel had a bloated aft end tapering toward a much narrower front—a bit like a stubbier, backward version of a Cardassian scoutship. But Dukat knew too well the design of this courier, and he spoke with the force of a curse.

"*Ferengi.*"

Natima Lang did not particularly enjoy these assignments, interviewing soldiers as they arrived home from the conflict along the border territories. The brown-uniformed troops who disembarked from their ships at the Mekisar military base outside of Cardassia City were usually exhausted from the long journey home, not to mention the horrors they had experienced on the front lines against the Federation.

Natima knew that her world struggled to keep up with the superior forces of the Federation troops; the Federation had more sophisticated weaponry, and their ships had much better tracking and dodging capabilities than any Cardassian vessel. But then, the Federation lacked something that Cardassia had in no short supply, and that was a particular brand of pride and self-respect that Natima knew was unsurpassed in the entire known galaxy. Cardassia would fight to its last breath over those territories. Whether it was the right thing to do, however, she could not say. She only knew that she was expected to retrieve appropriate sound bites from the returning soldiers to bolster the morale of her people, and she meant to do her job.

She scanned the careworn faces of those stepping through the platform portal, their rocky features revealing little emotion beyond simple weariness. She hoped to recognize someone, anyone, from the last time she had been here. It distressed her to think of those soldiers she'd come to know in any capacity being killed and never returning, but of course it was the reality, a reality that the Information Service always had to face.

When she'd been assigned to Bajor, easily the most violent and primitive world she'd ever seen, Natima had witnessed some of the most unspeakable things of her career. She'd enjoyed the challenge, at first, but was relieved that her request for a transfer back home had finally been granted. Bajor was a cruel place, with cruel people. It horrified her to see the aftermath of the skirmishes between Cardassian soldiers and the resistance fighters on that world, but perhaps the most upsetting revelation she'd had there occurred when she had discovered that she was beginning to relate to the Bajorans on some basic level. It seemed to her the very best reason to come back home, to focus her allegiance where it belonged; but her opinions regarding the Union had never been the same after the years she'd spent on Bajor.

With a small handheld netcam, she spoke to a few soldiers, who responded to her questions brusquely but supplied her with the patriotic phrasings she expected—and needed—to hear.

"My unit paid dearly, but the Federation's losses were even more significant. We will prevail."

"Cardassia will not sleep until we have wrested what is rightfully ours from the Federation dogs."

"The families of those who have not returned can feel proud knowing that their son, husband, father, or brother gave up his life to better our world."

Natima winced a little at the last one, for there were women in the military as well as men, but Cardassia was still mired in patriarchy. Females were seldom in combat, although there were a number in command. It was generally believed that women belonged in the sciences, situated as far away from physical danger as possible, for their roles as mothers were valued more highly than any other contribution they might make to the Union. While Natima certainly didn't regret that she wasn't stationed on the border along with these returning soldiers, she might at least have liked the option. As it was, she got plenty of disdain from her male colleagues at the Information Service, who had long tried to dissuade her from covering pieces that might place her in harm's way. It was foolish, especially considering that Natima had no children—and though Cardassian women were blessed with an especially long window of fertility, Natima's window was more than halfway closed.

In this press of nearly identical soldiers she suddenly saw a familiar face, one that it did her heart good to recognize, for it was the face of her old friend, a glinn named Russol. It was always a relief to see her acquaintances return safely, but it especially gratified her to see that Gaten Russol was still alive.

She put up her hand and called to him, and he turned, along with a few others who looked to see what the commotion was about. Russol smiled in instant recognition, for the two had shared a few exchanges at various press conferences. Natima had come to believe that Russol and she were like-minded politically.

"Hello, Miss Lang," he said, bowing slightly, stepping closer. "On assignment, I presume?"

Natima nodded.

"You look rather uninterested," Russol noted. "Do you find these interviews tedious?"

Natima was taken aback at his undercurrent of irritability, not sure if he was flirting with her, but Russol then smiled so warmly that she was compelled to smile back. Perhaps he *was* flirting.

"It's worth it to have run into you," she said, feeling bold. "It's always a relief to confirm that an acquaintance has come back safely from the front lines."

"They'll never finish me off, though it's not for lack of trying." His face twisted slightly, his eyes growing distant before he refocused on Natima.

She cleared her throat, fidgeting with the netcam in her hands. "Do you have any comments that you might like to share with the Union public?" she asked him.

Russol snorted. "No," he said, and his voice was unmistakably bitter. "I suppose I would have something to say, if I thought that anyone would listen to my opinions instead of execute me for them."

Natima was shocked; she knew from their past conversations that Russol had a bit of a radical streak, but she had not expected him to state anything so bluntly. She was not sure how to respond.

From the corner of her eye, she thought she recognized another of the men that were coming across the tarmac from where the returning ships were docking. Turning slightly, she identified the features of a man whose name did not come to her right away, but his profile and expression was immediately reminiscent of quaking regret, of a time that Natima generally took pains to avoid revisiting. Bajor. Terok Nor.

Natima looked away. This was Corat Damar, the former fiancé of Veja, Natima's old friend and colleague from her days on Bajor.

She tried to turn so that Damar would not see her, hoping to avoid an uncomfortable reunion. His memories of Bajor were probably even more unpleasant than Natima's, for it was on Bajor that he had lost the woman he loved. Veja Ketan had not died, but she had been injured so severely as to render her incapable of bearing children, which, according to Cardassian tradition, made her ineligible for marriage.

In a way, Natima had always thought, Veja's ultimate fate was worse than if she had died, for although she was alive and generally well, Damar could not marry her, and Veja was very unlikely to marry anyone. Some women in her position would have taken a lover, but Veja was not the kind of woman to indulge in such tawdry dalliances, and anyway, it was clear that there was no other man for her but Damar. Natima still spoke to Veja from time to time, and had learned recently from her that Damar had married and had an infant son. Veja had delivered the news with heartbreakingly false indifference. The entire subject depressed Natima so profoundly that she wished never to think of it, let alone to speak of it. Natima was unmarried herself, but she had never been especially interested in the prospect of marriage and children. Veja's life's dream had been to raise a family. The circumstances on Bajor had taken that from her.

Natima risked a glance in the hope that the soldier had gone away, but he was there—and he raised his head and looked at her. She saw the hardness in his expression go slack for a moment as he recognized her, hidden sorrow rising to cloud his gaze. Natima could not look away now, for it would be impolite to pretend that she had not seen him. She smiled quickly, but he did not smile back, looking very much as though he intended to go on his way without acknowledging her. Though it was rude, the possibility that she would not have to speak to him filled Natima with great relief.

"Miss Lang?" Damar called.

She could not reasonably ignore him in Russol's presence, not without a lengthy explanation that she would rather not give. She nodded to Russol.

"Another time, I hope," she said lightly, and he smiled, spreading his arm in a gesture of polite dismissal. Damar strode through the other soldiers in his unit to approach her.

"Hello . . . Gil Damar," Natima said, after searching his

uniform for signs of his rank. She was surprised to see that he was still a gil, for it seemed that his military position had been rising rather quickly back on Terok Nor, over a decade ago. She remembered, then, that he had been a favorite of Dukat—until he had fallen from the prefect's good graces, following the incident that resulted in Veja's injury.

"Hello, Miss Lang," Damar addressed her, his voice reflecting an edge that indicated a pronounced dislike. He had never made a secret of his opinion of Natima, and she knew that he would not have approached her at all without compelling reason.

"I am here on behalf of the Information Service," Natima said, raising her netcam. She hoped to keep the exchange relatively free from topics that would cause discomfort for either of them. "Perhaps you would like to make a statement—"

"Do you ever speak to Veja Ketan?" Damar interrupted.

So much for avoiding discomfort. "Yes," she said, keeping her voice hard and steady. "I still see her from time to time. She works within the fact-checking division of the service now, and mostly stays out of the field. She has a little house on Cardassia IV, but then she also stays in the Paldar sector, during the cold months."

"So . . . she is well," Damar said hollowly. "She is . . . does she ever speak of me?"

Natima coughed. "No," she lied. She did not wish to continue this line of conversation. "Tell me, Gil Damar, do you have anything to say to the people of Cardassia regarding the situation in the border colonies?"

"The border colonies," he snarled. "They are a waste of Cardassia's resources. I won't miss being there."

"So, you're not to be sent back, I gather?"

"No. I'm to be made glinn next service quartile, and then I'm to join a freight crew for a shipping operation."

Natima nodded. All of Cardassia's interstellar shipping concerns were overseen by Central Command. Officer on a freight crew was still "military" work, but it was a lucrative and therefore much coveted assignment; there were subsidies, contracts, even benefits, depending on the runs. Still, there was no glory in such work.

"Well then! Congratulations are in order regarding your new rank—and your new assignment," Natima said. She could hear how brittle and false she sounded. "I hear that serving on a freighter can be an exhilarating existence—plenty of travel, meeting people, experiencing new cultures—"

"I'm sure it will suit me fine," Damar said flatly. "But Bajor is where I would rather be." He spat on the ground, as if to illustrate his feelings on the matter.

Natima stepped back from Damar, speechless and disgusted at the gesture. Why would Damar want to return to the place that had nearly destroyed him? Natima herself had vowed never to go back to Bajor if she could possibly help it. Besides the danger, there was the remoteness, the climate, the awful smells—and the dust! Natima would never forget that terrible, choking dust, from the reddish dirt that turned to mud in the humid cold, thick and crusty like wet concrete.

"I would devote my life to the pursuit and execution of the insurgents of Bajor," Damar said, his expression icy cold, completing his statement without words. *Because of Veja.*

"But . . . the Bajoran resistance movement . . . it is only getting more dangerous," Natima said carefully. "We've practically tapped out the Bajorans' resources anyway. We might as well—"

"It's not Bajoran resources I care about," Damar snarled. "It's exterminating the people who live to make Cardassians suffer. I don't know why we haven't begun using biogenic weapons in the B'hava'el system yet, but I can tell you that if I were stationed on Bajor, any unit under my command would not fail to drive those terrorists out of the dirty little caves where they squat and scheme. They are a backward and violent people, and their existence does nothing to perpetuate humanoid progress."

Natima flinched. He was wrong to suggest biogenic weapons; that would give the Federation cause to finally put an end to the Bajoran annexation. The Union was already walking a fine line between occupation and genocide—a thing that the Federation was very unlikely to tolerate, since they couldn't seem to prevent themselves from meddling in other worlds' affairs. But Natima was not comfortable arguing with Damar. It was not only because she understood his personal stake in the matter, but because her own opinions concerning Bajor tended to lean toward the dangerous. Central Command did not always bother to distinguish the subtle differences between mild dissent and high treason. Natima decided to end this encounter; though she might seem brusque in doing so, she had nothing more to say to Corat Damar. "If you will excuse me, Gil—"

"Certainly," he said, and turned abruptly away from her to follow the rest of the soldiers to the transport station, where they would be sent home to their families for a night or two before heading off to their next assignments.

Natima thought, as she watched him go, of the word he had used to describe Bajorans—*backward*. It may not have been entirely inappropriate, in certain contexts, but weren't Cardassians also backward, in their own ways? For if Damar and Veja had still wished to marry, to raise a family, why could they not have taken in an orphan child to raise as their own? Natima knew only too well the dire conditions of the orphans left behind on Bajor to fend for themselves in a hostile, alien society—not to mention those abandoned children who lived right here, in the Cardassian Union. But it would have been unthinkable for someone like Damar to defy the social constructs of what was acceptable as a traditional Cardassian family. She had dared to broach the subject with him once, and had always regretted it. Damar was a man who did not take tradition lightly, no matter how irrational it might have appeared to an outsider—or to someone like Natima, who had once managed to glean a sense of her world through the eyes of an alien observer, at least for a moment, and had not much cared for all that she'd seen.

Of the regularly stationed assignments the Obsidian Order had to offer, the surveillance post at Valo VI was easily the quietest. For those agents who preferred a little solace now and again, a short stint on Valo VI was a welcome respite. But to be sent for more than a few months was cause for concern, especially among the older agents who were not yet ready to turn in their sigil. The long-term post to Valo VI was synonymous with retirement. It may have been preferable to death, but for an Obsidian Order agent who had grown accustomed to a lifestyle of unpredictable chaos, being stationed indefinitely at a static listening facility was as near death as one could get while still breathing.

Dost Abor suspected that his own circumstances were different. He had committed no error that he was aware of to have warranted his placement on Valo VI for such a very long time, and he was far enough from retirement age that it made little sense for him to have been put out to pasture so soon. His conclusion was that Tain perhaps considered him a threat. Abor figured he had two alternatives. The first would be to prove his mettle to Tain by accomplishing a breakthrough that could not be ignored and that would guarantee his placement back in the field, where he belonged. The second would be to kill him. It was not entirely beyond the realm of possibility, though it would be something of a trick. Abor felt fairly certain that nearly every agent had entertained such thoughts from time to time, but Tain still sucked air.

This facility, housed beneath an allegedly impenetrable force field on a rather miserable asteroid, was one of many that was unknown to those outside the Order, Cardassian or otherwise. Although there had been a single security breach at this facility some years ago during which an operative had been killed, no data had been compromised, and Abor's superiors had shrugged off the incident as an inconsequential break-in by Bajoran scavengers looking for an easy target. Enabran Tain had never been particularly concerned about Bajoran comings and goings, since he, like most Cardassians, considered them to be a vastly inferior species that posed no genuine threat to the sanctity of Cardassia—unlike Gul Dukat, who couldn't even get a handle on their pathetic uprisings.

Deep in the bottommost level of the Valo VI Facility, Dost Abor had taken a moment away from the monotony of his post to answer a call from another of his colleagues in the Order, a man named Kutel Esad. Abor had been acquainted with this man since before his recruitment into the Order, when the two were both in their culmination year at school, but Kutel's needle-sharp face had changed very little in all those years. It had often been said that Kutel was old before his time, both in appearance and in outlook, and now, in late middle age, he had finally grown into his cautious nature.

"*Hello, Dost,*" his old friend greeted him. "*You indicated in your communiqué that there was some item of business you wanted conveyed to Tain?*"

"Indeed, Kutel," Abor said smoothly. "In reviewing transmissions sent from the Ministry of Science at approximately the time of the object's disappearance—"

"The object?"

Abor hesitated with some impatience. He had forgotten, of course, that Esad would not know what he was talking about without a bit more explanation. "The Orb, I mean. The object I recovered from the ministry's storeroom."

The item in question had been stolen from the Order sometime during the upheaval that followed the assassination of Tain's predecessor, and had landed in the hands of the Ministry of Science on Cardassia Prime. There it had lain, almost forgotten, except for a single report of a disturbing reaction experienced by a young scientist, many years past. The item had not been seen since, not until Dost Abor ordered a thorough search for it, which had yielded results earlier in the month.

Esad nodded now as he remembered. *"Yes, the Bajoran artifact. Tain had it refiled within the Order's collection, but we have never been able to glean anything of value from any of the so-called Orbs. I must tell you that he was puzzled why you went to so much trouble to locate this particular object."*

"The item itself is of no interest to us," Abor told his friend. "It is who last handled it that might be of some relevance."

Esad did not answer, only rearranged his features to convey dubious expectation.

Abor went on. "I have quite a lot of time to review old transmissions, messages that have been encrypted, intercepted, and then filed away to be decoded at another time. The last time I was stationed here, I happened upon an old one, sent approximately twelve years ago, that had originated at the Ministry of Science with a researcher named Kalisi Reyar. Her father is Yannik Reyar. Do you know him?"

The tight line of Esad's mouth pinched together. *"He is Enabran Tain's military go-between,"* he said briskly.

"Correct," Abor replied. "Yannik Reyar received a

transmission from his daughter regarding a matter that she felt concerned the Order. One of our tracers flagged a few terms it felt warranted our attention, but the second check found nothing of immediate interest in the transmission and filed it away to be reviewed at another time. I was the one tasked with reviewing that message to determine its relevance, and I learned something that I found to be a bit curious."

"And what might that be?" Esad's tone indicated that he was indulging his old friend.

"It seems that his daughter was the person who gave authorization for our object to be removed from the science ministry's storeroom, the last time it was taken out—before it became classified and then misplaced."

Esad nodded, but his expression still held no interest.

"That last encounter with the object coincided with an outcropping of rumor surrounding the Oralians."

Esad made a face now, expressing his disgust regarding the followers of the so-called Oralian Way. The ancient faith had supposedly experienced a resurgence in the past decade or so, a surprise to many who had previously accepted that the followers had all been killed in the settlements on Bajor, where they had been relocated prior to the annexation of that world. Modern Cardassians were not sad to see them go, for their religion was an impediment to progress, a throwback to a time of foolish superstition and a cumbersome theocratic government. Recent reports indicating that groups of Oralians had begun to meet in secret was puzzling and perplexing to Central Command. Many believed that these groups were simply comprised of young, rebellious people, experimenting with forbidden nostalgia that they did not actually understand.

"Enabran Tain is fairly certain that the rumors surrounding the Oralian Way are just that—rumors," Esad said.

"They may be only rumors, but even if they are—the

inception of those rumors coincided with the disappearance of that Orb."

Esad nodded slowly. *"Have you reviewed the files regarding
the Ministry of Science's records on the object?"*

"Yes. The last scientist to handle the object was a
woman named Miras Vara. I believe she was the one who
misfiled it in the first place."

*"The ministry claimed that it was misfiled accidentally. They
are not known for their efficiency, as anyone can attest—"*

Abor interrupted the other agent. "Miras Vara disappeared at the same time as the object. She did not misfile it
by accident, Kutel. She took pains to hide it. Now, why do
you suppose she would have done that?"

"I have no idea," the other agent replied. *"But if you have
a theory, I suggest you enlighten me, because I am sure that Tain
would love to hear it."*

Abor hesitated, deciding how much he wanted to elaborate. "She is affiliated with the Oralians," he said. "I am
sure of it."

Esad chortled lightly. *"Your certainty will not go far with
Tain. But if you can prove it, Dost, then I suspect Tain might
have reason to congratulate you."*

"I don't want congratulations," Abor said. "I want to be
back in the field, where I belong."

Esad smiled. *"Well. I will let Tain know of your, ah, suspicions, and we'll see what he has to say."*

Abor returned his smile with cordiality. "I will look forward to his reply."

2

Thrax watched a string of the little orange-hued people as they unloaded the shipping containers from the open maw of their ship's hull, making fairly efficient work of it, but Terok Nor's security chief was wary of them nonetheless. Under his gaze, one of the creatures broke away from the others and strode across the cargo bay toward him.

"I am DaiMon Gart," said the oily little man, indistinguishable from the rest of his crew.

"DaiMon," Thrax acknowledged curtly, wondering if he might have met this particular Ferengi before—their names were as similar as their ugly faces and their loudly patterned outfits. Thrax manufactured a thin smile. "It's a pleasure to do business with you, sir."

"Oh, no, the pleasure is entirely mine," Gart said eagerly. "In fact, I wonder if your commander might be interested in working out a trade agreement with my little venture. I noted that you Cardassians have been doing business with the Lissepians for quite some time . . . but did you also know that the Lissepians have been secretly tacking on a surcharge for their refueling costs? They are also notorious for overcharging their clients for unstable cargo. We Ferengi have no qualms about taking on virtually anything you want transported—even through Federation space, if necessary—and I do mean *anything*."

"Ferengi have few qualms, I've found," Thrax said mildly, though he was certain that Dukat would have no interest in striking up a "bargain" with Gart, or any other Ferengi. They were an intensely avaricious people—annoyingly so, in fact, with a reputation for deceit.

A noisy scuffle caught his attention, interrupting the flow of shipping containers through the short brigade of Gart's crew.

"Tell your men to resolve their disputes somewhere other than on my station," Thrax said sharply.

"Quark!" The DaiMon shouted. "Do your job, you ungrateful wretch, or you'll be tossed out the airlock with that load of replicated *gree* worms you've been trying to feed us!"

One of the Ferengi shouted back to his DaiMon. The man, presumably Quark, carried one end of a long shipping container, assisted by a shorter Ferengi who grunted as the brigade came to a halt. "Those *gree* worms are not replicated!" Quark protested. "I spent a fortune on them, I'll have you know!"

Another of the Ferengi spoke up. "I've had those *gree* worms, and they're not only replicated, they're awful! He's been lying on his expense reports, DaiMon!"

"Why you—" Quark shouted, dropping his half of the shipping container to lunge for his crewmate's excuse for a neck.

"Enough!" Thrax roared. "If you damage that equipment, I can guarantee that Gul Dukat will charge you double for it—and what you don't have in currency, he'll be happy to take out of your hides!" If there was one thing the security chief had learned during his years on Terok Nor, it was the effectiveness of making threats on the prefect's behalf. Dukat had a reputation too, after all.

The two Ferengi immediately went back to work, but their argument continued, whispered now.

Gart began his pitch again, perhaps thinking that if he grinned wider, exposing more of his filed teeth, Thrax would believe him sincere—but behind him, the sniping Ferengi were back at it, their voices rising even louder than before.

"Quark! Kurga!" Gart turned and shouted. "I warned you!"

The smaller of the two Ferengi, the one with a mournful expression that appeared to be permanent, pointed to the other. "He is trying to cheat you, Gart! He overcharged you for that last run of synthale, and I have evidence that he has really and truly been trying to poison you! He wants to—"

"Stop it at once!" Thrax demanded, just before Quark made another clumsy attempt to swing at his crewmate. Thrax was not the sort of man to draw a weapon without worthy cause. He stepped closer to the line of squabbling aliens and reached out to grab one of the Ferengi by the ear, which caused the most horrible screeching noise Thrax thought he'd ever heard. The other men in the line promptly dropped their containers with a collective clatter and clapped their hands over their ears. Thrax recognized the efficacy of such a squeal in the realm of defense. For a people with hearing so much more sensitive than his own, the sound had to be excruciating. Indeed, despite his own rather mediocre hearing, Thrax's head seemed to be splitting in two because of the horrid sound, and he quickly let go of the man's ear. The screaming ceased, but the scuffle threatened to continue before the Ferengi named Quark dashed through the cargo bay and out into the corridor.

"Good riddance," Gart snapped, and turned back to Thrax. "Now, about our negotiations—"

"Don't press your luck," Thrax said. "Just unload the cargo and get out of here. Unless you want my people to unload it for you."

The threat—that he would have the Ferengi's ship searched, undoubtedly uncovering vast quantities of stolen supplies or expensive contraband—did the trick.

"Of course, yes, it's a pleasure," Gart said meekly, and turned back to his crew, who had quickly and quietly resumed their work.

Thrax watched them carefully until the last container was unloaded, wondering if the fight was really a means to distract him while another of the Ferengi robbed the station blind. He'd better find this Quark right away and get him off the station as expediently as possible. The last thing Terok Nor needed was an unattended Ferengi; the Bajorans gave him enough trouble as it was.

Natima ran a finger over the edge of her glass. The bit of *kanar* she'd already sipped had gone straight to her head. She would not have chosen *kanar* for herself, but when she'd arrived, Russol had already put in the drink orders, leaving Natima to accept whatever was brought to her.

Natima liked the restaurant he'd chosen. It was dark and pretty and too expensive. She could remember the first time she had come here, to celebrate her apprenticeship with the Information Service. She'd had no family with which to come, and so she had come alone, to toast her own unlikely success.

Most people followed the career trajectory that had been laid out for them by their parents when they were children. Natima had been left to find her own path after being turned out by the orphanage where she'd grown up on Cardassia II. She had applied for the apprenticeship and gotten it, beating out several others with familial connections to the Information Service. It was the proudest and most exhilarating moment of her life, not likely ever to be replicated. It was the first time she'd felt herself to be a true member of the Union, self-sufficient and able to serve.

It was impossible not to remember that sensation as she sat here, across from Russol, sipping *kanar* like any other Cardassian—but deep inside she felt different, and she would always feel different. It was a topic she would never be comfortable discussing with someone like Russol. Another orphan might understand, perhaps, but very few grew up to be productive members of society. Natima didn't have much chance of speaking to another, at least not one from her own world. On Bajor, it had been a different story.

Natima brought herself back into the present, mentally filing away volatile topics for another time. "I don't much care for *kanar*," she said, being truthful, but also playfully irritable.

"I apologize, then," Russol said, and in his earnest reply Natima saw that he had not asked her here in order to be coy. She frowned slightly into her drink. Of course he would have no romantic interest in her—no man ever seemed to. She supposed she scared them away, but she was too old and set in her ways to feel more than a moment's regret. She'd been ignored by better.

"It's not a problem," she said. "It won't hurt me to try something new." She took another sip, no longer caring quite so much if she became a little inebriated.

"Miss Lang," Russol began.

"Call me Natima," she said, not so much to flirt with him, since he'd made it clear that wasn't his purpose, but to eschew as much of the yoke of formality as possible. Natima found it tiresome after a while, trying to keep up appearances. It had never come naturally to her, as she'd never had anyone to teach her the nuances of appropriate social behavior from the time she was a child; it had all been learned by trial and error, with sometimes embarrassing results.

"Natima, it has come to my attention that you're . . .

not in full agreement with the direction the military government has begun to take in the past few decades." He looked at her uneasily.

Natima narrowed her eyes, reflexively searching for traps. "Everyone has their own ideas about the way things ought to be run," she said ambiguously, and took a larger sip of her drink.

"Yes, I suppose it's true, though most decline to discuss it."

"Certainly in a place as public as this one," she said, lowering her voice slightly.

"So . . . you would be more comfortable if we discussed this topic elsewhere?"

Natima considered it. What was he asking her, exactly? Did Russol's dissent go deeper than mere complaints coming off the front lines? She wasn't sure how to respond, but some string of curiosity deep in her mind had been plucked, and she could not pretend she did not hear the humming.

"It . . . it depends," she said, again ambiguous. What might she be getting herself into?

"Natima, I've done quite a bit of checking up on you, and I believe I can trust you," he said, looking into her eyes. "I've reviewed the stories you've done in the past, and though it was often subtle, I've definitely detected a . . . tone from you, and from your stories. I feel as though a person like you . . . could be useful in what I am trying to do."

Natima swallowed before answering, trying to keep her voice indifferent. "This is starting to seem a little dangerous," she said airily, and finished her drink.

"It is dangerous," Russol admitted. "You and I both know that Central Command has eyes and ears everywhere. They probably already know what I'm up to. If they don't, then it's a given that the Obsidian Order does."

Natima wrinkled her nose at what seemed to be a proclamation of defeat. "Then why are you pursuing . . . whatever it is you're pursuing, Glinn Russol?"

"Because I love Cardassia," he replied without hesitation. "And I feel that preservation of her most basic ideals is worth the risk of execution. I don't have a family, and neither do you. I feel that my first obligation is to Cardassia. I wonder, Natima, if you might feel similarly?"

A man came around to their table to ask after their order, and Natima did not hesitate to request another *kanar*. Russol's raised eyeridge made her smile. "I think I've developed a taste for it," she said, indicating the empty glass in her hands.

Russol watched her, waited, and she made her decision.

"I agree that this topic might be best discussed elsewhere. Where and when would you like to meet?" The words rang slightly in her ears as she spoke them. If Russol was indeed trying to trick her, then she had probably just implicated herself. But she studied his gaze once more, and felt assured that he was not. Either that, or he was in the Order. She knew their agents trained to be as convincingly sincere as Russol was now being.

"I have a few friends I think you might be interested in meeting," Russol told her. "I am hoping that they will benefit as much from the encounter as you will."

The steward brought Natima her second drink, and this time, she downed it in a single draught.

Mora Pol was clearing up his desk for the night—a mere formality, but one that gave him some sense that he still maintained a shred of control over his own life. He felt overwhelmed by despair this evening—not a new sensation for him, though it was especially crushing tonight. The system he had been working on for over six years was finally complete. It was the sort of thing that should have given any scientist some measure of triumph, but not for Doctor Mora—for the system in question was a weapon, to be used against his own people.

Collaborator. Murderer.

He pushed the thoughts away and tapped off the lights in his laboratory, a space he shared with the Cardassian scientist with whom he had been working these past six and a half years. He headed for the door, intending to go to his cramped quarters at the far end of the building.

Mora was the only scientist who lived in the building in addition to working in it, for he was the only Bajoran left at the Bajoran Institute of Science. The name, of course, was a holdover from the days before the Cardassians had taken over this world, and the Bajoran scientists who had once worked here had gradually disappeared, one by one, until only Mora Pol was left. His job was to conduct research, but his primary task was to keep the Cardassians convinced that he was still one of their allies, one of the few Bajorans who remained allegiant to the occupying forces that had invaded their world. The Cardassians who ran the institute had decided, some years ago, that it might be easier to assure Mora's continued loyalty if he did not leave the institute, and so it was here that he made his bed. He had, at first, been allowed visitors on a very limited basis, always with a Cardassian ear strategically placed so he could not reveal anything sensitive to his family when they came. But Mora knew that it was humiliating for them to be associated with a collaborator, and so he had long ago asked them to stop coming. He thought they would return if he were to request it, but he could not bring himself to do so.

His self-disgust had blossomed over the years, was finally coming to full flower. He'd never set out to hurt anyone, had cooperated with the Cardassians because he worked for the government, and even now, the few corrupt Bajoran figureheads that still remained—Kubus Oak and Kan Nion came to mind—continued to insist that they comply with Cardassian policy. Mora had been so afraid for so long, he'd fallen into the habit of willing, even eager compliance. He'd saved his own life, but he was starting to believe the price had been too high, after all.

"Doctor Mora?"

He started a little as his name was spoken suddenly from somewhere in the darkness of his lab, and he put the lights back on, exasperated. "What is it, Odo?"

The shape-shifter was in his tank, the vessel where he regenerated each night and where Mora often implored him to remain so he would stay out of the way of the other research that was conducted here. Mora's lab partner, a woman named Kalisi Reyar, did not much care for Odo's active presence in the lab while she was reviewing her notes. Odo had become more of a side project for Mora in recent years, since his research with Doctor Reyar had begun to take precedence over everything else he was doing. The tests and drills he ran with the mysterious life-form had slowed to a near halt.

Odo's "head" was glimmering in its partially solid state, the rest of his mass a stretching, shining, amorphic liquid. The effect was unsettling, though Mora had seen Odo in this semi-humanoid state many times.

"Doctor Mora, now that your project with Doctor Reyar is concluded, will you and I resume our work?"

"Odo, please. If you're going to speak to me, I'd prefer it if you would become completely humanoid. When you do that . . . it unnerves me."

The liquid spilled out of the tank and Odo's shape defined, the nearly transparent quality of his "face" instantly hardening into the appearance of an oddly smooth-featured Bajoran, his tall, stiff body seemingly clad in a plain jump-suit—a concession to Bajoran and Cardassian notions of propriety. Odo had difficulty perfecting the form of a convincing person, though there were times when he was feeling especially confident that his bone structure looked more realistic than usual; when he was nervous, the shape of his jaw and the curves of his ears appeared particularly unfinished. Mora had discussed it with him many times, which seemed to give the shape-shifter even more difficulty in maintaining his appearance. The scientist did not mean to aggravate him about it, but it frustrated him somewhat that Odo's progress in that area had stalled so significantly.

"You and I will resume the old schedule of testing just as soon as my superiors deem it necessary," Mora said briskly. "In the meantime, you can continue to study on your own, and we will work together for a few hours in the evenings, when my other responsibilities don't take my attention from you."

He felt a little sorry for the creature, supposing him to be lonely without the same regimen of nearly constant supervision he'd enjoyed in the beginning. Odo had always seemed withdrawn, and really, he was essentially still a child. His appearance and voice suggested an adult male, but Mora knew better. He would probably not be able to live the life of an adult for at least another ten years or so, a thought that actually gave Mora quite a bit of comfort—for, as long as the shape-shifter needed him, the Cardassians would need him, as well. Doctor Yopal, the director of the Institute, had always maintained enough curiosity regarding Odo that Mora doubted very much she'd ever put him back on the shelf where he'd sat for so long before Mora had been assigned to him. And what else could be done with him? He was almost helpless without Mora, and even Yopal wasn't cruel enough to just turn him out—unless, of course, she decided to assign a Cardassian scientist to work with him. That possibility did trouble Mora from time to time, but he felt somewhat assured that it was unlikely to happen on Yopal's watch.

"You must regenerate now, Odo," Mora instructed the shape-shifter.

"I have been regenerating for many hours," Odo told the scientist, and Mora frowned.

"Then you may access my comnet link to study. I need to go to bed now. I will see you in the morning. I will probably have time to do some work with you tomorrow afternoon."

"Good night, Doctor Mora," the shape-shifter said in his gravelly fashion, his voice heavy with a trace of what seemed to be sadness, though Mora could never quite tell if it was reflective of actual mood.

Mora headed to the small, dark room that was barely bigger than a closet—his home. He took off his shoes and coat and sat on the edge of his small bed, trying to push from his mind the duties he would have to perform in the next few days. He would help with the implementation of Doctor Reyar's project, an anti-aircraft system that could target and eliminate Bajoran terrorist raiders as they left the atmosphere. Mora had done his best to stall the work for as long as he could without making it obvious, but now there was nothing more he could do—at least, nothing that wouldn't result in his own execution. The system would go up with or without him, and what would happen to Odo if Mora was gone?

Yes, I must think of Odo, he told himself, finally slumping onto his cot and falling into a troubled sleep.

Dukat knotted his hands beneath his desk, fighting to keep his expression free of contempt as the Ferengi stepped into his office. Quark, he called himself. Dukat wondered if he should have asked Thrax to attend this little meeting. He didn't want to seem mistrustful, to put the creature on the defensive, but one couldn't be too careful when it came to Ferengi. And what did this one intend, now that his ship had stranded him on the station? Dukat wished very much that he could avoid even addressing the topic. He had considered having the man arrested on some trumped-up charge or other, but Thrax was strangely reluctant to make arrests under what he considered a "dishonest" premise. It was a trait that had led Dukat to consider his reassignment more than once.

"You've asked to speak to me?" Dukat began.

"Yes, Your, uh, Highness. You see, I don't want to go back to my homeworld. There's trouble waiting there for me. I don't really have many options at the moment, and I'm wondering if it might be possible for me to . . . stay . . . here."

Dukat did not answer him. Quark had a crafty look to him, his eyes bright with it, but at least he wasn't going to cower and bootlick, as Dukat had half expected.

"I have money," the creature insisted. "My father left me an inheritance. It's just a matter of getting the bank on Ferenginar to transfer the funds to a local depository so I can access it. I could rent a room from you, maybe even start a business here. You'd do well to have a savvy entrepreneur such as myself on your station." Quark grinned, exposed his pointed teeth. "I could bring in travelers from all over the galaxy, give a bit of notoriety to this spot. Maybe you'd be able to establish better trade relationships if your station had a little more to offer. Maybe you'd be able to—"

"I don't really like Ferengi," Dukat said.

"Well, I suppose you're not alone in that," Quark said smoothly, "but I must tell you that my people have been victim to a great deal of slander and misrepresentation. We're trying to make our way in the galaxy, just like everyone else, and we have no interest in conflict—all we want is to make a little money for ourselves. The truth is, fortune generally follows a Ferengi whenever he sets up a business venture on another world. You might be surprised to learn that on some worlds, Ferengi are considered good luck."

Dukat stared. "Is that so?"

"Yes, it's true," Quark said. He hadn't been so bold as to sit, but he leaned on one of the chairs in front of Dukat's desk, the picture of casual arrogance. "Many people regard matters of economics to be something of a mystery, but it's not like that to my people. Wherever we go, prosperity goes with us. A wise man might be looking for a way to share in a bit of that prosperity—"

"If you're going to stay here," Dukat interrupted, "I'm going to need to see the money up front. I'm not talking about credit, either. I'm not talking about a thumbscan on a padd, or a signature. I'm talking about hard currency, Mister Quark."

"Currency, sure. I can get you that. I can do whatever you want. Just let me stay, Mister Dukat. Let me—"

"It's Gul Dukat."

"Gul Dukat, right. So, you'll let me stay, won't you?" The Ferengi had assumed a begging posture, his wrists pressed together in a strange demonstration of supplication.

"Hard currency," Dukat repeated.

The Ferengi nodded again, his hands clasped together now in what Dukat perceived as feigned gratitude. "Would you consider working out some kind of a deal? Perhaps we could conceive of a system where you might offer some kind of a discount—reliant on my timely payment, of course—but then if I were to go into delinquency, you could charge a penalty. It would be a clever way for you to make a profit from—"

"I'm not interested in making a deal," Dukat told the Ferengi. "I just want to see my money. By the end of the day, preferably. Otherwise, there are plenty of transports out of here with a reasonable likelihood of providing you passage on credit."

Quark did not look happy, his bright eyes narrowing slightly, the massive ears on either side of his head seeming almost to droop. Dukat dismissed him, feeling comfortable that he would not have to see more of this Ferengi after today.

The Ferengi stopped at the door, turned to look at Dukat again. "I wonder if I might be able to interest you in something other than money. You see, the crew of my freighter left me several crates of unreplicated foodstuffs in the cargo bay—goods of the very finest quality—but I don't know if I have the means to unload so much product without a go-between. Perhaps you'd be interested in—"

"I have no use for Ferengi fare," Dukat said with some disgust. What the Ferengi called food, Cardassians paid good money to have exterminated.

"It's not only Ferengi cuisine I've got in there," Quark insisted. "I have contacts and suppliers all over the galaxy. I routinely purchased all kinds of foreign delicacies—anything I could get below cost, I acquired—although my DaiMon didn't always care for cuisine from Benzar, or Andor. A man such as yourself probably has a much broader palate than an idiot like Gart, though, am I right?"

Dukat sighed. "I don't think so, Mister Quark."

Quark looked even more unhappy than he did before. "That's perishable cargo," he muttered to himself. "There must be someone around here who can appreciate—"

"I'm sure you'll do fine. Now, if you don't mind . . ."

The Ferengi nodded to him, somewhat compulsively, before finally taking his leave, and Dukat let out the breath he had been holding. He found the Ferengi to have something of an objectionable odor, a smell that reminded Dukat of Bajor's swamps—of moss and muck and the larvae of biting insects. He couldn't imagine that anyone would have an interest in food offered by this man, not unless it was a person who was starving to death.

Doctor Mora's primary job was to calibrate the equipment for Doctor Reyar as she prepared the computer systems on Terok Nor, to process the new transmissions from the surface. He was somewhat in awe of the station, and it certainly felt strange to have left the walls of the institute, walls with which he had grown contemptuously familiar in the past seven years.

"Doctor Mora, must I again remind you to concentrate on your work?" Reyar's crisp voice interrupted Mora's thoughts as he looked around the computer core, its strange colors and severe angles such a far cry from Bajoran design. The air was hot and dry. He felt as though he were in the epicenter of the Cardassian mind, surrounded as he was by these foreign terminals and flashing streams of Cardassian alphanumerics. Would the whole of Bajor someday look like this? Mora hoped he would not live to see it.

"I . . . apologize," he stammered, and turned back to his work, slowly pecking at his keypad. He knew Cardassian characters well enough now, but his fluency would always be stilted. It might have been different if he had learned the language as a child instead of as an adult—pointless to even think of it; he suffered enough for not being Cardassian. And there was the matter of the Cardassians' eidetic memory, though Mora had long since learned that it was less developed in some than in others—and Reyar fell into the category of those who struggled. He felt reasonably certain that her intelligence and ability at rote memorization were somewhat on a par with his own, but that did not still his fear of her. Of all of them.

Mora helped her develop the recognition software that would process telemetry from each of the scanning stations that had been built on Bajor's surface. Erected by labor crews of Bajorans that had been recruited from the hill territories of each continent, the towers would transmit constant scans of Bajoran airspace, searching for non-Cardassian flyers. If the system detected an unauthorized craft, particle beam weapons would lock onto the transgressor and blow it out of the sky. The system would go online at the end of this week, but Mora had an idea to get word to the resistance before then. It was a long shot, and it was dangerous, but Mora felt that he had to take the chance. His cousin, a farmer in the village of Ikreimi, had always claimed to know someone who was affiliated with the freedom fighters. If Mora could send word to his parents, asking to have his cousin come and visit him at the institute, he might be able to pass on some valuable information before it was too late . . .

"Stand up, Mora," Reyar instructed him. Puzzled, he did as he was told. She took out a small scanning device and began to wave it up and down the length of his body.

He cleared his throat. "May I ask what you're doing?"

She smiled to herself, clearly pleased. "I suppose you thought I brought you up here for your expertise, hm?"

He cleared his throat again. "I'm your . . . lab partner, Doctor Reyar. You needed an assistant . . ."

"I needed a cooperative Bajoran, to enter your biospecs into the new system's recognition software."

Mora was puzzled. "But it's an anti-aircraft system. Why—?"

"There's another aspect to it that perhaps you weren't aware of, Doctor Mora." He could tell by the delightedly smug expression on her face that she was about to tell him what it was, though she'd obviously taken some pains to conceal it from him. How like her, to seek pleasure by making him uncomfortable.

"I recently decided to add another function to the sensor sweeps," she went on. "As you know, it took me a long time to fine-tune the targeting sensors so that we will avoid accidents involving Cardassian aircraft, to compensate for the effects of Bajor's highly variable atmosphere . . ."

"A great many tests," Mora said.

"Yes, Mora, more tests than I had anticipated. How odd, that every time I thought I had adjusted it perfectly, it seemed even more misaligned than it had been before." She gave him a hard look.

Mora felt sick. He shouldn't have been so obvious in sabotaging her calibrations, though he'd done his best to make each change appropriately subtle. Of course, Reyar had her suspicions, but Mora knew that Yopal wouldn't listen to a word of it—the director of the institute had never cared for Reyar. "Oh?" he finally croaked.

"Yes, well, never mind that. I confess, part of what took me so long to perfect this system was my own distraction. Halfway toward completion I had the idea to combine this project with another that I envisioned, and I shifted much of my focus to that. Yopal barely knows anything of it—I cleared it with the prefect, of course, no thanks to our esteemed director." She smiled now, her self-satisfaction back in full force.

"Are you going to tell me about it?" he said, as politely as he knew how.

"It will target moving objects on the surface," Reyar said, obviously pleased with herself.

"Moving objects? Like . . ."

"That's right. Not just aircraft leaving the atmosphere, but smaller objects. An object as small as a person. In fact, it's designed to locate people who attempt to cross proscribed boundaries. Bajoran people." She smiled. "That's part of why we've come to the station, Mora, and why I abandoned the idea of deploying a satellite network in favor of a ground-based detection grid. You see, those signal towers will alert officials here on Terok Nor any time an aircraft has been shot down. But it will also alert personnel here when unauthorized Bajoran travelers have been detected in the regions that are known to be frequented by terrorists. That way, Dukat can deploy troops to investigate a particular region, instead of just having them wander aimlessly around in the hills and forests as they've been doing all this time, using less reliable sweeps from their aircraft—or even handheld tricorders. This system is simple, really. So simple, I don't know why anyone hadn't thought of it before."

Mora caught his breath. "Not everyone can be as brilliant as you are, Doctor Reyar." He could not look at her in the eye, knowing that she was waiting for his reaction, and in truth, he was finding it difficult to conceal his horror. He had not counted on something like this . . .

"So," he said carefully, "it will work on the same principles as a tricorder?"

Reyar frowned. "No," she said. "The targets are too broad. In the future, I plan to remedy the imprecision of this system, but for now, these physical sweeps should be more than sufficient to help pinpoint the locations of terrorists."

"Terrorists," Mora said. "But if innocent civilians were to trip the system . . ."

Reyar's frown went deeper. "If a civilian remains within the boundaries designated for Bajorans, he has nothing to worry about. It is designed to target terrorists. If a Bajoran is carrying proper identification and a permit when he is picked up, he will, of course, be set free."

"But," Mora said, "people make mistakes. Children sometimes run off into the forests—"

"The system will not target children," Reyar said firmly. "I saw to that. You are the template, Mora, an adult male. We are going after the resistance, Doctor, not children. *We* are not terrorists."

She went on, explaining that Cardassian-sanctioned Bajoran ships would continue to function unmolested, and Mora bit his lip, bursting with questions. The system would be unaffected by children, but at what age did Reyar assume that Bajorans suddenly became dangerous? Was it based on physical sweeps, on DNA, or on some other property? And might the resistance simply begin to rely on children to run their errands for them? That wasn't unheard of, though Mora actually knew very little about the resistance. He had never met anyone in the resistance as far as he knew, only heard rumors about them. His heart sank further in his chest as he realized that the plan he had worked on for so long would not be feasible with such a sensor system in place. He doubted very much that the Cardassians would allow his cousin to obtain a travel permit—possibly his parents wouldn't be eligible, either. There was nothing he could do while sequestered at the institute, which, while not entirely remote, was a small distance away from the villages. As a probable target for terrorist activity, it would likely be placed beyond the perimeters of Reyar's no-travel zones.

He kept his expression flat, desperately considering alternative possibilities as he turned back to his work. He felt the hot, eager flicker of hope slipping away from him. He put his head down and tapped at his padd, trying to formulate some kind of a plan, immediately talking himself out of anything he could think of. He would have to be clever if he meant to do something, and he wasn't sure if it was the sort of cleverness he could deliver. These systems were going to go online, and there was nothing he could do to warn the resistance about it. He was no spy, no rebel. He was just an invisible man in a lab coat, without much of a soul left.

3

Ashalla was cold today, colder than it would normally have been in Tilar, where Winn Adami had grown up, colder than in Relliketh, where she had spent five years in a Cardassian prison camp. But Vedek Winn felt warm inside today, for she had come to the Shikina Monastery at Ashalla specifically to be in the presence of the Orb, and today was the day that would finally happen.

After all that she had been through in her life, she felt that she deserved the attention of the Prophets. It had taken her the better part of the past year to get permission from the rest of the Vedek Assembly to view the Tear of the Prophet, the Orb of Prophecy and Change, the most valuable and revered object on all of Bajor—and its most closely guarded secret. As the most junior member of the Vedek Assembly, Winn had to wait for many weeks before she received word of her "clearance," but now that she was here, her resentment at being made to wait was beginning to dissipate.

Vedek Winn awoke in the bedchamber at the Shikina Monastery with heady anticipation; she could not wait to find what important truths about herself the Prophets would reveal. Winn had always known that she was destined for something important, and after the years in the prison camp, her conviction had grown even stronger. The

Prophets had arranged it so that she would survive that experience intact, but with a furious, unwavering desire to see herself vindicated for what she had been put through. The Prophets did not choose just anyone to be captured, tortured, humiliated, released, and then almost immediately chosen for the Vedek Assembly. Winn had been quite sure for some time now that she was meant to be a mouthpiece for Them, and this would be the first step toward proving it.

She brushed her soft, light hair before donning the modest headpiece of her order. These days, only Jaro Essa had the privilege of seeing her without it, and she took some measure of pride in that knowledge. She had always worn her robes casually when she was younger, often forgoing the traditional headgear, but after being stripped of her vestments at the prison camp, Winn felt that she would not take them for granted again, that her physical presence was to be carefully guarded from anyone except for the very few to whom she submitted her trust. Right now, Essa was the only person who fell into the category.

She belonged to Essa now, as much as she could belong to another person. He was an influential man; though he held no power under Cardassian authority, he was powerful nonetheless. It made Winn proud to think of her Essa: he was honest, he was true to Bajor. He had gained his reputation by his own merits, not by licking the boots of the despicable aliens who had come to try to steal this world. But the Prophets would eventually see the Cardassians away—Winn believed that as surely as she believed in her own potential. And when that happened, Jaro's star would rise along with hers.

A soft rap came at the door, and Winn presented herself to the monks who were to take her to see the Orb.

"Vedek, I come to inform you that we cannot take you to the Tear of the Prophets this morning, for there is to be—"

"Cannot take me?" Winn repeated, with fierce politeness. "But . . . I have waited all this time already." It galled her that this underling apparently had the authority to deliver such a message to a member of the Vedek Assembly.

The monk went right on speaking as if he had not been interrupted. Her irritation with his insolence made Winn miss the first part of his message. ". . . or what there are of them here at the shrine. We have received an encrypted message from Prylar Bek at Terok Nor—"

"Prylar Bek? What could this possibly have to do with the Tear of the Prophets?"

"An emergency council of the Vedek Assembly," the monk stated, repeating the first part of his message. "You, of course, are required to attend. It must be done immediately. There is not time for anyone to travel, and we cannot rely on communiqués, even encrypted ones. Prylar Bek insisted it was imperative that the Cardassians not hear the content of his message, for it concerns the kai herself."

Winn swallowed her bitterness and followed the aging monk as he lurched his way down the glossy, echoing corridor of the monastery. He took her to a chamber where she was met by another member of the Vedek Assembly, an old, unlikable woman named Sharet Ras. Winn nodded to her with the appropriate measure of deference, thinking that perhaps someday she would be in a position to make the other vedeks feel like children, as Vedek Sharet often seemed to like to do.

Soon they were joined by seven other vedeks of the assembly, with Sharet presiding as the senior member. There were several core members away, but as the Shikina Monastery was currently home to the main body of the Assembly, it would be up to the attending vedeks to conduct the meeting, to hear the message, and to make whatever decisions might need to be made. In spite of her disappointment, Winn had to consider that perhaps it was the Prophets' doing that she should happen to be here at this time.

"Prylar Bek has sent us a coded message in the hand of a mock prisoner smuggled off Terok Nor," Vedek Sharet informed the others, not wasting any time. "He has learned from someone on the station that a new detection grid could put the life of the kai—and, indeed, the lives of every Bajoran—in grave danger. The grid is purported to be almost ready—it will be operational within the week. He has insisted that the shrine where she has hidden must be completely evacuated, for the Cardassians will be sure to find it just as soon as the new system goes online."

"Who is his source?" Vedek Preta demanded. "How can we even be sure that the coded message is genuine? This could be a trap to bring the kai out into the open."

Winn had been thinking much the same thing, but something in her constitution wouldn't permit her to speak—not only because she was the youngest member of the assembly, nor because her first concern had been for the kai. Her anxiety was for the resistance fighters who would likely be targeted by the technology in question. There had been a time when Winn had disagreed with the rebellion, but times had changed. The Vedek Assembly's positions had changed. Of course, the kai was a symbolic beacon of hope for Bajor, but she did not hold the same importance to its future as did the resistance. Winn was suddenly eager to contact Jaro Essa.

Vedek Sharet smiled patiently. "We must come to a quick conclusion, my brothers and sisters," she said. "We must decide which poses a greater risk: evacuating the kai—preferably here, to the Shikina Monastery—or doing nothing."

"Bek is a trustworthy man," Vedek Marin said. "We must do this."

The other votes were cast, with four of those in attendance voting to reject the warning as a trap, and four opting to immediately inform the kai of the possible danger and to arrange to have her secretly transported to the Shikina Monastery. It fell to Winn to cast the deciding vote, which pleased her not a little. After a brief moment of reflection, she decided to warn the kai, for she ultimately felt that Kai Opaka was good for Bajor. She wondered if the kai would ever learn of Winn's role in the vote. *How will I reply when she thanks me?*

The decision made, some monks were recruited immediately to take the message to Kendra, so that Ranjen Stassen could be contacted at the shrine of the kai. Winn was relieved that the ordeal was over, and eager to resume her scheduled appointment with the Orb. But Vedek Sharet had other ideas.

"Vedek Winn," she said, with a gentleness that Winn surmised to be false, "I think it is best if we do not take anyone down to see the Orb just now. There has been so much excitement for a single day . . . and you must have heard that an Orb experience is not something to be taken lightly. I sense, Vedek Winn, that you are not ready for such an experience today. We will speak further on the matter tomorrow."

"But . . . Vedek, after all the time I've waited, I am more ready today than I will ever be," Winn protested, but she could see a kind of finality in the eyes of the old woman. She would not be getting her chance to see the Orb today—maybe not even this week—especially if the warning concerning the kai turned out to be genuine. The "excitement" would not be ebbing any time soon. As she returned to her rooms, Winn thought to herself that the warning had better turn out to have substance; if she'd been prohibited from seeing the Orb without cause, it would certainly make her regret her vote.

Russol met Natima at her house with a skimmer, a means of transportation that she supposed he felt was more discreet than public transport. But Natima knew only too well that if Russol had been marked as a possible dissident, it wouldn't matter how he chose to travel; the authorities would know where he was going before he even got there.

Natima was taken to the residence of a retired archon, where she was greeted in the lobby of his impressively large house by one of his many servants. The furniture was rich and heavy, the art expensively austere. She was surprised that one so wealthy would have associated with government nonconformists; she had always supposed that rebellion stemmed from desperation, from the young, the poor, or men like Russol who'd been forced to take part in conflicts that they did not agree with.

There were many people here, seemingly from all walks of life and within every age category beyond young adulthood, though most of the people she saw were nearer to her own age. There were only a few women, and most of them seemed to be someone's wife. It may have just been the backdrop, but everyone Natima saw seemed to come from wealth or prestige. She supposed she should have felt out of place, but she mostly only felt curious. She was uncomfortable speaking too freely to anyone she met, though the conversations she overheard quickly confirmed that these people were indeed radicals; she no longer believed Russol was trying to trick her. Staging something on a scale like this, with so many other people involved, seemed highly unlikely.

It took some time before the "meeting" came to order, though the lack of organization and leadership made it unlike any meeting she'd ever attended—more like a confused congregation at a party. The guests had been called to gather in a large, glassed-in room at the back of the manse, overlooking the expansive grounds, stone gardens, and cultured cacti. Russol and the host tried to maintain direction over the crowd, but as various well-dressed figures stood to speak, others would cut in and still others would stand to disagree, the resulting arguments and side arguments quickly giving way to chaos.

"The heart of our problems rests on Bajor," one man kept insisting. "The costs of the Bajoran venture have long outweighed the profits. And when those resources have run dry, the market for those products that are reliant on Bajoran raw materials will crash, and the economy will suffer for it."

This at least seemed to resonate with most at the meeting, but the solutions were another matter. "Cardassians will never accept an abrupt conclusion to the annexation," another man cut in. "We must first find an alternate source of those materials that now come from Bajor—for when the Bajoran minerals have all been mined—"

"The problem is that Central Command is not pacing the removal of those materials!" interrupted someone else. "Bajor has more than enough resources to sustain Cardassia for many generations. But Central Command has been striking trade agreements with other worlds that do not make long-term economic sense for us. They are only interested in short-term wealth, where they should be providing for Cardassia's long-term needs."

"But the Bajoran resistance—the conflicts with the locals have become more than the current prefect knows how to handle. The Information Service refuses to report the truth on the matter of Bajoran terrorism—"

Natima flinched internally. When she'd been on Bajor, she had been one of the primary media censors. Her objective had been to downplay the violence on that world, reporting instead on the perceived successes of each Cardassian venture.

The arguments continued, and Natima began to feel exhausted just listening. She caught Russol's eye and tried to convey to him her feelings. *Why did you bring me here,*

Russol? This group has no direction, they are only united by their sense of frustration, but they use it against one another. Russol looked back at her, and Natima saw a shift in his jaw that seemed to indicate he did not disagree with her.

"Friends," Russol called out over them. "We've come here tonight at great risk to ourselves. We may not all agree on each and every strategy, we may not even be sure what it is that we want to change—only that change is what we all desire, in the Union's policies regarding Bajor. We need people like you if we are going to bring about that change." He swept his arm out in a gesture to indicate everyone in the room, but Natima felt as though he might be speaking directly to her, as though he was addressing the look she had just given him. The room was mostly silent now, and Natima finally felt herself able to listen.

"Every day this annexation continues, more lives are lost, and another piece of Cardassia's soul is chipped away. We need to make our domain reflect the integrity and hope that each of us carries inside, for the Union that *could* be—the Union we can see, in our hearts and minds, the pride of which inspires us toward greatness. We need people who believe that a sound government, a solid economy, and a world we can be proud of is worth the risk of being called *dissident*."

Natima felt a surge of inspiration. She did indeed believe that Cardassia was worth fighting for; she loved her world and she loved her people. It was the tactics of its politicians and soldiers that she disagreed with. Over the years, she'd come to understand that the desperate times before the annexation had warped the sensibilities of the modern Cardassian. The traditions and customs that had sprung from necessity during those lean times, the rigid definition of what constituted a family—Natima would like very much if those definitions could be retooled to better fit the conditions of the present. Not only because she was an orphan, but because of something she had learned on Bajor.

Natima had only met one Bajoran insurgent, but that meeting had been enough to learn something about the whole of them, she believed. The terrorists had bucked their old social proscriptions, the castes that had once defined their society, and they had bucked the proscriptions imposed upon them by their occupiers. They had done it to preserve something more inherent than tradition—it was a sense of self that they clung fast to, a deep-rooted definition of what it meant to be Bajoran. Natima had been envious when she had recognized it, and she was envious still, for she felt no such connection to her own world— not anymore.

She longed to revisit it, the Cardassian patriotism she had enjoyed before her time on Bajor. She hoped that perhaps Russol would be the one to resurrect it, Russol and this group of squabbling dissidents. Fifteen minutes ago, it had seemed impossible to her—but now, as she watched the group of people around her, rapt at Russol's words, she allowed herself to hope that it might be true.

B'hava'el had just begun to dip in the valley below the foothills, and Li Nalas knew he'd do best to get back to camp before the sun got any lower. It was a long walk to the camp, which was situated in the sparsely vegetated valley below him, and Li didn't relish the idea of sleeping out in the open. It was warm now, but once the sun went down behind the valley's rim, it would not be.

He looked across the narrow ridge for Mart, the teenager who had joined his cell only a few months before. Mart had been awestruck to join the movement alongside the famed Li Nalas, and it was all Li could do to keep from shattering the illusion for the youth, intending to let him down gently, as he had tried to do for most of the others in his current cell. His fame was merely the stuff of legend, rather than the substance, but it wasn't always easy to dissuade people from believing otherwise. He'd had more than his share of luck, that was all.

"Li!" called Mart, squatting at the edge of a nearby bluff. The two were concluding the day's surveillance, even though the Cardassians had not been sighted in this valley for decades. Mart's panicked expression as he hurried to join Li suggested that the time had come. "There're flyers coming in this way!"

Li instinctively hunkered down with his back to the steep hillside behind him, though it did him no real good. What did they want over here? As far as they knew, this was deserted outback. His cell usually camped here in the summertime, moving toward the cities in the winter, when resistance activity went up.

"Looking for us, maybe," Mart said. His voice was steady, but his eyes, glassy and green, reflected deep fear—and changed to beseeching as he turned to look at Li. He really believed that Li could keep him safe, that Li Nalas was the folk hero everyone made him out to be.

Li figured he'd do his best, though that probably wouldn't be worth much. "Come on, Mart, we've got to take cover. It looks like we'll be spending the night here. If we can get to the wooded area above the bluff before the sun goes down, we'll be okay." The flyers were coming from the direction just beyond their camp. Li turned just before he noted that the thrum of the Cardassian engines had changed; the ships were landing.

"What are they doing?"

"Probably putting down ground troops," Li said. This was unusual. The Cardassians usually sent their patrol ships out to the same clearings over and over, where they disgorged confused soldiers with clumsy handheld scanners. This was different. Those flyers seemed to know exactly where they were going, and where they were going was uncomfortably close to home camp. Li reached for his comm, to send a clipped warning back to the others, but the ships were so close to the encampment, there was no way they didn't already know. Li squinted at the faraway Cardassian craft, no larger than children's toys at this distance, the burn from their engines causing a blurry haze all around their thrusters. They hadn't landed at all, Li could see now. They were hovering.

There was a sudden, brilliant gust of firepower, like a light show from the gratitude festival, eerily silent before the sound waves had a chance to travel across the valley. Mart gasped and Li cried out, the sounds lost to the quick, drumlike bursts that followed the explosive visual display. The flyers shot straight up into the air, having completed their mission, black plumes of smoke rising in their wake.

Mart looked ill. "That was . . ."

"That was our camp," Li confirmed, his voice strained in its softness. "But . . . maybe they weren't all there. Some of them were probably patrolling . . ."

"We're the only ones still out on patrol, you said so yourself half an hour ago!" Mart cried. "They were all there, and you know it!"

Li silenced him with an upheld hand, for he could hear more aircraft activity overhead.

"Come on!" Li snapped, all too aware that there was nowhere to run. The bluff stretched on narrowly for *kellipate* after *kellipate* before there was a suitable place to climb down, and after that it was only the openness of the valley, a place they had come to think of as safe through the years.

We all should have known better. Mirel, Orthew, Baj, Tel . . . They all would have been at camp, making dinner, making plans. His friends.

The flyer was practically over their heads already. Li pulled Mart along into the low-growing shrubbery that clambered up and down the sides of the steep bluff, but the flyer's sensors had apparently picked them up, and Li wrapped his arms tightly around himself, anticipating the fiery blow, expecting to see the Prophets at any moment.

To his surprise, the sudden, noiseless blast actually felt quite cool.

When he regained control of his senses, he found himself in a dark, cramped chamber, surrounded by painfully bright blinking lights, yellow and turquoise. Mart heaved raggedly at his side, looking as bewildered as Li felt. Li tried to shake off the muddled feeling that had come with the sudden transport, but he was lucid enough to know that they were inside the Cardassian ship. He and Mart were behind some kind of translucent curtain, and Li scrambled to his feet, glimpsing a uniformed soldier just outside the shimmering field that separated them. "Hey!" he shouted, doing his best to pound against the nebulous surface of the containment wall, his fists springing back oddly from the impact.

The soldier turned, impassive.

"Where are you taking us?" Li demanded fiercely.

"Quiet!" The Cardassian snarled. "Save that energy for the labor camps!"

Li turned to regard Mart, whose face was a mask of disbelief and fear. Li looked away from him before he registered the disappointment in the youth's expression. Of course, the legend of Li Nalas was a fraud—Gul Zarale's death had been an accident—but despite his protests, he'd been assigned the role of hero. Mart would have come to see it for what it was, eventually. Everyone had to grow up, sometime. It was just too bad it had to be like this.

Kalisi Reyar avoided the gaze of her lab partner. She knew that he was secretly taking pleasure from the news she had just received: she was to leave the Bajoran Institute of Science immediately, reassigned to a medical facility on the other side of the planet. She had argued with Yopal, the institute's director, though it made her feel frustrated and embarrassed for the Bajoran to overhear her protests. Despite the great success of the new detection grid, Kalisi was unable to glean any enjoyment from it. Her name had been barely a footnote in the comnet reports, all the glory going to the director of the institute, a woman who barely had anything to do with it.

Kalisi knew that Yopal was silently scornful of her inability to re-create the corrupted research from memory. The director had also mentioned to Kalisi, more than once, that it had been negligent and foolish not to keep more backups that were separate from the institute computer system. Reyar had kept only a single isolinear rod, stolen during the sabotage. It was a tack Kalisi had employed to safeguard her work from theft by her rivals. It had not yet occurred to her, being new to Bajor at the time, that terrorists might be bold enough to attempt to destroy her work. Add to it the ongoing humiliation Kalisi had suffered at taking such an unprecedented amount of time to reconstruct her data—her memory had never been as well-developed as her colleagues', and that truth was readily apparent to her coworkers, though Kalisi had always taken pains in the past to conceal her handicap. Yopal didn't want a researcher impaired with such a weakness to work on her staff, and now that Kalisi had finished her assignment for Dukat, the director was all too eager to dump her off somewhere else.

In a way, she should have been glad. She had often felt cursed, having to work alongside a Bajoran—a male scientist, no less—and she had labored to make his existence as unhappy as possible without resorting to overt torture. If Mora Pol was an accurate representation of his species, it was a wonder they'd ever crawled out of their caves.

Yopal seemed to like him, though for what reason, Kalisi couldn't imagine. Perhaps as a reminder of what they strove toward. At least at the medical facility she would be working exclusively with Cardassians. The hospital was presided over by the illustrious Doctor Crell Moset, a man whose name had begun to carry weight back home on Cardassia Prime, from what little Kalisi had gathered on him. But still, it was an indignity to be sent away to a hospital when her particular line of expertise was better suited to the facility here.

While Kalisi gathered up her things in the lab, Mora was pretending to fool around with the shape-shifter in the tank while it "regenerated." He poked at it with some kind of electrical probe, but Kalisi knew he was watching her, and she kept her back to him, even when she heard someone else enter the room.

"Hello, Doctor Mora, Doctor Reyar." It was the institute's director. Kalisi supposed she had come in to deliver a smug good-bye, but Yopal scarcely acknowledged Kalisi and instead began to speak to Mora regarding his next project. Kalisi kept her back turned as before, pretending not to listen, but smiling slightly when she heard what the director had to say.

"You're to begin work immediately on improving anti-grav efficiency for the transports that go back and forth from Terok Nor. This is going to be a very time-consuming project, as Dukat wishes for this to be done within a very tight window. I don't anticipate your having any extra time to work with Odo."

"But . . . Doctor Yopal, I know I don't have to remind you, Odo is sentient. It doesn't do him good to simply sit in his tank with no interaction. I need to be able to see him—to speak to him—even if it is only a few times a week—"

"We'll do the best we can," she said crisply.

There was nothing Mora could say except to mumble a response.

"Very well, then. Oh, and Doctor Reyar?"

Kalisi turned, concealing her smile. "Yes, Doctor?"

"Your transport is here. You probably don't want to keep it waiting."

"Thank you, Doctor." Kalisi was finished anyway. She had only remained in the lab to listen to what the director had to say to Mora. She took her things and walked out, uninterested in further pleasantries. She stepped outside into the cold damp, wondering what the hospital would be like. Well. She'd know shortly.

Kalisi had very few things to be loaded into the shuttle's cargo compartment, only a small valise with her work clothes, a few document and padd cases. The vanity she'd possessed as a younger woman was all but gone now. She'd had no time for a personal life here on Bajor, a fact that hadn't troubled her when she'd believed her work would propel her to glory within the Union. Lately, though, she was starting to experience real pangs of regret for her decision to trade a family on Cardassia Prime for a career on Bajor. This transport seemed to symbolize her defeat, the certainty that she would never experience the notoriety in the scientific community that she had hoped for. She could expect to live out her twilight years calibrating biobeds on an occupied world. The thought was anything but welcome.

She was the only passenger on the tiny vessel, and she tried to strike up a conversation with the pilot regarding her destination, but quickly found him to be less than garrulous. She satisfied her boredom by looking over some reading material on her padd, but the novelty of her uncertain situation made it difficult to concentrate.

After what seemed like only a very short time, Kalisi looked up to see that the transport had continued to rise, as though the pilot meant to break out of the atmosphere. But that couldn't be right, could it? His authoritarian silence unnerved her to the point where she did not feel comfortable asking questions, but when the shuttle did not drop, she dismissed her awkwardness.

"Where are you taking me?" she demanded, just before the shuttle broke through the very highest clouds in the Bajoran sky, swiftly and calmly riding the turbulence out into the dark of open space. "I thought I was just going to the hospital at Huvara Province! Why have we taken this . . . unlikely route?"

The pilot, seated behind a security compartment, spoke to her through a comm system, his eerily disembodied voice no more talkative than it had been before. "We are making a required stopover."

"A stopover!" she exclaimed. "Offworld? Why was I not informed of this before I boarded?"

The pilot had nothing more to say, and Kalisi had no recourse but to ride in angry, terrified silence while the little skimmer took her not only from Bajor, but out of the B'hava'el system altogether. Her mind raced with questions, but there was no one to answer them. She clasped her hands together and waited.

4

He was too close. No Cardassian had ever come this close to the Shakaar cell's hideout before, at least, not anytime before last week. He wasn't close enough to guess where the hideout was, necessarily, and his scanning equipment couldn't possibly reveal its location, for the hillside surrounding the caves was riddled with kelbonite. But he was still too close. Kira Nerys would have to get him before he got even a linnipate closer, just as she had gotten his two companions. The bulky Cardassian rifle she had lifted from one of the slain soldiers was slowing her down, and Kira knew that she was going to have to ditch it. She could come back for it later, she decided, even though Shakaar had been insisting for over a week that nobody leave base camp until they could confirm or deny the rumors they had been hearing. She was sure to get an earful from him when she returned to camp, especially when she told him that she didn't know where Bestram was.

She pitched the stolen rifle at the base of a tree with distinctive branches. She had been to this spot many times in her life, countless times, and she would be back again, to get that rifle, just as soon as she finished her job here.

She set off again, lighter now, clutching her phaser pistol in one hand and walking the way she'd learned years ago, the way that kept the needles and leaves and bits of bark and the papery seed hulls of the blackwood trees silent beneath the soles of her soft old boots. She could hear his footsteps, though they were a ways off; she would hear him long before he would hear her, and no matter how precise his scanning equipment, she would be the one to shoot first.

She stopped walking as she heard a subtle shift in the echoing crunch of the soldier's footfalls, edging for a large tree. He was headed vaguely in her direction, and although he probably knew exactly where she was, if she held completely still, she could still manage the element of surprise. He would approach as quietly as he knew how, but it would not be quiet enough. He would get within striking range, but she would be well protected behind the trunk of a wide tree. Before he even had a chance to aim, she would charge; he'd be dead before he realized she was coming.

She let her breath out in tiny increments, held her body as still as stone. His footsteps drew closer . . . and when she heard the telltale whisper of dry brush less than a body length away, she sprang out from behind the tree, already firing.

She did not miss. His body jerked as it staggered backward, his phaser falling, and he let out a single dying groan before he landed, and then he was silent and motionless on the floor of the forest. The birds chirped overhead, and Kira scrambled forward, phaser still trained on the dead soldier, to strip him of his weapons and comcuff. She stopped for a moment to listen, but she heard nothing more. Her companion, Bestram, was nowhere in sight, and neither were the Cardassians who had chased him off in a different direction.

Loaded down with equipment, she made for the tree where she had stowed the other phaser rifle, and then beat it back to the Shakaar cell's hideout in the nearby mountain, a mountain so low it was scarcely more than a hill, nearly invisible behind the grand, old-growth trees that surrounded it.

She took the chance that there were no more soldiers around and ducked for the entrance, a tiny, camouflaged opening in the rock that led to a system of tunnels, some of them natural, some of them blasted out by the network of resistance cells that operated in this region. She had to squat down on her haunches to avoid bumping her head on the low ceiling of this passageway, one that had been carved out a little at a time by another cell, the nearby Kohn-Ma. She shimmied along, grunting with the weight of all the equipment she pushed ahead of her, wishing that she had walked around to the more accessible west entrance, but then she remembered that the Cardassians had come from that direction—there could have been more of them, waiting for her. She swallowed her doubts regarding Bestram. He must have gone around, she told herself, though she doubted very much that it was true.

After a long time, she turned a blind corner where the passageway widened and she was able to walk upright at last, her knees and spine creaking a little as she rose to her full height. Kira was small in stature, probably the smallest person of any who used these burrows, but the northwest entrance tunnel still felt claustrophobic to her. She had often wondered how some of the larger men managed to tolerate the press of rock all around them—to say nothing of the darkness. She was nearly to her cell's main hideout now, the place where they lived, ate, slept, bathed, and plotted together. Kira had always thought of it as a warren or a den; it was rough and sometimes depressing, but it was home. For now, anyway.

"Shakaar!" She called out to the leader of her cell as she came into the primary chamber of the Shakaar cell's camp. "Has Bestram checked in?"

Mobara was the only member of the cell in the primary chamber, working on a piece of equipment at a table in the main tunnel, near where the cell's comm system was usually kept. Lupaza and Furel were back in Dahkur, where they had been visiting some friends, and nobody had heard from them in days; it was part of the reason Kira had wanted to go back into Dahkur with Bestram, to ensure that they were all right. Mobara put down his tools and began to relieve Kira of the equipment she carried, stopping to examine a tricorder. "Shakaar told you not to go out, Nerys," Mobara said absently, turning the tricorder over in his hands, already laying out a plan for how he would put it to use.

"I know, but—"

Shakaar emerged from another of the tunnels, with Gantt just behind him. "Nerys—I told you not to go out!"

"I know, but— Bestram, have you heard from him?" She was too anxious about the missing young cell member to argue with Shakaar about going out.

Shakaar looked tired. "I haven't heard anything," he said, wiping his face with one of his rawboned hands. He had been awake for at least two days and nights, manning the long-range comm system, fielding the reports that were coming in from all over the planet. He looked to Mobara, who had been attending to the shortwave system. "Did you hear from him?"

"I didn't," Mobara said, and turned to Kira once more. "Do you think he could have been behind you?"

Kira shook her head. "No, I'm sure he wasn't. He took off in another direction. Three soldiers came after me, the rest followed him." She took a breath. "I think he was making for the ravine, so maybe he'll come in by the western route."

Shakaar nodded, but his expression was grave. The knots of tension in Kira's stomach tightened as she realized that if Bestram had taken the western route, he would have beaten her here by a healthy margin. He'd either taken cover somewhere else, or—

Or he didn't. Kira took another breath, tried to think of something she could say or do to sound encouraging, but nothing came to mind.

"So they found you," Mobara said.

"Yes," Kira said. "But what were we going to do? We'll starve in here. We have to be able to get to the village for supplies—"

"We'll do that when it becomes absolutely necessary," Shakaar said firmly, "and after we've rigged a way to transmit false life signs, or some kind of a shielding device . . ."

"I'm working on one right now," Mobara said. "It should be ready within a week. If you and Bestram had just waited to speak to us about this . . ." His tone was uncharacteristically scolding.

Kira said nothing, feeling mildly defensive, but mostly afraid for Bestram. She'd feel responsible if he didn't come back, even if it *was* his idea to go out in the first place. But why, then, had she been able to go out by herself earlier this week, with no sign of a Cardassian anywhere? When she'd told Bestram about it, he'd been eager to sneak out past Shakaar, believing the enemy patrols had been redeployed elsewhere. But he was wrong. The Cardassians had found them anyway.

Gantt spoke up in a low voice. "We've gotten more bad news since you've been gone," the stoic medic informed her. "The comm chatter says Li Nalas has been killed." Stunned, Kira looked to Shakaar for confirmation.

"Is it true?" she asked him.

Shakaar's voice was solemn. "It's what they're saying on the comm—that his entire outfit was wiped out three days ago, somewhere in the outback."

This was the fifth report they'd gotten of a cell being taken out completely. The cells in Jalanda, Renday, and Elemspur were also said to be gone—not a single member left.

Shakaar continued. "There was a report . . . someone claims that Jaro Essa is confirming he heard it was a new Cardassian detection grid."

"Is that what's taking down the raiders?" Mobara wanted to know.

Again, Kira looked to Shakaar. She hadn't heard anything about raiders. He looked as surprised as she did.

"The Kohn-Ma cell have lost five of their aircraft," Mobara explained. "Five of their *men*. That's more than half their cell."

"When did you hear that?" Kira asked with some urgency. She had become friendly with one of the Kohn-Ma cell members . . .

"I heard it an hour ago, from Tahna Los," Mobara said. "The rest of the Kohn-Ma are still in the city, and Tahna put in a call to me to see if we were still here."

"I heard reports of other raiders being shot down, as well," Shakaar said, his voice troubled. "But I didn't hear that Jaro Essa said anything about it. . . . I thought it might be another of their propaganda plants . . ."

"We shouldn't take any chances," Gantt said.

Shakaar nodded. "We won't be launching any of our own raiders anytime soon. At least, not before we know what happened with the Kohn-Ma's ships," Shakaar said.

"So what should we do?" Kira asked. It wasn't enough for her to sit here and listen to all the frantic gossip coming from the comm. She wanted to act—to get outside and confirm what was happening.

"We'll do nothing until we've gotten more information. First thing, we wait for Bestram. We give it the usual fifty-two hours before . . ." He trailed off.

"Before the search party?" Kira finished for him.

Shakaar shook his head. "Not this time," he said. "This time . . . I think this time will have to be different."

Kira swallowed hard and met Mobara's gaze, found

fear there, too. She had the distinct sense that things were changing, big things.

"We can't just stay in these caves forever," Gantt pointed out. "If there's a system monitoring Bajoran movement, we'll all have to go back to the city, get fake papers—blend in, somehow . . ."

"Not me," Kira said firmly. "I'll stay here."

"I'd rather stay here, too," Mobara said. "I think I can figure out a way to temporarily mask our biosigns so that we can get from place to place, at least in the short term. With careful planning, we can still—"

"But how are we supposed to plan full-scale attacks with temporary masks?" Gantt argued. "If we're being targeted at this location, we've got to leave."

"We'll have plenty of time to figure that out later," Shakaar said. "For now, we gather information. We work on getting in touch with the rest of the cell, making sure everyone is all right."

Kira swallowed. "What about the Kohn-Ma?" she asked.

Shakaar shrugged. "They can do what they want," he said. "But if there are only four of them left, they might just feel as though it's over for them."

Kira felt her resolve harden. "No," she said. "They won't feel that way." Kira didn't know Tahna Los especially well, but she did know that he wouldn't give up, even if he was the only one left in his cell. She knew it because it was how she felt about the Shakaar.

Quark was less than thrilled that he'd had to give up such a large quantity of gold-press latinum to the pompous Cardassian who ran this place. It was a lucky thing he'd had that emergency stash at the bottom of one of the crates Gart had unceremoniously unloaded when he'd marooned Quark. Buried under a quarter-ton of rotting vegetables, the latinum had been safely shielded from his nosy shipmates. He remembered the way the prefect's eyes had widened when Quark had presented him with a full brick, despite his obvious revulsion to the smell coming from it. It pained Quark to leave it on the gul's desk, but he took comfort in knowing that he'd made a sale.

Quark grinned, thinking of the possibilities. He'd left home a lowly freighter cook, driven from the beautiful swamps of Ferenginar by a ridiculous accusation that was, sadly, true. But he'd been listening, from the beginning, from his very first day boiling the morning snail juice for Gart's idiot crew. Listening for that faint, come-hither breath of opportunity, seeking out the entrepreneurial brave—and now she had come panting after him like a two-strip dabo girl, and he had the lobes to take action.

He patted the vest pockets containing his remaining strips and slips, and settled down in a chair in his new quarters, his grin souring slightly. The Cardassian hadn't gotten all of it, but the loss had hurt. And yet, what other recourse did he have? Where else could he possibly go? Dukat obviously didn't want him here, but latinum bought welcome, he'd found. Even with Klingons, to some degree. It was too bad Dukat hadn't wanted the perishables, but Quark already had an idea or two.

He'd known about the occupation, of course. No self-respecting businessman would travel the starry seas without knowing who had the power where. In the B'hava'el system, the Cardassians carried the big stick. They'd run over some backward agri planet to "borrow" most of their resources, to boost a sagging economy at home—not a bad business plan, considering the payoff, though not so hot for the Bajorans. He'd seen plenty of Cardassians, but until his little tour of his new home this morning, he'd never seen a Bajoran before, not up close. In some of those pale faces he'd read crazed desperation, barely concealed; in others, utter, total defeat.

He'd been sent by a gaunt-faced "merchant" to his newly assigned lodgings, to find not much at the far end of a bleak, curving corridor—a bunk, a table, basic replicator, outdated computer console—but it was comfortable enough for someone who'd just been ejected from a tramp freighter. Quark was in no position to complain—he hadn't expected Risa.

He quickly set about contacting his family on Ferenginar to inform them that he was still alive, but of course his fool-headed mother was apparently too busy with some trivial female pursuit to answer a transmission from her beloved eldest son. He left her a message, and then one for his idiot brother Rom, and then he waited. There wasn't much he could do now, not until he'd arranged for his funds to be transferred. He didn't have a padd; he had virtually no assets besides his few crates of delectable odds and ends—*milcake* mix, *sargam* filets, caviar, pickled *plomeek*—and his brilliant business acumen. Which was awesome, of course, but it didn't pay the bills, not yet. There were his personal effects—at least Gart had tossed out Quark's bag along with the refrigerated, "poisoned" containers—but nothing he could consider much of an asset. At least not among Cardassians.

Except the disruptor, maybe. Quark looked over at his bag, considering. You never knew when you might need to defend yourself. Of course, on a place like this, a single disruptor pistol was brittle reassurance—especially since he had never actually fired the thing. In any case, he couldn't imagine a need for it. He had been blessed with the gift of gab.

The little console in front of him chimed to indicate that one of his messages was being returned, and Quark fumbled around a bit with the alien keyboard before he managed to access the image of his mother, her wizened face showing deep concern. Quark was disgusted to see that Ishka was wearing some piece of fabric swathed around her neck.

"Moogie!" he cried out, embarrassed. "Take that thing off!"

His mother looked down, and then plucked at the scarf. *"Sorry, son. I was just trying it on. I forgot it was even there."*

"Ugh." There was nothing more terrible than seeing your own mother in clothing. It wasn't so bad when other women did it—it was suggestive, of course, but suggestive wasn't necessarily horrifying. Quark remembered when Gera had put on his jacket, once, after he'd taken it off—a bold gesture, one that should have been upsetting, but she'd looked oddly cute in it . . . He promptly buried the thought. The sub-nagus's tart of a sister was why he'd had to leave home in the first place.

Ishka got right to business. *"Quark, what has gotten into you? A Cardassian station! Haven't I told you about those people? They have no interest in profit at all—they're almost as bad as the Klingons, but with less scruple! All they want to do is plunder, and then plunder some more. No head for business!"*

"That's enough!" Quark shouted. His mother had such nerve, trying to tell him—the eldest male!—what to do. "All I need to hear from you is that you've made sure Rom has transferred all my accounts over to the Bank of Bolias."

"Son, I'm not so sure your brother can handle your request. Maybe it would be better if I just—"

"Rom has to do it," Quark said firmly. Of course his mother knew that Rom was an idiot, as stupid as any Klingon when it came to matters of money, but there was no one else. Cousin Gaila would have skimmed, and there were no other close male relatives to whom he could turn.

"For Exchequer's sake, Quark, it's a simple request. I don't approve of what you're doing, but if I can just put in the call to the bank for you—"

"Put in the call?" Quark said, a little sick at the thought of it. "Please tell me you're joking."

His mother pursed her lips beneath the hook of her nose. *"Of course I am,"* she finally said. *"I'll contact your brother right away. And don't worry, I'll see to it that he doesn't miss anything."*

"Good," Quark said. "I've got big plans for this station. I'm going to be rich in no time."

His mother continued to look fretful. *"But . . . son . . . Cardassians? There's a war going on there, isn't there?"*

"Not exactly," Quark told her. "But even if there was, don't forget the Thirty-fourth Rule of Acquisition." *War is good for business.* That'd shut her up.

"Don't forget the Thirty-fifth Rule, either," Ishka reminded him. *"'Peace is good for business.' Couldn't you come back to peaceful Ferenginar, carry out your plans close to home?"*

"Moogie, I've got cases and cases of unreplicated food, and I'm on a station full of starving Bajorans."

"Quark, don't get mixed up in the local politics! Aligning yourself with the Bajorans—"

"Who said anything about alignment? It's supply and demand. You should see some of these people, Moogie. They're ugly enough as it is—tall, straight teeth—"

"And what makes you think they have any money?"

"Some of them do. They're bound to! They have vendors on this station, and I've seen Bajorans patronizing them. But you can't eat money, can you? From what I've heard, there are food shortages on their planet, and they don't seem to have a pair of decent shoes between a dozen of them, let alone a replicator. If they have the money, they'll pay. Believe me, Moogie."

"The Cardassians won't stand for it. You'll be killed."

"The Cardassians don't have to know," he said, lowering his voice from force of habit, though he'd already checked and double-checked the channel's security. The Cardassians were good, but not that good. "Besides, I've got an idea for a legitimate venture. You wouldn't believe what passes for leisure here. These soldiers—they've got nowhere to unwind! I'm going to change that, though."

His mother frowned, her eyes moist. *"So, there's no way I can convince you to come home?"*

Quark shook his head firmly. "I figure it'll be at least another decade before it's safe to show my face again. The sub-nagus isn't likely to have forgotten me."

"Maybe if you'd just married his sister," Ishka said sadly.

"She was engaged," Quark reminded her. "Anyway, I'll never get married. I'm not like Rom."

There was silence for a moment as Quark read his mother's disappointment—because of no more grandchildren, or because of Rom in general, he couldn't say.

"How is Rom, by the way?" he asked guiltily. "And that little baby of his . . . what was his name? Gob?"

"Nog," his mother said sharply. *"He's just fine, and he's hardly a baby, Quark. He's a lovely little seven-year-old. A brilliant boy."*

"Takes after his mother, does he?" Quark muttered.

Ishka cleared her throat. *"I'll send the money your way,"* she said. *"I mean, Rom will."*

"Thank you, Moogie," Quark said again, and signed off the transmission. He stared at the blank screen for a moment, allowing himself a moment of nostalgia for his home, back on beautiful green and wet Ferenginar, the air so moist and temperate, not like the arid heat on this station. At least his room had separate climate controls, though he couldn't get them to even begin to mimic the humidity he craved. His sinuses were parched. He decided to go to bed. With any luck, his money would be available in the morning. Until then, he had nothing to do but maybe try to make some Bajoran contacts, and he wanted to be rested before he made his way back over to the Bajoran side of the station. Rested, and armed.

Kalisi didn't know whether to be relieved or terrified when the flyer finally slowed, came to orbit of an unknown world. She had no idea where she was. Her knowledge of star charts was scanty at best. She'd never had any desire to study the geography of space, and had paid only brief attention to that part of her education, learning just enough to satisfy her requirement for graduation. She only knew that below her was a very small, very dark planet, distant from its minor sun.

The sharp-faced pilot did not address her, only tapped his comcuff. "Two to beam down," he said aloud, and Kalisi felt the cool rush of the transporter beam. When the sensation passed, she found herself in a long, brightly lit hallway, the pilot ushering her toward a door at the end.

"This way, Doctor Reyar." He did not sound unfriendly, exactly—in fact, there was no detectable emotion in his tone whatever. There was no one around, but she knew they were being watched. She could feel it.

Obsidian Order, then.

The pilot led her down a set of curving steps and into a large vestibule that housed a great many computers, floor-to-ceiling units with dozens of screens on each row, lit up with flickering characters and intermittently changing live feeds. There were shots that Kalisi recognized as public gathering places on Cardassia Prime: the Hall of Records, the upper levels of the Assembly building, the grounds of the Ministry of Science. Other feeds depicted scenes that Kalisi surmised were from other worlds, so alien was their appearance. She had scarcely blinked when she was greeted by a middle-aged Cardassian man whose features were as broad as the pilot's were pinched. He stepped forward, ushering her into a small room off to one side. He closed the door behind them, leaving the pilot outside.

"Doctor Reyar," he said. He flashed an unnervingly handsome smile. "Forgive me for bringing you here under such mysterious circumstances. Discretion was of the utmost importance. But no matter. We'll have you to your required destination in no time at all. But first—if you don't mind—I have a few questions for you."

Kalisi's initial reaction was anger, but she recognized the futility of it, and worked out a kind of smile. "Of course," she said, choking slightly on the words.

The man gestured for her to sit. "We would have done this on the surface of Bajor, but you see, my duties do not permit me to leave this facility. Not without the say-so of my superiors." He smiled again, and Kalisi could not suppress a shiver, for although the room was well-appointed, if small, it was cold here—colder even than on Bajor.

Kalisi sat, feeling an odd mix of indignity and fright as she waited for him to explain her kidnapping. Her father had ties to the Order, which should have insulated her from danger, but the isolation of this facility was anything but reassuring. Kalisi knew the sorts of tactics the Order employed to extract information from their interviewees. Her gaze darted nervously about the room. She didn't see anything that resembled the fearsome interrogation equipment she had always imagined, but then, perhaps her imagination was lacking. Maybe such a device was something so thoroughly innocuous that it had already been administered to her, without her even noticing.

"Doctor Reyar, I'll not keep you guessing. This matter concerns an old colleague of yours, from the Ministry of Science."

"The ministry," Kalisi repeated, trying to think of anyone suspicious she had known at the old facility.

"Yes, a woman named Miras Vara. You were quite close to her at one time, were you not?"

"Miras!" Kalisi exclaimed. Miras was hardly the sort of person that warranted the attention of the Obsidian Order. But then, perhaps Kalisi had been wrong. Perhaps this was not the Obsidian Order at all? Nobody had identified it as such; in fact, this man had not identified himself in any fashion.

"May I ask what this is about?" she said, feeling a little less frightened, a little more confused.

The man hesitated, and then spoke again. "Doctor Reyar, you contacted your father some years ago regarding Doctor Vara, and her strange behavior following an incident with a Bajoran artifact."

Kalisi immediately remembered. "Yes, I did," she admitted. "But I have not seen Miras in years. Not since . . ."

"Not since she disappeared, following that incident."

"She . . . disappeared," Kalisi repeated—a statement, but then she wasn't sure if she had known it. She had been so busy with her research at the time—so determined to be recognized by the Cardassian Board of Scientists so that she could develop her prototype on Bajor . . .

"That's right," the man said. "No one has heard from Doctor Vara since you notified your father about that object. And no one has been able to find the object, either. In fact, some time ago, I sought to retrieve it from the Ministry of Science, where it had been . . . misplaced for a good long time. But do you know what I found, when he went to remove it? Remove it legitimately, I might add, with proper permit and credential?"

"What?" Kalisi asked in a small voice, for she had not quite puzzled out what any of this had to do with her.

"The object was gone!" he said, in mock surprise. "Gone, after it had been confirmed that the director at the science ministry had relocated it, at last. *You* knew, before any of this occurred, Doctor Reyar, that the object held some significance. You knew enough to tell your father that he would be wise to inform Enabran Tain about it, didn't you? Now, I would like you to tell me anything you know regarding Doctor Vara's disappearance, Doctor Reyar."

His eyes glittered. Kalisi shook her head. "Please," she insisted. "I don't know! I haven't spoken to Miras in ages. I had no idea she was wrapped up in any . . . missing object. I . . . my father is Yannik Reyar, can you contact him, please? Does he know I'm here?"

"I know who your father is. I don't need to call him."

Kalisi felt ice in her veins. It was so terribly cold in this room—was that part of this man's interrogation technique? *Was* this an interrogation? She was afraid, and being scared made her angry. Who was this person?

"I've told you all I know," she said, realizing as she said it that she'd told him nothing. "I'm to be sent to Doctor Crell Moset's hospital. If I don't arrive there, my father will know that something has happened to me."

The man laughed then, the threatening tilt of his countenance abruptly vanishing. "My dear, you sound so grim!" he exclaimed. "Of course you'll be taken to Doctor Moset's hospital. It's a pity you couldn't help us. But if you remember anything at all . . ."

Kalisi stood, dazed. Was this really coming to an end? "I'll contact you, of course," she said, though she did not know his name, nor even the name of this planet where he apparently resided. "But who . . . ?"

"My name," he said cordially, "is Dost Abor. If, at any time in the future, you remember anything at all about your friend, you need only to contact your father in order to find me."

"Anything at all," she promised, wondering now what had actually happened. Had she imagined the cold, the way his eyes had shone, watching her cry for her father? Had she imagined her own fear?

Any citizen of the Union could be called upon at any time to assist the authorities in matters concerning the good of home and state. Which authority—homeworld police, the Order, Central Command—didn't really matter; authority got what it wanted. It seemed she'd been called upon, that was all.

Of course that's all. Miras Vara had gotten herself into some kind of trouble. It made sense that someone would want to talk to her old acquaintances. And she didn't know anything; she hadn't even *thought* of Miras in years . . .

She forced a laugh at herself as the pilot beamed them back up to the shuttle. *I should have been a writer of enigma tales,* she decided. She'd been slightly inconvenienced, at worst, and she'd overreacted. That was all. But then—that cold, handsome smile.

Dost Abor, she thought. She'd remember the name.

OCCUPATION YEAR THIRTY-FIVE

✦ ✦ ✦

2362 (Terran Calendar)

5

There was no more smoke, the explosion's resultant fires having long since died, but everything smelled of burnt composite and chemicals, the stink rising from the blackened ground. There was nothing left of the house—scarcely even rubble. The Bajoran device, whatever it was, had reduced the Pa'Dar home to little more than a large heap of fine dust.

Kotan Pa'Dar stood at the edge of the site with his personal aide, scarcely able to look at the mound of ash. A slight breeze stirred the dust, and Pa'Dar felt his eyes and throat ridges ache, wondering if the bones of his wife and son were in that dancing tide of particles. It was a mere fluke that Pa'Dar himself had not been home when the attack had occurred. In the days that followed the incident, contemplating his life without his family, he had wished that he had been home, sometimes so fervently that he could not sleep. He wished he had gone with them, wherever they now were.

Yoriv Skyl, who had been Pa'Dar's assistant and closest friend for the past four years, was now doing his best to provide consolation, but Pa'Dar found that he wished the other man would simply remain silent, as he could hardly bear to concoct responses for him.

"The others at the settlement continue to insist that your

son may not have been here when the attack occurred," Skyl said. "Every man in our vicinity has been instructed to look for an eight-year-old Cardassian child, and with so few of our children on this world, it will only be a matter of time—"

"Please, Yoriv. This isn't necessary." Pa'Dar found it ironic that his own house should be the one to be targeted. He had been sympathetic to the plight of the Bajorans almost since the beginning of his term; he had originally come to Bajor in the role of scientist, not conqueror, and during his reluctant political tenure had done his best to see to it that the Bajorans under his direct governance were treated fairly. But the terrorists did not distinguish, only worked to create the biggest impact with their violence. And who better to attack than an exarch?

Pa'Dar and Skyl were supposed to be discussing the particulars of a new dwelling that would be built here, directly atop the ruins of the old, but Pa'Dar was far from enthusiastic about the idea. He did not want to live on this spot anymore; in fact, he wasn't even sure he wanted to live on Bajor anymore.

With that thought, his adjutant fielded a transmission that had come to his padd. It was Dukat—Pa'Dar knew it from the first silky word as the prefect greeted Pa'Dar's aide.

"Yoriv."

Skyl turned slightly, to keep Pa'Dar out of the frame. Pa'Dar watched impassively, sure that his assistant would know to keep him out of any exchanges with the prefect. Especially today.

"Hello, Prefect. Is there something I can do for you?" Skyl's round face was the picture of helpful supplicant.

"Yes. You can remind Pa'Dar that the reports concerning drilling estimates in Tozhat were to be in my hands as of yesterday."

"Prefect, perhaps you've not heard of the tragedy that

occurred here four days ago—we are still dealing with the aftermath."

"Of course I am aware of it," Dukat said. *"I am the one who ordered that the site be assessed right away for the approval of a new structure. I wanted the affair to be managed as seamlessly as possible, to allow Pa'Dar to put the incident behind him—after an appropriate opportunity to grieve, of course."*

"Yes, of course, and for that, I know the exarch is grateful. You're most gracious, to extend such a courtesy when I know how you're counting on that data . . ."

Skyl went on, handling the prefect with his customary aplomb. Pa'Dar was grateful for his assistant's capabilities, for he himself had never been much of a politician when it came to handling Dukat's demands—many of which Pa'Dar disagreed with directly. Pa'Dar had been acquainted with the prefect for a long time, and the rivalry and dissent between the two men had only increased over the years. It didn't improve the situation that certain members of Pa'Dar's family served on the Detapa Council, and it was no secret that the council was often in direct conflict with Central Command. As the civilian government started to exercise more influence over the military, Dukat's position weakened—and he had Pa'Dar to vent his frustration on.

As Skyl continued to field Dukat, Pa'Dar had another look at the ruins of his home, and made a decision. Skyl finished his call and turned to Pa'Dar with apology in his expression.

"Business does not rest, Kotan. I will facilitate those reports for you—all that they will require is your thumb-scan. None of it is of such consequence that you need to trouble yourself with it immediately."

"Thank you, Yoriv. But if I may make an observation—it seems to me that you do my job even better than I do."

Skyl looked worried. "I don't mean to imply that your

input is unnecessary, Kotan. I only meant that perhaps, at a time such as this—"

Pa'Dar interrupted him. "You misunderstand me, friend. My father insists that he can eventually get me nominated for a seat on the Detapa Council if I return to Cardassia Prime. There are two members of the council who will likely be retiring soon, due to their age. . . . I wouldn't have considered it before now, but it seems to me that the Bajorans no longer appreciate my efforts here."

Skyl appeared to understand, now. "And so . . . my services will no longer be required?"

Pa'Dar almost smiled. "They will be very much required, Yoriv, for I intend to recommend you as my replacement. I have little doubt that the prefect will approve, since it seems to me that your relationship with him is far better than mine has ever been." He did not add that it was unlikely that any other, more experienced politician would want the position. Where once a man might feel that his political career could be secured by serving a few terms on Bajor, most now felt that it was not worth the risk. That skepticism was not likely to abate in the wake of this current tragedy.

Yoriv was speechless, and for a moment, Pa'Dar thought perhaps the other man didn't wish to take the position. But Skyl broke into an earnest smile, a smile of gratitude, and Pa'Dar felt, for a moment, something almost like relief— but it was gone again with another slight breeze, the dust of his heart and home spinning up into the ever chill wind. If nothing else, the thought of leaving Bajor at last was of some consolation. That comfort was small indeed.

She was only imagining that she could hear the whistling of the wind outside, Kira knew. In fact, nobody in the Shakaar cell was sure what kind of weather was going on beyond the dense, soundproof rock, though they'd received a report that there was a strong storm front coming in. Unusual for this late in the spring, but deep in the cave, there was no way to confirm what was really happening out there. Refractory minerals in the surrounding hillside, so effective at concealing them from Cardassian scanners, likewise made their own tricorders useless, unless someone maintained a tricky relay system that would have to be periodically recalibrated from outside. Where the weather was concerned, it was easier just to crawl through the tunnels to have a look at the sky. Sometimes Kira looked forward to doing the weather report, just to glimpse the outside world, but she didn't want to do it today. She was tired after another sleepless night.

Nobody went outside much anymore, and not for longer than absolutely necessary. After the detection grid had first gone online, they thought they had already defeated it; Mobara had come up with small individual devices that were supposed mask their biosigns, make them less distinguishable from the surrounding flora and fauna. The tech, as it turned out, wasn't entirely reliable, a fact driven home during that harrowing week last year when Kira had been cut off from the rest of the cell for seven days while being hunted by Union troops.

More recently, Mobara had cobbled together a rig that generated a scattering field over a small area, making them invisible to the sensor towers, and within the field the cell was able to travel in small groups—up to a point. If someone happened to accidentally wander or be forced outside the perimeter of the field, Cardassians were usually upon them within minutes. That was how well the grid seemed to work.

Although, Kira reflected, *it doesn't* always *work*. Even without Mobara's gadgets, there were still times when Dahkur's resistance fighters succesfully crept through the hills undetected, and Kira had often been among those lucky few.

But unless and until they could discern a pattern to those failures in the grid, it was in the relative safety of the caves that they made their homes, living off emergency rations and making gradiose plans to knock out the sensor towers.

The few active cells left on Bajor were dealing with the grid in much the same way as the Shakaar, but her cell heard about those things only through word of mouth. They had lost long-range contact with the other resistance groups over a year ago, although nobody was sure how it had happened—probably just a communications tower on Derna that needed maintenance, and no way to get to it. The Cardassians' anti-aircraft system was still fully functional, but that was an assumption only—one nobody in the Shakaar cell dared to challenge.

Kira set about boiling some water on the makeshift unit her cell used for a stove. This unit could produce heat without the danger of toxic emissions, as long as it was functioning properly. Drinking water was collected from a runoff point in an underground stream below them, one of the same streams that carried off any non-compostable waste and irrigated the artificially lit gardens Shakaar was always trying—unsuccessfully—to coax into producing enough food to make supply runs less necessary.

It was important to check the snowmelt every so often in the spring to ensure that the water levels were sound; they needed enough water to last them through the summer, but too much melt too soon meant they'd have a flood on their hands. The detection grid had turned even that tedious errand into a venture of uncertainty, and nobody had been able to check the rate of runoff in almost a month. Kira was all too aware of it every time she took a drink of water. Would this be the month they'd all die of thirst in this cave? Or the night they'd all drown in their sleep when the subterranean streams beneath them began to swell, filling the chambers with icy water?

The water in the pot began to bubble, and Kira tapped the contents of a Cardassian-issued ration pack into the little saucepan she was using. Most people ate these things straight, but Kira preferred to make a kind of soupy porridge from the crushed contents of the packets. It wasn't what any Bajoran would call delicious—the Cardassians' idea of food took quite a bit of getting used to—but you could live on it.

It was early, and the rest of the cell was still asleep, or possibly out in the larger chamber, grumbling about failed plans. Nothing had been going well lately, not for many months. Only a very few minor operations had been successfully carried out by the Shakaar cell over the last year, working in conjunction with what was left of the Kohn-Ma cell, a group Shakaar Edon didn't always see eye-to-eye with. The Kohn-Ma cell had fewer qualms about "friendly fire" than did any other cell Kira knew about, even if it involved civilians—even if it involved children. Kira didn't like it, but she had always taken it to be a necessity of fighting a war. Shakaar seemed to feel differently.

Kira ate quickly. She didn't want to be scolded for having her packet of rations so early in the day. The cell members were each supposed to be living on just one of these things every twenty-six hours, but Kira had decided she'd make another run back into one of the local townships herself, tomorrow, after the storm cleared up, to resupply the cell with food and other necessities.

She didn't know why, but she'd been the luckiest in her outfit as far as these supply runs went. Every time she reminded Shakaar or Lupaza of it, they'd insist that luck only went so far—*"How do you know your number isn't about to come up?"* Kira insisted it was only because she was more careful than the others, the ones who hadn't made it back, though she knew it was certainly not true. She could be just as clumsy as anyone else—last time she hadn't made it back to the warren until long after the Cardassians must have found the false life sign and moved on to find her signal—but somehow, she'd made it clean.

Kira had just about finished her meal when she jumped at a voice that seemed to come from nowhere. "Nerys!"

She turned to find that someone stood in the tunnel that connected with the northwestern entrance, the one used by the members of the Kohn-Ma cell. It was Tahna Los, a handsome but cocky young man who was not much older than Kira.

"You scared the *kosst* out of me," Kira grumbled, and quickly finished her food.

"I need you for a minute."

"You *need* me, eh?" Kira smirked, pretending to flirt. It always disarmed Tahna, who, despite his good looks, was notoriously clumsy with women.

"Really, Nerys, this is serious. Someone has to go and do the weather report in an hour. Biran wants me to do it, but I can't get through those little tunnels like you can. All you have to do is look out—"

"I should have known," Kira said. "Serious, huh? Please, Tahna. I'm busy."

"Busy eating, as usual," Tahna snorted.

"Well, maybe if I gain some weight, you'll stop pestering me to slither through that little crack in the rock. Your cell should have widened that fissure a long time ago."

"Biran says we can't. He said if we try to open it any further, it'll cause a cave-in."

"Sure," Kira muttered. "Fine, I'll do the weather report. But this is the last time this month. I've done it four times in a row."

Kira followed her friend through the hole that had been chipped away in the rock, reluctantly letting him pass into the arm that led down to his own cell's hideout. She headed back through the winding passage until the ceiling abruptly dropped to the height of her chest, and she was forced to crouch. The rock scuffed her clothes, and dust crumbled into her hair.

It seemed to take an eternity to scuttle through the squat passage. She kept expecting to hear the wind soaring through the trees as she came closer to the tunnel's mouth, but she heard nothing, and when she finally came upon the opening, she saw why.

There was no storm today. The sky had minimal cloud cover, and the air was moist, but warm. A perfect day.

And I'm spending it inside a hole in the rock. She squinted out at the sky, the blue color beyond the clouds so impossibly uniform. She did not want to go back inside. It was such a beautiful day, reminiscent of her childhood, and early summer days playing springball with her brothers.

She crouched there for a few moments before she found herself poking her head farther out of the tunnel, her neck and shoulders and waist following. She just wanted to stand up and stretch before reentering that cramped passage. She stepped out onto the ground, still wet from the rain the night before, and let her joints expand for a moment. Nobody had ever been caught this close to the tunnel; the kelbonite shielded them until they got to be a few paces away. Of course, there was always the chance of being spotted, but Kira felt certain that there would be no soldiers nearby. These days they were sent out only if the detection grid was tripped; otherwise, they stayed in their stifling barracks where they could . . . do whatever it was Cardassian soldiers did in their free time. Kira didn't care to speculate.

She took a few steps forward, acknowledging a desire to run out into the open and enjoy the day, enjoy the natural beauty of her world. She inhaled deeply. She could smell the rain-soaked spice of the wild *salam* grasses, the pitch from black rubberwood pines.

Maybe I should go home, too.

Not forever, just until they could figure out some way to beat the grid. Gantt had talked extensively about going back to his family instead of waiting around for nothing to happen. Some of the cells had disbanded, she knew, the members slipping back to their families, back to their old lives. But Kira didn't accept that the resistance movement was beaten. It was a temporary setback; they'd find a way to—

She froze. A rustling in the trees, just ahead of her. She immediately ducked, crouch-stepped backward to the cave, eyes wide and watchful, and then she saw it—not a Cardassian soldier, but a lean cadge lupus, its lips curled back over its sharp yellowed teeth. Kira froze, and the animal licked its lips, its ribs showing, its belly undoubtedly empty. Would it follow her back into the cave? She didn't want to chance it. She reached for her phaser—and it wasn't there.

Don't run.

She'd never faced one alone, but everyone knew basic safety. Never try to outrun a cadge lupus. You could try to charge it, make noise, make big movements; sometimes— often—that drove them off. Otherwise, look for the tallest tree you could climb and get off the ground. Kira acted. She lunged at the animal, swept with her arms, making the fiercest sound she could muster. Unfortunately, it came out sounding weirdly shrill and decidedly harmless. The lupus didn't budge, only continued to growl at her, the grizzled fur on the back of its neck spiking with aggression.

If it leapt for her, went for her throat, she'd be dead. If it followed her into the tight cave, she'd be trapped, unable to run in the narrow passage.

Kira spotted a tall tree with low branches, not too far behind the animal. She didn't stop to think, only took an enormous breath and ran for it. She sprinted so close to the lupus she could have reached out and patted its head. She must have confused it, for she reached the tree and was shimmying up the trunk before the beast came after her.

She reached a branch high off the ground, tried vainly to catch her breath as she perched on the peeling wood where it joined the trunk. The lupus paced the ground below, growling and whining.

Think. If the lupus went away soon, maybe she'd still have a chance to get back into the passageway before her biosign tripped the grid. But if not . . . she'd be better off letting the animal have her. Better that than bringing Union soldiers down on the warren.

How could she have forgotten her phaser? It was Tahna's fault, catching her off guard while she was in the middle of cooking breakfast, trying to conceal her meal from the others in the cell—after this, she'd never eat more than her fair share in a day, she vowed it to the Prophets a hundred times over.

Finally, the lupus seemed to lose interest in her, and it skulked off silently into the forest. But Kira knew better than to move right away. It would stay close, watching to see what she'd do. How long should she wait? Half an hour? Ten minutes? How long until the detection system locked onto her—if it hadn't already—and she'd end her life as a Cardassian practice target up in this ridiculous tree? She recalled her earlier thoughts, and decided that if the lupus meant to have her, so be it. It was better than the alternative. She edged toward the trunk of the tree, reminded anew that coming down a tree was a much more difficult undertaking than climbing one.

The clouds were creeping in, the perfect day beginning to turn into something else again. Fine droplets of rain had begun to fall by the time she reached the ground, and she dashed for the nearby cave entrance, squirming considerably as she fought her way through the hateful passage, imagining the creature slipping through the dark behind her. She would not be doing the weather report for a good long time after this. And the supply run? She'd be using the west entrance, thank you very much, no matter how risky it was said to be.

To her great dismay, Lupaza was waiting for her when she finally made it back to the primary chamber. The older woman held the remains of Kira's ration packet in her hand. These wrappers were not composted—like most products manufactured by the Cardassians, they were made without consideration for the long-term impact of their existence. The wrappers were usually pitched into one of the streams, where they would wash up at a point not far from Dahkur town with the rest of the cell's trash. Scavengers usually picked those things out and found ways to reuse them.

"Girl!" Lupaza exclaimed. "I've told you and told you . . ."

"I know, Lupaza, but I promise I'm not going to be hungry again until tomorrow. I feel a little sick, actually."

"Where have you been? Weather report again?"

Kira nodded.

"What's it doing out there? Rain, like they said?"

"Rain, like they said. You know—you'll think I'm crazy, but I'm going back to bed."

Lupaza shrugged. "I've always thought you were crazy, Nerys."

"Thanks."

Kira slid past the older woman and walked to the sleeping barracks, where the rest of the cell was still asleep. She settled down onto a wide pallet that held the slow-breathing forms of Shakaar, Latha, Chavin, and Mobara. Chavin was snoring. Kira wondered, as she tried to relax into elusive sleep, how she'd managed to escape detection this time. Without even a false life sign! Was it because she was too close to the kelbonite? Or was it really just luck? Probably, it was the kelbonite. Otherwise, wouldn't the Cardassians have found their hiding place by now? Kira didn't know, and she was too tired to properly consider. Her mind raced for a while before she finally started to drift, just as the others began to stir.

"Wake up, lazy!" Chavin chided her, pulling the blankets away, and Kira waved him off, too tired to challenge the insult. Thankfully, the others finally left, and Kira could sleep. She dreamed of a pacing cadge lupus, and a tree that was somehow sinking into the ground, lowering her to the animal's waiting jaws.

OCCUPATION YEAR THIRTY-SIX

✦ ✦ ✦

2363 (Terran Calendar)

6

Dukat was exhausted when he disembarked at the docking ring of Terok Nor. The funeral had been spectacular, one of the biggest Cardassia Prime had ever seen. Dukat had expressed polite condolences to Gul Darhe'el's family, but he secretly felt that the whole thing had a certain ostentatious crudeness about it. Darhe'el was hardly worthy of such an honor, and regardless of his character, there were some Cardassians, Dukat among them, who felt that death was a solemn occasion, not the appropriate time for garish displays. Darhe'el's family apparently felt differently. Gul Darhe'el, rot his petulant soul, would certainly have approved.

The funeral had been tiresome, and his few days at home had been less than peaceful. Athra had brought up the idea of moving to Terok Nor yet again, a topic he thought they'd closed long ago. A military ore processing station was no place for children. She knew that, and if she was so lonely, she might be a bit more welcoming when he did get time away, might make an effort not to argue over subjects long decided—and their bed had been cold for much of his stay. The bittersweet pride he usually felt upon seeing how his children had grown had too quickly faded, the lost years telling in their watchful young eyes. Two of them were in secondary training already . . . Even his habitual visit to Letau had failed to rouse his spirits. He had been bone-weary since before the long, cramped flight back to Terok Nor.

He was greeted, as he filed off the transport ship, by several members of his staff, all vying for his immediate attention regarding every manner of station business. Dukat tried to wave them off, but at least one glinn had news that Dukat knew he'd do best not to ignore: Legate Kell was on the comm, calling for the third time this afternoon.

"He knows how long it takes to travel from Cardassia Prime to Terok Nor," Dukat complained to Glinn Trakad, as they started for operations. "I saw him on Cardassia Prime not twenty-six hours ago. What could possibly be so important that he needs to contact me before I can even get my bearings after such a long journey?"

The dull-witted Trakad had no answer for him, and Dukat sullenly recalled the loss of one of his favorite aides, Corat Damar. Dukat sorely wished he could find another officer as loyal and agreeable in person as Damar had been, but then, of course, in the end, Damar had chosen his personal life over station business. Enough time had passed that Dukat supposed he was willing to forgive the younger man for it, but the recollection was still irksome.

Kell was waiting for him on the comm when he arrived in his office and put on the lights. The room felt cold and deserted, after only two days, but he heard the environmentals kick on as he sat.

"Legate," Dukat addressed his superior. "I didn't expect to converse with you again quite so soon."

"Dukat, it has recently come to my attention that you have changed religious policy on Bajor," Kell said. "Again."

"Ah," Dukat replied, a smile spreading across his face. "And this . . . concerns you, Legate?"

"You know perfectly well it does!" Kell snapped. *"When you abolished religious counsel in the work camps and placed restric-*

tions on the open practice of the Bajoran faith, I thought it was one of your more intelligent decisions. Now you've reversed it. Explain yourself!"

Dukat's smile didn't waver. "You have my reports. You're aware that there has been a measurable drop in terrorist activity since the implementation of the new sensor sweeps."

Kell scoffed. *"A drop, perhaps. But not an end."*

"Restoring the Bajorans' religious freedom demonstrates that they can only benefit from abandoning the insurgency," Dukat pressed on. "Besides, I have found that it is useful to give the Bajorans something precious to them, once in a while."

"Useful?"

"Yes. So I can threaten to take it away again."

Kell shook his head, his expression conveying annoyed disapproval. *"There was a time, Dukat, when you understood how dangerous rampant, unchecked spirituality could be—when you recognized it for the cancer it is, and didn't hesitate to excise it."*

Dukat's eyes narrowed. "I have not forgotten," he said tightly.

"And yet now you're using the Bajorans' religious freedom as part of some self-serving strategy, as if running Bajor was a game of kotra."

"Violence is down. Productivity is up. If the annexation were indeed a game, I daresay I am winning."

"But you haven't won yet," Kell pointed out. *"Cardassia can scarcely afford to risk Bajor's long-term usefulness on your overconfidence."*

Dukat was growing weary of the conversation. "I assure you, Legate, Bajor is under control. *My* control. Will that be all?"

"For now," Kell said, *"But this conversation is not over."* The legate abruptly cut the connection, and the prefect stared at his now-empty holoframe for a moment, imagin-

ing the day when Kell would pay for every slight, every obstruction, and every wasted moment he had ever caused Dukat.

That day will come soon, he assured himself. *This I vow.*

Mora was still flushed with pride regarding the reception Odo had received, though it had been several hours since the Cardassian dignitaries had left the Bajoran Institute of Science. Mora had induced the shape-shifter to take on the forms of several animals, but it was the so-called "trick" he'd done with his neck that had garnered the most reaction. Mora couldn't quite gauge why the Cardassians had responded as they had, but he didn't much care. That his work was being considered important was the best outcome he could have hoped for.

Yopal had insisted that Odo be put aside for months at a time while Mora attended to other matters that interested the Cardassians. In the past two years, Mora imagined he had only worked with Odo the collective equivalent of a few weeks. Being idle seemed not to have a physical effect on Odo, but it concerned Mora nonetheless, if for no other reason than that he could not use Odo as an excuse to avoid collaborating on Cardassian projects. But that was probably going to change, now. The occupation leaders, including Gul Dukat himself, had been so impressed with Odo, Mora was now beginning to hope, even to believe, that he might be able to work exclusively with Odo once again.

It was with these cheerful thoughts that he was running his customary bioscans on Odo's signature tonight, when the shape-shifter assumed his humanoid form and began to ask questions.

"Doctor Mora, have I been here for a long time?"

Mora was a bit taken aback by the question, until he recognized that Odo might not have any concept of what was meant by "a long time." Ten minutes might feel like a long time to the shape-shifter, or it might not feel like much time at all. They'd discussed the concept, of course, but it occurred to Mora that he'd never actually questioned Odo about his feelings in the matter. "What do you think, Odo?"

Odo looked away from Mora. "I am thinking, Doctor Mora, that I have been here for long enough."

Mora had to stop what he was doing in order to reexamine and internalize what the shape-shifter had just said. The coordinates denoting Odo's mass—many times greater than when he could still fit in a handheld beaker, so many years ago—flashed by on the screen of his padd, but it was as though he didn't see them.

"What . . . could you possibly mean by that, Odo?"

"I would like to leave this place."

"Leave?" Mora was so surprised, he laughed. "Odo, where do you presume to go?"

"I am very unhappy here," Odo replied, and the tone in his voice undeniably reflected it.

"Unhappy! Odo, you have never given me any indication before that you were not happy."

"Haven't I?"

Mora took a step back. In a rush, he came upon the uncomfortable realization of what Odo was telling him; the many times that Odo had appeared to be sad, or even hostile. Mora had taken care never to acknowledge those reactions as anything but awkwardness on Odo's part, a fumbling, perhaps, for the correct response, never to be considered at face value . . . but in his heart, perhaps Mora had known it. And yet, what could he have done? Odo was his life's work. Mora had ignored Odo's misery out of necessity. For a fleeting moment, it filled him with deep shame, but his own sense of self-preservation chased it away.

Odo went on. "I want to live as a Bajoran lives, Doctor Mora." He seemed uncomfortable as he said it.

Mora spoke stiffly. "Well, Odo, I'm not sure if you know exactly what that entails. In fact, typical Bajorans . . . don't enjoy most of the comforts that you and I do. It's a harsh world out there, and—"

"Doctor Mora, I . . . do mean to leave."

"Odo!" Mora exclaimed, feeling himself growing angry. The shape-shifter had never spoken to him so firmly before. "You aren't ready to leave! Nowhere near it! You and I still have years of work ahead of us . . . many things to do . . . before you could even consider it!"

"But, Doctor Mora, there is no way for you to make me stay."

Mora was stunned at what he was hearing. "Odo, are you trying to imply that you . . . would simply walk out, on your own?"

"You would not be able to prevent me from it," Odo said. "But I wished to tell you before I go."

Mora tried to steady his breathing. He was at least grateful that Odo hadn't simply run away, but the very idea . . . that he somehow believed Mora would ever condone his leaving the laboratory. He raised his gaze to meet that of the shape-shifter, and Odo quickly dropped his own. He had learned humanoid expression just well enough to have picked up some affectations almost naturally, but still, he would never blend into the general population. People would always know there was something naively peculiar about him, even if he learned to perfect his humanoid form. He'd be lucky to last a week in the real world.

"Odo. You must reconsider. It would be very dangerous out there for you. If I could escort you into the outside world, I would do it, but you know I'm not permitted to leave the facility . . ."

"I am sorry about that, Doctor Mora. I wish you could leave, too."

Mora saw, then, that Odo had felt even more of a prisoner here than he himself had. He could sympathize with his wanting to leave, but if there was any way to stop it from happening . . .

There isn't. He'd worked with Odo long enough to know what his capabilities were . . . and to know that the creature could be surprisingly obstinate, when the mood struck him.

"Odo," he finally said, "I must emphatically insist that you stay."

To Mora's chagrin, the shape-shifter merely shook his head from side to side, still not looking up.

"So. You would leave me. The only person who has ever shown you any kindness, the only person who cares about your well-being . . ."

Odo was silent, but Mora could see that he was just as determined as before. He let out a frustrated breath, feeling sick with defeat. If Odo was gone, there was nothing to keep him from collaborating with the Cardassians, or, rather, to keep him from having to acknowledge that was what he'd been doing all along. Working with Odo, he'd been able to forget the rest of it, at least for a time. He tried a different approach.

"You will find that the Cardassians out there, they will not be nearly so pleasant as those you have met inside."

Odo was silent for a minute. "Doctor Reyar was not so pleasant," he said.

Mora laughed sharply. "Doctor Reyar is a *hara* kit compared to the Cardassians you are likely to meet outside the facility."

Odo seemed to consider this. "I will be careful," he said firmly. "I can take care of my own needs. I can travel as an animal to avoid them, if it is necessary."

Mora's heart sank as he saw that cautionary tales were unlikely to change Odo's mind. He wondered, then, what the Cardassians' reaction to him would be. Of course, Odo was not a Bajoran, and he would not register against the detection field that existed outside most of the boundaries. He would likely be able to travel wherever he wanted without stirring up the Cardassian troops . . .

The code, he thought, and the rest of a plan suddenly came together.

"Odo," he said, "if you are determined to do this . . . I would ask that you would do one thing for me."

Odo did not answer, only appeared wary—at least, Mora thought he looked wary. It was not always easy to tell. He went on.

"I'm not permitted to leave, as you know. I can only contact my family very sporadically, and those exchanges contain nothing of substance. I would like for you to deliver a message to them."

"Of course, Doctor Mora," Odo said, seeming relieved, "I would be happy to do it."

"Thank you. I hope you will stay at least another twenty-six hours, Odo, so that I can get . . . get all my notes together," he said, fumbling for an excuse. He felt a deep ache of misery as he said it, revisiting the unhappiness he had been living in almost exclusively since he had been forced to work as a collaborator. Now his most important work—a creature he had come to feel great affection for— was going to leave him. He would have no one, no respite from his loneliness. But if Odo could deliver a message to the Ikreimi village, if Keral's claims of knowing someone in the resistance had any merit at all, maybe then, some degree of the self-loathing he had come to experience could be dialed back, at least to tolerable levels.

Odo blinked at him, slowly and deliberately, and Mora realized he was looking at a free man, a creature with nothing on his conscience and a limitless future. And for just a moment, Mora resented him so deeply that he could hardly stand to look at him.

Natima had been called to the Information Service's headquarters in Cardassia City for her latest review with Dalak, the director of her department, and as she shifted in a stiff-backed chair in front of his small metal desk, she could tell by the tone of this encounter that he was probably going to be transferring her. There had been rumors of changes made, and he had that distracted, irritable air he acquired when he was forced to reshuffle assignments. She hoped he'd send her to Cardassia II. She had grown up in an orphanage there, but that wasn't the reason she wanted to return. She'd made contacts in the past few years, people who had come to seem to her almost like family.

Of course, Natima wasn't sure what it was like to have a family, so she couldn't make the comparison with any certainty, but she had become very close to a few of the people within the rough organization that was beginning to take shape. In particular, Gaten Russol, though Natima had no romantic interest in the man. No, he was definitely more like a brother to her—or at least, her estimation of what a brother must be like. A brother that she had come to deeply trust and respect. He currently lived on Cardassia II, along with a handful of others within the nascent dissident movement that Natima was helping to organize.

It seemed that Dalak had other things in mind for Natima, however. It took her a moment to fully grasp what he had said when he uttered the words, "Terok Nor." It was a name that was immediately familiar—and immediately repugnant.

Natima sat forward in her chair, her hands spread across the surface of the director's desk. "No, no, Mister Dalak, you promised you would not send me to Bajor again. You said I—"

"I never promised you any such thing," Dalak said crisply. "In fact, I am certain that I warned you this day might come. Come now, Miss Lang. It's been years since that incident on Bajor. Decades, even."

Decades? Could it really have been that long? Natima supposed it had. How had she suddenly come to be so old?

"Besides," Dalak went on, "I'm not sending you to Bajor, specifically. Terok Nor is a thoroughly modern Cardassian facility, in orbit of the planet, with the strictest of security measures. You will be safe there and uniquely placed to report on the annexation from its command post."

"Yes, of course," Natima replied, though it wasn't so much the issue of safety that made her loath to return to the B'hava'el system. It was the politics, the gross display of manifest destiny that she feared would someday drive her people into ruin. Could she safely keep her opinions silent in such a place? Especially with that degenerate prefect residing in the very same facility?

"It's a temporary post," Dalak assured her. "You'll be there less than a year."

Natima fell back into her chair, unhappily accepting the inevitable. This was her career, and though it was increasingly coming into conflict with her evolving ideals, there was no other profession she cared to pursue. She would go where the service sent her.

It was late, and the bar was closed for the night, but Quark was still at work, as he often was, tallying his daily receipts at one of the tables. He checked every number at least three times against his earlier totals. He was not a man to make mistakes in his ledgers, because he never failed to check his totals thrice.

Quark heard the footfalls of someone approaching the door long before they entered the bar. One of the Bajoran workers, wiping up a puddle of spilled *kanar*, flinched as an expressionless garresh jostled past him, as if he was not even there. Quark frowned. He had taken pains to project the image of neutrality, but sometimes it galled him to see the way the Bajorans were treated.

"Quark, you have a call," the Cardassian told him. "Something appears to be wrong with your comm line—"

"I closed it down for the night," Quark snapped, and then quickly checked himself. He couldn't afford to express any attitude. He gave a strained smile. "So I could get a moment's peace while balancing my account books," he finished. "Thank you for informing me. I'll take my call now."

He watched the blank-faced garresh leave his bar and chased the Bajoran worker off before he activated his comm. The call was from Ferenginar, and Quark felt sure he knew the origin of the communication code—it was his cousin Gaila, doubtless looking for a handout. Now that Quark was beginning to enjoy some monetary success, he could look forward to every leaf and twig of his family tree coming along with their grubby hands outstretched.

His bar on the station had grown from a little gambling post in one of the storefronts on the Promenade to the largest business on the station. Quark's had quickly overtaken the replimat as the popular place for Cardassians to drink and dine—no great accomplishment, but he wasn't going to argue with success—and he'd plowed his profits back into his black market business, *and* created a fund to pay off anyone who might venture too close to his fledgling enterprises. Besides the foodstuffs—and the Bajorans were a nut-and-root type of people, mostly cheap vegetables and bird flesh—he oversaw a goods exchange, and he had a line on some utilitarian art from the surface, which he sold on consignment at one of the shops. Carved wooden bowls and tatted shawls were popular with the station soldiers; they liked to send them home to their families. He could get a piece of pottery that would sell for twenty slips on the station in exchange for a half-slip bucket of root soup. He was making money hand over fist, and of course his mother had to brag about it, telling tales that had reached the ears of many less-fortunate relatives and acquaintances. As it was, Quark had already taken in his penniless idiot brother and nephew, after Rom's marriage had finally failed, and he wasn't especially interested in showing anyone else the same degree of altruism.

Gaila's ugly mug was spastic with excitement, and he didn't bother with any pleasantries. *"Quark! Aunt Ishka tells me you've begun turning quite a profit these days! I wonder if you wouldn't be interested in fronting a potentially very lucrative endeavor."*

"I'm already fronting a lucrative endeavor," Quark told his cousin. "It's nice to talk to you, Gaila, but I've got things to do."

"Your mother also tells me," Gaila went on, as if not listening, *"that your brother and nephew have come to live with you. That you took them in entirely out of the goodness of your heart—"*

"There's no goodness in my heart," Quark hastily interjected.

"That's not what Aunt Ishka tells me!" Gaila said. *"She says you're becoming soft. I hear you're selling food to those Bajorans at cost. I hear you're—"*

"You hear nonsense, then," Quark snarled. His first instinct was for self-preservation—to deny outright that he was selling anything to the Bajorans—but he couldn't back down from an accusation like that. "I may have lowered my prices somewhat, but you can't gouge the Bajorans when they've got next to nothing to pay with. I wouldn't sell anything if I didn't make it accessible, and I'm selling plenty. You've got to know your market, cousin. I'm sure there's a Rule of Acquisition that says something about that . . ." He racked his brains, but could not think of an appropriate Rule. Perhaps he should make one up.

"*I know the rules, and I've got a better idea for profit in the B'hava'el system,*" Gaila said.

"You want to come *here?*" The last thing he needed was Ferengi competition—especially from his lousy cousin.

"*That's right. Food is one thing, but weapons—the Bajorans would pay well for them, wouldn't you say?*"

Quark snorted. "And I thought I was taking a foolish risk."

Gaila ignored him. "*Would you loan me the latinum to get it started? A munitions consortium, that is. Think of it, Quark! If the Bajorans have a little money to spare for a bit of food now and again, they'll have money to spare for guns and ammo, no question. I've been listening to the newsfeeds from Bajor since you got there, and the resistance will stop at nothing to—*"

"I don't know, Gaila." What his cousin was saying made sense, but Quark wasn't entirely sure he wanted to get involved. Of course, with his black-market goods business, he was already into the occupation pretty deeply, but he had a strong feeling that on a list of Cardassian punishable offenses, food-someone-might-eat and weapons-someone-might-shoot-at-you-with were not quite equal. "It sounds pretty dangerous."

"*I'll buy you your own ship when I start to make profit,*" Gaila promised. "*I mean, in addition to paying you back, with interest. You name the rate you're comfortable with.*"

Quark frowned. The danger seemed a little less dangerous when he started thinking about interest rates. Gaila was a relative, of course, so he couldn't go much higher than eighteen percent . . .

Gaila began to smile toothily, reading Quark's silence in his own favor. "*Do we have a deal?*" he ventured.

"I don't think it would be a good idea for you to be coming and going on Bajor," Quark said. *It wouldn't be good for either of us if he was caught.*

"My associate will take care of the face-to-face business with the Bajorans," Gaila promised. *"All transactions will take place outside the system. You'll never see either of us."*

"Well," Quark said, thinking he could live with that arrangement, "I'm thinking about twenty percent."

"Twenty percent! Quark, I'm family!"

"You told me to name my—" Quark stopped speaking, staring in horror at the blue light that had flickered on his keypad. "I have to go," he said, and jabbed his finger at the disconnect. Someone was trying to listen in on his conversation.

Quark snapped his console shut with shaking hands. He reviewed, in his mind, the last few lines of the conversation. *We were only talking about financial matters, nothing to implicate me.* Thrax had been trying to catch him at his black market business for three years now, but Quark had been far too careful. His stupid, prideful boasting may have changed all that. If he hadn't been so quick to defend himself; if he'd just denied Gaila's implication that he was dealing with Bajorans—well, if Thrax had indeed heard his conversation, Quark's only recourse was to construct a convincing lie. He put his ledgers away and began to close up the bar, already working on his alibi.

Since the presentation at the Bajoran Institute of Science, Dukat had thought often of the shape-shifter, Odo. He'd heard about the creature years before, of course, and had always meant to go see it—the discovery of a new sentient life-form was inherently interesting—but he'd had more urgent matters needing his attention, and indulging a mild curiosity on Bajor's surface hardly seemed worth the time. Now that the resistance was finally—*finally*—firmly in hand, he'd arranged a presentation at the institute for some of the occupation leaders, to report on the new detection grid—and to make a show of Bajor's safety, of course. The mere fact of inviting them was proof, and he'd overseen preparations himself, discussing with the director his ideas for the visuals, his feelings on how the material should be presented. As an afterthought, he had asked her to include something about the life-form.

Doctor Yopal's presentation on the sensor and tracking systems had been brief and not overly technical, as he'd recommended, and had been well received. Too long a presentation, and the guls and legates attending might start to regret the trip, which would have been entirely counterproductive. Another scientist spoke more specifically on the systems' impressive attendant weaponry, and Dukat had been positively gleeful, watching the grim, irritable faces of his detractors as they were forced to recognize his success. But the nondescript fumbling Bajoran who'd introduced himself last had stolen the show. Or rather, his shape-shifter had.

Dukat had displayed the same polite interest as everyone else, but he had no doubt that they were all just as astounded as he. The Bajoran had gone on about density and mass and theoretical subspace phasing, but all attention had been on the "man" that stood next to him, tall and lean and of strangely unmolded face. The being had shifted through a number of different forms, becoming a whole series of animals, a chair, a table, a pair of boots; at the Bajoran's urging it had done tricks with its skin and flesh, stunning and amusing the rapt audience.

Afterward, several of Dukat's departing guests had asked what he planned to do with the creature. He had managed some ambiguous answer, wondering that himself. The research had shown Odo to be impervious to any common injury, and capable of fantastic physical strength. There had to be some military application, something that would advance Cardassian interests—and therefore his own rank and reputation, a most agreeable corollary.

He leaned forward in his office chair, tapped in the code for the institute. A moment later, the director's face flickered onto his screen.

"Gul Dukat," she said. She looked pleased to see him.

"Doctor Yopal," he said. "I wanted to commend you once more on your management of the institute's presentation."

The scientist hesitated, then frowned in seeming irritation. *"Do you not remember telling me already?"*

She was flirting. Dukat sighed inwardly. Sree Yopal was attractive, he supposed, but he would never meet a Cardassian female as lovely as his Athra, at home and patiently waiting for him. To have an indiscretion with another Cardassian woman . . . he found the thought distasteful.

"Although I was surprised you let the Bajoran present Odo," he said, entirely ignoring her less-than-subtle advance. The message would be clear. "Surely, you've turned the project over to a team of our own . . . ?"

Her face smoothed, became a mask. *"Actually, the shapeshifter has left the institute."*

"What? What do you mean? Who authorized a transfer?"

"No one, Gul. Odo left of its own volition."

"And you just let it go?"

Yopal cleared her throat. *"Short of placing the entire institute under a high-density containment field, there was no way to keep the shape-shifter, if it did not wish to stay."*

Dukat had to consciously relax his neck and jaw to speak. "Where did it go?"

"I do not know. Perhaps Doctor Mora—"

"You will have him forward all research regarding the shape-shifter to me immediately."

"Yes, sir," she replied.

"And . . . Doctor Yopal, I have good news for you."

"Oh?" She cocked her head.

"Yes, Doctor. Your assignment on Bajor has come to an end. You may return to Cardassia Prime."

The woman's smile vanished. *"Prefect,"* she said faintly, *"you are . . . too kind. But I—"*

"No need to thank me," he said, fully aware that thanking him was the last thing on her mind. He knew her type all too well. She was driven and committed, and leaving Bajor was anything but a reward to her, especially so abruptly. She would be unlikely to enjoy as much prestige in a Cardassian facility. But losing the shape-shifter was not a mistake that Dukat could let go unpunished. He cut the transmission off, already thinking ahead. What had the Bajoran doctor said?

"Odo has expressed great interest in learning more about his species . . ."

Where might such a creature go? Who would it talk to, if it sought information about other worlds? A Bajoran farmer, raised by generations of Bajoran farmers?

It will come here, Dukat thought, suddenly certain of it . . . though Dukat would do what he could to ensure the visit, to see to it that Odo understood where its best chances lay.

He put a call in to the base nearest the institute, waited while a surprised garresh went to find his commander. It shouldn't be too hard to find the creature, considering its appearance. He'd have it monitored at a discreet distance, and once he was sure of its whereabouts, he could decide how best to draw it in, bring it to Terok Nor. Then he could take all the time he needed, to decide how Odo might best serve the Union. It—

He, he reminded himself. *It identifies itself as "he."*

Dukat smiled. A sentient creature that could turn himself into a book on a shelf, an insect on the wall . . . Perhaps *he* might serve best as one of Dukat's team.

". . . which was how I ended up spending half my residency on the station at Hetrith," Doctor Moset said. "That's when I really shifted my focus. The creature died, eventually, but I kept it alive long enough to learn everything about it. By the time I went home, I was ready to apply for my second doctorate. And after all that work, they put me *here*. Even Hetrith had better facilities, and it was a frontier station."

He leaned against the biobed that Kalisi was calibrating, his long arms folded, his tone light in spite of his words. She'd found Crell Moset to be a man who took most things lightly, his most common expression one of amused detachment. They were alone in the contagion ward, the beds empty, the day staff excused. In the weeks since Kalisi had come to work at his hospital, Moset had taken to seeking her out sometimes in the late afternoon, talking a bit about himself as she went about whatever menial work she'd been assigned. Complaining about his lot in life, which was so much better than hers, she occasionally felt like throttling him.

After a few days to consider her options, she'd decided to encourage the doctor. For a relatively young, unmarried woman it was not the wisest choice, she knew, to become involved with a superior. But for such a woman with few prospects, in her personal life or her career, there were worse mistakes.

Like not *becoming involved with one*, she thought, tapping at the open control panel on the bed's back. Second time in a month she'd had to reset the circulatory diagnostics. The equipment wasn't the best, but at least it was *his* hospital, his research facility. She was just someone qualified enough to fix it.

"I mean, how many times have you had to reset these

things?" Moset asked, his thin line of a mouth curving slightly.

"You seem to do just fine with what you've been given," she snapped, a sneer in her voice.

He studied her a moment, perhaps making his own final decision on the matter. He had a fine, high brow and extremely thin lips. Not a bad-looking man, although his hair was an atypical brown, rather than black. He was tall, which she liked. She didn't know his personal situation, but doubted it was relevant. He'd been working up to something since the day she'd arrived.

"That's right, Doctor Reyar, I do," he said, meeting her gaze directly. "I've done important research in my time here."

Kalisi went back to her work. She felt the heat in her voice, felt its warmth. It felt good, to say what she wanted to say. To know what effect her irritation would have. She was an attractive woman, she knew, well-educated and fine of feature.

"How nice for you," she said, not looking away from the bed panel.

A beat later, and his hand was on her shoulder. His fingers were long and tapered, his hand warm through her tunic. It was so cold here, always so cold . . .

"I see how hard you work," he said, his voice low in his throat. "I appreciate it."

She turned to him then, letting her anger carry her. "I'm a weapons engineer, Doctor. I designed and implemented the detection grid that has made Bajor safe for us, that has finally halted the insurgency. And because of a single mistake I made, years ago, the Ministry of Science has given me no credit for my work, for my research. My reward for getting the systems up and running is to be sent here, to fix biobeds for *you*."

She'd stepped over the line, but she didn't care, and the

doctor's heat was coming back at her, his bright eyes flashing with it.

"You think I want to be here? My specialty—my passion—is nonhumanoid exobiology. I had just begun to establish myself at home and the ministry tells me I'm needed *here*, running research projects on an inferior species, giving inoculations and treating diseases as though I'm some, some *medic*. At least you get to go out in the field. I'm here every night, every single night, all alone—"

He was suddenly so close to her that she could smell him, the astringent scent of sterilizing hand cleanser, an expensive hair oil. His gaze was brilliant, piercing, and focused entirely on her. His hand slipped around her lower back and he pulled her roughly closer.

She fought him for a just a moment and then allowed herself to be kissed, to feel the crush of his narrow mouth against hers. He was a brilliant man. She would work at his side, find a way not to be forgotten. He pushed his hand into her skirt, and then her only thoughts were of the flesh.

7

Although the occasional alien pilot came through Quark's bar, as well as the odd half-breed from regions unknown, the vast majority of his clientele looked identical to him: dark, slicked-back hair, uniformly gray skin, and indistinguishable shiny gray military uniforms. Sometimes, if one of the Cardassian regulars struck up a conversation with him, Quark had to engage in a moment of panicky brain-wracking in order to place the man—was it someone he'd talked to before? It took time to recognize a particular Cardassian, and even then, Quark didn't go much by faces; a man's voice, his mannerisms, the verbal expressions he frequently used—that was the way to tell, in an ocean of bland gray people.

Women were a different matter. Quark came up from the cellar after the lunch rush one fine, lucrative day to find that there was a new face in his establishment, a female face. He'd seen Cardassian women before, but they were always either uniformed or accompanied by a male. This woman was neither. She was dressed in a long, green gown—not a scientist or a soldier, and apparently nobody's wife, either. The dimple in her forehead was painted bright blue, something that Quark was reasonably certain indicated that she was not married. The other men in the bar had taken notice, too, a group of noncoms and a couple of glinns at the bar all stealing looks.

Quark saw that his brother was headed toward the woman's table. Quickly he elbowed his way ahead of Rom and approached the lone Cardassian female.

"Hey," Rom protested, but Quark ignored him. He flashed his best sales smile at the woman.

"What will you be having, then, miss?"

The woman lifted her face to him, her throat long and graceful, accentuated by the ridges that ran down either side of it. The neckline of her dress dipped down low enough that Quark could see the alien peculiarities of her pectoral bone structure; a scoop, identical to the one on her forehead, was plainly visible just above her breasts. Quark swallowed, noting to himself that he had never seen quite so much of the Cardassian anatomy before; he found this woman's to be surprisingly agreeable.

"A Samarian Sunset, please," she said, her voice cool.

"Right away," he said, and dashed back to the bar.

"Brother," Rom said. "Your elbows are sharp." He rubbed his side.

"Sharper than your wit," Quark grumbled, mixing the drink. "Can't you see there are a half-dozen customers who haven't been waited on?"

"I was trying to see to that woman back there—"

"I'll handle her, Rom. You take care of those soldiers in the corner."

"Oh. Okay, brother."

On his way back to the woman's table, Quark nearly tripped over one of his Bajoran day laborers, a scrawny man who had gone blind in one eye. The man looked up from where he had been scrubbing the floor, his ruined eye disarmingly cloudy and dead-seeming, and Quark scowled at the sight of him. "Out of my way," he barked, shoving the crouched old man with his knees.

"Forgive me, Quark," the man said huskily.

Quark felt a little nauseous, regarding this poor creature.

Since that conversation with Gaila, he'd gone out of his way to show the Bajorans no mercy. He had his reputation to consider; for a businessman, "soft" was like a curse.

"Ferengi do not forgive," he said sharply. "I can't have my customers stumbling over a bag of bones on their way to the tables. Do your job, or it's back to the mines."

"Of course," the man replied, following it up with a coughing fit.

"And try to control your coughing! This is a place of relaxation—we don't need to be confronted with the specter of your various . . . maladies!"

Quark stepped over the Bajoran and set the drink down in front of the pretty woman, smiling broadly. He tapped the side of her glass with a fingernail, and the clarity of the glass was suddenly overtaken by a reddish cloud that dissipated into a soft, orange glow.

"One Samarian Sunset," he announced with a flourish.

"Thank you," she said, eyeing the Bajoran man on the floor. She seemed troubled, but Quark could not be sure, going by her mysterious expression alone. Maybe she didn't like Bajorans. He could not take his eyes off her. Her skin wasn't so much gray as the pale, metallic hue of the Ferengi sky on a spring morning. Her eyes sparkled like gems.

Quark put his hands together and watched her as she took her first sip. "Is it to your liking?" he asked eagerly.

She smiled, and cleared her throat. "It's fine, thank you, Mister . . ."

"Quark, the proprietor of this humble tavern." He spread his hands.

"Well, Mister Quark. I'm Natima. Natima Lang. It's a fine place, your establishment. The last time I was here, I remember thinking that the station was sorely lacking a nice place for . . . food and drink."

"The last time you were here?" Quark cocked his head.

She took another sip. "When I was a much younger woman than I am now." She laughed softly.

"You look plenty young to me," Quark said honestly. Cardassians hid their ages well.

She snorted a ladylike snort. "Thank you, Mister Quark, but . . . I doubt the Cardassians in here would agree with you. You might have noticed they can't stop staring at me."

"Because you're so attractive," Quark said, again in earnest.

She laughed again, louder this time. "It's because they can't figure out what a female civilian my age is doing in a place like this, without a male escort."

Quark slid into the seat opposite hers. "I'll admit that very question occurred to me, as well."

She set down her drink, stared at it. "I'm with the Cardassian Information Service. I've been sent to report on the state of the annexation. I was on the surface of Bajor, years ago, and now . . . I've been sent back, though I'll be staying on the station this time."

Quark nodded. "So I can look forward to seeing you again?"

She smiled, meeting his gaze evenly. "Yes, I suppose you can." She gestured to the soldiers that surrounded them. "If they will tolerate it."

Quark shrugged. "Who cares what they think?"

"Women have their roles within my society," she said, and sounded rueful, though Quark couldn't imagine why.

"Isn't it that way in every society?" he asked. "I mean, besides those Bajorans—they've got nothing in the way of civilized societal structure. Their women just run around, willy-nilly, doing any old thing the men do—"

"I think I'll be going now," the woman said briskly. "I've finished my drink." She stood up.

"Oh," Quark said, filing the information away. Feminist, probably. He could work around that. "Well, please do come back."

"Thank you, Mister Quark." She said it with a worrisome air of finality. She fished a slip of latinum from a pocket concealed in her dress and dropped it on the table before turning to go.

Quark didn't want it to be over, but he had no line at hand. He was reduced to telling the truth.

"Wait. It's . . . lonely on the station, sometimes. Perhaps I could offer you another drink . . . at half price?"

She stopped for a moment, actually seemed to think about his offer before shaking her head. "No," she said finally. "I'm hardly so lonely that I've been reduced to chatting all night with a Ferengi."

Quark picked up the latinum, rubbing it absently as he watched her walk out. She'd overpaid. He had been insulted, but only slightly. And she was staying on Terok Nor. He'd see her again.

Natima, he thought, and smiled his best sales smile, even though there were no customers at hand to see it.

It was late morning; Sito Keral had overslept. His family was already gone, his wife and daughter having done him the courtesy of giving him an extra hour to sleep after a particularly late night. Keral appreciated the extra rest. He wasn't young anymore and couldn't function well on just a few hours sleep. But he needed to get out into the fields to join in the harvesting. In these lean times, it was imperative that every able-bodied individual in Ikreimi village divert the sum of their energies toward maintaining the municipal crops.

He quickly dressed and sat to pull on his old boots, thinking of how nice it might be to someday have a new pair. One could not acquire such goods in his village. There was a single road that led from Ikreimi into Dahkur City, where a Bajoran traveler might take a transport to any handful of locations that would offer such things as boots, factory-made clothing, agri equipment . . . But that was reliant on money, not only for the goods themselves, but for travel permits, to protect the bearer from the Cardassian troops who inevitably appeared when an unregistered traveler left the boundaries of the village. The soldiers did not discriminate between terrorists and civilians without authorization. For Keral, working now only to sustain his family's most basic needs, consideration of new boots had become as distant a dream as a free and independent Bajor.

Keral plotted a course to the *katterpod* fields as he closed the front door behind him, hoping to avoid the attention of the others in the village who might accuse him of shirking his responsibilities. Squabbles in the village had lately been erupting into vicious and bitter conflicts. Keral did his best to settle them between others, and avoid them on his own behalf, but he was not always successful.

He had to step over a trickle of foul water that spilled from a broken pipe into the gutter as he left the house. Another project on an always-growing list. Over the splash of water, Keral could hear the beating of running feet—a child's steps. He stopped to find the source, saw the lone figure of a smallish boy turning the corner of the street a moment later. It was one of the Sorash boys, out of breath as he approached. Keral was instantly concerned—children weren't supposed to be unattended in the village, not since the detection grid had gone online. The systems did not detect children, which made it perfectly safe for young ones to venture into the forest—except that their parents could not go after them, not without bringing Cardassian soldiers into the village. Fences had been built, boundaries carefully marked, but still, a child without an adult escort was always cause for anxiety.

The boy came straight to Keral and started talking, the jumbled words interspersed with gasping.

"Calm down," Keral told the boy, whose proper name he could not remember—there were three boys in the Sorash family, so close in age they were difficult to tell apart. "Where is your mother? What is it you are trying to tell me?"

"A stranger," the boy said between breaths, "in the center of town. He says . . . he is looking . . . for you. My mother sent me to—"

"A stranger?"

The boy looked uncertain, his eyes wide. It was very unusual to receive outside visitors anymore. The Ikreimi village, situated between Dahkur city and the hill territories, was remote, surrounded entirely by forests that were off-limits to Bajoran travelers. Keral couldn't imagine what specific business this traveler might have with him, business that would have earned him a travel permit . . .

Keral tensed, his gut knotting. He hadn't thought to ask the obvious. "Is he Cardassian?"

The boy shook his head. "Not a Cardassian," he said. "But he looks . . . funny."

Keral raised his eyebrows. An alien visitor? A Bajoran with some disfigurement, perhaps—a member of the resistance?

"What does he want with me?" he asked, though he imagined that if the boy knew, he would have said so.

"He says he knows your cousin," the boy told him.

"Pol?" Keral relaxed somewhat, for it was conceivable that his cousin, a man who worked for the Cardassians, might have the means to deliver a message to his family. Mora Pol's family lived in the next village past Ikreimi, so this visitor, whoever he was, must have come to see Keral first, perhaps hoping the word would be passed along.

Keral followed the boy, whose name he thought might

be Tem, to the center of the little town. A flagstone-lined patch, now overrun with weeds, had once functioned as a public square, but the village lacked the time or the resources to maintain the space. There were several cracked stone benches that had been erected at approximately the time of Ikreimi's founding, many hundreds of years ago. Sitting on the nearest bench was a man with an unnatural sheen to his features—an alien, Keral surmised, though one not of a sort he could remember seeing before. His mouth and nose were roughly formed, his ears curiously simple. What struck Keral as strangest, though, was his vague resemblance to Mora Pol, the man this alien purported to know. He wore his hair pushed back, like Keral's cousin preferred, and was dressed in a simple worksuit. Keral thought he had seen Pol wear similar clothes, before he had been prohibited from leaving the institute.

Keral bent down to Tem. "Go straight to the fields," he instructed him, and the boy nodded, not needing to be told, scurrying back to where his mother worked.

"Hello," Keral said to the stranger. "I'm Sito Keral, and I understand you have been looking for me." He extended his hand as the other man rose to his feet. The alien looked at Keral's hand for just long enough to confirm to Keral that the gesture was unfamiliar to him, but he did eventually take Keral's forearm and shake.

"I am Odo," he said, his voice like unpolished stone. "Doctor Mora has a message for you. Only for you."

"I'm listening," Keral told him.

"Not here," Odo said. "In private."

"All right," Keral agreed, though to his thinking the issue was moot, since the town was nearly deserted. Everyone was harvesting. He gestured back in the direction of his house, not entirely comfortable with the prospect of inviting this strange person inside, but unable to think of an alternative.

Odo looked at everything as they walked, as though studying each tree, signpost, and cobblestone for an answer to a particular question.

"How is Pol?" Keral asked, striving to be polite.

"He is . . . well," the man answered, though he did not pause in his ongoing scrutiny, moving in a jerky and almost birdlike fashion. "Doctor Mora is a very intelligent man."

"Yes," Keral agreed. "He was always bright. He and I . . . we both came up together, studied together in the same levels at school, but Mora had much more of a natural inclination toward science and mathematics than I did. It was within the realm of his *D'jarra*, of course, to be a scholar, but nobody expected anyone from this family to go so far."

Odo had no answer for him. He seemed to be startled by everything he saw, as though this was his first encounter with a Bajoran town. Keral's curiosity grew.

"How did you know him?" Keral asked. "Did you work together?"

"Doctor Mora worked with me," the man said, but did not elaborate further. Keral decided to forgo any more questions until this man could deliver the message he had promised.

They reached the farmhouse, Odo standing stiffly aside as Keral opened the door. Keral gestured him inside, and the alien awkwardly ducked his head in acknowledgment, stepping past him. A stranger, indeed . . . although Keral sensed no malice about the creature, and Pol had apparently trusted Odo at least enough to send him to his family. These were strange times; Keral would reserve judgment for now.

Once they were inside, and Odo had looked around for a moment, he began to speak, clearly reciting something he had carefully memorized. "Mora is functioning reasonably well, but he has limitations. His mother and father might like to know that he is thinking of his grandfather today, it being the thirteenth night of the seventeenth moon."

"The seventeenth moon?" Keral interrupted, confused. These words held no significance for him.

Odo went on. "At the time of the twenty-third Gratitude Festival, Mora was inclined to compensate for the thirty-second rule of the oracle of twelve . . ."

Keral was dumbfounded, listening to the alien rattle off strings of meaningless names, dates, and places, references to long-dead relatives. Odo was almost finished with his litany before Keral understood what was going on—his cousin had sent a message in code.

"Odo," Keral said carefully, "Did Pol explain to you the significance of this message?"

The alien man, whom Keral was beginning to find oddly naïve, shook his head from side to side.

"Do you think you can repeat this message?" Keral asked. He walked to his desk, found paper and a graphite stylus.

The alien stared at his rudimentary tools before continuing. "Certainly. Mora is functioning reasonably well, but he has limitations . . ."

Keral listened more carefully this time, dredging up some long-buried memory, the number code that he and his cousin had made up as children. Of course, it was mostly Pol's doing, for he had always been the smarter of the two, but Keral thought he might be able to remember just enough of it . . . He asked the alien to slow down, to repeat the longer sequences, and carefully transcribed them. When Odo had finished, Keral asked him if he could repeat it once more.

As Odo recited the string of words and numbers a third time, it occurred to Keral what it was exactly that was most unusual about this man. He didn't blink, at least not in a way that seemed to come naturally to him. The third recitation concluded, Keral stared at the strange man for a moment.

"I thank you, for delivering Pol's—Doctor Mora's—message to me," he said, setting the scrap of paper on a nearby table. "I wish you well on your travels."

The alien stood, unmoving, still staring at the stylus in Keral's hand.

Keral didn't mean to be rude, but perhaps Odo needed clearer direction. "You may go now."

Keral wasn't sure if the man understood, until he spoke. "I have nowhere to go," he said in his gravelly voice.

Keral was disarmed. "Well," he said. "You, ah . . . you might be able to stay in the village. I could try to find you lodgings. I have to get to the harvest today—perhaps you could help."

"The harvest," Odo repeated. "I would like to help."

Keral supposed there wasn't any harm in it—an extra pair of hands was always welcome at harvest time. He glanced again at the piece of paper, knowing that he had no time to pore over it now—the harvest would not wait. "Well, then. I will take you to the fields. Come with me."

The alien obeyed him without another word.

Quark was in a foul temper already when the emaciated Bajoran man, with his one clouded eye, stumbled with a tray of dirty glasses, those left behind by the table of customers who had just departed—the bar's only patrons this morning. There was nobody in the bar to witness it, and the man managed to catch himself before he lost control of what he carried, but Quark was not feeling like an optimist. He had yet to make profit on drink sales today.

"That's it!" Quark snapped. "It's back to the mines with you."

Rom began to jabber from behind the bar. "He didn't break anything, brother. It was my fault he stumbled.

I didn't finish cleaning up where Gil Rike'la spilled his synthale."

"Gil who?" Quark grumbled, before deciding it wasn't important. "Listen, you," he said to the old Bajoran, whose name had escaped him, "I've given you more than enough chances. I realize you're old and . . . and . . . decrepit . . . and all that, but I can't have you stumbling around my bar."

The man's voice was little more than a croak. "I'm sorry . . . I . . ."

Quark couldn't stand the sound of it. "Enough!" he yelled. "I don't want to hear it. Just . . . get out of here. Go back to the mines!"

"Can I . . ."

"Get out!" Quark screamed, and the man scuttled off.

Quark's chest was still heaving when someone behind him spoke up. "That man is too old to work in the mines."

"And what would you know about it?" Quark sneered, before he could catch himself, before he realized it was a woman's voice. "Natima," he said, turning and smiling. It could only be the Cardassian beauty; no other female had spoken to him in . . . in quite a while. "Miss Lang! How lovely to see you. Would you like a drink?"

"I'm not sure," she replied. "The atmosphere in here today—it's a little heated for me."

"No, no, not heated, not heated. This is a calming place, a place to unwind," Quark insisted. "Please, first drink's on the house. What would you like?"

The graceful Cardassian hesitated for a moment before taking a seat at a nearby table. "I'd like a Samarian Sunset," she said.

"Of course, of course," Quark said, snapping his fingers at his brother. "Did you hear the lady?" he shouted, and Rom nodded from where he stood, fumbling at bottles and glassware.

Quark sat down next to Natima. "So, tell me, Natima—may I call you Natima?"

She drew in a breath. "I don't see why not," she said, guarded, but not too wary. That was good, Quark thought, or at least he hoped it was.

"Tell me, Natima. Most Cardassians I've encountered think I'm too soft on the Bajorans. You seem to have another opinion."

She looked uncomfortable, and he decided he'd better change the subject. "Forget that," he said. "Let's talk about you."

"Me?" she said. "What would you want to know about me?" Still guarded, though she didn't look ready to bolt quite yet. Rom arrived with her drink, and Quark took it from him, wanting to ensure that he would be the one to produce the drink's famous effect. He tapped the glass with a resounding *ping* and presented it to her.

"You just strike me as someone with a story to tell," Quark said. "I can spot those types, being in the business I'm in."

Natima half smiled. "Restaurateur?"

"No, no, the business of people. I'm a people person, you see."

Her expression went unmistakably sour. "Ah. It would seem that the *Bajoran* people in here might think otherwise."

There it was again, that odd sympathy for the people her own kind had disfranchised. "It's not like that," Quark insisted. "That man—he's an employee, and I expect a certain level of competence in those who work for me. The Bajorans in general, well, some people would say I've been quite . . . benevolent toward them. Compared to the treatment they receive in the mines . . ."

Natima shrugged. "It wouldn't be difficult to improve upon those conditions," she said, as though she didn't care, but Quark felt certain he could read genuine compassion in her tone. It was an in, and he ran with it.

"It's just a show," he said, lowering his voice slightly. "I mean, when I'm cruel to them like that. You don't think—" He grinned in disbelief, sat back, shaking his head. "It's merely a scare tactic. I'll be sending my brother out to tell him he'll be back tomorrow. You're right, he is too old to work in the mines. I think it's terrible, sending the aged to work in that place. I imagine Dukat tries to be fair with his policy, but . . ."

"It's a shame any Bajoran has to work there," Natima said.

"You're right," he said quickly. "I agree with you completely. I've said it all along, in fact."

She turned to him, her expression careful . . . and hopeful? "Have you?"

"Yes," he said. "In fact, when I first came to this station, I noticed immediately how hungry the Bajorans looked, and . . . and . . ." He trailed off, remembering his boast to Gaila. Someone had been listening; perhaps this lovely woman had been sent here to trick him into confessing. He took a breath, feeling as if he'd just sidestepped an audit.

"And what?" she asked.

"And . . . I said . . . those people ought to . . . eat more."

"Oh," she said, dropping her gaze and quickly finishing her drink.

Quark cleared his throat, watching her as she looked into her empty glass. He sorely wanted to be wrong about her, but probably she was just one of Thrax's minions. If it was true, it was a terrible shame. He stood from the table, excusing himself abruptly and going off to wipe down the bar.

"Brother," Rom said to him, "did you mean what you said—about the old Bajoran? Do you want me to . . ."

"No," Quark snapped, and then looked up at the door-way, where Natima was just leaving, her gait so poised she seemed to float. "Yes," he said, scarcely recognizing his own voice. "Yes, go and tell him."

Rom gaped, confused.

"Go!" Quark shouted, and his brother scrambled to attention.

Rom left the bar, and Quark, wiping the spot he'd wiped twice already, let out a breath he hadn't realized he'd been holding.

8

The numbers of people who came out to these meetings at Vekobet were dwindling. Kalem Apren headed up the meeting, as he always did, which was held in the basement of his own house, as it always was. This house had belonged to his wife's father, who was from the influential Lees clan, members of whom had held powerful positions in Kendra government for generations. These days, there were only a few people of Kendra who still believed in trying to maintain leadership, only a few who harbored the most fragmentary sense that hope could still be alive, though it had grown increasingly dim these past three years, the years since the detection grid had gone up. The resistance had very nearly ceased to be, further lowering spirits.

The grid had put great constraints on the lives of ordinary people. It didn't always deliver immediate results, and in the first few months of their implementation, some people chose to take the risk of traveling through unauthorized territory to see family, friends, or lovers from whom they had been separated. Some of these had been fortunate enough to discover flaws in the system—gaps in the detection grid that opened up at measurable intervals as the sweeps cycled. But more often than not, Cardassian skimmers and flyers appeared immediately, and the offending wanderer was caught and taken away before he could entirely register that he had been discovered. Nowadays, nearly everyone treated the system with healthy respect; some people were afraid to travel even within its boundaries. At first, nobody was entirely sure which areas were considered "safe" zones, and the Cardassians had no mercy or forgiveness for anyone who accidentally found themselves in a region that had been deemed off-limits. Now the boundaries were often marked with improvised indicators, to remind people to stay within the demarcated zones—or expect to wind up in the ore processors at Terok Nor. Children were kept close at hand, for there were many stories regarding little ones who had wandered off, their frightened and desperate parents going after them, despite the danger, never to be seen or heard from again.

Kalem was among the few who could afford a Cardassian travel permit. Many people with access to permits preferred not to use them, for the Cardassians often still came when the grid was tripped; the soldiers took great pleasure in harassing citizens, even those bearing permit receipts and proper documentation. But Kalem still traveled often, used his freedom on behalf of as many people as he could. He delivered food, messages, gifts, payments, and vicarious love for anyone who asked him. It was exhausting, but he felt it was his civic responsibility, and he acted without complaint. He had earned the respect and gratitude of many, but his efforts to organize a more effective body of self-government had gone more unrealized than ever before, with many honest people frightened into complete submission.

The basement of his house currently held twelve people, including Jaro Essa and himself. All that was left of what had once been a much larger society of self-proclaimed leaders who represented various aspects of Kendra society. Kalem tried to draw strength from the twelve tired, weathered faces he saw in the low light; none of them were ready to give up, despite growing evidence that the Cardassians' grip was only tightening. They stood together in the candlelight, relying on the long-held assumption that the windowless basement would keep them safe from Cardassian scrutiny. It was illegal for unauthorized Bajorans to assemble publicly, which was why the meeting had to be conducted at a residence, but Kalem had no doubt that the Cardassians would cheerfully ignore the details of their own rules in order to prosecute Bajorans suspected of trying to govern themselves.

"Minister," an elderly woman addressed him. She had long been trying to organize a more communal method of distributing rations, with very limited success. The collaborators in the town were opposed to her efforts, all of them accusing her of trying to put them out of work, and she lived in fear of being turned in. She began to inquire after his own support of her proposed methodology, and Kalem felt a sudden stab of despair. He looked to Jaro Essa, who stood next to him in front of the small throng of people. Jaro's face was downturned, his somber dark eyes deeply pensive. Kalem knew that the other man's attitude had always been more pessimistic than his own, that he couldn't rely on Jaro to assuage his own creeping despondence regarding the seeming futility of what they were trying to do. He felt disconnected from the words he spoke, as if he were hearing someone else's voice.

"My thoughts on the matter are that if anyone is willing to participate in a genuine effort to conserve rations, then those people are all entitled to a portion of the inventory, no matter how many family members or how much space they devote to food storage. We have to rank food consumption on an individual basis, rather than household . . ."

She nodded along, took up speaking again, but he couldn't focus on her words. Just a few years ago, this basement would have been packed with people, bursting with ideas that could have genuinely contributed to the cause. Now it was all about basic survival, any thoughts of driving off the Cardassians kept to themselves.

Kalem had not heard from anyone in the Valo system in a very long time. It was rumored that the communications tower on Derna had malfunctioned, and because no unauthorized Bajoran ships were allowed to leave the atmosphere, there was no way for the resistance to get to the towers and repair them. Kalem's hopes of somehow persuading Jas Holza to help bring in the Federation were growing dimmer by the day. His plan to reach Keeve Falor was even more distant now. For all Kalem knew, neither man was still alive.

The meeting limped to adjournment, and Kalem escorted his guests to the door as they hesitantly left for their own homes. Jaro Essa lingered behind, as he sometimes did, and as Kalem turned to him, he saw that the old major was sporting a slight smile. News about the resistance, perhaps? Jaro had never actually fought in the resistance himself—by the time a genuine resistance movement began to take shape, he felt that he was too aged to be of any use to the fighters—but he made it his business to keep up with what they were doing, and to pass word back and forth between cells when he could.

"I wanted to let you know," Jaro told Kalem confidentially, "that I heard from a very reputable source that the resistance cell outside of where Korto used to be is still operational."

Kalem nodded, his dark mood improving slightly. "The kai's son is still alive?"

"Yes," Jaro confirmed. His voice lowered even more. "I wanted to tell you before I announced it to the others. I wasn't sure if we should spread word among the people, or if it was better to keep this news confidential."

"Thank you," Kalem said, and he heard himself sigh

with some relief. "Let's keep the spread of this information restricted to a few key individuals . . ."

Jaro nodded. A little bit of good news went a very long way, and the health of Kai Opaka's son was better news that Kalem might have hoped for tonight. If Kai Opaka's son were to be killed, it would be devastating for the morale of Bajor. It was bad enough that the legendary fighter Li Nalas was dead, along with scores of resistance cells scattered across the planet. If Opaka Fasil were to be killed, something inside of Kalem—and more than a few others, he suspected—would wither and die. Bajor desperately needed heroes right now, even if their deeds were symbolic rather than actual. In times as dark as these, any hero would do.

It was late, and Keral was exhausted, but he didn't want to go to bed until he'd made some headway on Mora's code. He'd spent the entire day in the fields, and now that the sun was down, he was crouched at the family's dining table with a sputtering candle, struggling to work out some kind of plausible key for the cipher brought to him by the alien visitor.

The numbers were easy; it was the words that had him confounded. Did each letter stand in for a numeral? Were the words themselves relevant? They had to be, otherwise Keral wasn't sure if the numbers made any sense. If he was right about the number parts, he had bits and pieces of what *might* be a message . . . or it might be gibberish. He clutched at the thinning hair on his head, wishing he could just somehow force himself to understand. *Couldn't you have made it any simpler, Pol?*

Keral heard a rustling behind him, and turned to find his eleven-year-old daughter approaching, her steps light. Jaxa's blond hair had come loose from her braid, tumbling about her shoulders and making her look very much as she had when she was a little girl. It put a lump in Keral's throat to recognize how quickly his daughter was growing up, especially when faced with how impossibly clever she was becoming. Some of the things she came up with—Keral could scarcely believe she was his own child. She was more like the Mora side that way, Keral's mother's side. They were all a clever people, many of them learned. How Keral wished he could do more for Jaxa than this primitive village—she could have gone so far!

"Jaxa," he whispered. "Why aren't you in bed? It's another early morning tomorrow."

"I know, Pa. That's why I'm up. You need to sleep, too. Could I help?"

Keral chuckled. "I doubt it, though I wish someone could. Of course . . . you might be better suited to figure this out than I am."

Jaxa peered over his shoulder at the sheets of paper he'd spread across the chipped wooden table. "What is this stuff, Pa?"

"I'm not sure, honey," he admitted. "Maybe it's nothing. You know the funny man I brought to the harvest yesterday? It's from him. He says he knows my cousin, a man you've never met—a very smart man."

"Mora Pol—he's a scientist," Jaxa said, picking up one of the scraps of paper.

"That's right," Keral confirmed. "I've told you about him before."

Jaxa traced a finger along one of the lines on the paper she was looking at. "'Sensors towers,'" she read. "'Aircraft?' 'Coded engine signature.'"

He smiled. "It's a lot of gibberish, I know."

"Mora made the detection grid?" She looked at him, frowning. "The towers . . . ?"

Keral answered carefully. "He has to work with the Cardassians, honey. He has to do it in order to stay alive. It isn't his fault . . ." Keral trailed off, thinking.

"Maybe he's given you an override code," Jaxa suggested.

Keral started to nod, feeling a surge of excitement. He shuffled through the pieces of paper, snatched up the one with the numbers that followed the reference to a traveler's array. He read the sequence, remembering something Pol had once told him, about programming . . .

"It's a backdoor password," he said. "He always built them into his programs, in case he needed to get back in."

His excitement faltered. "Except . . . how am I supposed to use something like that?"

Jaxa was still looking at the same sheet of paper. "Someone would have to take the code to the resistance," she said.

"Mora remembered that I knew Kohn Biran," Keral said. He felt like he had to catch his breath, suddenly. If it was true, if it was an override code of some sort, probably with instructions on how to approach . . . His cousin had passed a huge responsibility on to him. Could he do this? Crack the code, and get it to Kohn Biran? Keral had a rudimentary idea of where the Dahkur resistance had gone. They had taken to the mountains after the grid had gone online, the low range visible beyond the western forest. Of course, this was assuming they hadn't all been killed.

He held out his hand for Jaxa to give him the scrap of paper. "You go to bed," he instructed her gently. "And thank you for helping me. Right now, we both need some sleep."

Even as he said it, he knew sleep would be impossible. His cousin, he realized, was counting on him to do this thing, which indicated that Pol believed Keral was capable. He hoped that Pol's faith would be enough to see him through, for Keral wasn't sure if he had any for himself.

Alone in her quarters, Natima's voice trembled ever so slightly as she introduced herself, setting forth her credentials to the man on the screen. The channel was hardened, but if the station's prefect learned her business, her intentions, she would be as good as dead. She chose her words carefully, using phrases she'd worked out with Russol as she presented herself to Tozhat's newest exarch, a man named Yoriv Skyl. Skyl had recently come to replace Kotan Pa'Dar, the man who had been exarch when Natima had lived in the surface settlement, years before.

Natima had never been formally introduced to Kotan Pa'Dar, though she had seen him in those years when she was on Bajor, at the occasional press conference, and once she had passed him on the streets between the habitat domes of the settlement. She had also seen him on Cardassia Prime, since he had returned from Bajor. Pa'Dar's wife and young son had been killed in a terrorist attack, and he had resigned from his post shortly afterward. There were many dissidents who were convinced that Pa'Dar was one of them, that he attended some of the off-planet meetings under an assumed identity, but it had never been confirmed. It was Natima's understanding that Yoriv Skyl, the man who had replaced him here on Bajor, was a close acquaintance of Pa'Dar's. She hoped that meant that Skyl could also be sympathetic to the cause, but his expression was giving her nothing.

Skyl was a heavyset man, slightly younger than Natima, but with close ties to the Detapa Council, Cardassia's civilian government. Russol knew him in some capacity, though not well enough to be sure of his political leanings. Still, after speaking with Pa'Dar, Russol agreed with Natima that the evidence for Skyl's receptiveness was strong enough that Natima should contact him.

"You say Glinn Russol sends his respects, through you," the exarch said. *"He is an honorable man. I've met him many times, on Cardassia II. But I find it strange that he would fraternize with a member of the Information Service, let alone ask one to deliver a message."*

"My employment has no bearing on my allegiances," Natima said. She took a breath, reminded herself that just because her job had taken her far from home, there were still things, however small, that she could do to help the movement. "I wish to speak to you as a citizen of Cardassia only."

Skyl's lips thinned. *"I would prefer to speak to you in person."*

"That would be preferable to me as well," Natima said quickly. "So, you'll meet with me?"

He nodded slowly. *"Yes, time permitting. I will see you sometime next week, if that conforms with your schedule."*

"I can make it comform," Natima said.

She signed off the transmission, and regarded another call that had been holding, one from within the station. Could it have been security, listening in and demanding to meet with her in regard to her business with Skyl? Even as she thought it, she knew better; security would not bother with the courtesy of a call. She considered letting the transmission go to her message system, but decided that she could use a distraction. In fact, the call came from Quark, the man who owned the bar.

"Miss Lang!" the Ferengi declared as he appeared on her screen. *"I'm so glad I've caught you in. I was wondering . . . if you might have some time this evening, if you would care to have a drink with me, perhaps, or even a walk around the station? If you could use the company, that is."*

Natima hesitated. She could, indeed, use the company, and the idea of a walk was appealing. She spent most of her time reading feeds from Bajor, correcting copy, doing her job. She didn't feel comfortable roaming the station in her free time, which both irritated and shamed her. She hadn't expected to feel so intimidated by the constant stares of Cardassian men, as they silently assessed her status, but she'd come to feel quite isolated in the short time since her transfer. A tour of Terok Nor would be nice.

But with Quark? She wasn't sure what to make of the Ferengi. She'd heard stories about them, of course, but had never personally known any. And she didn't know him well enough to decide if he was trustworthy, or if he was as greedy as the stories made out. But he interested her, on some level; perhaps it was the reporter in her, curious about another culture, or perhaps it was just the invitation to be with someone from whom she didn't have to fear exposure as a traitor. At least, she assumed not. Quark clearly had dealings with the Bajorans that were not looked upon kindly by the prefect.

"Maybe just one drink," she said, and he nodded eagerly.

"I'll see you in the bar, then," he said. He grinned broadly, exposing his filed teeth. *"I'm looking forward to spending some time with a beautiful lady."*

He promptly ended the transmission, and Natima sighed. Perhaps it was simply the flattery. Even from this odd little alien man, someone whom she did not find physically attractive in any way—but then, she had never been one to be tripped up by a man's good looks. The few times in her life she had ever been drawn to a particular man, it had been the measure of his integrity that had called to her. And while she found it difficult to believe that a Ferengi bartender would have much of that, she supposed she could stand a night of listening to someone tell her she was youthful, attractive, whatever else he was going to say in trying to woo her; in truth, her ego could use it.

The Bajorans of this village had been kind to Odo, and he understood that they were appreciative of his assistance with their harvest. But he also wondered how much of their acceptance was a result of his remaining in his humanoid form, at least while anyone was present. Nobody had asked him to approximate the shape of anything else, nobody had instructed him to revert to his natural state, nobody had insisted that he hold still while they waved a tricorder around him or poked him with an electrified probe. He found it refreshing, though the children in the village made him ill at ease—they all tended to stare and whisper whenever he was around, something the adults at least refrained from doing.

He had been given leave to rest at an abandoned farmhouse, and offered meals at a communal table. Odo had no need for food, but he understood that it was a necessity and a social activity for Bajorans, and so he joined them as often as seemed appropriate. He still did not know what he meant to do, now that he had left the institute, but he was satisfied that he'd made the right choice in leaving. Doctor Mora had turned away from him, after giving him the message to carry, and had told him not to bother returning until he was ready to continue their work. Odo had grown used to Mora's manipulations over the years, had come to understand that the doctor did not have many choices. Odo enjoyed having choices. He liked the variety of people he was meeting, and was beginning to understand that while he was quite different from the Bajorans in some ways, there were also distinct similarities. They spoke of their feelings with such freedom, smiled and laughed and cried with ease, embracing their lives . . . It was all foreign to him. He had amassed thousands of facts, of definitions, of data threads in his years at the institute, but had learned little of the ways of people, and found this new situation quite appealing. Doctor Mora had been comparatively quite subdued, and few of the Cardassians he'd met had ever bothered to speak to him of their personal lives.

On this day, the people of the town had continued their shelling of *katterpod* beans, their primary staple food. When the sun had risen, they had gathered at the enormous mill to work, as they had for the past two days; most sat outside in the cool, early light, shelling beans for various purposes, while a few worked inside, carrying some of the shelled beans to the millstones; they would be ground into flour that could be used to bake a type of flat bread called *makapa*.

Odo's unsurpassed strength in operating the massive millstones seemed to be valued by the Bajorans, who tired much more quickly than Odo and required a longer rest between work periods. He was therefore working the mill, an apparatus that years before had been driven by water. For reasons that Odo did not entirely understand, the water no longer flowed with any regularity, and the equipment now had to be driven by brute strength. He was pleased that he could assist. Doctor Mora had often asked him to perform, but never to assist.

Two Bajorans who had accompanied him inside the old building were beginning to quarrel about their method of shelling the beans. "If you stack them like that, the beans on the bottom will be crushed," said the first man.

The other man made a face. "They won't be," he insisted. "It's much more efficient to do it this way. And anyway, the crushed beans can go into the flour bin. You have to account for a few crushed beans in the harvest."

His companion shook his head. "We can't justify the possibility of spoilage," he said. "Crushed beans are twice as likely to mold if they've sat for more than a day."

"They won't sit," his friend argued. "I'll have all these shelled by this afternoon, at the latest."

"You say that, but you don't know your limits. I've been watching you, and your pile only disappears when you've got a helper with you. By yourself, you won't be able to shell this entire heap by tomorrow. You have to lay them out to shell them."

The other man was beginning to look angry. He started to reply, but first he looked up and caught Odo's eye, and the shape-shifter realized he'd stopped turning the stones in order to stare at the men, a behavior he remembered

Mora specifically instructing him not to do. He dropped his gaze.

"What is it?" one of the men asked, his tone unfriendly. "Do you have an opinion about *katterpod* stacking, Odo?"

Odo shook his head from side to side. "No," he said. "But I do have an opinion about conflict in the face of hunger."

The man narrowed his eyes, and his companion spoke up. "What's that supposed to mean?"

Odo chose the words in his customary careful manner. "I only mean that the particulars of the food harvest shouldn't be a matter of such dispute. What matters is only that it gets done, because your survival depends on it. Is that correct?"

The first man nodded slowly, and looked at the other. "I'll help you shell this pile when I'm done with mine," he said.

Odo went back to pushing the stones, happy that the unfriendly tone had gone out of the man's voice. Several times since he'd come to Ikreimi, he'd witnessed unpleasant interactions, and he was coming to learn that a third party could sometimes redirect their intentions. He was as polite as he knew how to be, and often asked to be corrected if he was in error; and somehow, the things he said to them seemed to make them stop to reconsider their conflict. He couldn't say why he did so, he only knew that he felt relief when the arguments ceased. It reminded him of the things Doctor Reyar had used to say to Doctor Mora—unkind things, things that had filled Odo with unwelcome tension.

The two men both turned their heads at once as another man entered the mill. It was Sito Keral, the man Odo had originally come to the village to see. He looked frantic.

"What's with you, Sito?" one of the men asked him. "You were supposed to be here nearly an hour ago."

Keral's face was all downturned lines. "Ver, I'm sorry, but I don't know what to do. Jaxa's gone!"

Odo ceased to walk, loosening his arms, remembering the small girl with yellow hair. She had smiled at him the day before, at the midday meal.

"Gone! What do you mean, gone?" Ver asked.

"She's run off toward the mountains, into the forest," Keral said.

"What would make her do such a thing?" the other man cried out. "Isn't she old enough to know better by now?"

"It's my fault," Keral said miserably. "My cousin sent me a message that indicated she could . . . she could . . . But now—" The man had run out of breath.

"Your cousin, the collaborator?" Ver said.

The fear and panic in Keral's eyes gave over to rage. "My cousin is a good man!" he shouted. "The message was for the resistance. That is why Jaxa has gone—she is trying to help!"

"For the resistance!" Ver exclaimed. "She'll never get to where they are hiding by herself!"

"Someone must go after her," Keral said, pleading. "Ver, your uncle has papers. Couldn't you ask him to . . ." He trailed off.

The other two men looked at each other, an unspoken note of impassive defeat passing between them. It was clear enough, even to Odo, that Ver did not want to ask his uncle to perform this favor.

Again, there was conflict here, and Odo thought he knew how best to solve it. He stepped forward. "The detection grid will ignore me," he said. "I'll go."

"Go where?" Keral asked, looking a little surprised. He seemed not to have been aware that Odo was even present.

"To get Jaxa," Odo replied promptly. "I'll look for her and bring her back."

Keral had water running over the lines in his face—tears,

of course—but he had a look in his eyes of hope. Odo recognized it as he recognized it within himself. Hope, the feeling that what is desired is also possible; that events may turn out for the best. He'd long known the definition; to see it was compelling, to say the least.

Odo left the mill at once, without looking back, and without waiting for a reply from the others, for it seemed to him a matter of some urgency. Children were important to the Bajorans, and ill-equipped to be alone. He was pleased that he could be of further assistance to these kind people.

9

Natima liked the look of Quark's smile as he gazed at her across the bar. It was at once friendly and lascivious, and she felt that the look on her own face probably mirrored his. She remembered, with slightly embarrassed pleasure, the holosuite experience from the night before—and what had come after the holosuite, in Quark's quarters.

It was late, the establishment mostly empty. He leaned across the polished surface, over the remains of the two Samarian Sunsets in front of her. Quark refused to charge her for her drinks, a matter that seemed to entirely astound his brother Rom and the Bajorans who worked there. Apparently, Quark didn't have a reputation for generosity. Natima knew better.

"Will you have another drink?" Quark asked her.

Natima smiled. "I don't think I can handle any more this evening," she told him. "I feel lightheaded."

"I do, too," Quark said, "and I haven't had a drop."

Natima's smile grew broader, probably more foolish. Quark glanced over her shoulder then, looking toward the door, and his eyes went wide, his smile disappearing.

"I didn't do anything!" he cried out. She turned around and saw that Thrax, the station's chief of security, had just entered the bar and was making a beeline for where she sat. She shifted nervously. Had Quark made a mistake in his black-market transactions? Or was it Natima he was after? She wasn't sure which option would be more unhappy for her.

She got her answer quickly enough as the tall man stopped by her chair. "Miss Lang," he said coolly. "I'd like it if you'd come with me to the security office."

Natima cleared her throat. "May I ask what this regards?"

Quark was gaping. "What do you want with her, Thrax?"

Thrax's already menacing expression grew even more so. "Mind your business, Ferengi."

"I am minding my business," Quark said. "The lady's business is my business."

Thrax's forehead creased with mocking curiosity. "Is that so?"

"It's not true," Natima said quickly, rising to go. "He has nothing to do with me." She wouldn't be responsible for getting Quark in trouble—Cardassian politics were not his concern.

"Natima!" Quark said, clearly hurt.

"It's all right, Quark. I'll see you later this evening."

"You will?"

"Yes." She said it with firm finality, trying to convey to him not to get involved, but he continued to look concerned, and she hoped very much that he would stay out of this, whatever "this" amounted to.

She followed Thrax across the Promenade to the security station, and took a seat in his cramped office. She drew a deep breath, reminding herself to be careful, not to let him intimidate her. But his manner of interviewing her was not threatening at all. In fact, he was oddly pleasant, a tack Natima presumed was meant to disarm her.

"Miss Lang," he said. "It's come to my attention that you have contacted the exarch at the Tozhat settlement."

"That's correct," she told him, thinking there was nothing suspicious about it. "On Information Service business," she added.

"Oh?" Thrax said. "But that isn't what you told him. You said that you spoke to him as a citizen of Cardassia only."

Natima felt her face darken with alarm, to hear him recite the exact words she had spoken to Yoriv Skyl. Had he been listening to the entire transmission? To all her transmissions?

He smiled. "There is nothing that goes on here that escapes my attention, Miss Lang."

"What is this about?" she demanded. If he meant to arrest her, she'd rather he just get on with it. She had no interest in playing shadow games.

"I'm only satisfying my curiosity," he told her. "I'm a man who likes to stay on top of people's intentions. I'm especially curious to know something. You mentioned a name that is familiar to me. Glinn Russol."

Natima sat frozen, terrified at the prospect of incriminating her friend.

"Is this the same Russol who bears the first name of Gaten?"

Natima didn't know what to do. "I . . . I . . ."

Thrax nodded. "I thought so," he said. "Well. That is all I'll be needing to know from you, Miss Lang. You may go now."

Natima stood up on shaky legs, confused.

"Oh, and, Miss Lang?"

She turned back to him, tried not to look as though all she wanted to do was get away from Thrax and his stifling office. "Yes?"

"I'd appreciate your discretion about this meeting. In return, I will happily keep the contents of your transmissions to myself." He paused. "You'll do best to avoid discussing your business with your new Ferengi friend. I know what he's up to. He thinks he's clever, but he makes plenty of mistakes. Mistakes that could easily come to the attention of Dukat, if he isn't more careful."

Was this a threat? "Th—thank you," she replied, and left the security office, her heart hammering.

Doctor Seia Trant led this day's trip to another work camp, another Fostossa vaccination for another tired line of grubby, sullen workers. It was the third time Kalisi had been sent along on one of the excursions to manage the equipment, to set hyposprays, and to see that the camp medical systems were compatible with Crell's. This camp was a few hours from Moset's hospital; it had some local name she'd already forgotten. She disliked the trips, disliked looking at the sickly workers, disliked Trant's knowing smirk whenever Moset was discussed, but she didn't see that she had a choice. Someone had to assist, and Moset had been locked in his lab for days, finishing up some radiation study for the science ministry.

Today, there had been little for Kalisi to do. The camp's system was already compatible with the hospital's—they were both obsolete—and medical files had been downloaded, backed up, sent off. She could either wait in the shuttle or assist Trant with the inoculations, which would at least get her back to the warmth of the facility that much faster. She sat at the counter behind the generally glum-faced Trant, refilling hyposprays, ignoring the smell of unwashed flesh and sour breath as the Bajorans filed into the room, ten at a time, staring around themselves like dumb cattle. A handful of soldiers stood by, most of them looking over the two female doctors with smirks of their own.

Kalisi watched another thin old man step up to Trant's table, as weak and tired looking as the rest of them. He slouched on the low stool, took his injection without comment, stood, and was motioned back out again by a soldier with a rifle. It was galling, how little these people appreciated what was being done on their behalf. Crell Moset had spent years studying Fostossa, had found a vaccine for a disease that had killed thousands of these people in the early years of the annexation. She had yet to hear a single appreciative word.

A worker sat down, a female with dead eyes. Hypo, stand, next. A man with a scar. Hypo, stand, next. A young woman with a babe at one pallid breast; neither looked well. Kalisi looked away, unhappy with the pity that welled up in her. At least at the institute, the only Bajoran she'd had to see was Mora Pol. Fumbling, frightened Doctor Mora, with his pet plastic man and his pedestrian mind. For him, she'd felt contempt. For these dirty, sorrowful people she couldn't help but feel pity, in spite of what they'd done to the Union, what they'd done to her *life* . . .

"How many more are there?" Kalisi asked.

Trant shot her a glance. "Eager to get back to the facility, Doctor Reyar?"

The looks, the smiles, that was one thing; with that insinuating tone, Seia Trant had overstepped her bounds, and Kalisi was no novice to professional malice.

"Are you implying something about my relationship with Doctor Moset?" Kalisi asked, loudly, brightly, and was rewarded for her candor. Trant looked away, her face darkening.

"If I've offended you—" Trant started, but was interrupted by a wild-faced man a few people back in the line, dirty and greasy-haired, his teeth bad. He had stepped out of line, was staring at the two doctors with an expression of disbelief.

"Crell Moset? You work for Crell Moset?"

One of the soldiers stepped forward, a hard-faced glinn with a scarred temple ridge. "Back in line."

"Moset the butcher? Is that who sent you here?"

The glinn raised his rifle. "Back in line, *now*."

The Bajoran lunged past him, grabbed at one of the hyposprays on the table, his expression crazed. Kalisi and Trant both stood and backed away as the other soldiers came running. The Bajorans scattered.

"What's in these?" the man shouted. "Another infection? *Poison?*"

He shook the hypospray in Kalisi's face, and then the soldiers were on him, knocking him down with their rifles, holding him down while Trant stepped forward and injected him with a hypo she'd pulled from somewhere, something that instantly halted his struggle, calming him into a glassy-eyed stupor.

Two of the soldiers carried the mumbling madman out while the glinn barked instructions to the workers, shuffling them back into line, calling off work code numbers.

Kalisi looked to Trant, who was calmly stepping back to her place, checking the tray of vaccinations.

"Seems like there's one at every camp," Trant said, sighing. "Doctor Crell Moset, evil scientist."

"What? Why?"

Trant shook her head. "They're superstitious and ignorant, these people. They don't understand how advances in medicine are made. How advances in *anything* are made."

Kalisi nodded, remembering Mora's puffy, stupid face. "I've noticed that," she said. As they went back to their work, she tried to picture it—Crell Moset, the work-obsessed, silently passionate man who fancied that he had a good sense of humor, as some kind of mad genius . . .

Bajorans, she thought, and refilled a new hypospray.

When she'd left home that morning, it had seemed like a grand adventure, a daring, heroic journey that would end with hugs and *jumja* cake, rewards for bravery . . . And Sito

Jaxa had managed to hold on to that fantasy while the sun was still in the sky, imagining the surprised faces of the dashing resistance fighters when they realized a little girl had saved them, imagining the ride home in one of their flyers, the stories she'd be able to tell her friends at school . . . She'd darted and hidden, pretending that there were enemy soldiers after her, and for a while she'd walked by a stream that had small fish in it, and she'd stopped twice to eat the snacks that she'd packed for herself—all the while dreaming and pretending, acting like a little girl, doing all the things she had imagined she would do if she ever got to explore the forest on her own.

Jaxa had longed to go back into the forest for what seemed like an eternity. When she had been very small, children of the village could run into the forest and play together whenever they liked, and Jaxa thought she remembered going into the forest all the time, though it was a very long time ago in her short memory. Jaxa wasn't sure exactly how old she had been when the rules had abruptly changed, when children were suddenly kept close to their parents at all times, when punishment for wandering off suddenly became severe and frightening— frightening because the children understood immediately that there was serious danger waiting for the entire village if they ever disobeyed. Fences had been built, warning signs erected. None dared challenge them—until today, when Jaxa had been so sure she was setting off on an auspicious adventure, one with the happiest of endings.

Now the sun was setting, and it was much colder than Jaxa had thought it was going to be. Even though the early fall days had been hot lately, the forest night was chilly, and too cold for sleep—as if Jaxa could have slept anyway, with the fears and regrets that were reeling in her head. What had she been thinking, sneaking away like this? Well, her pa always said she was rash. She'd made a foolish decision, a childish decision, and now she was likely going to freeze to death for it.

She huddled miserably in the dark, hiding beneath the exposed roots of a rubberwood pine, thinking to herself that she should have reached the mountains by now, anyway. She thought it would be so easy to find them—the tips of the tallest peaks were clearly visible from Ikreimi village, but here, with the trees so close overhead, she could only catch glimpses of them, and even then it appeared that they were moving farther away, not closer. She had most likely been walking in circles. Now she only wanted to go back home, but she didn't know which direction that was, either. She had badly misjudged her own abilities, her own sense of direction. Well, how could she have known? She had scarcely ever been out of the village, not since she was a little girl, going to the city with her mother and father before the grid went up. It had seemed so easy, then, but what had she known at that age?

Jaxa was alone, frightfully alone. The old road she'd roughly paralleled all day had badly deteriorated until it finally gave way to tangled forest. Jaxa had seen no footprints; the branches and weeds grown across the path were undisturbed. It especially surprised her, considering her assumption that the alien visitor, Odo, had traveled this road. She supposed he must have come by another route. The forest appeared entirely devoid of humanoid activity, now and for a very long time past.

But with that thought, she heard something. A rustle in the low branches. Something moving toward her, something big. She froze, her eyes open wide in the darkness. She tried with all her might to see what was making the noise, but she could only see the dark gray shadows of the trees around her, and the brilliant, cold stars wheeling overhead.

Another, nearer rustle, and she thought she saw one of the shadows moving, thought she heard the sound of padding feet. A soldier? She tried her best not to breathe, holding herself in a small, tight ball, knowing it would do no good. If a soldier had come, he would have equipment that would tell him exactly where she was. She heard a sound, then, that she could not at first identify. A low, rhythmic grumbling.

It's a hara *cat.*

The fear changed. The animal didn't need sensors, it could smell her plainly. She could only hope that it had already eaten, that it hadn't been stalking her, as *haras* had been known to do when food was scarce. Jaxa's breathing grew tight with quickly mounting dread. Would it hurt when the *hara* pounced and dragged her from beneath the tree? Or would she simply go into shock, numb to the animal's inevitable attack? The animal growled, and Jaxa froze in fear.

But now she heard another sound. Something was running, crashing through the underbrush. Something very, very large, larger definitely than the *hara.* Jaxa began to cry, and then she screamed when she heard the terrible sound of the *hara* as it howled in furious pain. Something was attacking it. A cadge lupus? She could hear the thrashing of the foliage around her as the animals struggled, and she covered her face with her hands. The sounds were coming closer, close enough that she could see them now, two shadowy forms locked together in the moonlight.

A violent shift of shadow, and the *hara* let out a strangled, plaintive caterwaul, disengaging from the attacker. The other animal allowed it to run off, its crash through the brush quickly fading.

Jaxa stared at the watching shadow, frightened. She didn't know what it was. It was massive, somewhat doglike, but it was not a cadge lupus and certainly not a *tyrfox,* unless it was the biggest *tyrfox* Jaxa had ever seen—and she had seen plenty of them around the *porli* pens back at Ikreimi.

The unknown animal slowly approached, and she pulled her legs as tightly to her chest as she possibly could, but she knew it was no use. It was heading straight for her, a big shadow that seemed to be . . .

Changing? Jaxa rubbed her eyes. Probably it was just the starlight, but suddenly there was no animal before her. There was a person. A man.

"Jaxa," the man said, and she thought she recognized the strange pitch and quality of that voice. He came closer, and she confirmed it. The alien visitor. The man who had brought her father the code.

"Odo!" She exclaimed, so grateful to see him that she scrambled out from under the tree, leaping to her feet and throwing her arms around his neck. "How did you find me?"

He pulled away, seeming to recoil from her, as though he was slightly afraid of the physical contact. She held him tight anyway, and he finally let her.

"I looked around," he said simply. "It's time to go back now. Your parents are waiting."

Jaxa was only too happy to agree.

Until Doctor Cul finally showed up, the institute had been in chaos. Doctor Yopal had left abruptly, her only good-bye a hardcopy of the transfer orders, sitting atop her empty desk. Kalisi Reyar had never been replaced, which left only three Cardassian scientists, a handful of techs, and Mora Pol. Nobody seemed to have an idea of when Yopal's replacement would be coming—if there was a replacement at all. Mora could not leave, so he didn't, but the other three scientists seemed not to know if it was still prudent to show up every day. No one told him anything.

For five days after Yopal's sudden departure, Mora had been slowly but obediently continuing the research into the project to which he had been assigned. Engineering had never been his forte, but redesigning hydraulic systems wasn't so terrible—dull, but not a reach—which had given him time to implement a small plan. Alone at night, with no director to look over his shoulder, he had found his way into the institute's long-term records—in particular, those of Kalisi Reyar. Mora had worked with Reyar long enough to have learned most of her passcodes and datastrings, and now, with no direct supervision, with the other scientists bordering on insubordination by missing shifts and not bothering with their security measures, he was able to make a genuine mess of what was left of Reyar's research in the institute's mainframe. A little more time, and he might be able to delete all of it permanently.

He'd been thinking, since Odo had left. It had occurred to him that Odo might not have been successful in delivering the message to his cousin, and even then, the resistance might never be able to disable the systems. But those systems were going to need maintenance someday, and when they did, nobody would be able to find the original schematics. If he could ever hack his way out to the mainframe's relay, he'd make it so they wouldn't be able to find Reyar at her new assignment, either. It was a small thing, his plan, but it distracted him from his unhappiness over Odo's departure.

It was on the fifth day after Yopal had left that the institute was finally introduced to its new director, a man this time. Mora could tell immediately that the three Cardassian scientists left at the institute deeply resented being put to work under a man. It was apparent to Mora that things here were about to get a lot less efficient than they had once been—not least because of his own efforts to sabotage the record-keeping.

Mora quickly found Cul to be surprisingly friendly, even kind. One of the first issues the slightly built Cardassian man addressed when he greeted Mora was whether the Bajoran might prefer to go home.

"I would like to see my family," Mora admitted cautiously. "But then, I would require a permit to find my way back to the institute."

"Oh, no, Doctor Mora," Cul said cheerfully, "I meant that perhaps you would prefer to return home permanently. This situation is less than ideal for you, being the only one of your kind here. There must be something you would prefer to do in the city of Dahkur, which would not require you to travel."

"Oh," Mora said, and felt a brief burst of something like fever, hot and dizzying, but wonderful, too. And then he thought of Odo. Mora still felt half certain the shapeshifter would return to the institute once he had learned how difficult it was going to be for him to get along in the outside world, and Mora could not let him come home to a Cardassian stranger.

"If it makes no difference to you," he said, "I . . . would prefer to remain here, if I could."

Cul was surprised, but he nodded. "Certainly, Doctor Mora. I didn't realize you were so committed. I admire you for your allegiance to the Cardassian cause."

"Yes, sir," Mora said, ashamed.

"If only there were more Bajorans like you," Cul went on, and started to speak of his future plans for the institute, but Mora had stopped listening. It occurred to him then that he'd finally been offered the chance to leave, to stop collaborating—the thing he had wanted for so long—and he hadn't taken it. His heart sank, realizing that he had probably made a mistake, but it was too late to change it. He had a feeling that Cul would be unlikely to offer again.

And Odo left me, he thought, but then thought of his small plan, his project, and felt some measure of reassurance. He remembered Daul Mirosha, the last Bajoran who had worked here, and how he had given up his life to liberate the Gallitep mining camp. Mora knew he could never do anything so heroic and dangerous as that, but perhaps, with less supervision, with more freedom under the new direc- tor . . . perhaps he could make a few more changes, imple- ment a few more small plans. Perhaps it was time to set his fear aside and take advantage of his position at the institute. He'd earned it, after all.

10

The little girl tried to make conversation as Odo made his way back to where he remembered the village to be, but Odo did not seem to know the right things to say to her, and he knew that she thought him odd. It made him anxious to return to the village, to hand her off to her parents and escape the curious nature of her comments.

"If only I hadn't lost my way," she said wistfully, looking out at the tops of the trees, outlined in the misty blue of the approaching morning.

"But you did lose your way," Odo told her matter-of-factly.

The girl seemed annoyed. "Now who is going to take this message to the resistance?" she asked him.

"I don't know," Odo said, "but your father was very afraid for your safety. Someone else will have to do it."

"Why don't the sensors detect you?"

"They probably do. But they don't react to me, because I'm not Bajoran."

She scrutinized him. "You look kind of like a Bajoran."

Odo cleared his throat uncomfortably. "You should not have taken such a risk," he told her.

Jaxa snorted angrily. "Sometimes risks are worth taking," she told him.

Odo had no reply. He supposed she might be right. The

idea was often implied, in the Cardassian histories he'd read, but he had no personal experience in the matter.

The sun was casting its brilliance across the day, and Jaxa seemed to grow even bolder in her queries now that it was not quite so dark. She changed the subject. "That big animal in the forest. The thing that chased the *hara* away from me. What was it? Where did it go?"

"It was me," Odo said, wishing she hadn't asked. While he hadn't made any effort to explain or demonstrate his nature to the people he'd met, he had no plans to hide it, either; he'd simply hoped to avoid the conversation. But she had asked.

"I knew it!" Jaxa said, excited. "How did you do that?"

"My unique nature allows for it." It was his standard reply, the one he and Mora had given to the various Cardassians who had come to view him at the institute.

"Oh," Jaxa said, seeming puzzled by the answer. "Well . . . what kind of animal was it?"

"A riding hound, native to Cardassia Prime." He replied as promptly as he would have to any question from Doctor Mora. "I learned it from studying three-dimensional motion images in the database at the Bajoran Institute of Science."

Jaxa frowned. "Could you be other animals, too?" she wondered.

"Yes," Odo said, again wishing she hadn't asked. He did not like the idea of changing his form on demand for her, or anyone else. It made him feel uncomfortable, especially since he wasn't sure how to go about refusing. It had only just begun to occur to him that he *could* refuse, if he wanted to, but he had never done so before, and he didn't know what kind of reaction a refusal would produce. He preferred an atmosphere of agreeable serenity, if it was possible to maintain it.

Jaxa tripped on a piece of root jutting above the surface

of the dirt path, and Odo quickly caught her by the elbow before she stumbled. As she regained her footing, her face tilted to the sky. "Look!" she exclaimed, and Odo raised his head to see a crooked line, soaring through the clouds. "It's a sinoraptor," she said.

"A sinoraptor," Odo repeated, watching the thing in the sky.

"A bird," Jaxa said.

Odo knew what birds were; egg-laying animals that could fly—or at least, some of them could. He recognized that he had seen birds go by as he was coming through the forest to the Ikreimi village from the institute, but he hadn't paid them much attention.

"Could you be a bird?" Jaxa asked him.

"I don't know," Odo said. "I've never tried it before."

"If you can be anything you want," Jaxa asked, "how come you're a person all the time? I only saw you be a person at the village."

Odo grunted before he replied. "I suppose it's because I have the most practice being a humanoid," he said.

"Why?"

"It's what Doctor Mora wanted me to be more than anything else."

"Oh," Jaxa said. "But . . . what do *you* want to be more than anything else?"

He looked up at the sky, watching the sinoraptor as it came closer, considering her question. "I don't know yet," he finally answered. "What do you want to be more than anything else?"

Jaxa already knew the answer. "A soldier," she said. "To fight the Cardassians and make them go away."

Odo was curious and surprised, but not terribly. He knew there was conflict between the Bajorans and the Cardassians, though he did not fully understand how it had come about. It did interest him, however, to recognize that a child would already know to be angry at the Cardassians. He supposed the conflict might have run deeper than he originally suspected, and acknowledged to himself that Doctor Mora may have been right—he still had a great deal to learn before he could ever truly "fit in."

It's not that I don't trust her, Quark reassured himself as he struggled with the locking mechanism behind the door panel. *It's just that if Thrax has been listening to her transmissions, and if she already knew that I was selling black-market goods . . .* Everyone made mistakes, it was a fact. An innocent slip of the tongue, and he could lose all that he'd worked for.

The door slid open, allowing him to ignore the meandering, unpleasant train of thought that had been plaguing him since his affair with Natima had begun, that had induced him to visit her empty quarters. She was on Bajor for the day, on business, visiting some grand high muckity-muck, so there was no reason for him to be ashamed of his minor break-and-sweep; she'd never even know that he'd been in her rooms.

Her quarters were quiet and spare, generic, lifeless without her. Quark produced a device from the pocket of his waistcoat and began to sweep for listening devices, but the readout quickly confirmed that her rooms were clean. He went through her desk, found hard copies of statistics and a box of isolinear rods labeled with boring, work-related titles. Nothing with his name on it, anywhere.

She said it had nothing to do with me, he told himself, and felt that flicker of unpleasantness once more, which he'd positively identified as guilt. But then, when he'd asked her about it, the night after Thrax had interrogated her, it seemed to Quark that perhaps she had protested just a little too much. She was hiding something. Quark had decided he'd better hack into her computer, just to be sure.

He settled in front of her console, bringing up the datastrings of her last several transmissions, looking for any visible markers to suggest that they had been monitored. He was shocked to discover that Thrax had been listening to all of them, and he played back the recordings, carefully reading the transcripts as he went.

There was nothing there to implicate Quark, he was certain, but he was disturbed that Thrax had been listening in. What did the security officer want with her? Something to do with her job, maybe? Quark hoped that whatever it was, she would be safe. On the other hand, he considered, maybe Thrax just listened to everyone's transmissions. Quark was sure that the security chief had tried, numerous times, to eavesdrop on his own communications, but Quark didn't skimp on tech; he had the very best—well, close to the best—modules and wire blocks, to keep his private business private. He decided that when Natima got back, he'd talk with her about upgrading her hardware.

He was ready to leave, but there was a padd next to Natima's console, open to a page with a particular line of characters, and he couldn't help but take a peek. It was in plain sight, after all. It was an acquisition code; Quark knew it immediately—he received similar sequences constantly from the military personnel who came through the bar and put their orders on their government-issued accounts. This one was probably from Natima's place of employment, the . . . Information people, whatever-it-was. She must have been ordering something just before she left. But this sequence included something extra to make it stand out from those that Quark dealt with every other day of his life. This one was complete with a passcode.

Quark drummed his fingers on her desk, frowning, thinking. With the passcode that was now in front of him, he had the means to access Natima's company acquisition accounts. If Quark was careful with it, he might be able to manipulate the sequence so that any purchases he made with it would not be attributed to Natima. Cardassians were notoriously sloppy with matters of finance. Quark knew that well enough; there were several customers that he regularly skimmed from, and they had never even suspected it.

No. He couldn't betray her. Although . . . he could certainly help a lot of Bajorans with this information. She hadn't said as much outright, but he knew how she felt about the occupation, knew that she sympathized with the Bajorans. If she had the know-how, she would certainly be using her account to help them. He could use the code to order goods under an assumed Cardassian persona, or maybe . . . just skim *enough* that nobody would even notice. She would never even have to know—and if she did, would she necessarily disapprove, considering all the good the code could do for the Bajoran people?

He let out a breath, chiding himself for his weak rationalizations. He was a Ferengi, and Ferengi lived to make profit. If he didn't take advantage of this opportunity, why, it would almost be immoral. He'd answer to the Blessed Exchequer if he ignored this code—and for what? The sake of some Cardassian female? He wasn't about to let a woman wreck his chance at success again, not after what had happened with Gera on Ferenginar.

"Right," he said, and fished another padd from the pocket on his waistcoat to copy the characters, quickly, before he changed his mind. Guilt was for hew-mons, not Ferengi, but still, he couldn't help but remind himself that just because he *had* the code didn't mean he had to *use* it. And if he did use it, he'd use it for good. If he made a little profit from doing good, where was the harm?

Upon returning Jaxa to her parents, Odo was immediately insistent that he be the one to deliver the message to the resistance cell in the mountains. The man named Keral was grateful, but wary. His wife seemed especially afraid while Keral was drawing Odo a sort of map. Using a little stick, he had scratched out a picture on a slice of parchment, and Odo had done his best to commit it all to memory.

These people, Odo was beginning to deduce, were very afraid of the Cardassians. Odo wondered if Doctor Mora had also been so afraid of them. He knew that there was something unspoken between Mora and Reyar, but he had never quite placed it as fear. He did not understand why anyone would be deliberately unkind to another person, but he felt more aware of his own differences than he ever had before.

Odo had finally found an appropriate surface for regeneration: a wide rock with a slight depression. It was flat enough that he could spread himself out, but the raised edges were high enough to keep him from trickling to the forest floor in his liquid state. He was exhausted, having traveled for most of the day, and although he was very close to the mountain pass, he needed time to rest before he could go any further.

He had spent the day experimenting, taking on the appearance of various flora and fauna, some of the inert forms he encountered along the way, as well as animals he remembered from the laboratory database. The question of the child Jaxa had resonated with him: *What do you want to be more than anything else?* Odo had never considered it before, but now, as he settled into the shallow, concave well in the rock, he decided he did not care to be in solid form; being a liquid was relaxing, and felt the most natural.

The only trouble was that being a liquid didn't lend itself to interacting with humanoids, and for some reason that he could not explain, he found humanoid interaction to be deeply compelling, to be preferable to being on his own. How he had hated the long hours and days he remained in the laboratory with no interaction from Doctor Mora! He craved the company of others, though he was not sure why; he only knew that he disliked the sensation of going for such lengthy, bleak stretches without it.

So, despite his preference for being in his natural state, while in the company of others, he would have to remain as a humanoid, as long as he could stand it. He did not want to give anyone reason to emphasize his differences, for it seemed that the Bajorans and Cardassians hated one another solely because of the contrasts between them. Odo was far more dissimilar to either race then they were even to each other—they were both humanoid; they were both solid—and yet, they clearly despised one another. For that reason, Odo knew he must remain as a humanoid if he wanted to avoid being similarly despised.

He had not been regenerating long before he was stirred from his state of pleasantly senseless liquidity. Something was moving through the forest. Odo manifested a few sensory organs in order to investigate comfortably.

It was a humanoid, coming through the forest. The clomping of approaching boots was accompanied by a series of chirps and clicks, indicating that the traveler carried several pieces of noisy equipment. Odo held completely still while the intruder passed him. It was a Cardassian male, dressed as a soldier.

Odo wondered how best to approach the situation. He did not feel especially afraid, for although the Bajorans feared the soldiers, Odo wasn't sure if their weapons would have any effect on his physiology. He believed he could not be contained in any way, and felt calmly confident in his ability to escape, should the situation warrant it.

The soldier continued to tramp back and forth, patrolling the region in a chaotic crisscross, as though trying to confirm his suspicions about something. It was possible that Odo had left some sign of his passing, that the soldier was interpreting as evidence of another person in the area. Without thinking much more on the subject, Odo decided to make his presence known. He wasn't doing anything wrong, and if he simply presented himself as a traveler, perhaps the soldier would then go away and allow Odo to continue with his regeneration.

Odo twisted his body into his humanoid form and stepped out into a small clearing where the soldier would be likely to see him. The soldier did see him, an expression of surprise crossing his ridged face. He pulled his weapon clumsily from its holster.

"You there!" The soldier called out. "State your business! Do you have a permit to be in this region?"

"No," Odo said. "I am merely traversing from one location to another."

"Travel is strictly prohibited through this area, unless you have authorization from the prefect." He stopped short after a moment, and holstered his weapon as he came closer. "Are you Odo'Ital, the shape-shifter?"

It was Odo's turn to be startled. "Yes."

"I have been instructed to bring you to the prefect," the soldier told him. "Come along with me immediately."

"But . . . I am traveling," Odo said. "I don't want to go with you."

The soldier drew his phaser again. "It's not for you to decide," he said. He seemed angry, though Odo didn't know why.

Odo decided it wasn't a good time to attempt to puzzle out the soldier's motives. He was no longer feeling quite so confident that the Cardassian's weapon would indeed be harmless to him. He decided he'd better change his form, though he wasn't at first sure what he should become.

The Cardassian took a step back as Odo shrank, and then expanded, transforming himself into a bird. A great bird with a massive wingspan—a sinoraptor, like those he had seen with Jaxa. He spread his wings, and then uncertainly moved them, testing his abilities in this form. The structure of his tapered bones was too heavy, and he hollowed them, feeling his body lighten with the shift. The soldier looked astonished. Although he had purported to know of Odo's shape-shifting abilities, apparently he had not expected to see the ability displayed.

Before Odo knew it, he was flying, his wings lifting him up over the treetops, over the head of the bemused and frightened Cardassian soldier, who seemed to have quite forgotten what his phaser was good for.

Natima shifted uncomfortably in the straight-backed chair of the waiting room, but it wasn't only the chair that made her squirm. Being on the surface again had brought up memories. Not all of them were unpleasant—far from it— but she had been so much younger when she'd been here before, still full of idealism and conviction, the indulgences of youth. Being here made her feel quite old, and not a little depressed at the steady passage of time.

A male secretary in a glinn's uniform finally nodded at her, and she rose from the stiff chair and walked to the exarch's office without further ceremony. His office was as dark and dusty as the rest of the Tozhat settlement, a place that she remembered as being clean and well-lit, nothing like the shabbiness she saw around her now. As she knew from her research, Central Command refused to appropriate any monies toward the maintenance of the mostly abandoned Cardassian colonies.

"Exarch," she said to the man who sat in the dim room at a broad wooden desk of Bajoran design. He looked fatter in person.

"You may call me Yoriv." The man was polite, but not entirely friendly. He gestured toward a chair and she sat, doing her best to seem at ease.

"Certainly, Yoriv. I am here on behalf of Glinn Gaten Russol, someone who has assured me that you will be sympathetic to the requests he has asked me to put to you."

"Miss Lang, I remind you that I feel some reluctance in discussing political matters with an information correspondent."

"Please, Yoriv. I understand your reticence, but I only have a message to deliver. There is nothing that you must say."

The smile he gave her was small and patronizing, as if she'd already wasted his time. "Well then, deliver it."

"Russol understands that a council is to be held on Terok Nor in the coming months," Natima said. "The civilian leaders here will have the opportunity to present their opinions regarding the status of the Bajoran venture. Russol wonders if you might be likely to voice an opinion in favor of withdrawal."

"Withdrawal!" Skyl snorted, apparently forgetting that Natima had excused him from the necessity of reply. "Central Command would never be in favor of withdrawal, not now that the resistance is finally straggling to an end."

Natima spoke slowly, respectfully. "Russol believes that perhaps you are the sort of person who might understand that the Cardassian economy has begun experiencing a downturn, and will likely continue to plummet if the return of Bajoran resources continue to slow, as it has lately begun to do. Russol has long felt that the needless deaths of our troops on this world has not been sufficiently justified by the short-term success of the annexation." She took a breath, for she had just made a bold statement. She hoped that in doing so, she would convince Skyl that she was not trying to trick him, but it seemed to backfire.

"Do you honestly believe that I would discuss my

intentions with a member of the Information Service?" he asked her, his tone even less friendly than before. "By trying to draw me into this conversation, it seems you might be attempting to coerce me into making a statement that would be looked upon very unfavorably by Central Command."

"As I said before, Yoriv, there is no need for you to make a reply, if you don't choose to. I am merely here as a messenger."

"Fine," Skyl replied. "But you might want to tell Russol that the next time he wants to send me a message, he would do best not to employ an information correspondent to deliver it."

"I understand," Natima said, and stood to leave, the meeting clearly over.

"Miss Lang," he said, before she reached the door, and she turned to look at him. "As a correspondent . . . you must be aware that the average Cardassian citizen doesn't regard the deaths of the soldiers here to be needless and tragic, despite the mere temporary nature of Bajoran benefits. Those soldiers are heroes, not martyrs."

"Yes, I do know," Natima replied. "But Russol thought that perhaps you felt differently—that, being on the surface, you would have firsthand knowledge regarding the violence, and the speed with which the resources here are being depleted."

Skyl laughed. "The state of Bajor's resources has been a matter of much speculation," he agreed, "but their actual status is unimportant. What matters is the people's perception of their necessity. If Central Command decides that Bajor's resources are spent, then they will be. If they decide otherwise, then it will be as they say."

Natima was speechless. Skyl's mocking tone seemed to indicate that he agreed with her and with Russol, but he was clearly not going to say so. She nodded to him with an uncertain expression of feigned politeness, and left, wondering if she had learned anything of value.

Dukat had been intrigued by Mora's extensive "notes" on Odo'Ital, although the proper format was lacking; the man was far from fluent in Cardassian. Still, Dukat had managed to skim over most of the high points in the past weeks, since his team had trailed Odo to a village in Dahkur. Odo measured as highly intelligent, but had received no formal education, had been taught only from institute files and by the Bajoran scientist. Not that Dukat doubted Mora's loyalty—the Bajoran had assisted with the sensors and weapons that had effectively shut down the Bajoran insurgency—but it did make him doubt Yopal's good sense. Why hadn't she assigned a Cardassian scientist, even a team of them, once she'd realized Odo's potential? What if they could clone him, create a race of shape-shifters, working for the Union? Regardless of his future applications, someone should have been giving him a proper Cardassian education when he was still young enough for it to imprint.

Too late, of course, but Dukat was not a man to dwell on past mistakes. What mattered now was coaxing Odo to Terok Nor. Dukat knew he'd find inspiration for future plans once he actually met with the creature, but he hadn't had time to follow up his initial plans, of late. There had been the yearly financial report to prepare, a problem with the processors that had caused them to miss their quota for more than a week—nothing to scoff at, when there was a growing push at home for the flow of metals and foods and building materials to increase, now that the rebels had quieted—and there was a girl, always a girl: a tender young beauty he'd rescued from the processing center, wise beyond her years, plucked straight off the transport from the surface.

Dukat had been busy. He'd twice tried to contact the

glinn he'd tasked to monitor the shape-shifter's movements in the past week, and twice been told that he was unavailable. He hadn't focused on it overmuch, but he wondered at a man who would dare try the prefect's patience.

A third day, a third attempt, and the garresh working communications couldn't put him through fast enough. When the glinn finally showed his face on Dukat's office screen, he did not look happy.

"Why have you not returned my calls?" Dukat asked.

The glinn tightened his jaw. *"Sir, I regret to inform you that my men—that I have lost track of the shape-shifter."*

"How long ago?"

"Sir. We have been searching for its tracks without rest—"

"When?"

The glinn took a deep breath. He looked exhausted. *"Four days, sir."*

"Did I not explain to you that he was to be closely monitored at all times?"

"And we did, sir. We have. It left the village in Dahkur, and we tried to follow it, but it approached one of my men. When he asked it to go with him, it—it turned into a bird and flew away. He was . . . startled, sir."

Startled. Dukat said nothing, and the glinn was quick to fill the silence, his desperation lending him voice.

"How can we track a thing that becomes water, or a stone, or a snake? With all respect, sir, we don't have the technology to keep it under surveillance."

Dukat hovered between anger at the glinn—impertinence on top of incompetence—and a kind of weary resignation, that he should have the only sharp mind, it seemed, in all of Central Command.

"It chooses to be a man," Dukat said, patient through gritted teeth. "It seeks out the company of other sentient beings. Go to the towns, ask questions. Cover the whole province, if you must. Someone will have seen something."

The glinn nodded sharply. *"Yes, sir."*

"And report back as soon as you've established his whereabouts. Do not approach him, or try to contain him in any way, do you understand? I will not indulge your ineptitude twice."

He cut off the transmission, shook his head. If Odo were ever to come to Terok Nor, it would have to be of his own volition. For now, keeping track of him would have to do, if his soldiers could manage it without his direct supervision.

Dukat picked up the padd with his schedule for the day, turning his attention to other matters. Truly, it was a wonder he ever got anything done.

11

When she got the upgrade memo from the science ministry, it was all Kalisi could do not to scream. She read it three times, her blood pressure steadily spiking.

. . . and you will receive the newly calibrated RV7 models and have them installed before the end of the next quartile . . .

She read it again, then stood, agitated, pacing her small closet of an office. Only the year before, Cardassia Prime had gifted Doctor Moset's facility with a brand-new computer system, state of the art—and backwards compatible with their outdated hardware. Since her arrival at the facility, Kalisi had spent countless hours elaborately reprogramming the system to get their aging equipment online and networked. And now the science ministry had actually come through with new hardware for the lab. Hardware that was, of course, incompatible with last year's computer system.

Kalisi couldn't stand it. She went to find Crell.

It was midweek and late, so she headed for pathology, fuming all the way. She exchanged nods with a few other workers, but no pleasantries; they all knew what she was to Moset, and his blatant favoritism had distanced her from anyone she might have looked to for friendship.

He was happy to see her, in his distracted and quirky way. They hadn't been lovers for long enough to breed too much familiarity, and he seemed to enjoy listening to her complain. She ranted about the ministry for a spell, as he nodded appropriately, shaking his head in shared frustration. She didn't expect him to offer any solution, and wasn't disappointed. He had been distant lately, in a way she'd come to recognize as a precursor to some new twist in his research.

"Well, it won't be for much longer," he said finally, smiling his thin smile. "This might be among the last upgrades we'll have to suffer."

"What do you mean?"

"You're an educated woman," Crell said. "You can see that the resources here on Bajor are dwindling."

"Yes, but the projection for dropping below quota is still decades away."

Moset leaned against the metal table behind him, cocking one eyeridge in a melodramatically cryptic expression. "That's just what they *want* you to think."

Her irritation was no pretense. "What do you mean?"

"That's propaganda, newscasts aimed at home. From what I hear, Cardassia will pull out of here less than a generation from now. Possibly within the next five years." He smiled with faint distraction. "I'm hoping for sooner, rather than later, of course."

Kalisi was surprised. She'd heard rumors, but hadn't believed them. Crell was well-respected, though, and had earned a number of influential friends in the science ministry and Central Command. If he believed it, he had reason to.

"What will happen to the Bajorans?" she asked, not sure why it was the first question that came to mind.

His playfulness fell away, his demeanor suddenly uncharacteristically grave. "Considering the declining state of their society and their ecosystem, in my estimation they'll be lucky to die off quickly."

As if to illustrate his point, a lab assistant wheeled a cot through the room's far entrance, a cadaver, mostly covered by a sheet. A Bajoran woman. Her skin was nearly white beneath the bright lights.

"If you'll excuse me, Doctor," Crell said, nodding at her. "I have some work to do. Perhaps we can continue this conversation at a later time?"

Kalisi nodded, already backing toward the door she'd entered by, as the assistant parked the corpse in front of Crell. She wasn't particularly squeamish, but wasn't interested in watching a dissection, either. She turned, thinking. She still had to decide how to handle the ministry's "gift." It was reprogram again or reject the computers . . .

She glanced back at Moset as the door slid open, and saw the Bajoran woman twitch.

Kalisi stopped, peered closer at the body as the door slid closed again. The assistant had disappeared, and Crell was pulling back the sheet to expose the woman's bare body, so strange and smooth, no ridges crossing her midriff. Kalisi was sure she had moved, like a shiver, when he had lifted the coverlet.

He tapped at a recording panel and lifted his scalpel, leaning over the naked alien.

"Subject is mid-20s—ah, 26, I believe, no history of disease before end-stage Fostossia—"

There! The Bajoran's hand this time, a spastic movement.

"Crell," she said, forgetting herself as he brought the blade down.

He paused, looked up at her.

"She's still alive," Kalisi said.

He blinked, frowned. As though he was still waiting for her to get to the point. "Yes?"

"I thought—I mean, I suppose . . ." She wasn't sure what to say, not sure what was happening. He acted as though performing a vivisection on a living person—a

Bajoran, but still a person—was something he did every day.

He smiled, straightened slightly. He glanced about, confirming that they were alone.

"You have a tender heart, Kali," he said. "This woman is already dead. Terminal coma. The disease was untreatable by the time she came to us. Better we learn something from her death, don't you feel?"

Kalisi took a step back to the table, unable to look away from the Bajoran's face. She saw it now, the quiver of her thin nostrils, a slow beat at her temple.

"What could you hope to learn?" she asked.

He gestured to the woman's flat belly. "More about their reproductive systems, for one thing."

"To what purpose?"

He smiled again, what she thought of as his teacher smile. "Ultimately, our work here is about finding ways to improve the health of the Bajoran labor force. To maintain optimal productivity. Gestation and child-rearing generally hinders the productivity of the parents."

Kalisi shook her head. "You're devising ways to sterilize them?"

His smile took on an edge of excitement. "Think. For the Union, there's no need for another generation of Bajorans—and really, it does them a kindness. Spares them from having to watch their children starve to death, once we're gone. *And*, it means a more effective work force while we're still here."

He leaned over the woman and made a swift, deep incision across her lower belly. Blood pulsed and pooled, slid over her bare hips to the table beneath. He lifted the flap of tissue, gestured at the wet red inside the bleeding gash, as though Kalisi would recognize the dying woman's womb.

"That's the problem," he said, nodding once. "They breed like voles, pregnancies one right after another, with rapid gestation periods. An effective sterilizing agent solves it. Getting it to them would be a simple matter—we add it to one of the Fostossia boosters; they're all required to have them. The issue is isolating the right component. I've already tried several formulas. There were promising results in the viral carrier, but those subjects all developed tumorous cysts. Obviously, we want to treat these people as humanely as possible."

The body on the narrow table between them convulsed sleepily and gave a ragged, guttural exhalation—the last sound it would make. The blood ceased to pump, the woman's thin, alien face relaxing.

"Horrible," Kalisi said, unable to help herself.

"This one stayed unconscious, at least," Crell said, with no emotion save for the affable tint that usually colored his voice. "Your reaction strikes me as slightly hypocritical, darling. You've devoted your entire adult life to designing weapons that target and kill them."

Kalisi stared at him. "Since my detection grid was installed, combat deaths of both Bajorans and Cardassians have been reduced exponentially. My work has *prevented* unnecessary suffering."

Her lover nodded. "As will mine," he said evenly. After a moment, he leaned in and resumed cutting, and Kalisi left him.

The ground unfolded beneath him, broad and green and thick with shadows. Odo was tired—he'd had so little time to regenerate—but decided it was for the best that he just approach these resistance people now and be done with his task. In the short time since he'd left Mora's care, things had happened so quickly, the environments and faces and rules constantly changing. He wished for time to assimilate his new experiences, to draw conclusions, but away from the laboratory, he'd discovered that time moved differently;

it seemed that there was not always opportunity to stop and think.

A final stretch of his wings, and he landed in the mountain pass that Sito Keral had told him of, hopping across a fallen tree, fluttering for balance. He became a small *tyrfox* that could amble effectively over the rocky ground.

It was exhilarating to fly, but being a bird was not easy. Flying was new to him, and tiring—not to mention a little frightening. Odo had never been exposed to such great vistas of height before, nor the perpetual biting wind that came with it. His experience until recently had been limited to what the laboratory had been able to provide. The possibilities of what he could do, what he could be—it was more to consider, more to process. The sooner he had finished his errand, a favor that he felt he owed the kind villagers, the better.

It took him only a short time to find the small opening in the rock, concealed by thick brush, but he could see that the brush had been pushed aside sometime recently. Someone had come through here, though it surprised him that a humanoid would clamber through such a tight passage. He transformed into a vole and entered the chamber, which immediately plunged into dense blackness. He adjusted his eyesight and made his legs longer, guessing that the distance to the resistance fighters within was considerable.

He traversed the tunnels for a long while, noting that there was more than one passage to go through. He heard many things—water and insects, other small, warm-blooded bodies moving through the dark. Finally, he heard voices, melodic whispers on the dusty air, and he followed the sounds. When he'd found the tunnel that seemed to definitively lead to the source of the conversation, he morphed back into a humanoid.

He hesitated, listening for just a moment. The voices were raised in argument, he was sure.

"Kohn Biran?" He called out into the tunnel. There was an abrupt silence, and then a lone voice responded, strained and careful.

"Who's there?"

"I come from Ikreimi village, to deliver a message from Sito Keral."

Another beat of silence. "I know you, friend?"

Odo was not sure how to respond. "We have not met," he said finally.

"Perhaps you should introduce yourself," the voice said.

"I must warn you," Odo called before entering the passage, "my appearance is . . . unusual."

The man said nothing else, so Odo entered the tunnel, which was larger now, so that he could expand to his usual height as a humanoid, and made his way to a much larger grotto; dimly lit with a few rudimentary torches. Its furnishings were plain and rough. A table—piled high with wooden dishes and the components of mismatched computer systems—some stools, heaps of bedrolls along the uneven walls. Two men were in the room, standing next to rough wooden benches, their posture tense—whether because they did not expect a visitor or because they had been quarreling, Odo could not say.

"I come with important news," he said, the words he had memorized.

"And what might that be?" one of the men asked, and Odo recognized his voice as the one that had called to him from the tunnel. This must be Kohn Biran, the cell's leader. Odo deduced that he was older than the other man, his heavy beard and thick, wild hair streaked with silver. The other man was no less unkempt, but appeared slightly younger.

"The anti-aircraft component of the detection grid. There is a way to reprogram it."

"Go on," Kohn Biran coaxed, looking at his companion.

"A code sequence may be entered to override the program's diagnostic," Odo continued. "It will alert the system to recognize Bajoran flyers in the same category as Cardassian craft, allowing raiders to leave the atmosphere unharmed. This is a procedure that would have to be performed on each tower individually; it will not be effective for the system as a whole."

The two men began to speak excitedly. "The comm relays—we can finally send people out to repair the comm relays—"

"We can regain contact with the others—"

". . . And if it works, the towers in other provinces—other continents—can be disconnected—"

Kohn turned back to Odo. "What about the biosensors?"

"I have no information about how to disable that aspect of the detection grid."

"But you have the code sequence for the flight sensors?"

"I have it memorized," Odo told him, and began to recite the code he had carefully remembered. The Bajoran asked him to repeat himself once, and Odo complied willingly. "If there is any doubt about my integrity or ability, someone may be sent to Ikreimi to confer with Keral for himself," he suggested.

Kohn studied him for a long moment, his eyes clear and sharp, then shook his head.

"That won't be necessary, Mr. . . ."

"Odo," he said. He felt that something more was required, so he added, "And I appreciate your trust in me."

"Well, the resistance functions on trust," the man told him, extending his hand. Odo clasped his arm.

"I'm Kohn Biran, and this is Ma Jouvirna." The other man nodded his head.

"You are welcome to stay here, Mr. Odo. The rest of my cell has gone out for provisions. You must be hungry . . ."

"That will not be necessary," Odo told him, "though I thank you." Just as Mora had taught him. Thinking of Mora, he felt a thing he'd long known, but had only recently come to understand. Resentment, that was the word. So much to see and do, so much to experience, and Mora had wished to keep him in the lab, had wished to keep him from the world. He stared at the two men for just a moment longer before ducking his head to dismiss himself, and then he turned and backed out the tunnel, morphing again into a vole and scampering back out the tunnel, the way he had come.

Quark had welcomed Natima home with open arms, and their trysts had continued, to their mutual satisfaction. But today, this very day, Quark had received the bulk of the main transfer to his personal account, credit that he'd garnered using Natima's access code. And when he'd seen the damages, he'd realized that his time with Natima was over. The feeling was a weight in his chest, a tightness in his throat, strangling his responses to his customers as they made their orders. Quark wished very much that he could just be alone today, but the bar needed him; his profits weren't going to make themselves.

Not that I can't afford it, he thought, considering what he'd just earned. The thought was like an invisible jack-screw clamped down on his heart, for there was no way Natima wasn't going to notice what Quark had done. It had been one thing to make a few false purchases that her employer would attribute to Natima herself, but when that had turned out to be so easy, Quark could not resist using the code for further gain. He had concocted a false acquisition number for himself, and used her purchase authorization to make an order to a company that did not exist, payable to an untraceable account in the Bank of Bolias. Untraceable to anyone, of course, but Quark, for he had opened the account himself. It was foolproof—that is, it was foolproof until someone from the Information Service alerted Natima to the discrepancy on her purchase records. That day should be coming around any time now.

Quark tried to busy himself stacking and restacking the glasses beneath the bar, trying to hypnotize himself with the monotony of the activity, but he couldn't block out the creeping misery he felt. He wasn't sure what had come over him, but whatever it was, it was obviously built into his very constitution, and he supposed he just couldn't help himself. If only he could believe that would be a sufficient excuse for Natima! Somehow, he doubted very much that she would accept it.

"Brother!" It was Rom, coming up behind him so suddenly that Quark almost dropped the glasses he held in each hand.

"Rom, I wish you would refrain from ambushing me in my own establishment," Quark snapped. "What is it?"

"Uhhhh . . . it's that woman again. That Cardassian female. She's trying to find you."

"She's here?" Quark looked around, panicked. Should he duck under the bar?

"No, not this time. She's on the comm system again. She wants you to meet her in her quarters tonight."

Quark tightened his grip on one of the glasses as if he would crush it. He cleared his throat, and set the glass down underneath the bar, turning the other one over in his hands. "Tell her I can't, I have to work a late shift tonight because . . . because some Bajorans who were supposed to come for cleanup duty never showed."

The aged Bajoran busboy turned to gape as he overheard the lie.

"Get back to work!" Quark screamed, almost hurling the glass at the half-blind old idiot.

"But, brother, the Bajorans are right over there," Rom

supplied helpfully. "And she keeps calling and calling. This is the fourth time today."

"I'm aware of that, Rom," Quark said, as carefully as if he were speaking to a child—a thick child. "But I want you to tell her that anyway, because it is easier than telling her the truth, which is complicated. And also private," he added.

"Okay," Rom said, shrugging. "But . . . it feels wrong."

Quark's voice was tight. "Rom, unless you want me to throw you and Nog out on your lobes—"

"Fine, Quark, fine!" Rom replied, agitated. "I'll do it! But I don't have to like it!" Rom scurried off to answer the comm, and Quark set the glass down underneath the bar with a dull clang. If Rom's intolerable honesty kept up, he might have to have his brother arrested again. He didn't like to do it, but occasionally it was necessary to frame Rom for some minor infraction just to get him out of the way for a night or two. Of course, he always dropped the charges in the end, but still, it was a hassle that he would have preferred to avoid, and anyway, Thrax was getting wise to it. He licked his lips and steadied himself for a moment before a large group of soldiers entered the bar all at once, and Quark looked up with his customary smile, more artificial than usual.

"Welcome to Quark's," he said cordially. "What'll it be?"

The soldiers were not in the mood for conversation, which normally would have been preferable to Quark, but today he regretted it; the distraction of idle chatter would have been welcome. He poured several glasses of *kanar* and handed them around, accepted his payment on padds and in cash, and even stopped to rub his fingers over the currency, as he often did, almost as an unconscious inclination. But the sensation of hard latinum in his hands had little of its usual effect on him today.

It occurred to him that there wasn't much purpose to making profit when it was only going to be accompanied with such doubt. But he quickly chased the thought away, experiencing a surge of shame at the notion. This must be exactly what Gaila and his mother were talking about— going soft, losing focus of what was really important in life. After all, love was temporary; everyone knew it didn't last. Latinum, though—that was forever. Maybe it couldn't keep you warm at night, but . . .

Who needs it, he snarled to himself, and went back to the distraction of stacking glasses, reviewing in his mind the day's hefty revenue margin. If that wasn't enough to soothe his nerves, then nothing would.

Kira had been the first to volunteer for this one. She knew Tahna Los was furious that she was the one who had been assigned to reprogram the sensor towers, but since he had been out on a provision run when Kohn Biran got the news, Kira claimed the job for herself uncontested. The older members of the cell weren't especially eager to do it, but Kira and Tahna had built up a friendly rivalry between themselves, and she knew he was burning with resentment to think of her getting the credit for this job.

She worked her way across Serpent's Ridge, keeping to the thick undergrowth of the wooded hill as she headed for the tower. She moved quickly, but not with haste, finding the softest step, the deepest shade of the late afternoon. The days were getting shorter, but it was still warm out, still mostly green. She'd thought she was in good shape, but after so long hiding in the tunnels, she'd gotten lazy. Her ankles and back ached with the unfamiliar effort of staying unheard, unseen, and her adrenaline shot up at every sound, birds and small animals that she'd all but forgotten about.

Not that it would matter. She could be the fastest, quietest runner in the world, and if the sensors were able to pick her up, there would have been soldiers on to her by now. As with all of the active missions the cells took part in, she had to be carefully shielded for this venture, but there was always the chance that the shields would fail; despite Mobra's careful attention to detail, there was a first time for everything.

I'm small, though. Smaller than Tahna, anyway. And just small enough to make all the difference apparently. It was a suspicion that had grown within her for a long time, but not so much that she would have gone out unshielded.

She could see the automated tower less than a half tessipate ahead of her, rising from the apex of the winding ridge. Thankfully, this one wasn't too far from the tunnels; the next closest was eight, nine days on foot. Still, she was nervous. Even the dense cover of the woods high on the ridge felt too exposed, and she had to climb the tower, melt the panel lock, and plug in a whole series of carefully memorized passcodes and commands. What if the lock didn't melt? What if she forgot a number or a character? What if whoever had cracked the code in the first place had made a mistake?

I've hacked a hundred system panels, she told herself. *And I won't forget.* And if there was a mistake in the code's translation, there was nothing she could do about it, anyway. Worrying wouldn't rewrite it for her.

The sensor tower was a slender metal cage that rose well over the tree line, built of the dusky matte composites that the Cardassians favored, that they manufactured at a massive plant in the southern highlands. Surely there was no ambush, no reptilian squad hidden in the shadows, waiting for her to show herself. Kira took a deep breath and stepped out from the cover of the trees, moving quickly to the tower's base before she had a chance to second-guess the action. This wasn't a job to linger over.

She approached the tower and shifted her small pack to one hip before starting to climb, the structure's design creating its own ladder. The panel she wanted was about midway up, perhaps four times her height from the ground. Not a terrible fall, but bad enough. She concentrated on the rungs one at a time, holding tight, always looking up, and finally, the boxy computer relay access panel was in front of her.

An evening breeze blew, cool through the late heat of the day. She uncoiled her belt with one shaky hand, clipping each end to the tower's metal hook-rings, creating a simple sling she could lean against. She felt horribly exposed, sitting on top of the trees, and quickly reached into her pack and drew out a slender vial about the length of her index finger. She uncapped the vial, dripped its contents onto the duranium lock that sealed the panel. The solution hissed and reeked, the lock dissolving as the magnasite did its work. Kira turned her head away from the acrid fumes, ignoring the magnificent view, all too aware that it was still light enough for her to be seen. Early evening was the best time for one of their raiders to lift out, all of them agreed—the setting sun caused problems with the Cardassian visual systems—but for her own sake, she wished it was dark.

A thin *ting* as what was left of the metal turned brittle, and the panel was open, the tiny screen and keypads lighting up.

Access first, she told herself, using the trick Lupaza had taught her to memorize the long list of codes, breaking it down into mental pictures and associations. *2698178*, she thought, tapping it in carefully. Twenty-six hours in a day. Keltis had ninety-eight prophecies. Seven plus one was eight.

She touched the input bar and the screen blinked once, twice, a third time— And someone screamed, so loud and close that she lost her grip on the tower, fell back against the sling, her knees banging into the structure hard enough to hurt. The sound stretched impossibly long as Kira scrabbled for the metal rungs again, her breath coming in shallow sips, the alarm klaxon tearing through the empty canyon from the top of the tower. The scream rose and fell, alerting the world to her trespass.

Kosst! She considered running for almost a second, disregarding the impulse in less time. She could afford a few minutes. She forced herself to think of the entry code. *Twenty-six hours, Ninety-eight prophecies, seven plus one is—*

"One plus seven," she said, her voice unheard over the deafening screech of the alarm. She'd transposed two of the numbers.

Focus. You know this, you know the numbers, so you do it, just do it. She typed it in again, forcing herself not to hurry— and the alarm shut off in mid-scream, the last echoes falling away over the treetops as she called up the next set of numbers, and the next, working her way into the system. *Focus, the nine days of atonement, the slash-dot key, four halved was two, plus . . .*

As she watched the complicated command sequences flash by, she understood that without these codes, there would have been no chance at reprogramming the system. If it worked, Bajoran ships would read as Cardassian. The majority of the cells would still have to stay hidden, but their shuttles could be moved to Derna or one of the other moons, the communications equipment there repositioned. Everything could change.

7, characters ksi, 3, 3 . . . 9.

There. The last digit was in. She took a deep breath, watched the screen go blank, back to a waiting status. Had it worked? She didn't know how to confirm, and she couldn't risk staying any longer. Someone would come to see why the alarm had gone off, and she meant to be far, far away by the time they showed.

She unhooked the sling and half slid down the tower, giving herself a few more bruises in her hurry to be elsewhere. She thudded heavily to the forest floor, stopping only long enough to stuff her belt into her pack, grabbing her comm as she darted into the woods.

Shakaar spoke her name as soon as she tapped the switch, his voice riding waves of static. She kept moving, taking deep breaths, stretching her legs for a run. She thought she heard the hum of an approaching ship, a far-away drone in the rapidly cooling air.

"It's done," she said.

"*Is . . . safe . . . send up . . . raider?*"

"I have no idea," she said, and she was sure of it now: a ship was coming. She broke into a sprint, pumping her arms for speed, jumping over fallen logs and crashing through the underbrush, more concerned with gaining distance than with stealth. She tripped over rocks, slid down sudden drop-offs, ran and ran and finally stopped, unable to go any farther.

She doubled over, hands on her twitching legs, gasping for breath. The skimmer had been coming from the south, she was sure of it, and she was headed north. By the time they realized that someone had cracked the access panel, she'd be well out of reach.

She raised herself up, deepened her breathing, and heard something she hadn't heard in a very long time—the telltale sonic boom of a Bajoran raider as it prepared to leave the atmosphere, echoing out from behind the hills that hid much of what was left of the resistance.

Kira clenched her hands into fists, counting seconds, breathing through her open mouth so she could hear the roar of particle cannons firing. But she heard nothing. A brown bird, flapping through the brush. Wind in the trees. Her heart, pounding.

We did it, she thought, she *believed*. It was too soon to know anything for sure, but she couldn't help her belief. She started moving again, her breath coming more easily as she worked her way down the ridge. She even found the capacity to laugh as two more raiders went up, noisily scraping the sky as they broke through the sound barrier.

Dukat had just finished his weekly call to Athra and was feeling nostalgic for home. His wife was pregnant again, a happy result of his last brief visit to Cardassia Prime, and positively glowed with good health and humor. She had images to show him of the other children, stories of their accomplishments. This child would be their fifth.

Sixth, he thought, but quickly shook the thought. He did not often think of the son he had lost, a casualty of Cardassia's poor conditions before the annexation. Athra never spoke of him.

He sat back in his chair after his faithful wife had bid him a heartfelt good-bye; he wished he could be home more often. As it was, the extra day or two he spent on Cardassia whenever he went to present his periodic progress reports was all he could spare, often in conjunction with his reports to Command. Before the insurgency was under control, he'd been lucky to manage that. Perhaps with this birth, he would arrange to take a more substantial vacation, a week or so . . .

And, of course, a stopover at Letau as well. . . .

A signal at his door, although it was late. The operations center staff was minimal at this hour, only a few men moving about among the softly blinking consoles. He saw that it was Glinn Trakad, and sighed.

He motioned the soldier inside. "Yes?"

Trakad carried a padd, held it up. "Summary of surface transmissions for the day, quotas, incident reports."

Dukat nodded, reaching for the padd. Trakad brought it to him, stepped back as the prefect scanned the reads.

"Anything of interest?" Dukat asked.

"A malfunction with one of the sensor towers. Possible sabotage attempt."

Dukat glanced up. "In what way?"

"An alarm was tripped, suggesting that someone tried to access the diagnostic system with an unauthorized passcode," Trakad said. "And the lock on the tower's relay was tampered with."

"Has the system been compromised?"

"No. It's been triple-checked. Everything is in working order."

Dukat frowned. "So, someone tried to break in and failed . . . ?"

"Yes, but the alarm was shut down before the ground team arrived," The glinn said. "Not disabled, but turned off. They would have had to have a code to override it."

"But the system is still working?"

"That's right."

Dukat shook his head. "Contact the Bajoran Institute of Science at once. We will need to alert the engineer who designed the program to see if it is malfunctioning."

Trakad nodded.

"Anything else?"

"Several flyers—three, I believe—were detected leaving atmosphere late this afternoon, but air traffic says there were no ships scheduled for departure, no flight plans filed."

"Are there any ships currently unaccounted for?"

"You think the resistance stole them?"

"Well, without knowing all of the facts, I can't say, can I?" Dukat said. He smiled thinly at Trakad, printed the padd to show that he'd seen the day's reports. "Check airfield inventory. I want all of our crafts accounted for. And see to it that the security unit from that tower is brought here."

He handed the padd back to Trakad, who nodded quickly, a slight bow before leaving. Dukat waved him on, idly wondering if the few remaining insurgents were up to something. But no. The Bajorans were a cowed people, pacified once more by their religious amenities, submissive to the will of the Union. In truth, he couldn't afford it to be otherwise, with the pressure to produce more always weighing on his shoulders. In any case, he would take no chances, looking into any reports of potential resistance activity himself.

It was much like being a father, he often thought, overseeing a planet of children, some willing, some willful. It was a balance, knowing when to encourage, when to provide strict correction, but one he felt he excelled at finding. As the Bajorans grew, culturally, intellectually, they would come to appreciate him more, to understand the choices he'd made.

I'll be remembered here long after I'm gone, he thought, and smiled, leaning back in his chair once more.

12

Thrax, finished with his station business for the evening, closed out the reports on his office computer, relieved to have finished the tedious chore after an especially trying day. But he didn't shut down his system after the mainframe link was disconnected; instead, he put a personal call through to Cardassia Prime.

It was some time before the call was answered, and he began to wonder, with disappointment, if the party he was trying to reach might have left her new "office" already, but she finally responded to the call, her face filling the tiny screen and causing Thrax to break out into a foolish grin.

"Hello," he said to her, feeling the welcome tremble that always attended their correspondence.

"Hello," she replied, her voice musical and soft, projected from his faraway homeworld. How he missed it. How he missed her! *"To what do I owe this occasion?"*

"I know it has been a long time," he apologized. "My business here keeps me from contacting you as often as I would like."

"Just your business?" she asked. *"Not . . . threats?"*

"No," he said firmly. "There are no threats, I have told you. I am safe. I only wanted to let you know . . . I located a dissident on the station, someone who is to return to

Cardassia Prime tomorrow. A woman—a correspondent for the Information Service."

"What is her name?"

"Natima Lang. Do you know of her?"

"No, but I'll see what I can find."

"It could be helpful to do so. She is affiliated with Gaten Russol. But more interesting to you and me—she contacted a member of the Detapa Council here on Bajor. An exarch at one of the old settlements."

The woman's eyes shone with interest. *"Do you think he is a dissident as well?"*

"Time will tell," Thrax told her. "But I believe he may be."

"And you believe this is good news for us?"

He nodded. "If the Detapa Council continues to oppose the government to gain power, it could eventually wrest the Union out of the military government's hands. It seems that the handful of dissidents I have been tracking have begun to add more followers to their ranks—followers in the civilian government."

The woman nodded. *"This could be favorable for us. But the Detapa Council may be no more in support of us than Central Command has been."*

Thrax frowned before his face twisted into a rueful smile. "Have you always been such a pessimist, Astraea?"

She smiled back, embarrassed. *"No, Glinn Sa'kat,"* she admitted, *"only realistic."*

He laughed quietly. It always amused him that she continued to refer to him by his military title—even his colleagues on the station called him by his first name. But for her, it had become almost a sign of affection to maintain the formality he had shown to her upon their first meeting. "Well," he said. "I thought it might be useful for us to find out more about these people, the dissidents. If there is any question that supporting their cause could serve to help us in the future—"

"*I agree,*" she said. "*I don't suppose they could detest us any more than Central Command already does.*"

"One hopes not." Thrax fell silent.

There was so much he wanted to say to her, but he would have preferred to do it in person. He had never been able to convey his feelings regarding her, not even when he was with her, on Cardassia Prime. His support of her position within the Way was much more important than their personal relationship, a relationship that had started when he had discovered her walking in a near daze along the periphery of Cardassia City, trying to put some meaning to the frightening visions she had been having. If the Fates hadn't intervened that day, hadn't seen to it that he would find her there— But of course, Oralius watched over Her guide. It was meant that he would find her, and he hoped it was meant that he would be reunited with her someday on his homeworld—sooner rather than later.

Two quartiles, three at most, he promised himself. No more than another year, certainly. He would be done with this place, and with Dukat.

"*The Bajoran religious man we spoke of . . . he is still safe?*"

"I can't be certain, but I believe so," he told her. "The one they call the kai is still safe, and I believe the man from your vision has a connection with her. That is what Prylar Bek tells me, but he will reveal no more."

"*He is mistrustful of you?*"

"No," Thrax said. "I believe he trusts me now, since I gave him the information to get his kai to safety before the detection grid went online. But he is simply not at liberty to reveal information. It is much the same way . . . that I feel about you, Astraea. I would guard you with my life."

There was a moment of awkward silence while Thrax tried to think of another item of interest. "So . . . after the next Bajoran council, I think I will try to make a connection with Yoriv Skyl, the Tozhat exarch," he said. "To see if I can discern his leanings."

"*A wise idea,*" Astraea agreed softly, and there was another moment of silence. Their calls always seemed to be conducted this way, ending with strained pauses, loaded with unspoken emotions.

"May you walk with Oralius," Thrax finally said, and she smiled, though she looked disappointed, too.

She signed off with a recitation from the Book. "'*To speak her words with my voice, to think her thoughts with my mind, to feel her love with my heart.*'" Thrax repeated the words back to her, and she smiled, her eyes closing, as her image skittered from Thrax's screen. He sat back in his chair and paused to reflect, to think exclusively of her for a moment, then he abruptly rose and left the security station, heading to his quarters for the night.

Natima's eyes were dry, but she felt like weeping. The transport had already left the station, and there was no looking back now—not that she would have wanted to. Still, she was going back to Cardassia Prime entirely contrary to her appointment. Dalak would be furious with her for this insubordination, but there was simply no way she could have remained on the station, not after what had transpired earlier today.

She was the only civilian on this transport, which had little in the way of elbow room. There was a tiny commissary, small berths, two beds to a room, with a 'fresher that had to be shared—at least for the soldiers. Natima was lucky enough to have gotten a room to herself. Being a woman had a few perks, at least. She rested, as best she could, on the hard berth, and tried to shut her mind to the unhappy events that had unfolded earlier, but it was all she could think of.

Had Quark really believed he could hide from her

forever in the microcosm of Terok Nor? She had cornered him leaving his quarters early this morning, and had demanded an explanation—hoping against hope that he would actually have one. But of course, through his pathetic attempts to justify what he had done, Natima saw the truth: not only had he stolen from her, he wasn't even sorry he had done it.

She had threatened to turn him in to the authorities for his dealings with the Bajorans—or the very least, to turn him in for violating her acquisition number. She was going to have to explain it to the accounting department at the Information Service, a task she dreaded almost as much as facing Dalak regarding her sudden abandonment of her assignment. But then, she hadn't turned him in after all—she still wasn't entirely sure why.

How foolish she had been, to trust a man who pretended to have a romantic interest in her—a Ferengi, no less! She could only assume that he had been using her from the very beginning, and yet, she had not even turned him in to save her own reputation. She knew that it was dangerous to draw attention to herself this way. If accounting were to closely examine her acquisition codes, would they find anything that would point to her status as a dissident? Natima didn't think so, but she couldn't understand why she would even consider taking the risk for someone as dishonest as Quark had turned out to be. She supposed she was just a fool, in the end.

She was crying, now, which should have been a relief, but was mostly just a humiliation. She let herself cry softly for a few moments before pulling herself together. She would never go to Terok Nor again, or to Bajor, and if Dalak tried to make her—well, maybe she was done with Dalak, anyway. Maybe it was time to move away from the Information Service. She had long remained loyal to her employer in part because she'd believed that she owed her life's success to the Service. But would it be so terrible, to attribute her success to her own actions? Maybe this was the push she needed to go in another direction, the sign that it was time to move into another phase of her life.

Good-bye, Quark, she thought, and lay down again on the hard, empty bunk, wishing she could sleep.

Vekobet had several abandoned districts that were not beyond the boundary constraints, but they had fallen into ruin in the past twelve years. The desolation was due in part to destruction from skirmishes between Union and resistance forces, and in part to a lack of functioning utilities. But the population was inching toward expansion again, and most of the occupied houses in town were bursting at the seams with extended families. The older districts had to be considered for renovation, for the active portions of the cities were becoming dangerously overcrowded. Kalem Apren was helping to dig an irrigation trench in one of the newly reclaimed areas, having already helped to patch the roofs of three old houses that had fallen into disrepair. He was waist-deep in the muddy ditch when his wife Raina suddenly appeared, out of breath, her exuberance showing.

"Apren!" she cried out. "It's the comm! Someone is calling you—from off world!"

Kalem wasted no time in dropping the shovel he had been using and clambering out of the muddy, half-finished trench. "Excuse me," he cried hastily to the other men, though he did not stay to hear their reply. He raced after his wife through the old streets, stopping at brief intervals so that one or the other could catch their breath, occasionally locking gazes and laughing. Someone had repaired the long-range systems, unless Raina was mistaken, and Kalem knew from her expression that she wasn't.

Panting and gasping, he clutched at the receiver, hoping against hope that whoever had called would still be on the

line—it was a good twenty minutes to and from the outlying settlement from where he and Raina had just come—
but someone immediately replied to his greeting.

*"Apren! It's Jas Holza! What a relief to finally reach you
again!"*

"Holza!" Kalem exclaimed, hardly able to comprehend
such an auspicious occurrence. "It's been a long time!"

*"Yes—as you say. And I have good news for you, and for Jaro
Essa and all the others."*

"Do tell!" Kalem turned to Raina so that she could
hear the exchange, both of them struggling to contain their
excitement.

*"I have been in contact with an arms merchant named Hagath.
He is willing—even eager—to sell us some very sophisticated
weapons—things that could make a genuine difference in the
fight. If you and I pool our resources, and distribute these materials among the right people—"*

"Is this a secure line, Holza?" Kalem interrupted.

"Don't worry about that," Jas reassured them. *"You have
said that Jaro has information regarding the whereabouts of the
resistance cells on Bajor . . ."*

"What's left of them," Apren replied, and then quickly
attempted to redact his pessimism. "Yes."

*"Someone with a warp vessel will have to rendevous with this
man somewhere outside the B'hava'el system."*

Kalem closed his eyes, trying to rein in his frustration.
"That's impossible. Warp vessels under Bajoran control are
virtually nonexistent. The resistance uses sub-impulse vessels, but even those have been grounded by a Cardassian
detection system that—"

"There must be someone with access to—"

"You mean, besides yourself?"

There was a pause, and Kalem wondered if the connection had been severed before Jas spoke again.

"I can't do it, Apren. The risk is too great. You must find

someone in the resistance movement who can get access to a warp vessel. I have been in sporadic contact with this man for over three years now, and I know he will be willing to negotiate whenever we are ready, but someone will have to go to him to make the exchange. He is wisely unwilling to enter Cardassian occupied space. I will appropriate whatever funds I can for this purpose, and I know you will too—but you can't ask me to enter the B'hava'el system."

"If you won't do it, then it cannot be done," Kalem said, with unusual finality. "You can't imagine what has become of the resistance movement on this world."

"This is unlike you, Apren," Jas said. *"I have been trying to contact you about this matter since the last time we spoke—and I never would have expected to get this reaction, once the message finally got through."*

"I wouldn't have expected this from you, either," Kalem said coldly. "But I suppose we've both changed." He hesitated for a moment, exchanging a disappointed glance with his wife, and then he ended the call.

"We found the shape-shifter."

Dukat smiled at the glinn on his screen. "Of course you have."

"You were right, Prefect. It was spotted in another Bajoran village. He has already been ingratiating himself to the locals. It seems he settled a dispute between two men who were accusing one another of burning down a barn, or some such foolishness—" He stopped speaking, apparently realizing that this was more than Dukat had asked to know.

Dukat tilted his head in recognition of the acknowledgment. "And you've made no contact with him, is that right?"

"Yes, sir."

"Good. Now, I want you to withdraw as much as possible without losing sight of him entirely. Give him time to establish himself. A month, perhaps. Then you'll send in some of your men, to recruit new workers for Terok Nor."

"And we bring in the shape-shifter with them?"

Dukat regarded the glinn's pedestrian thought processes with mild distaste. Unable to see a step past the next. "Absolutely not. You will make it clear to Odo that he is not required on the station. But you'll also be sure he understands what happens at Terok Nor. That ships from all across the quadrant come here for trade and diplomatic purposes. And that as a . . . visitor, he would be welcomed here."

"What if it doesn't choose to accompany the new workers?"

"Oh, he'll come here. Perhaps not right away, but he'll come."

The glinn's confusion was apparent, although he was too well trained to question a superior. Dukat considered explaining it to him—that they might be able to catch and cage Odo, but that winning him, besides being infinitely more satisfying, was also their best chance to actually *keep* him. A glance at the office door stilled his urge to enlighten the dull man. Glinn Trakad stood there, a sweaty sheen to his forehead. The subordinate looked deeply unhappy as he tapped the door signal.

News he doesn't wish to deliver. Dukat gestured him in, commending the ground soldier once more before signing off. Trakad held a slender box in his hands, what appeared to be computer equipment of some sort. A portable relay drive, perhaps.

"Yes, Trakad."

"This is from that sensor tower in Dahkur." The soldier looked ill.

"And . . . ?" Dukat prompted.

"This was not a malfunction, sir. This was an attempt at sabotage. The surface inventory reports confirmed it. Several unaccounted-for flyers have been recorded leaving the surface, but no flyers have actually left. They were Bajoran ships, sir. There is a single capture of the saboteur's face—a Bajoran."

A close shot of a young redheaded woman's soft face snapped on, her expression absolutely intent, her eyes filled with fear. The capture had been taken a second or two before she'd fled for the woods, Dukat imagined, scampering away like some small, wild creature.

Dukat turned away from the screen, away from Trakad. And smiled. She was still alive, then—and as beautiful as her mother had been, though in a different way. Strong, where Meru had been fragile. The nerve it must have taken, to climb that tower, to dare such a blatant offense. It was outrageous, of course, totally unacceptable, but while he condemned the action, he could not help but admire her spirit, the foolish bravery of the young and romantic.

Still, I had hoped she would not continue down this road . . .

"Why haven't you contacted the engineer who designed the system?" he asked, turning back to Trakad. "This suggests that the detection grid is not working as it was supposed to."

"I have tried, sir. But it seems that no one can locate her. You dismissed the director of the institute, and their record-keeping system has been in quite . . . a disarray since she left. You did not immediately appoint a sufficient replacement, and—"

Dukat sighed heavily. It was no wonder that the man looked as though he'd swallowed broken glass. Nobody wanted to deliver news to the prefect that indicated the prefect had made a mistake. He finally turned around. "Well, then. We will have to send someone else to repair it, won't we?"

"I have already done it. Our chief of engineering assures me that he has overseen a complete recalibration, and everything is now functioning properly."

Dukat raised his forehead expectantly. Why then, did the man still appear to be so uncomfortable?

The soldier cleared his throat with some difficulty. "But . . . but the signals in Dahkur remain as confused as before, sir. More unauthorized ships reported taking off, and the anti-aircraft system fails to lock on to them—"

"Suspend all air traffic in Dahkur," Dukat ordered.

"Shall we shoot the raiders down manually?"

"No," Dukat said quickly, thinking of young Nerys. "Get me Basso Tromac," he ordered. Basso was the only one of Dukat's adjutants that knew the full extent of his interest in Nerys and in the rest of the Kira family. Basso would have to redouble his efforts in Dahkur right away. Dukat dismissed Trakad, and thought again of Nerys, wondering what she hoped to accomplish, wondering if he could somehow lead her away from the terrorists, to teach her to be a proper citizen of a Cardassian host world, before she got herself into real trouble. He had little spare time, of course, but he felt it was the least he could do for Meru's only daughter. Such a lovely, lovely girl deserved better than to huddle in the forest like a wild animal.

OCCUPATION YEAR THIRTY-EIGHT

✦ ✦ ✦

2365 (Terran Calendar)

13

Kira fought to keep her own terror in check as she rifled through the belongings of the chemist. She still could not entirely believe that she was here, on Terok Nor, a place most Bajorans would have done anything to avoid. It had been a hasty decision to come—a dangerous one—but this was an opportunity that could mean a significant advance for the resistance. It was long believed that Dukat employed a small, secret network of informants, and Kira was currently right in the den of one of them—the one who served as their direct link to the prefect. Vaatrik Drasa owned this shop, and he could walk in any minute and find her . . .

There were hundreds of things that could go wrong here. Coming to Terok Nor was easily the biggest risk Kira had ever taken—bigger even than Gallitep. But when the Shakaar cell caught word that there was a way to get someone on the station—and back off again—Shakaar had insisted that they had no choice.

Tahna Los had wanted to go, originally, but the Bajoran man who came to the Shakaar cell with the intel insisted that a young woman would be viewed with less suspicion. It was as though the assignment was made for her, and she'd been quick to volunteer. It was an opportunity they couldn't afford to miss.

So do it, already! Kira moved faster, looking through

Vaatrik's files, her fingers scrambling over his keyboard, looking for anything, anything. The man who had arranged for her to come here had insisted that there was a list somewhere in this shop. A list of eight collaborators, who were scattered all over Bajor. Take them out, their informant had insisted, and over half the Cardassians' intelligence infrastructure would fall apart.

She left the computer running a search and stood, considering the jars of herbs, powders, and drugs that lined the walls. She searched for some clue that one of them contained more than it seemed to, then checked her chrono. If Shakaar's informat—the man who'd gotten her onto the station—had done his job, Cardassian security would still be busy with the explosion he'd caused down in ore processing. But she didn't have time to search every jar! She had to get out of here soon, but would she get another chance tomorrow?

"Who are you?" someone demanded, and Kira took a step back, turning, her thoughts racing with the thunder of her heart. Vaatrik had caught her.

"Hello," she began, wondering with some doubt if she could try to seduce him. "I'm—"

"I'm calling security, unless you explain yourself right away." The Bajoran went for his comm, but Kira drew her phaser, reacted before she'd thought through the greater implications—and Vaatrik fell to the floor with a crash.

"Oh *kosst*," she whispered. She had just killed Vaatrik, and the door was wide open for anyone to see. Had he signaled for security? She had to get out of here right now. There would be no other opportunity, for this shop would be swarming with Cardassians in moments, and then she would never get off this station alive. She had failed.

"Rom!" Quark was in a foul mood when he opened his door. "You're supposed to be tending bar!"

"Frool is watching the till, Quark. I have to tell you—"

"Frool is not family, Rom. You get back there right away."

"But, brother—"

"No buts, Rom, Frool is probably robbing me blind even as we speak!"

"But, brother, there's a Lurian in the bar."

Quark's mood worsened. "Well, get rid of him!"

"But . . . brother, he's really . . . big. And . . . hairy. He says his name is Morn."

"All Lurians are big and hairy, Rom, no matter what their names are, and they're also bad for business." He waggled his fingers like a squawking puppet. "*Jabber jabber jabber.* Find someone to deal with him. Maybe you could plant something on him, get him arrested. Now that Thrax is away, it should be easy to concoct a simple frame job."

"Yes, but, brother—"

"Maybe I should get in touch with that Tarulian trader I did business with last year. We've got to make the best of our opportunities while Thrax is off the station."

"But, brother—"

"What did I tell you about *buts*?" Quark shoved his brother out into the hall.

"But, brother!" Rom shouted, just before Quark could slide the door closed. "There's a new chief of security now!"

Quark scowled. "What did you say?"

"There's a new chief of security now."

"I don't believe it," Quark muttered, and grabbed his jacket. "Come on, Rom. We're going to the bar. I'll take care of this Lurian of yours."

A new chief of security? Quark hoped his brother was mistaken—it certainly wouldn't be the first time his fool-headed brother was wrong about something. Quark wasn't sure if a new chief was going to be a bad thing or not. He'd just gotten Thrax sufficiently broken in, really. A new chief might be too quick to make assumptions about a Ferengi businessperson. Assumptions that might be correct, but that was exactly the problem. At least Thrax always gave him the benefit of the doubt, pretended that his race had no bearing on his likelihood of being a suspect for any particular crime. A new security chief might not feel quite the same way.

Rom continued with his blithering as the two made their way down the corridor of the habitat ring and onto the Promenade. "It's true, brother. Yesterday Dukat hired someone else, to look into a murder investigation."

"I'll give him a murder to investigate," Quark muttered.

Rom ignored him. "He's not a Cardassian, the new chief. He's a shape-shifter."

Quark wasn't quite listening as the two entered the bar, and he noted that the Lurian in question was indeed big, possibly the biggest Lurian he had ever seen. He sat at the far end of the bar, his massive bulk heaved over a single staggering barstool. Poor barstool. As to his hairiness, well, Quark was less alarmed about that than he was about the bigness, but it did make him seem especially menacing. He was talking up a couple of unwitting Cardassians seated near him at the bar.

In an instant, it dawned on Quark what his brother had just said. "Wait, what did you just say about the new chief of security?"

"Uhhh . . . he's a shape-shifter," Rom said.

Quark snorted. "There are no shape-shifters in this sector, you nitwit."

One of the Cardassians at the bar, a dal named Boheeka, turned away from the typically long-winded Lurian to interject. "It's true," he said. "He really is a shape-shifter. I saw him once, at the Bajoran Institute of Science. He can be anything he wants to be. He's one of a kind, they say. Nobody knows where he came from."

Quark felt himself go stiff with horror. "No."

"Yes," Boheeka said. "He could be"—he picked up a cocktail napkin—"this napkin! He could be . . . him!" He pointed to the Lurian, who had now fallen silent. An unusual state for a Lurian.

Quark looked frantically from the Lurian to the Cardassian. Was this a joke? A cruel, cruel joke? "Why isn't Thrax coming back?"

The other Cardassian shrugged. "Who knows? I, for one, won't miss him."

"Me either," added Boheeka. "He was arrogant."

Quark swallowed repeatedly, his throat having gone very dry. "He wasn't such a bad guy," he squeaked. At least Thrax was no shape-shifter, pretending to be a cocktail napkin so as to spy on a humble Ferengi proprietor.

A Bajoran woman walked into the bar then, drawing his attention; someone from the mines, probably, though they didn't often come into Quark's place unless they were looking for work. This woman's posture seemed to suggest otherwise.

"There you are!" she cried out, and walked straight up to Quark. She was pretty, young, with bright red hair and large, expressive eyes. If not for all the lumpy, cumbersome clothing, she might be something. He'd been thinking about hiring some dabo girls . . .

"I just wanted to let you know," she said, coming closer, "that I appreciated the opportunity." She came close enough then that Quark could smell her, a scent that was at once peppery and sweet, like Bajoran *nyawood*. With an almost imperceptible movement, she reached out her hand and pressed several strips of latinum into Quark's palm. The careful precision of the motion indicated that she did not want to make the transaction known to the Cardassians at the bar. Quark deftly slipped the latinum into the pocket of his waistcoat.

"Of course," he said, waiting to see what would happen next.

"I know that you have a lot of other Bajorans who want to work for you," she went on, "and I just hope that I made an impression on you . . . that you won't forget."

"Sure, sure," Quark said, thinking he might understand. These Bajorans! They always assumed he was going to be on their side, that he would be willing to concoct stories on their behalf, just because he had gotten himself mixed up with the business of selling supplies to them. He sighed. Well, at least there was the latinum, though it wasn't very much. He'd better get rid of her. "You did make an impression. But I'll have to think about it some more. There are quite a few others who are looking to work for me."

"Thank you," she said huskily. "Just let me know if . . . there's anything more I can do." She turned quickly and left the bar. Quark stared after the young woman, hoping he'd seen the last of her. She was sexy, sure, but something about her immediately suggested trouble, and he wasn't interested in getting mixed up in anything else—especially now that he had to worry about a new security chief.

One of the Cardassians at the bar let out a low chuckle. Quark turned to him, returning his lascivious implication with a meaningful grin, though he felt a little ridiculous about it. He'd never seen that woman before in his life, let alone had any sort of relations with her. Although he had, on occasion, taken part in such relationships with other Bajoran women, that was hardly the business of these depraved Cardassians. He cleared his throat and looked away, hoping to change the subject—particularly before the Lurian started to prattle again.

"So, ah," Quark said to the soldier, sitting down next to him, "tell me more about this so-called shape-shifter."

Rom suddenly materialized from somewhere in the back. "Brother!" he said urgently.

"What is it, Rom?"

"Brother—the Lurian—he's still here!"

The massive Lurian turned, fully capable of hearing Rom's warning, though the alien had almost nothing in the way of ears. Quark waved his hands. "Not now, Rom. We've got bigger things to worry about at the moment than Lurians." He turned to the hulk at the end of the bar. "No offense," he told him, and the Lurian shrugged.

Quark coughed and turned back to the Cardassian, hoping to trip him up somehow, for he was still working the angle that this was a ruse meant to make him look foolish, that there wasn't really any shape-shifter, and that Thrax would come walking through the door at any moment, the Cardassians in security all having a little laugh at Quark's expense. He could hope, anyway. But he had a bad feeling. The Lurian in the bar, the bizarre actions of the red-haired Bajoran woman, and the unconfirmed rumor of a new security chief—all seemed to mark the presence of some unhappy portent. Or, at the very least, the makings of *some* kind of change on the horizon. Things had been going quite well lately; a change could only be for the worse.

Quark scowled. The nerve of Thrax, resigning his post without even saying good-bye. It was enough to drive an honest man to drink.

Doctor Moset was excited. Kalisi could see it in the brightness of his eyes, the quick, efficient way in which he laid out their equipment, checked the hypos she'd prepared. Funny, how she'd stopped thinking of him as Crell, somewhere along the line. They continued to sleep together, but much of the passion had fled on her end, replaced with a kind of fearful awe. If he knew that she was less than present at their physical meetings, he didn't seem to mind. Nor did she, particularly. Moset had been given a free rein by Central Command, a license to do whatever he deemed relevant to achieving new medical breakthroughs. A man with that kind of power was not to be denied, not if she still hoped to salvage a name for herself.

He leaned forward now, the two of them waiting for the first Bajorans to file in. They were at a medical center outside the Jalanda manufacturing camp, to give the required annual Fostossa booster to the workers and their families. Moset had wanted them both to be here. A day they could reflect upon with pride, he'd said.

"Are you ready to make history?" Moset asked, touching her shoulder. The lab was overbright, accentuating his pallor.

Kalisi nodded. He knew what interested her, understood her motivations well enough; she sometimes wondered if he was manipulating her, reminding her of the things she most wanted those times she felt less than committed to his agenda.

A dozen, fifteen Bajoran children filed into the room, led by a pair of soldiers and a middle-aged Bajoran woman, her face pinched and fearful. The children, all young, were subdued, staring at the smiling doctor with the hypo in his hand. The oldest was perhaps in her early teens; the youngest still possessed the rounded cheek and jaw of a child half that age, his eyes wide with anxiety.

"Where are their parents?" Kalisi asked. The soldiers shuffled the children forward.

"Working," Moset said. "But they'll be in to get theirs soon enough; the gul is excusing them from the lines early."

Kalisi nodded at the older woman. "Who is that?"

Moset blinked at Kalisi, a vague smile forming. "Whoever watches them, I suppose. Really, how could I possibly know?"

Kalisi watched as the children lined up to receive their inoculations, their small faces drawn with fear. The first two were boys, who submitted to Moset's quick hands and gentle smile without flinching. The third was a girl, perhaps eight or nine, with a beautiful head of thick black hair, arranged in curls. Kalisi didn't generally find the Bajorans to have much physical appeal, but the child was quite lovely. She was crying, and as the Bajoran chaperone tried to coax her to approach Moset, the little girl fixed her tearful gaze on Kalisi.

"Is it going to hurt?" she asked, her voice quavering.

Yes, but not today, she thought.

"No," she said calmly. "It won't hurt a bit. I promise."

The little girl stepped forward, her terror barely under control.

"Listen to Doctor Reyar, she knows what she's talking about," Moset said, exposing his small white teeth, and reached for the child, who gave Kalisi a pleading look, a silent appeal for there to be no pain . . . and then he applied the hypospray, pressing it to her too-thin upper arm. A faint, brief hiss and it was over.

"All done," Moset said, smiling again, releasing her.

The child rubbed at her arm, dawning relief breaking across her face. She turned a beatific smile to Kalisi.

"It didn't hurt," she said.

Kalisi could not return the smile. She looked away, wondering where this girl would be the day she learned that there would be no children for her, ever.

Less suffering, she told herself. *A mercy.*

"You be sure to tell all your little friends," Moset said. "Inoculations don't hurt a bit. Nothing to fear."

The girl nodded happily, and Kalisi felt such a profound discomfort that she made an excuse about having forgotten the work code reader at the back of the lab, so that she might escape for a moment, to collect herself. To remember what was important.

It preoccupied much of her attention over the next few

weeks, remembering those things which had once defined her ambitions. She found a way to avoid Moset's embrace for much of that time. Luckily, it wasn't difficult. He was busy, running more tests, working pathology, preoccupied with refining his new formula. When they did meet, it was often in the course of work; she continued to handle the machinery, smooth over programming snags, set the systems to collate the results he wanted.

It was late, the night he signaled at her door, a look of hunger in his sharp gaze. He seemed pleased, as well.

"Crell," she said, stepping back to admit him. "Has something happened?"

"I've just gone through preliminaries on the cultures I've been running," he said, smiling widely as the door closed behind him. "Concomitant to the vaccines we gave, thirty-six days ago. There are no indicators of malignant cell formation."

Kalisi nodded, understanding the relevance. One of his early sterilization formulas had filled the wombs of twenty Bajoran women with cancerous cysts and tumors. They had all died very shortly afterward. The formula was supposed to make better workers out of them, while sparing them the burden of children, but death was hardly conducive to productivity.

"That's excellent," she said. "What about the component isolation? You've found a way to replicate it?" There was a problem with mass-producing one element of the formula, a hormonal inhibitor. Thus far, he'd only been able to generate small amounts. Until he could make more, planetwide inoculation was unattainable.

"I believe so," he said. He stepped toward her, reached out to stroke her neck, touching the ridges there in a way he knew she liked.

"But I didn't come here to talk, Kali," he said softly.

Kalisi let him pull her closer, not sure she had a choice

anymore. Not sure if she had ever had . . . but fairly certain that she'd lost her grasp of what had once been important to her, after all, and that she couldn't seem to get it back.

Lieutenant Commander Elias Vaughn did not immediately recognize the turning in his stomach as he walked from the ship's bridge to his quarters, but it wasn't troublesome enough to warrant much consideration. Today had been mostly the usual—various reports from contacts, along with his observations for his superiors in special ops—but then there had been something new, something unexpected. An alleged dissident from the Cardassian Union had contacted his ship's CO today, apparently from the Bajoran system. Vaughn could not imagine where this Cardassian had found the means to get in touch with any member of the Federation; he only knew that it was information that should be passed along. Alynna would want to know.

His stomach twitched again as he reached the hall of officer's quarters. It took a moment for him to identify the gnawing sensation—it was hunger. Simple hunger. Vaughn knew that his metabolism was beginning to slow, an unwelcome effect of his age—and sometimes, he had to admit, he got so busy that he forgot to eat. He found the revelation to be annoying—infuriating, even. His ninetieth birthday had come and gone, and he thought he might even remember turning ninety-one sometime in the recent past. They seemed so close together now, it was hardly worth keeping track . . .

He found himself feeling somewhat contemplative as he entered his quarters. He had taken care of himself over the years, but there was no denying that he was slowing down, that he had already slowed down—though he believed it was confined strictly to the physical realm. The very idea of diminishing mental acuity was enormously unwelcome. Still, seven decades in Starfleet was a long time by anyone's measure, and those years weighed only more heavily with the passage of time.

He didn't have time for food now, or for daydreaming; he put in a call to Vice-Admiral Nechayev, tapping his fingers impatiently as he waited for the transmission to engage.

"Elias," the cool-faced woman addressed him. Vaughn smiled pleasantly at her.

"Alynna," he replied. "I have a piece of interesting news. It may trickle down to you from my CO's weekly formal report, but I felt it was worth contacting headquarters on my own as soon as possible."

Nechayev gave him a nod. *"You're on the border, is that right? Gathering intel?"*

"That's right. A Cardassian dalin contacted our ship today. He was asking to be put in touch with someone of authority within the Federation. The captain sent it on to the politicos, but I thought it might be of particular interest to you."

"A Cardassian dalin," Nechayev repeated, interrupting. *"Regarding what, exactly?"*

"After a great deal of rather . . . strained conversation, he informed my CO that he is a dissident among his people, and he's seeking assistance from the Federation—specifically in the matter of the Bajoran occupation."

Nechayev looked surprised for a split second before regaining her traditional composure. *"Assistance?"*

"He claims to be in league with a group who oppose the occupation of other worlds. He mentioned the border colonies as well. He seemed sincere, but then— I trust you know something of the situation out there, Alynna."

"Yes," she said smoothly. *"I do."* She paused, seeming to consider. *"Remind me, Lieutenant Commander, what is the nature of your current assignment?"*

Vaughn was taken aback by her use of his rank. Was she reprimanding him for deviating from task?

"I am a mission specialist, gathering and analyzing intel along the Union-Federation border," he said evenly. "And if I may speak freely, Admiral . . . I thought, given your past experience with the Bajorans, you might be interested in information—"

"The Federation is not interested in the Cardassian Union's relationship with Bajor," Nechayev said. *"We are interested in their relationship with us."*

Vaughn was surprised, but hid it, studying her careful neutrality with interest. They were not close, he and Alynna, but had known one another for many years. He knew that she'd fought to see the Federation get involved with Bajor, after an intel mission she'd undertaken shortly before the Cardassian's occupation of that world. Perhaps her failure to do so had haunted her, somewhat, had made her the aloof, tightly composed creature she was now. Perhaps she simply preferred not to revisit a painful past.

"I am hereby reassigning you," Nechayev said. *"I'll put in the paperwork to have you sent back to Starbase 375. From there, you're to reestablish contact with this Cardassian as quickly as possible. Do whatever you can do to develop a relationship with him. Learn all you can from him, and report back to me."*

Vaughn nodded. "Am I to inquire about his world's relationship with Bajor?"

Nechayev looked surprised again. *"Bajor?"* she repeated. *"No, Commander."*

Vaughn arched one brow. "This man claims to want help from us. If his request is legitimate, can we afford to turn our backs on him?"

"The Federation is in a precarious position with the Cardassians right now," she said. *"This man surely has an ulterior motive, but he could still prove to be very useful, if he's handled carefully. We can't afford to misuse this opportunity."*

"Of course not," Vaughn said. "But if there is any

chance that he could give us something that would allow us to step in to the Bajoran situation—"

"*Let's let Bajor worry about themselves,*" Nechayev said, "*and we'll worry about the Federation.*"

"Yes, sir," Vaughn replied, though he did not like her answer. He disconnected the call, and stared at the replicator in the wall, no longer hungry at all.

Recently, Dukat had taken to spending much of his spare time going over surveys and estimates, seeking new sites for mining operations on Bajor's surface. In spite of the quotas he'd been meeting—sometimes even exceeding—he continued to hear rumors and to catch implications. The Detapa Council had become even more vocal in recent months; Kotan Pa'Dar and his lackeys wanted Cardassia to withdraw from Bajor. It was funny, how things changed; a few decades with enough to eat, and it seemed most of Cardassia had forgotten why they'd come to Bajor in the first place.

He sat at his desk in his private office, a well-appointed room adjacent to his quarters. It was from here that he usually spoke with family or with his political contacts—any conversation that he did not wish to be logged. It was also where he did most of his research, a place he was unlikely to be disturbed.

If they only knew what they were thinking of throwing away . . . Dukat scanned another list of estimates from the site in Rihjer, where there looked to be a heavy vein of duranium, relatively close to the surface. There were half a hundred locations just as promising . . .

The signal on his personal comm was most unwelcome, but he answered it, hoping it might be Odo. They'd had few casual conversations since the shape-shifter had come to the station, although Odo seemed to have an aptitude for his new position. The new man, Russol, spoke highly of his abilities. Dukat was more intrigued than ever, and took a certain pride in having the fascinating creature at his beck and call. He had made it clear to Odo that his door was always open.

"Sir, I wonder if I might speak to you a moment. I'm just outside your quarters."

Basso. Dukat looked at the handful of padds he still wanted to review. "Actually, Basso, perhaps you could—"

"It's about Kira Nerys."

Dukat sighed. He'd expected the visit, sooner or later. "All right. Come in."

He didn't stand, made no effort to express welcome to the Bajoran. "Yes?"

Basso took a deep breath. "I've waited for your instructions regarding Kira Nerys since her arrival here," he said evenly. "I did what you have been asking me to do for years. We found her, came up with a reason to get her here—she's *here.*"

Dukat waited, perfectly aware that Basso would get to the point sooner if he said nothing.

"Did you know she's a person of suspicion in the death of Vaatrik?"

"I've heard."

Basso looked surprised, but only for an instant. "Odo will be bringing her in for interrogation. Will you . . . shall I have Odo bring her directly to you?"

"That won't be necessary," Dukat said. "I'd prefer you not trouble the shape-shifter. Is that all?"

The Bajoran was obviously frustrated, and had apparently worked for Dukat long enough to feel entitled to speak freely. "I don't understand. You've had me searching for her since she joined the resistance. We have her, now, on Terok Nor, and you act as though—that is, you don't seem . . ."

Dukat let him trail off as he decided whether or not to

explain himself. He didn't need to, of course, but he wasn't without pity; in Basso's position, he'd probably hope for an explanation himself.

"You needn't concern yourself with Kira Nerys any longer. I'll see to the matter personally."

"But her connection with the Shakaar cell—"

"—isn't at issue, here," Dukat said. "She's on *my* station. And she can't leave without my knowing it. Let her pretend for a while, that she still has some control. When she starts to get desperate, I'll bring her in for a discussion about her options. By then, she'll be ready to listen to reason."

"You underestimate her," Basso said. "She's a terrorist. She might be here to assassinate you."

Dukat smiled. "Or you," he said lightly, and the way the other man blanched, he thought he'd discovered the root of Basso's concern. Considering the lure they'd used to draw her out, it was extremely likely that Kira had been involved with Vaatrik's death; he'd been Bajoran, but a collaborator with the Cardassians. She might not hesitate to kill another. Basso Tromac, for example.

"Don't take on so," Dukat said. "I'll oversee the matter myself. You trust me, don't you?"

Basso did his best to nod convincingly. "Of course, Prefect."

He left the office, the outer door of Dukat's living space closing a moment later. Dukat stared after him, thinking. After a moment, he tapped his system up and typed in a few commands, calling up two files on Kira Nerys. The first, her file as it had been.

Confirmed association with Shakaar and Kohn-Ma cells. Probable connection to events at Gallitep, to the destruction of several surface relay bases, to numerous counts of tech sabotage. Possible affiliations with other terrorist groups, including Gertis, Krim . . . The list continued. Her priority status was in the upper hundreds. He looked at the newer file, a file that he'd edited himself upon receiving the news that Kira Nerys had been recognized by the shuttle's computer.

Civilian runner for the Shakaar cell. A minor operative whose activities are limited to running errands for the terrorist leaders. May have participated in minor boundary/curfew infringements. He'd also dropped a digit off her status number, making her a low priority. Dukat altered the number again, lowering it further, then dropped it back into the system. The real file would stay on the self-contained system in Dukat's private office, for now. Had Kira Nerys set foot on Terok Nor with her actual file online, security would have been alerted immediately, the docking ring locked down. As it was, he and Basso Tromac and a single communications worker were the only people who knew who she really was, and he meant to keep it that way. He didn't need to be worrying about Central Command's reaction to his harboring a wanted terrorist, or Odo turning her over to the military police before Dukat had a chance to speak with her. Dukat hoped to eventually inspire a more personal loyalty in Odo, but thus far, the shape-shifter had proven himself to be quite pedantic about the rule of law . . .

"Best to keep you to myself, for now," Dukat said, looking at the capture of her face next to the doctored statistics. He still hadn't decided what course to take with her. In truth, he did not know what outcome he sought, only that he felt irresistibly drawn to the young woman, perhaps because of his history with her mother. His fascination with Meru's daughter had only grown over the years, deepening as time passed.

Ah, Meru! There were times he missed her terribly. Her death had been a tragedy, one he'd truly felt himself helpless to prevent. He was not a man who wasted time reconsidering the past, but there were times he wondered what might have been, if Meru had not betrayed him . . .

Dukat shook himself, closed the files on his screen, and picked up another padd, calling up the specs on a likely tritanium deposit in the northeasternmost corner of Musilla Province. He'd have his chance to indulge his personal life another time; there was work to be done, and he didn't want next month's quarterly report to be sent without at least five major projects at outline stage. The people at home needed to understand how vital the annexation remained. He could cite reasons of compassion for their extended stay—the fragile Bajoran government would collapse if Central Command withdrew, undoubtedly causing a civil war—but he felt that appealing to common practicality was a better bet. Bajor was a sustaining resource, one the Union mustn't dare release. As its prefect, he understood that better than anyone.

14

Odo had been swept into an investigation regarding the brutal murder of a Bajoran chemist on Terok Nor, and he wasn't sure he was up to the task. In the weeks since he'd come to the station, since the prefect had recruited him for security, he had struggled to learn the job. He had observed and restated information to people with differences of opinion, and thus far, the disagreements he'd overseen had mostly worked themselves out. Gul Dukat said he'd wanted Odo because of his reputation as a mediator in some of the Bajoran villages, and more recently, with some of the Bajorans in ore processing. But solving Bajoran disputes and puzzling out Cardassian criminal codes were hardly the same thing. A deliberate killing was something entirely new in his limited experience.

Having just come from an interview with the Ferengi bartender, Odo was struggling to keep up with the interface on the security office's computer. The system differed from the one at the Bajoran Institute of Science, and Odo had not yet become accustomed to its peculiarities.

"Anything from the Ferengi?"

Odo looked up as a Cardassian man entered the room. Dalin Russol had arrived at the station shortly before Odo himself, to shore up security after the previous chief had left. Russol didn't seem to be especially keen on accepting the position as chief himself, however, although he had allegedly been offered the position, and had thus far been encouraging Odo to accept the role. A year ago, Odo would have accepted the encouragement at face value, but he'd learned a few things about the nature of humanoids. Enough to know that he understood very little.

"Not sure," Odo said, and left it at that. The Ferengi had given him a story that turned out to be false. A female suspect had bribed him for an alibi, which Odo supposed could be an indication of her guilt. But he had a nagging feeling there was more to the story. He looked up at Dalin Russol. "I don't know if I'm the right person for this job," he confessed. "The prefect seems to want me to simply find someone to arrest as quickly as possible, without completely ensuring that it's the right person. I don't know if he and I . . ." He stopped, for he didn't know how to put voice to the rest of it.

"What?" Russol asked him, but then supplied his own answer. "You wonder if the breadth of your own moral bandwidth might not completely overlap with Dukat's? Is that it?"

Odo wasn't sure, but he thought this sounded something like what he wanted to convey. He nodded.

Russol smiled. "That is exactly why you must accept this position, Odo. My understanding is that Thrax was as fair as a man could have been, for being a Cardassian, but you—you're an outsider. You'll escape the biases my people have for these"—he spread his hands—"Bajorans."

"Your people seem to have a natural prejudice against them," Odo replied carefully, for he still did not fully understand what drove the two races to despise each other so.

"My people are offended by the Bajorans," Russol said, looking away from Odo. He locked his hands behind his back and raised his head, seeming very interested in the ceiling, though he kept talking. "Their culture appeared static to us. They had not progressed, by Cardassian standards, in many centuries. Their behavior . . . we found it unacceptable for them to have settled into a lifestyle of such lazy contentment."

"What could be wrong with being content?"

Russol laughed, a rueful sound. "Cardassians live for the pursuit of the next phase in every undertaking of their lives. It's never good enough to be merely content. Cardassians . . . scarcely know the meaning of the word, in fact." He looked at Odo. "So, you have another subject to interview for your investigation?"

"Yes," Odo said. He wondered at Russol's behavior, the words he had spoken. The man seemed not to agree with his own characterization of his people, but then, Odo supposed he was not all that well-practiced at reading people's intentions. One of the many reasons he feared he was ill-suited for the position in security.

Russol left him alone, and Odo continued his clumsy navigation of the computer system, looking for a file on a particular Bajoran. He found it after a few false starts: Kira Nerys.

Odo studied the image of the sullen-looking redheaded woman, and he revisited a nagging suspicion that had troubled him when he had interviewed her in person. She was familiar to him, but he couldn't place where he had seen her. In one of the villages? He was sure that wasn't it. He read her file, finding her to be loosely affiliated with the resistance movement, but her activity within the resistance was limited, and she had not been accused of any serious crimes. Of course, Odo suspected that Dukat could have her arrested simply for being associated with the movement, but he sensed that such action would have been arbitrary on Dukat's part. The thought of Dukat's nature brought him a resurgence of discomfort. The work of helping solve disputes, he believed, was good work; why would Dukat have asked him to stay, if he did not wish Odo to do his job well?

He studied her picture until the image seemed indistinct, blurry. He had looked at it too long, and now she didn't look familiar anymore. He shut down the program, trying to picture her as he'd seen her on the station today, when she'd given him her unlikely alibi. He could not shake the feeling that he knew her from somewhere. Perhaps it would come to him when he spoke with her again.

Kalisi Reyar returned to her quarters after a tiresome day, chilled and out of sorts, to see a message waiting on her companel—a transmission from Cardassia Prime. She hadn't had a call from home since . . . since she wasn't sure when. Her family had initially been proud that she'd left home to design Bajor's detection grid, but that had been when they'd all thought she would be away a few years, at most. Her father, in particular, had made clear his sorrow that his second-oldest daughter had not already returned home triumphant, to give him grandchildren and settle into a high office at the science ministry. Their last contact had been months before, an obligatory birthday message.

Kalisi took off her coat—she'd spent most of the afternoon outside in a cold and misty drizzle, trying to adjust the hospital's security feed—and told her computer to run the message as she sat to take off her boots.

A Cardassian woman she didn't recognize came up, smiling politely. She was well-dressed and spoke in a cool, clear voice.

"Doctor Reyar. My name is Tera Glees. I represent the University of Culat, on Cardassia Prime. As you may or may not have heard, we are expanding our campus to include a research department specifically designed to assist Cardassian colonies and annexations. We're in need of a professional to round out our weapons division, and are inquiring as to whether or not you'd be interested in taking a position with us. I've attached a file outlining a job description, with links to salary, housing, campus maps. I believe you'll find it comprehensive, but please feel free to contact me at any time with any questions you may have. I look forward to taking your call, and we thank you for your consideration."

Her eyes wide, one boot still in hand, Kalisi stared at the screen as the woman blipped off. She dropped the boot to the floor, stepped to her desk, and opened the rider, scanning the bullet points with disbelief. The pay and benefits were excellent, the opportunities suddenly limitless.

Weapons research. At Culat, which had produced some of the best and brightest minds in the Union. She could be done with Crell Moset and his brilliant, soulless eyes, done with menial mechanics and medical scanner debugging, done with the *cold*. She could go home.

She wanted to tell someone, needed to hear it out loud, but she had no friends at Moset's hospital. In a daze, she put in a call to her father. When his face appeared on her screen, stern and wary and so well loved, she felt like weeping.

"I've been offered a position at Culat," she said, before he could say anything.

"What? At the university?"

"Yes. They're opening a new research department and want me for their weapons team."

Her father smiled, then, and her heart warmed. She hadn't seen that smile in some time.

"The university at Culat is most prestigious," he said. *"You've accepted?"*

"Not yet," she said. "I've only just received the transmission."

"*Then why are you talking to me?*" he asked, still smiling. "*Call them back, accept the position. You'll be home, dearest. You'll finally be able to start working on that family you keep promising us.*"

Is it going to hurt?

No, it won't hurt a bit. I promise.

Kalisi stared at her father, hearing the little Bajoran girl's voice as clearly as if she was in the room. Seeing her frightened face, seeing her smile once she realized that the inoculation was over, that there had been no pain.

It didn't hurt.

"*Kalisi?*" Her father frowned. "*You* are *going to accept, of course.*"

"I—of course," she said, but her excitement, her *relief* at the offer was gone. "I have a few things to finish here first . . ."

"*What things? I thought you were working in a medical facility now. Surely they don't need your expertise on weapons systems to treat sick aliens.*"

Kalisi wasn't sure how to answer him. How was she to tell him that she'd begun to feel haunted by the spirits of a million unborn children? *Alien* children? She had always been his practical girl, his brilliant, focused one. How was she to admit that after all these long, cold years, struggling to make her name—*their* name—she was losing her focus?

She changed the topic, recalling something she'd been meaning to ask him about for some time now. "Do you remember when I asked you a few years back . . . if you could confirm that a man named Dost Abor was in any way affiliated with the Obsidian Order?"

Her father frowned for a moment, trying to recall the prior conversation, and then he nodded. "*Yes, indeed, I confirmed that he is an operative. He's stationed at an offworld listening post. But what makes you ask about Dost Abor?*"

"Kali?"

Kalisi turned in her seat, saw Crell Moset standing in her doorway. He'd apparently taken it upon himself to surprise her.

"Ah—" She turned back to the screen, smiling apologetically. "Father, my supervisor needs my attention. Perhaps we could speak more of this later?"

Her father had spent most of his professional career acting the diplomat. He needed no further prompting.

"Yes, another time. Be well, dearest."

The screen went blank, and Kalisi turned to face Moset. She did her best not to let her irritation show, it would only lead to sex . . . although his attempt to be playful by sneaking into her room suggested that it was already a forgone conclusion.

"That was your father?" the doctor asked. "Who is Dost Abor?"

Kalisi stood, smiling. "I did not hear you come in, Crell."

"Old boyfriend, perhaps?"

"Nothing like that," she said. "I've just come in. Have you eaten? We could—"

"Your father works as a liaison, doesn't he? Why would you be asking him about an old lover? Or perhaps he's another medical researcher . . . ?"

His tone was mild, a slight smile on his crease of a mouth, but there was a sudden sharpness to his gaze that made her stomach tighten. Her lover was an obsessive man.

The truth cost her nothing. "Dost Abor . . . is someone I suspected to be affiliated with the Order. Just before I came here, he asked me questions about a Bajoran religious artifact I once handled, at the Ministry of Science."

Moset leaned against her desk. "Why would the Order take interest—" He stopped abruptly, his eyes narrowing. "Was it one of the Orbs?"

Kalisi couldn't hide her surprise at the terminology Moset used: the "Orbs." She'd very nearly forgotten that anyone had ever referred to the objects as such, but she remembered now, Miras Vara had called the thing an Orb . . . an Orb of the . . . *Prophets*? Bajoran religious nonsense. "Why would you suggest that?"

Moset pursed his lips slightly, a knowing expression in his usually impassive eyes. "The Obsidian Order has been hoarding them," he said. "I believe they want to keep them from the Oralian Way."

"The religious fanatics?" Kalisi was puzzled; she knew very little of that particular organization—only rumors. "I thought the Union dealt with them decades ago."

The maddening expression, his "teacher" voice. Kalisi dropped her gaze from him as he replied. "The Union probably thinks so, too. But the Way lives still."

Kalisi couldn't help a sneer. "How could you possibly know that?"

He smiled. "I have a relative who has been involved with the resurgence of the Way for some time now."

"The resurgence? So you mean . . . younger people are practicing this faith now?"

"Yes, they have been rebounding in increasing numbers for at least fifteen years or so."

"Fifteen years!"

"Possibly longer," he said. "They are led by a woman— they call her the Guide. She has been around for fifteen years, at least—this is how long I have known of her, anyway. Her name is Astraea. She is said to be the successor to a line of religious guides who have the ability to channel their deity."

Kalisi did not reply except to wrinkle her nose fiercely. As a scientist she felt especially skeptical—even contemptuous— regarding matters of mysticism and superstition. But she was reluctantly interested enough to continue listening to Moset's account of the strange phenomenon.

"This so-called Astraea . . . I hear she was a ministry-trained scientist before she was chosen, or summoned, or whatever they call it."

Kalisi scoffed audibly, and Moset went on without hesitation, as though deliberately ignoring her reaction.

"She's had visions, they say. Maybe from one of those Orbs, who knows? My relative informed me that she met with this Astraea once, right on Cardassia Prime."

Kalisi frowned, feeling annoyed with him. "So. You have a relative associated with a dissident group, and you've not reported it? Do the authorities know about this Astraea?"

Moset shrugged. "It seems likely. The Obsidian Order does, anyway."

"Practice of this religion is illegal," Kalisi said. "It is your duty to share this information with Union officials."

He looked at her with an expression so patronizing, she wanted to scream. "This relative of mine is someone who means something to me, Kali. Sometimes our personal loyalties are as important as our allegiance to the Union. Wouldn't you agree?"

Kalisi did not reply, for his proclamation was nothing less than shocking to her. He smiled lightly and stepped forward, cupping her chin in one long-fingered hand, leaning in to kiss her, as if he believed he could erase her disdain with his physical touch. She did what she could to mask her distaste, but it was difficult. Her feelings toward this man had cooled considerably since she'd first met him, and this new revelation wasn't helping his case any. She'd assumed he was a patriot. Allegiance to the State was what being Cardassian was all about.

The kiss was passionate and lingering, and she felt her body responding in spite of her feelings. Still, she mostly wished he would go away.

When he finally pulled back, she said, "I've been offered a job."

He seemed annoyed that the press of his cool lips hadn't driven every other thought from her head, but he nodded with feigned interest. "Oh?"

"A position in weapons research, at the University of Culat."

Moset blinked. "Really? Are you going to accept?"

His tone was matter-of-fact. She hesitated, wondering what she should say, thinking of her father, thinking of the guided genocide that she had become involved with . . . Thinking of the Bajoran child, of course. She hated that little girl for what she'd done to Kalisi's carefully tended dreams, for making her reevaluate them so.

"No," she said, forcing a smile. "Not now. Our work here is too important."

"Are you joking?" It was his turn to look surprised. "You should take the job. Granted, what we're doing here is important, but now that I've found a way to replicate the hormone, we'll be able to synthesize vast amounts of the vaccine in a relatively short period. Within a year, every Bajoran on the planet will be made sterile. Anything else I do here will be . . . anticlimactic, I suppose." He shook his head. "I have a few friends who keep apprised of which way the wind is blowing; Cardassia probably won't be here in another generation, and I see no reason to linger to the disheartening end. If I were offered a university placement studying my true passion, I'd take it in a heartbeat."

"They'd let you leave Bajor?"

"After all I've done here? And with the inevitable withdrawal looming? We're not prisoners, darling. Of course they'd let me go." He touched her again. "We could go together."

Kalisi's thoughts were so far from their relationship that she flinched at his touch. She was thinking that she had to be mad, that she'd finally lost her mind, after all. It was the only way she could account for her sudden decision to act. To rid herself of that small Bajoran face in her mind's eye.

It won't hurt a bit, she thought, and let him slide his hands around her waist and up her back, arching to his touch.

15

"Have a seat, Odo." The prefect gestured to the chair opposite his desk, and Odo looked at it.

"No, thank you," he said. He preferred to remain standing.

Dukat's eyeridge rose, an expression that Odo believed conveyed surprise, though he didn't know why Dukat would be surprised. He decided maybe he'd better sit, after all.

"That's better," the prefect said, smiling now. "Would you care for anything to drink?"

Odo shook his head. "My physiology doesn't require it," he told Dukat, not for the first time.

"Oh, yes. Of course. My mistake."

Odo spoke. "My notes regarding the investigation are ready for your review. I still haven't found a definitively guilty suspect—"

"Forget the investigation. It's the death of a single Bajoran man. You did your best, didn't you?"

"Yes, sir." Odo wondered if Dukat meant to dismiss him from the position for his failure to solve the murder. "I wanted to be sure that I had the right person, you understand, and I haven't satisfactorily—"

"Don't trouble yourself, Odo." Dukat shook his head slowly, folded his arms across his chest. "It's difficult business, running a place like this, and trying to keep order in place on the whole of Bajor at the same time. Sometimes, certain things have to be overlooked, I suppose."

"Murder?"

Dukat went on as if he hadn't heard. "My superiors assign more responsibility to me than I believe I can accept. Events I have no control over . . . especially not with the limited funds and resources I am appropriated."

"Indeed," Odo mumbled, wondering why Dukat had called him here.

"If they would only agree to send a new survey team!" Dukat had unfolded his arms, was gesturing with his hands in the air. "There are brilliant profits to be made, Odo!"

"Profits," Odo repeated. He thought he knew what the word meant, though he couldn't remember hearing of it from any of the Bajorans he had known.

"Yes," Dukat said. "Profits. Monetary wealth."

Odo nodded. "You can exchange these things for goods and services . . ."

"And power, yes." Dukat nodded. "Ask the Ferengi if you need a better explanation." A corner of his mouth curved upward as he said it, apparently amused. "You'll make an excellent chief of security if you have no motivation for profit for yourself."

Odo considered this. "Why?"

Dukat continued to smile. "Because profit is what drives men to immorality."

"Immorality. So. The Bajorans . . . they fight your soldiers and steal from you—for profit?" Odo already knew that they did not. Although he was still not entirely certain why they did fight the Cardassians, he knew it was not for profit. He was curious to see what Dukat's estimation of the Bajoran motive amounted to.

Dukat's smile slipped away. "In a roundabout sort of way," he said.

Odo noted the lie to himself. He no longer doubted that Dukat had a shifting sense of integrity. He had come to feel, lately, that his attraction to the Bajoran people had much to do with their general lack of facade. He believed them, when they spoke.

"It is topics just as this one that I fear will prevent me from performing my duties to your satisfaction," he told the prefect. "Though I have lived among humanoids for some time . . . I still find your motivations to be puzzling on occasion."

Dukat nodded. "You were, in a sense, raised by a Bajoran," he observed, "but you are not a Bajoran, and you never will be."

Odo said nothing, feeling an odd pang of something like regret, and Dukat smiled again.

"Well, Odo," he said, "if you have questions, you'd do better to ask me than anyone else."

"Yes," Odo said, but he thought he'd probably be better off leaving his questions unanswered than to seek Dukat's advice.

He waited to be dismissed, but the prefect wasn't done with him, continuing to speak about political matters that held no interest for Odo. It was difficult to remain captive to Dukat's speech when Odo didn't understand half of it and couldn't begin to imagine what would constitute an appropriate reply, but he realized, after a time, that Dukat wasn't in the least bit interested in Odo's opinion. He wanted an audience. In his own way, Odo decided, Dukat was just as lonely as he himself sometimes felt.

It took the prefect a long time to finish his diatribe, and when he finally seemed to run out of steam, Odo took his leave of the Cardassian, seeking out the Ferengi bartender. He found him where he expected him to be, tending to his establishment, making animated conversation with the people who frequented the place. Odo regarded the Ferengi with curiosity; here was a humanoid who looked quite distinctly different from the Bajorans or the Cardassians, and yet, Odo knew that Quark was more like the others than he was like Odo. There was nobody on the station even remotely like Odo—not even the Lurian.

"Can I interest you in an image capture?" The Ferengi spoke without quite looking at Odo, wiping glasses and lining them up behind the bar.

"No, thank you," Odo replied automatically, without fully comprehending what the Ferengi had just asked him. "That is . . . What do you mean?"

"You've been staring at me such a long time, I thought you might like a permanent keepsake of my countenance."

Odo frowned. He knew that he was supposed to be fostering an atmosphere of authority here, and it wouldn't do to have this Ferengi speak to him this way, especially not in front of the Cardassian patrons. "I just wanted to let you know . . . that I'm watching you." He did his best to sound menacing, though he wasn't sure if his effort had any effect until the Ferengi responded.

Quark turned and smiled so wide it looked like it must be painful for him. "I invite you to watch away," he said lightly, spreading his hands. "You'll find that I'm a lawabiding resident of the station, as eager to maintain order as anyone else."

Odo narrowed his eyes. "I doubt that very much," he said, his voice hard. He studied the Ferengi's expression, looking for indicators of dishonesty. He had watched the Bajorans so carefully that he was learning to distinguish among the subtle nuances of their facial repertoire. The Ferengi was different, but not by much. The alien's grin quavered, almost imperceptibly, but Odo could see that he was frightened. He turned back to the rows of brightly colored glasses that framed the bar, suddenly very interested in rearranging them.

"I've come to ask some advice," Odo said, hastily changing his tone. "Dukat suggested that you could elaborate something for me."

"What might that be?" Quark asked him, turning back to face him again.

"Profit."

This time, the Ferengi's smile was genuine. "Well! You've come to the right place!" Quark insisted. "Have a seat—this could take me awhile."

Odo didn't need to sit, but he knew it would make the other man more comfortable, and so he sat, listening intently as Quark launched into a very detailed explanation of interest rates, investments, profit margins, and supply and demand.

"They say the market is driven by an invisible hand," the Ferengi told Odo in a near whisper, as if he were about to share something very confidential. "But we Ferengi know better than that. The market is driven by greed, pure and simple! Greed is the original renewable resource, Constable—may I call you Constable? It is the thing that literally makes the universe expand."

"The universe expand?"

"Whatever—it's an expression," Quark said. "All you need to remember is greed. Greed equals profits, in the long run. You see?"

"Yes," Odo said, though he actually didn't. Apparently, greed was the need to . . . acquire things. Things that humanoids used to . . . make themselves comfortable. Odo had little perception of the humanoid estimation of "comfort," though he imagined it was something like what he felt when he was regenerating. Still, humanoids seemed to require a great many things to maintain their comfort. Odo wondered if perhaps Dukat was right about Odo's own need—or lack of it—for profits. All that Odo required to be comfortable was a suitable vessel for regeneration—

and perhaps, the company of at least one agreeable person. As the Ferengi continued to gabble about profits and acquisition and luxury items, Odo thought that it might take him a very long time to understand humaoid motivation, after all.

Kira noted that the Bajoran side of the station seemed a consolidation of the very worst effects of the occupation; the tightly-packed living quarters and strict regulations gave it the appearance of the worst ghettos in the cities planetside, only more desperate, somehow—probably because there was very little chance of escaping. Throngs of people drifted about the darkened Promenade, most of them with a gaunt and miserable set to their features. Kira wondered how long it would be before she started to look just like them—or maybe she already did.

Not much longer, thank the Prophets. A few more days and she'd be slipped onto a transport, and then she'd be home.

Many Bajorans were sitting, or even lying along the Promenade, some of them with rough blankets spread out offering food and wares for sale, some of them simply resting after a hard day's work in the ore processors. Farther back, a few people had lit cooking fires in old shipping containers, for there were only a handful of replicators on this side of the station, and the mine workers were not allowed to have food in their sleeping quarters, since it was thought to provoke fights and encourage the voles that lived in the maintenance conduits. Kira sidestepped the idle bodies of young and old as she passed.

She walked past several shops, including that of the slain chemist and his wife, and a fairly clean eatery that was primarily patronized by some of the upper-echelon Bajorans who lived here. People who had just received their wages might come here to waste a week's pay on a single meal, but the clientele was mostly composed of

Bajoran merchants, overseers, and probably criminals. Just beyond it was a humbler establishment, a bare room that served weak teas and soups on acceptance of Cardassian-issued ration cards. It was here that Kira was to meet with the constable again. She would have preferred to avoid this encounter, but she had little hope of evading him on this self-contained facility, and to ignore his summons was to invite further attention to herself. It was best to find out what he wanted.

She supposed she should have been afraid that Odo was going to arrest her, but she also supposed he would have done it less ceremoniously than by sending someone to find her and ask if she would meet him at this location. Why not just burst into ore processing with a phaser? No, Kira felt somewhat confident that this meeting concerned something else, though what it was, she could not say.

She spotted him, sitting erect at a table, looking around the room in an unnatural, abrupt manner. He had no food in front of him, which made her feel inexplicably nervous, as though he did not expect this interview to last long. "Don't you want anything to eat?" she asked him, taking the seat opposite him.

"No," he said. "I only want to ask you something."

"I've told you all I know about Vaatrik," she said. "What more do you want with me?"

"My investigation into the chemist's death is over," Odo told her, and she felt herself tense further at the welcome news. Was this about the resistance, then? She had admitted her involvement with them, though she had done it to keep his attention from Vaatrik's death. She believed he would not turn her in, though she was not sure why.

"Go on."

He blinked. "Were you ever . . . at the Bajoran Institute of Science?"

Kira was immediately puzzled. "Excuse me?" She

scoured her mind for the reference—she had heard of it, of course, but then . . .

"The Bajoran Institute of Science. Have you ever been there?"

Kira did not know how to answer. She had confirmed to the alien that she was in the resistance movement, so it shouldn't condemn her any further if she admitted that she had been there once. Many years ago, the Shakaar cell had broken into the facility. They had used the institute's transporter for the mission to Gallitep. But how could this alien know anything of that incident? She felt fear creep in; perhaps he *was* about to arrest her.

"Never mind," the alien said, and stood to go. He nodded politely at her, a kind of stiff bow, and took his leave.

Kira stared after him, not sure what to make of his question. The heavyset Bajoran who operated the eatery approached her, then. He was corpulent, obviously in league with the Cardassians to be so overfed; Kira hated him immediately.

"Only patrons sit here," he said.

Kira scowled, annoyed at the slight. "What about him?" she asked, tossing her head in the constable's direction as he went out the door.

The man snorted. "He works for the spoonheads! He can do what he wants."

Kira stood to go. "So can I," she said menacingly, staring the man down for a moment, but then recognized the foolish bravado for what it was—fear, masquerading as defiance. She turned from him sharply, heading for the exit. It appeared she'd gotten away with killing one collaborator. Better not to press her luck.

Dukat saw Gil Trakad through the crowd, such as it was, and sighed. There was only a small turnout for Merchant's Day, a quarterly event on the station in which free samples of food and drink were passed out to the Cardassian populace, but there were enough people around that it was no place to discuss business. And from the eager expression on Trakad's wide face, it could only be business.

Trakad spotted him and hurried across the Promenade. Dukat started walking as soon as Trakad reached him, steering them toward a quieter spot. They stopped near the entry to Quark's—the Ferengi bartender did not participate in Merchant's Days—and Trakad started speaking in a low, quick voice.

"I've got information," he said. "I've been monitoring the private channels for transmissions of interest, and—"

"Keep your voice down," Dukat said, glancing around them. There was no one close, but he disliked having confidential discussions in public. One never knew who might be listening.

Trakad spoke in a stage whisper. "Dalin Russol sent a message to a point outside Cardassian space. To coordinates that are listed as a possible Federation contact."

Dukat cocked an eye ridge. "Really? When was this?"

"Yesterday, at precisely 2200 hours."

"What was the message?"

Trakad shook his head. "Encoded. But no code is unbreakable."

"Indeed not," Dukat said, starting to smile. In spite of an exemplary record, Dalin Gaten Russol had remained something of an enigma since he'd come to Terok Nor. No matter the conversation, he kept himself removed from it, spouting clichés of patriotism in answer to any direct question. Dukat had half thought him another plant from the Order—they were always dropping their agents clumsily on his station—but perhaps Russol was something else entirely.

"Make an isolinear recording of the transmission and

bring it to my office immediately," Dukat said. He'd had no small experience with code breaking. He would decipher it himself.

"Immediately, Prefect." He turned his smile to Trakad. "Depending on what the dalin had to say, perhaps we can revisit the idea of upgrading your quarters."

Trakad bowed as he backed away. "Thank you, sir."

Dukat waited a moment before turning and heading back to operations, reprioritizing the rest of his day as he walked, smiling faintly at the passing familiar faces. He had too much to do; his walk to the Promenade for lunch had been his only break in what felt like days. There was the famine in Hedrikspool Province to manage, thanks to a *katterpod* weevil infestation that wasn't discovered until days before harvest. The surface commander summit was coming up, and he was expected to attend, to dispel rumors that a withdrawal was imminent. There were still the daily reports to get to, and a depressingly low weekly ore output to bury in the numbers . . .

As he stepped into the turbolift, turning to face the door, he saw Dalin Russol walk out of the security office, his head high, his shoulders back. A man with a purpose. He quickly disappeared from sight, but Dukat smiled again as the door slid closed, deciding he'd get to that recording sooner rather than later.

Kalisi considered her options carefully before acting, enjoying the feel of her mind at work again—looking for the best angle, the most propitious path. For the first time since leaving the science institute, she felt like herself, or the self she was before she came to Bajor. Like a woman willing to do whatever was necessary to achieve her goals.

When she felt comfortable with her plan—as comfortable as she could feel, considering the risks she meant to take—she contacted the university representative, double-checking the time difference to be sure she could reach her directly.

Tera Glees was again impeccably dressed, her tastes simple and expensive. Kalisi smiled politely.

"Ms. Glees, I'm so pleased to meet you."

The woman smiled in turn. *"Doctor Reyar, thank you for returning my contact. Have you had a chance to consider our offer?"*

"I have," Kalisi said. "I would like very much to work at the University of Culat. However, I'm currently invested in a project I can't afford to walk away from at this time. Might I inquire if you mean to keep the position open much longer?"

The representative tilted her head slightly. *"How long would you need?"*

Kalisi tried to read the woman's face for some indication of how much she could get, but Glees was impassive, her expression carefully controlled. Kalisi went with the truth. "I am uncertain at this time."

Glees' smile went flat. *"Unless you can be more specific, I'm unable to promise anything . . ."*

"Of course," Kalisi said. "Perhaps I might inquire again, once I have a better sense of my time frame."

Glees nodded. *"That would be best."*

"Might I ask—have you contracted anyone to head the exobiology department?"

Glees blinked. *"We have not. That is, the university already has Doctor Revel Panh on main faculty. He will probably lead the research branch, as well."*

Kalisi nodded. "He is renowned. Who is your exobiology specialist? You have one, of course."

Glees hesitated just long enough to let Kalisi know she'd chosen the right tack. The representative obviously took great pride in her school; she did not like any oversights to be pointed out. *"Why do you ask?"*

"Only because my immediate superior is Doctor Crell Moset," Kalisi said proudly. "You know of him? He's been awarded commendations on several occasions—" She allowed a fleeting look of surprise to cross her face, of realization. "You could get him. He is eager to return to Cardassia Prime, to pursue his research."

Glees looked surprised. *"Doctor Moset is available?"*

"He is," Kalisi said, then smiled. "But don't tell him I said so," she added lightly.

Glees' eyes narrowed. *"Why not?"*

Kalisi shrugged. "Oh, of course, tell him if you *wish*. I only meant to say that Doctor Moset is a great man, but of fragile ego. He's quite proud of his reputation. You know how it is for men in the sciences . . ."

Glees nodded, catching on. Figuring it out for herself, exactly as Kalisi wanted. *"He might be insulted that we did not contact him of our own initiative,"* she said.

Kalisi nodded gratefully. "You understand."

Glees offered a wry smile. *"Too well."*

Kalisi didn't want to overplay. Time to end the call. "I hope very much that I'll be able to finish this project in short order, and that the weapons research position will still be open," she said. "Work at the University of Culat . . . I am truly honored."

Again, just the right thing to say. Glees's smile was sincere. *"Contact me as soon as you know anything."*

The two women broke contact, Kalisi pleased with her performance, the first step in the small charade that would end with her freedom—from Bajor, from Moset, from her ghosts, new and old. It wasn't too late for her, not yet.

Quark's bar was entirely empty, and he stared glumly at the people outside as they passed his entrance. He usually closed his bar for this event; it was Merchant's Day, the ridiculous Cardassian tradition that requested all the sell-

ers along the Promenade to provide free samples for the
soldiers. It was supposed to bolster business, but all Quark
could see was one great big handout. That wasn't business,
it was charity, and Ferengi most certainly did not advocate
charity. Not only was it against the law on his homeworld,
he could expect to wind up in the Vault of Eternal Des-
titution in the next life if he were to participate in such
blasphemy. The very word was profane, and the idea of it
made his gorge rise.

Quark's back was to the door, his arms folded irritably across his chest, considering that he might as well have
closed today, when someone entered, and Quark turned to
see the new Cardassian soldier from security approaching
the bar with long, determined strides. Quark broke into his
best-rehearsed smile. "Welcome to Quark's," he said, but
the Cardassian did not answer.

"Well, what'll it—*ugh!*" he gurgled, as the big man
grabbed him by the front of his shirt and pulled him up off
his feet, almost over the surface of the bar.

The Cardassian spoke with no inflection. "Morn tells
me that you refuse to serve him. He's planning to file a
formal complaint."

"M—Morn?" Quark asked, through quick, hyperventi-
lating breaths.

"The Lurian," the man said, with slow and deliberate
anger.

"Is . . . he . . . a friend of yours?"

"I could care less about him," the Cardassian said coldly.
"I'm doing my job."

"You're Dalin Russol, aren't you? I don't think we've
been properly introduced." Quark tried to smile, but the
Cardassian said nothing. *What is his problem?* "Lurians are
bad for business," Quark squeaked. "Nobody will want to
come in here if he's hovering at the end of the bar like a
ghoul, talking everyone's ears off . . . and he wants to drink

on credit!" He coughed, strangling. "But . . . maybe we could work something out."

The Cardassian continued to glower forcefully as his grip tightened on the front of Quark's clothes. "I have heard about you," he finally said through his teeth, his voice a thin, tight line of fury. "From my very good friend, Natima Lang."

Quark inhaled sharply. "Natima," he said, the fear temporarily forgotten as he revisited his shame. "How is she? Is she well?" His labored breath slowed as he pictured her, so graceful, so clever and beautiful. He had never met another woman like her, and he didn't expect he ever would again.

"Don't you even speak her name," Russol hissed.

"Please," Quark begged. "You must tell her—*auch!*" He squealed as the Cardassian went for his ear. *"Please!"* he cried out. *"Not the lobes!"*

Russol continued to twist and pull while Quark struggled for his wits, anything he could give this man to make him stop this overt torture. "Wait!" he cried out, "I hear things on the station all the time . . . *ow!* . . . please stop! *Listen to me!"*

Russol loosened the pressure on Quark's ear without letting go entirely. "What kinds of things?"

Quark's head was bent uncomfortably where Russol gripped his lobe. "I heard . . . Dukat talking about you with his . . . *ow!* . . . one of his henchmen. He was talking about . . . the Federation or something . . ."

"The Federation?" Russol let him go abruptly, dropping him. "Tell me more, Ferengi, or I won't just twist your ear, I'll cut it off."

From his huddle on the floor Quark cradled his ear, panting with relief and fear. "His lackey said something about you . . . talking to a Federation person or something . . . and then Dukat told him to make an . . . an isolinear recording of the conversation."

"When was this?" Russol demanded.

"Just now," Quark said. "Not ten minutes ago."

Russol turned to leave, appearing very troubled, but he before he left he turned again. "I'm not through with you," he said menacingly.

"Could you just tell Natima that I never meant to—" Quark stopped as he saw it was no use, Russol was gone. In another beat, Quark saw a massive shape in the doorway, and his first instinct was to shoo him off—it was the Lurian. But any business today was welcome business, and Quark smiled at the hairy alien instead, gesturing for him to sit, thinking that maybe letting this man have a drink on credit wouldn't be the worst thing that he had ever done.

Odo was beginning to feel better suited to his new role as he crossed into the Bajoran side of the station, though he could not say why. He liked working with Dalin Russol, and the Bajorans here seemed to accept Odo's authority, for the most part. Perhaps they believed that he was preferable to Thrax, his predecessor—this was Dukat's estimation of the situation. Odo hadn't seen any particular evidence of this, but he surmised it was a likely possibility. He was not a Cardassian, after all.

Odo found the red-haired woman named Kira in the same place he'd interviewed her before, sitting at a table in the eatery with a cup of tea in her hands. It was at her request that they met this time, though he couldn't imagine what she wanted with him.

She wasted no time in telling him. "Constable," she said in an urgent whisper, "do you know anything about my transport off the station?"

"What?" Odo did not immediately follow. "You were . . . leaving the station?'

"Of course I was leaving," she whispered, looking around. "It was arranged that a Cardassian gil was supposed to transport me off the station, but he never came. He was supposed to pull me out of ore processing last night."

Odo shook his head from side to side. "I don't know anything about it," he said. "Probably, though, the Cardassian pocketed the money and left. Motivated by profit, of course," he added.

The woman only stared at him, no less angry and frantic. "It's . . . a possibility," she said, "but it's just as possible that he was found out, and something happened to him."

Odo frowned. "Are you concerned about him?"

"Of course not! I need to get off this station, don't you understand?"

"I don't know anything about it," he repeated.

She sat back in her chair, looking down into her empty cup. She still seemed angry, but there was something else in it, too. Distress. Odo wanted to help her, though he wasn't sure why. Helping her would certainly welcome chaos here, and Odo had no desire to bring more chaos upon himself.

"Why are you fighting the Cardassians?" he suddenly asked.

She looked up from her cup and laughed, though it was not a happy sound. "Because," she said. "Because everything the Cardassians have, they stole from us. From my people—from *me.*"

Odo considered it. "It has been suggested that the Bajoran people asked the Cardassians to come to Bajor," he said.

Kira shook her head. "Suggested by Cardassians, I'm sure." Her eyes flashed, expressing a depth of emotion that he could scarcely imagine. "You see how we're treated. You think this is something we want?"

It certainly seemed unlikely, but he did not see how his opinion mattered, one way or another. He could only do his job, which was to correct injustices as defined by Cardassian law . . . which quite suddenly seemed terrifically unfair. Shouldn't he be allowed to discern fairness based on the specifics of any given situation? Shouldn't everyone?

He spoke before he had a chance to think further. "I can help you," he offered, having no idea how he would go about it.

"Help me?"

"Get off the station."

Her eyes widened slightly, her expression of anger softening somewhat. "How are you going to do that?" she asked.

"I don't know," he admitted. "But . . . I'll find a way."

16

Only two days after Kalisi contacted the university rep, Doctor Moset walked into the hospital's main computer room with a broad grin on his narrow face.

This is it, she thought, and relaxed. Finally. The waiting had been uncertain.

"There you are," he said, walking over to where she sat, running the weekly diagnostics on the security system. "You'll never imagine what happened this morning."

Kalisi was the picture of innocence. "What happened?"

He sat next to her, looking around to be sure they were alone. One of the nurses had been in to check something, but had left promptly when he'd seen Moset come in. No one else was within earshot.

"I was contacted by the University of Culat," he said. "They've offered me a position in exobiology, specializing in nonhumanoid. A *chair*, Kali, if it works out. And . . . I've accepted."

Kalisi widened her eyes. "Crell! How wonderful!"

He took her hand, squeezed it in his own thin, sleek fingers. "We could work together, darling. You must call them back, ask if the weapons position is still open."

She met his gaze, her own filled with manufactured hope. "I'd like that. But—" She shook her head. "The vaccine . . . there's the batch recovery in just a few more weeks.

If we want to replicate the master samples, we should start with a new synthesis."

Moset frowned. "Perhaps I could arrange to come back for a time . . ."

"No, Crell," she said, firmly, lovingly. "I will stay. I've already explained that I have a project to finish before I can consider their offer, and you've accepted. I will see to it that the master vaccine samples are properly adjusted."

He reached out to touch her face, fingers spidering over her skin. "It is my work, Kali. I couldn't ask to stay . . ."

"You're not asking, I'm offering," she said. "Truly, is there anyone else you would trust with the documentation of the process? To see it through?"

She waited, watched him think. She was prepared to lie outright to get him away—create some false family issue she needed to resolve before she could return home, or even suggest that she wanted him to make a place ready for her, calling on the archaic tradition in which a man creates a suitable home for his affianced before she will agree to marry him.

Funny, though, how neither of us has mentioned marriage . . . She suspected that he would, before much longer. Or not. In some ways, she knew nothing at all about Crell Moset.

He finally shook his head and answered her question. "You know there isn't."

"Let me stay," she said. "I'll finish the work, I'll record everything . . . And then I can meet you at Culat."

Moset beamed at her, impulsively raising her hand to his lips, dry as desert grass. "What would I do without you?"

So far, so good.

She smiled back at him. "Does this mean I'll meet your cousin?"

"My cousin?"

"The one you were telling me about, who walks the Oralian Way."

Moset grinned ever wider. "Did I say it was a cousin? I don't recall."

She laughed. "I thought you had," she said, and went in another direction, wanting to defer his suspicions. "Ever since you told me about the Way, I've wondered . . . You say the current leader was trained at the Ministry of Science?"

"Yes."

"As was I," she said. "I am curious about when she was supposed to have worked there. Perhaps I knew her."

Moset smiled. "Perhaps you *are* her."

His attempts at humor were oblique and rarely funny. "What do you mean?"

"Only that when you told me you'd handled the Bajoran artifact—Astraea was alleged to have received her call by touching one of those Orbs, at the ministry. And she is about your age, I believe. You would have trained around the same time." He chuckled, then turned mock serious. "Tell me, Kali, are you secretly speeding away to Cardassia City when you're not with me, leading an ancient religion in your spare time?"

Miras. Instantly, she knew. Her friend from school, who'd borrowed Kalisi's clearance to look at the Orb, who'd suffered some sort of hallucination that day the computers had glitched . . . *Astraea is Miras Vara.*

She'd planned to use the information about Moset's relative as her leverage, but if it was true, if the secret leader of the Oralian Way was Miras . . .

She had to pretend admiration at his clever jest, but her laugh was real. Crell Moset had just inadvertently provided her with exactly what she needed to ensure that she could achieve all of her objectives.

I will be free, she promised herself, and laughed again.

Making his way through the corridor near the empty habitat ring, Odo was startled when someone grabbed his arm. Without thinking, he dissolved into a liquid from his shoulder to his wrist, removing himself from the clutching fingers. He was considering his response when he realized that it was Dalin Gaten Russol.

"Odo!" The Cardassian appeared unhappy, his movements anxious. "I need your help."

Odo took a step back. The urgency in Russol's voice was troubling. "What's happened?"

"I . . . I need you to do something for me. There is an isolinear recording in Dukat's office. I need that recording. My life depends on it, Odo. Possibly more than my life."

Odo blinked, a conscious action that did not, of course, come naturally to him. It was something that he often remembered to do only when he was beginning to feel distress or confusion. It was one of the first habits he'd been taught. "What is more important than your life?"

"I can't explain it, Odo. Just understand that this matter is of the utmost significance."

"I'm sure I can retrieve it for you," Odo said, and something occurred to him then—something vaguely related to the idea of profit. *An exchange . . . of goods—or services.* He spoke slowly. "But I will need you to help me with something, as well."

"Anything I can do for you, Odo, I will do it. Just get me that recording by the end of the day."

"I will get it for you now, if you like. But there is a Bajoran woman who needs to get off the station," Odo said. "Do you think you could assist her?"

Russol looked surprised for a brief moment before he nodded. "That's almost too easy," he replied. He looked sidelong at Odo. "A Bajoran woman, eh? Why, may I ask, is this particular Bajoran important to you?"

Odo frowned. He was unsure of the answer himself. "It seems to me . . . if you are unwilling to share more information about your isolinear recording, then perhaps we can agree to keep our motives to ourselves."

Russol nodded, a smile spreading across his face. "Agreed."

Dukat was ready to see her, or rather, believed that Kira Nerys might finally be ready to see him. He'd watched the feeds from the processing levels off and on since her arrival, watched her shoulders begin to slump as she saw her future unfolding, grit and grease and no way out. Whatever rebellious spirit had dared her to come to Terok Nor, it had certainly been diminished. He didn't want her broken, just receptive.

He summoned Basso Tromac to his office, considering how the meeting might unfold: young Nerys, frightened and alone, brought before the prefect, a man she'd been raised to fear and even hate, who'd loved her mother in secret, taken care of her as she had taken care of him. Nerys would never know that part of it, of course. That would be . . . counter-productive, in any case. But he saw a real opportunity here, to act as a father figure to the girl. Perhaps his could be the firm, guiding hand that would lead her away from her vain struggles, lead her to accept a better life for herself. Surely, it was what Meru would have wanted.

He sighed, wishing that was his only interest. In truth, he also sought distraction from the steady decline in Bajor's export quotas. Until Kell and the Council finally relented, sending what was needed to keep Bajor profitable—surveyors, geologists, researchers to study pharmaceutical possibilities in the flora; the list of possibilities were endless—there would be no respite from the dropping figures. Bajor would serve Cardassia well for at least another generation, but until the Union was willing to invest, the statistics would tell a different story; would show, in fact, that the planet was beginning to run out of nonrenewable resources.

And the blame would be laid on me. He disliked the thought of how it might read in the story of the Union, the one dutifully memorized by schoolchildren. He could see how it would look, where the implications would fall . . .

A signal at his door, and then Basso Tromac walked in. "You wanted to see me, Gul?"

Dukat smiled, his thoughts returning to Nerys. "Yes. I think our Bajoran guest has squirmed long enough. I want you to bring her to me."

"Here?" Basso asked, his expression giving the rest of his thought away—*and not your quarters?* Puerile of mind.

"Where else?" Dukat asked, his smile sharp.

Basso nodded. "Of course. Right away."

He left the office and Dukat sat at his desk again. But perhaps he should be standing when Nerys was shown in. Which would be least threatening to her? It was his attention to detail that often won him the things he sought, and disarming the Bajoran girl of lifelong prejudices would be no easy task. This would only be the first session of many, he was sure, but first impressions were often the strongest.

He turned to his computer, calling up her file—calling up both of her files, after a moment's thought, the original and the one he'd personally edited. Perhaps presenting her with evidence of his sincerity would be a good beginning. A handful of internal memos popped up—authorization requests, mostly—and he quickly answered them, only pausing over one. A waste processor needed replacement, a costly and time-intensive task, and while it needed to be done, he thought it might be put off awhile—

There was a noise, close behind him. Dukat turned, stylus in hand, the briefest pulse of instinctive fear clenching his gut—

—assassination—

—and he saw a vole, fat and sleek and holding something in its jaws, disappearing into the air conduit by the door. Another refugee from the storage bays, an ever-present nuisance that continued to thrive in spite of maintenance's best efforts. The voles arrived in cargo containers from home, lived on the refuse left out by the Bajorans, by careless shopkeepers. Terok Nor represented the very pinnacle of Cardassian technology; that they couldn't rid themselves of a few voles was an utter embarrassment.

Overcome by disgust, Dukat threw his stylus after it. He picked up a padd from his desk and threw that, too, but the gesture was a futile one. The vole was gone.

His lanky, leaning form, his thin blade of a smile, his strange precision in even the smallest of tasks . . . Crell Moset was gone, packed and returned to Cardassia Prime. It hadn't taken long, once the gears had ground into motion, moving the science ministry's complicated transfer process along. There had been a formal reassignment of staff, a small, private dinner attended by a handful of colleagues, and a final, inevitable night of passion with Kalisi. She had enjoyed the sex. His efforts were sincere and practiced, making it easy to forget the rest of it—what she'd read recently about his experiments with polytrinic acid, for example, on living Bajorans. Or the radiation tests, or the additive to the Fostossa vaccine, or a dozen other things she'd learned since first submitting to his caresses. Her body responded in spite of her thoughts and, she had to admit, because of them, the darker feelings adding a flavor to their coupling that had frightened her, afterwards, but had, at the time, been extremely stimulating.

Only hours after their final, lingering kiss, the very morning his shuttle left atmosphere, she set to work. She destroyed every existing variation of the sterilization component and spent several hours wiping its formulation from the records before she set the machines to work up a new synthesis. Or, rather, the old one. The one that lacked Moset's additive. On the chance that someone might later try to recover his work at the facility, she altered the lists of chemicals taken from inventory over the past year. Finally, she replicated the original masters and issued the commands necessary to begin full facility batch fermentation. The Bajorans would receive the Fostossa vaccine, nothing more.

It didn't take long to tear it all down, his brilliant solution to the Bajoran question; she'd managed it in only a few hours. With Moset gone, much of the research facility that adjoined the hospital had been shut down. Another doctor would reopen in a few weeks, someone doing a study on botanical medicine or something equally uninteresting. Kalisi was not bothered by anyone as she worked. Anyway, she had higher clearance than any wandering aide who might wonder what she was doing, running the entire system and every outlet from the computer room, searching each database for particular files that might have been cached away. By midafternoon, she was certain that there was no trace of Moset's recent work left anywhere in the system. She could do nothing about his personal hardware—he'd taken his work padds with him, of course—but she had reason to hope he wouldn't be around to use them for very much longer.

She sat in his private office, looking around at the empty spaces where the doctor had kept his eccentric memorabilia: an anatomical model of a Cardassian heart; a holo of his mother and grandmother, sharing a single stern expression; a complete set of the works of Iloja; and his prize, an extensive collection of beetles from different worlds. The room still felt like him, though perhaps that was because parts of her still ached from his heartfelt farewell, and she could still smell his breath in her hair, feel his hands on her body . . .

She shivered, a mix of revulsion and heat that she did not attempt to explain to herself. What mattered was that her first objective had been met. She wasn't sorry that she had acted, although she knew that if the rest of her plans didn't work out, she'd just signed her own death warrant, deliberately destroying legitimate research of use to the Union. Would Moset come after her personally? She didn't know. More likely, the ministry would insist on a trial, the doctor their main witness against her. Because her guilt was incontrovertible, a trial, too, would mean her death.

Why had she done this thing? Why would she willingly place what was left of her career in jeopardy, risk bringing shame to her family, risk her own execution? She had thought upon it often since the day she'd assisted in sterilizing an entire community of Bajorans, and had come to realize that she did not wish to spend the rest of her life haunted by what she had helped Crell Moset create. She could still have children, might even choose to do so if she met a fitting suitor to sire them; she might, she might not . . . But the understanding that she had the choice was important for her, as a woman and as a Cardassian, as a responsible member of the Union. As little as she cared for the Bajoran people, she didn't want her name to be associated with the sterilization of a species. If it was true, what Moset said, that allowing them to bear young would doom tens of thousands of them to slow starvation, then she'd just created an apocalypse for them. But their future was not set in stone. And if he was wrong, she'd left them a choice, and that did not seem to be such a great evil. They would probably choose incorrectly, anyway. They were an illogical people.

Her reasons no longer had bearing, which was a relief;

she could stop thinking about that aspect. It was done, and if she hoped to survive the aftermath, she needed to act.

From the empty office, she put in a call to her father, using his secure channel, breathing deeply as she waited for the relays to go through. She was no longer certain she understood what evil was. She'd always believed it to be a deliberate thing, a conscious decision—one man chooses to kill another for personal gain; he is evil. Working with Dr. Moset had taken her certainty away about a number of things. He did not wish the Bajorans any harm; he simply saw them as a factor in his equations, another variable to be quantified and managed. He had his formulas and his experiments, he looked at the numbers, he decided how best to fulfill his purpose, and acted accordingly. It was cold and brutal, science without sentiment, and it was who and what she had been before coming to work with Doctor Moset. Evil? May as well attempt to apply morality to mathematics. The only thing she knew with any certainty anymore was that she never wanted to see Crell Moset again. She wanted her last chance at a real life, that was all.

She shifted in the doctor's chair, deciding how much to tell her father while she waited for the last pickup. When his face finally appeared on her screen, she was ready.

"Father."

"Kalisi!" He smiled encouragingly. *"I've been waiting to hear from you. You've accepted the position at Culat, haven't you?"*

"I am about to," she said. "My supervisor here asked me to finish the project I was working on, but I'll be done quite soon, and free to return to Cardassia Prime."

"That's wonderful," he said. *"You'll alert me as soon as your transport is scheduled, of course. We'll want to be there to meet you, and—"*

"Father, I need help."

He stopped talking, stopped smiling, his expression at once wary and concerned. *"What is it?"*

"There is someone—someone who poses a threat to me, should I return home."

"In what way?"

"My position at the university would be compromised," she said. "This man acted as my superior."

He waited, but she offered nothing more—nor did she have to. She was a single woman of viable age, attractive, and her father was no idealist. He sighed unhappily, probably presuming some manner of sexual blackmail.

"What would you have me do about this?" he asked.

"Your contacts at the Order," she said. "You've used them before to have people . . . removed."

He frowned. *"I will do whatever I can to protect you, child, but you overestimate my status. I have no rank within the Order."*

"But if you had something to offer them, something of value . . . They will occasionally trade a favor for information, isn't that so?"

She already knew that it was, and he nodded slowly, his eyes full of questions.

Kalisi smiled. "Contact Dost Abor. Tell him that if he can find a way to help me with my problem, I can tell him what happened to Miras Vara."

"Miras—the girl you went to school with?"

"Please. I will explain it to you as soon as I return." She smiled again. "I'll be in Culat, Father. We'll have time."

Yannik Reyar hesitated, then nodded again.

Almost home, she thought.

A load of pulverized ore rattled and thumped endlessly along the belt, the sound lost beneath the constant roar of the giant turbines that filled the massive room. Heat waves trembled up from the floor. Dozens of dirty, sweating Bajorans stood over the line, sorting the rock with torn fingers, sending the results on to the belt that ran to the turbines; there, the ores were ground and dropped to the smelters. Another group of Bajorans shoveled the rejected material to a different belt. The air was hot and thick with dust, hard to breathe, even with the nose filters. It was hard to *think*.

Kira paused long enough at her shoveling to wipe a forearm across her brow. The result was a viscous gray smear of mud. Dust covered everything, made the workers look like some childhood perception of *borhyas*.

We are *ghosts*, she thought, too tired to fight the depressing concept. *At least, I am*. It was only a matter of time before someone decided to point out that Kira didn't belong on Terok Nor. Since the day the pilot hadn't showed, she'd been tense, waiting for some heavy hand to come down on her shoulder, to drag her before the prefect or into an interrogation room. She'd spent her "free" time meditating, trying to prepare herself. She was determined that they would learn nothing from her, but she was afraid of what they might be able to pry from her mind, with their drugs and devices. She was afraid of the pain, too, afraid of being tortured to death. She didn't want to be scared, and told herself that worrying about it was pointless, but she couldn't help it.

The days had stretched, though, and her immediate terror gave way to other fears—like becoming one of the cowed, desperate people she'd met on the station, most of them just trying to keep their families alive. Terok Nor's Bajoran populace had few resources and were worked to the point of exhaustion, the better to keep them from organizing in any effective way. The people she'd met had the solace of the shrine but no real hope, and every day she stayed, she feared for her own failing will. Drag herself awake to work, break for food, more work, a scant meal, then back to the inadequate shelters for not enough sleep. It was almost enough to make her wish for discovery.

The shape-shifter had promised to help her, but she

knew better than to pin any hope there. Odo didn't strike her as a liar, but he worked for the Cardassians; he owed her nothing. He hadn't turned her in, but she thought his willing blindness was the most she could expect. If she wanted to go home, she'd have to find her own way.

The rock blurred past her, her arms aching as she hefted another scoop of slag, tipping it onto the belt. These were the thoughts that cycled through her mind while she worked, repeating themselves endlessly and uselessly. She knew she had to come up with some kind of plan, but there was no forest to hide in, no caves to which she could run, no city in which to lose herself among its wretched populace; she was so far out of her element, she felt she didn't know how to look for the opportunities she'd need to escape, or even change her situation.

One by one, the men and women around her stopped working, looking toward the section's entry, where the Cardassian "managers" usually lingered, close to the heat but out of the worst of the dust. Kira stood up, saw the tall, grim-looking Cardassian security officer coming her way, and realized that the wait was finally over. She'd thought it might be a relief, but she was wrong. She was terrified.

She had to fight the urge to turn and flee, in spite of there being no sanctuary; this was Dukat's station, and she'd been stupid, stupid to think she could come and go as she pleased. One or two of the workers moved closer to her, and for a brief, hysterically hopeful second she allowed herself to think that she might be saved, but she also knew better. She made herself step forward, not wanting anyone else to be dragged away with her.

The Cardassian grabbed her by the upper arm, pulling her back toward the entry. The watching guards smirked, one of them shouting at the workers to return to their stations, his voice amplified to be heard over the turbines.

She had to half run to keep up with him, his viselike grip unyielding. He walked her quickly through the "clean" room, where sharp blasts of air took off the worst of the dirt—wouldn't want the interrogator to get his hands dirty—then out into the relative coolness of processing's main corridor, walking them toward the hub. The main hall clanged and thundered with the sound of heavy machinery, but it was infinitely quieter than in the channeling room.

"Where are we going?" she asked.

The security officer didn't answer, just kept walking, giving her his profile. His insignia marked him as a dalin, and he was handsome, by Cardassian standards. They favored a wide head, a tall, muscular frame. She was a strong woman, she knew that, but he was so much bigger than her—her head barely came up to his chin—she couldn't see how she could take him. She'd had some training, but learning how to throw and roll with a willing partner wasn't the same as trying to toss a full-grown, armed Cardassian to the floor. It took a very well placed kick to take one of them down, a blow to one of the bony ridges on their face, but in the position she was currently in, he had too much the advantage. She'd have to free her arm from his grip and face him before she could get the drop on him, and she didn't see it happening—not with so many of them swarming around.

Accept it, just accept it, she told herself, but she couldn't stop trying. "Did Odo send you? I spoke with him, before . . . Are you taking me to see Odo?"

"Quiet," the Cardassian snapped, and then they'd reached the end of the main hall. He nodded at a lower-ranked soldier standing near the lift—the garresh saluted promptly—then he dragged her inside.

When the door closed, shutting out the clamor, she felt that she could hear herself think again. The relief was physical, as if she'd been plucked out of a vast, rattling machine. The lift would let out at the Bajoran sector of the habitat ring. Maybe, if she could slip away, she could . . .

. . . *I could what?* she thought, looking up at the discreet camera in the lift's ceiling panel. *Sneak onto a shuttle? Tiptoe past the recognition software?*

The lift came to a stop and she was pulled out, the dalin acting as though she was a package he was carrying. And a sudden horrible thought occurred to her, as they moved past the fenced wards, heading for the inner lifts. The ones that led up to operations. To Dukat's office.

Comfort women. There were several on the station. She'd seen them—Bajoran women walking the Promenade in elegant clothing, their expressions dumb with sedatives or shame. Dukat was well known for his preferences—young, pretty, willing to provide. She'd rather die.

"If you're taking me to be interrogated, you could at least tell me," she said, grasping for some clue. "Is it Odo? Is he—"

His grip tightened, cutting off her words. *"Quiet!"*

The Bajorans they passed looked away, went about their business, plodding to or from some assigned destination. Kira felt ill, and as they neared the ops access lifts, she started to think she might actually vomit.

"I feel sick," she said.

"That's too bad," he said, not looking at her as they passed the lifts, heading for the crossover bridge to the outer ring. The docking ring.

Were their interrogation rooms in the outer ring? She didn't know . . . but the dalin was a security officer, Odo was head of security . . .

Kira kept her mouth shut, concentrating on keeping up. They walked to the access corridor, entered it. The hall's design, like the rest of the station, was stark and cold, maybe to balance the dreadful heat, and they walked straight through two security checks, the soldiers saluting, the dalin nodding in turn.

He was going to let her go. Or, he was going to shove

her out of an airlock. Either way, she was through with Terok Nor.

I'll come back the day the last Cardassian leaves, she promised herself, latching on to the thought; it implied that she would survive this, somehow.

They turned a corner, and there was a small group of Bajoran men and women waiting at one of the station's wide, rolling locks. None of them looked well. Kira recognized one of them from her ward, a woman who suffered respiratory problems associated with breathing heavily particulated air. Jaryn, something like that. Even with the nose filters, a lot of the workers suffered chronic conditions.

The officer shoved her into the line, just as a Cardassian pilot stepped out of the lock, his expression bored.

"Is she going to the hospital, too?" he asked, nodding at Kira.

"No. This one is to be released in the Dahkur Province. By order of Dukat."

Dukat?

She looked at the dalin, back at the pilot. Were they exchanging some silent information? Was it a trick? The pilot nodded, started filing the other passengers in. As the dalin turned to leave, Kira stepped after him.

"What's going on?" she asked, keeping her voice low. "Why are you—"

Before she could speak another word, he'd gripped her arm again, roughly turning her back toward the moving line. "There's a two-minute delay on the security captures in this sector. Keep your back to the cameras."

She nodded, recognizing that she was being given a tremendous gift. "I—thank you," she said.

He hesitated, finally looking at her. "Thank the shapeshifter," he said, and then walked away.

17

Thrax had been doing this sort of thing for a very long time, but somehow, his years of experience made it no easier for him. He was always fearful of getting caught, hence the elaborate tactics he took to avoid arousing the suspicion of Central Command—or worse, the Order. He didn't have it in him to be comfortably sly; that sort of manner was better suited to the man he was about to make contact with.

He approached the Public Hall of Records, looking for his contact but knowing that Esad would not make his presence known until Thrax reached the agreed-upon point of encounter. He entered the great building and went to the third level, where copies of modern works of poetry were kept, along with recent literature. He removed an isolinear rod from a shelf in front of him and plugged it into his padd, perusing with feigned interest.

A voice behind him made him jump. "Is this any good?" a man asked.

Thrax turned, his breath hitching. He half expected to see a stranger, but instead he saw the thin, jagged features of Kutel Esad, the man who had served directly under Enabran Tain for the last nine years of Tain's tenure as the head of the Obsidian Order. Esad was holding in his hand an isolinear recording, identical to those that were used

here at the Hall of Records, but Thrax knew that this particular recording did not belong here.

"The collected works of Maran Bry," Esad said, pretending to read it from the label on his isolinear rod.

"Bry's work is not for everyone," Thrax said. He tried
his best to sound natural, but his voice hardly sounded like
his own.

"Is it for you?" Esad asked him. The wiry man, though
he had a reputation for his cautiousness, maintained his
cool composure in the face of Thrax's readily apparent
nervousness.

Thrax recited the lines of one of Maran Bry's more
controversial poems that had been agreed as code to pro-
ceed with the exchange. His voice wavered, though he had
chosen the verse himself. If he delivered the words incorrectly, would Esad carry through with the exchange? The
older man was well known for his strict insistence on careful adherence to procedure, down to every last detail. Even
though he knew Thrax's face by sight, he did not trust that
the Order wouldn't place a surgically altered plant in his
place—if their interest in the Oralian Way warranted such
a measure.

*"The cold hands of a foreign morning/press themselves within
my breast/isolating me from the comfort of my world's motherhood."*

Esad handed him the rod. "You would appreciate this
better than I," he said, and turned to go.

Thrax removed the rod that he had inserted in his padd
and replaced it with the one Esad had just given him. He
read for a moment, and then removed the rod, placing it
back on the shelf for Esad to retrieve later. He pocketed his
padd and walked as quickly as his legs could take him without actually running. He needed to get to Astraea right away.

Kalisi Reyar sat and waited, and waited . . . and waited.

After her conversation with her father, things had happened quickly. She'd been contacted by Dost Abor almost immediately, an extremely polite message suggesting that she pack her things and expect transport within the week. She was ready within hours of the transmission. There was little to pack, no mementos she wished to keep; Bajor had been a long, embarrassing discomfort, beginning to end, and she'd felt only relief at the thought of leaving.

Even if it was to come here again, she thought, looking around at the small, cold room where she'd first met with Dost Abor, on his dark, hidden world. It was as unpleasant as she remembered, but it was also her last stop before home. She could stand it a little longer—although it had been hours since she'd given the agent her information, hours of fidgeting and second-guessing, of looking over her padd with virtually no interest, and she was starting to wonder what was taking so very long. Starting to worry a little.

What if the story didn't check out? She'd given him the information about the identity change, Miras to Astraea, and detailed what Moset had told her about the ancient religion holding meetings in Cardassia City. In the Torr sector, he'd said. Surely, they had enough to find Miras Vara by now. Kalisi felt a dull pang of guilt. Miras had been a sweet girl, but no great mind.

She had been sitting alone for the better part of the day when Dost Abor finally walked in. Kalisi stood up, eager to be finished, to be escorted back to the ship.

"May I go now?"

Abor smiled. "Not quite yet, I'm afraid."

He gestured for her to sit again. Kalisi did so, feeling the worry bloom anew. "Didn't—you weren't able to confirm my information?"

"We were," Abor said. "Your information may well have been good a few days ago. But unfortunately, our agent found nothing but a shop that sells replicator parts, where we had anticipated finding a hideout for Oralians. Perhaps someone warned this Astraea that we were coming. Perhaps your information was not correct in the first place."

Kalisi didn't know what to say. She felt that she should apologize, somehow, but that was ridiculous. It wasn't her fault that Miras had run. It should have been a quick, simple affair to find her and bring her in. If the Order couldn't manage even that, then how was Kalisi to blame?

"Because we were unable to benefit from this information," Abor continued, "I'm afraid we can't help you with your problem."

Kalisi wanted to protest, but understood the way things worked within the Order. "Of course," she said, feeling a kind of numbness settle over her.

Crell Moset, alive and well and waiting at the university. Waiting for the documentation of his vaccine work . . . and for me. What happened when she didn't contact him? When he found out that his sterilization formula had been destroyed? Would he bother to go back to Bajor, to re-create his death vaccine, and she'd have risked everything for no gain? She couldn't go into hiding, she had family to consider . . . But there'd be no position at Culat, no future at all once he reported her sabotage, and that she couldn't bear.

I'll kill him myself, she thought, but knew she didn't have the nerve. The will, yes, but she was no killer . . . unless . . . If she could pretend to care for him a while longer, perhaps he would be willing to listen to her explanation . . .

At the thought of being with him again, she decided she'd rather have him dead. Her father would help her, he had other friends—

"I understand, you know," Dost Abor said, drawing her back to the chill room.

"Understand?"

"That you felt you had no choice."

Kalisi blinked, felt her cheeks darken. How could he

know about her relationship to Crell Moset? Or was he referring to the destruction of Moset's work? "What do you mean?"

"Now, Doctor Reyar—may I call you Kalisi? Kalisi, you strike me as a woman with a conscience. It's understandable, that's all I meant to say. I believe that someone warned Astraea."

She started to shake her head, understanding and disbelief creeping through her veins. "No," she said.

"Perhaps you saw an opening, a way to finally recover your career, after your sad showing as a weapons designer," he said, his sympathy exaggerated. "You remembered an old friend, thought that gaining from her inevitable capture was no great evil. All for the good of the Union, after all. Why you'd want your lover killed is beyond me, but perhaps you've taken another."

Abor smiled, his teeth shining in the dim light. "Or perhaps he wasn't *satisfying*. In any case, you made your choice. And then you thought twice about your decision."

"No," she said again, shaking her head more violently. "No. I want to speak to my father, right now."

"Now, Kalisi," Abor said, his voice soothing. "In spite of certain methods we're sometimes forced to employ, the Order is, at core, a gentle organization. Our interests are the same as yours—we seek to acquire knowledge that will benefit the Cardassian people."

He raised his hands, gestured vaguely at the room. "This facility acts as an information filter, as a research center, sometimes even a laboratory. We have several just like it seeded throughout the galaxy, places we can gather data without fear of harassment by Central Command. For the agent who chooses to utilize the resources here, there is no end to what can be accomplished."

She said nothing. She was a citizen of the Union, she had done nothing wrong—

—*negligence, sabotage*—

—and surely her fear was an overreaction. She'd been frightened last time, too, and it had been for naught. Even as she told herself these things, however, she remembered that she wasn't a stupid person, nor did she believe in self-deceit. Not in matters where someone else held such immediate power over her.

"The Order does not appreciate having its time wasted," Abor said, his voice as cold as she knew it would be. "Nor do we care to have our agents put in potentially danger-ous situations, because our informant is unable to decide whether or not she wishes to help us." He drew a breath, and then his voice became carelessly cordial again. "I've been at this facility for far too long, I suppose," he told her. "It's hard . . . to see what is perceived as a way out of an unpleasant situation, only to learn that your credibility has just been compromised, perhaps beyond repair."

She saw the phaser in his hand, and thought that her father would be heartbroken and furious, and then she wondered if she would have had children. She hoped the Bajorans would take advantage of what she'd given them. Funny, that her last living thought would be of them, but then—

Dost Abor fired, and Kalisi Reyar didn't think anymore.

Kira stepped onto the shuttle with the rest of the passen-gers, helping the wheezing man in front of her take his seat before she took her own. The shuttle was small—there were seats for only twenty—but not quite full. It had obvi-ously been in commission for some time, ferrying small groups to and from Bajor's surface; the seats were worn, the paneling faded. There was only one Cardassian aboard, the pilot; apparently, the riders were too sickly to warrant a guard.

Kira settled into her seat, tense and watchful. No one

spoke, but Jaryn, the woman she'd met on her ward, smiled at her, her eyes kind.

Almost out of this, Kira thought, watching the shuttle door, waiting to hear the telltale rush of internal air that signaled they were ready to leave. Kira was starting to feel like she could breathe again when a Bajoran man stepped on board. Compared to the other Bajorans on the station, the balding man was well-dressed and clean, and his face had a hard, superior look. As he scanned the seated passengers, his expression suggested that the sight of so many sick people disgusted him—and when his mean gaze reached Kira, the smile that broke across his face told her the rest of it.

Collaborator.

"Kira Nerys," he said. "You're to come with me."

Kira stared at him, not moving. She feigned confusion. "Who?"

His hand dropped to his belt, and she saw the disruptor tucked there. "Just get up."

She unbelted and stood, trying to keep her face a blank. Inside she seethed, her fear finally overwhelmed by the revulsion she felt, looking at him. A Cardassian had helped her escape; this *Bajoran* was taking her back.

The shuttle pilot stepped out from behind the partition at the front of the small vessel. He looked at the Bajoran man, at Kira, back to the Bajoran.

"Get off my shuttle," the pilot snapped.

"I'm taking her with me," the collaborator said, nodding at Kira.

"No, you're not," the pilot said. "She's going to Dahkur, Dukat's orders. Now get off before I *put* you off."

"Dukat's—" The Bajoran drew himself upright, his expression imperious. "Do you know who I am?"

The pilot looked him up and down with disdain. "You're a Bajoran. That means you're nobody."

The passengers all held quite still, perhaps aware that they weren't in any shape to protest. Kira felt her temper flare.

"Oh, for fire's sake—" The Bajoran man reached for the padd tucked into his belt, tapped a few keys, presumably calling up his identification. He handed it to the pilot, who accepted it as though it might be a bomb.

While the pilot read, the Bajoran man grabbed her by the arm, the same place the dalin had gripped her, and she winced, pulling away.

"Now, Nerys, don't be like that," the Bajoran said, and it was all she could do not to punch him. Who was he, to be so familiar?

"This appears to be in order," the pilot said reluctantly.

"You said she was supposed to go to Dahkur," the Bajoran said. "Is that where the rest of them are going?"

The pilot shook his head. "One of the testing facilities. A hospital."

The Bajoran spoke in her ear, his voice soft. "You're lucky I came when I did, then. They like to do experiments on pretty little things like you. You didn't really think he was going to take you to Dahkur, did you?"

Kira recoiled from him, her skin crawling. She looked out the open door onto the empty docking platform, saw that there weren't any other soldiers. The collaborator had come alone.

"He said she was to be released in Dahkur," the pilot insisted sullenly, still hesitant to answer to a Bajoran. "Dukat's orders."

"Who told you that?" the Bajoran asked. "You'll have to come with me to the prefect's office, immediately. This needs to be resolved."

The shuttle's captain shook his head, handing the padd back to him. "I've just received clearance for departure. I'm on a schedule. You got what you came for, didn't you? I'll be back in twenty-six hours, I can make a report then."

The balding man released Kira to take the padd back. "You have no choice in the matter," he said. "Whoever told you that this . . . this *woman* . . . is to be released was not acting upon Gul Dukat's authority, I can assure you. The prefect will want to speak with you directly."

The pilot didn't care for the way things were going. "Let me see your identification again," he said darkly, backing up a step. The pompous collaborator stepped forward, and Kira realized her opportunity had come.

She didn't stop to think. As the Bajoran held out his padd, Kira stepped forward and took the phaser from his belt, the motion fast and fluid. He squawked, turning, and she pulled back with the phaser and hit him with it, as hard as she could.

The weapon glanced off his left temple with a dull *chunk*, splitting the skin, but he was on the floor before he'd started to bleed, out cold.

The Cardassian dropped the padd, grabbing for his own phaser, and Kira stepped back, flipping the weapon against her palm. She pointed and fired, releasing a brilliant blast of light in the small cabin.

The pilot fell, the smoking hole in his chest telling her that the phaser had been set high. The passengers were trying to get up, talking, their voices high with fear.

"Hey," Kira called, keeping her voice low but pitched to carry. "Calm down, please. I'm taking us home, okay? Just—just buckle in."

She hurried back to the open door, spun it closed, her heart racing. She turned, looked at the two bodies crumpled by the partition. One dead, the other only stunned— she could see that the Bajoran breathed still. She raised the phaser, thinking that it would be the second Bajoran she'd killed in as many weeks.

Second collaborator, she told herself, and that she had no choice. She fired at close range before she could consider it any further. She didn't *want* to consider it any further; only wondered, for a brief glimmer of a second, what could motivate a Bajoran to turn on his own people like this.

A few of the passengers turned away—Jaryn among them—but most looked on, their faces still frightened but calm once more. A man wearing bandages on both of his hands started to weep.

"Thank you," he said, and Kira could think of nothing to say to that, nothing at all.

She stepped over the dead men to get to the cockpit, hoping she could handle the shuttle's controls, thinking that she'd find a way.

OCCUPATION YEAR THIRTY-NINE

✦ ✦ ✦

2366 (Terran Calendar)

18

The Oralians still met in the Torr sector, in an underground shrine that was conspicuously adjacent to the Cardassian theater—hiding in plain sight, among the most prominent features of Cardassia City. It was here that Thrax Sa'kat met with Kutel Esad late one evening, long after Cardassia City had fallen silent for the night, with only a few of the civilian city guard out, idly patrolling the sector. Thrax was still a soldier of Central Command, and Esad was still an agent of the Obsidian Order, but their status did not mean that they weren't cautious when they made the exchange of the curiously bulky object, draped with a cloth and tied about clumsily with a piece of rope.

"This is the one?" Thrax inquired.

"I do not know if this is the object that Astraea first encountered at the Ministry of Science," Esad replied. "Retrieving this item required a great deal of haste on my part, for although Enabran Tain is no longer the head of the Order, his successor is not exactly a fool."

"No, of course not," Thrax said, gratefully accepting the object from his friend. The bundle was heavier than it looked.

"I was able to confirm one truth about this item which you may find helpful," Esad told him. "These objects had designations among the Bajorans—each was said to be for a specific purpose. I do not know what designation the others in the Order's collection bear, but I know at least that this one was known as the Orb of Wisdom."

"The Orb of Wisdom," Thrax repeated. "I believe Astraea will be pleased."

Esad seemed uncomfortable with something, and he regarded Thrax. "Have you told her that you intended to retrieve this item for her?"

"Not exactly," Thrax confessed. "A very long time ago, I may have implied that I would try, but . . ."

Esad's lips thinned. "If I may give you some advice, Thrax . . ."

"Certainly. Your advice is always welcome."

"That object . . . should not remain on Cardassia Prime."

Thrax involuntarily clutched the object tighter. It had been his intention that the Orb would be a gift for the followers of Oralius—for Astraea.

"But . . . the Guide should have the Orb, Kutel. It was the Orb that brought her back to us, that returned Astraea to Oralius once again. Don't you suppose it was meant to be here, where she is?"

"The object belongs to the Bajorans," Esad pointed out.

"But there is no way that you or I could possibly return this to Bajor," Thrax argued. "I believe that Oralius meant for us to have it."

Esad was silent for a moment. "I fear that it will put Astraea in danger," he said.

"Then why did you agree to retrieve it?" Thrax protested. "I don't understand, Kutel."

"I don't either," the other man admitted. "When I originally came into possession of the Orb, I thought you were right—I thought that those who walked the Way should have it. But then . . . then I . . . I touched it, and I was . . ."

"You . . . opened it?" Thrax was stunned. Astraea had

told him that nobody else had been able to open the case, nobody but her.

"No," Esad said. "I didn't open it. It happened when I placed my hand on the case. It didn't happen immediately. I lifted the item, and then . . . it seemed . . . as though I was beginning to . . ." He trailed off, looking embarrassed. "I was overcome," he said finally. "With the feeling that it should be taken from Cardassia Prime, right away."

Thrax continued to clutch the Orb case to his chest, looking at the sheepish face of his friend. He did not want to listen to what Esad was saying, but he felt a strange, reluctant pull . . .

"The Orb is for the Oralians," he told Esad firmly, and turned to carry the heavy case into the shrine. Esad murmured a good-bye as Thrax let himself inside the ground floor front, a small, darkened shop that sold replicator parts. It was surprising to Thrax that a man as normally business-like as Kutel Esad would so quickly succumb to mystical ideas regarding the Orb. Although Thrax believed very strongly in the power that the item possessed, he had been under the impression that Esad was much more skeptical of it himself. Esad was a practical man. Overly cautious, perhaps.

Thrax carried the item down the back stairs of the shop, into the office where Astraea met with individual followers. He set the item on her table and began to tug at the wrappings that Esad had hastily swaddled around the case. As the item was revealed to him, his breath hitched in his chest. Its appearance was appropriately impressive, and he wondered where it had come from. Had the ancient Bajorans fashioned this splendid case for the precious relic that resided inside?

The object belongs to the Bajorans.

Ignoring the voice in his head, he put his hand gingerly on the case and waited to be overcome, as Esad had described himself. But the case was cold, and Thrax felt nothing. He smiled to himself, in part with relief to have been released from the worry that Esad had planted in his mind. He pictured how pleased Astraea would be when she learned that his efforts had finally produced this happy result, and then he left the shrine, reassuring himself once again that it was the safest place for the item, at least for now.

It was dark and still in this part of the city. Kira Nerys checked her scanner as she approached the improvised holding facility, and it quickly confirmed what she already suspected: there was a Bajoran life sign behind those walls, but it was fading fast. Tahna would not hold out much longer.

Kira had come here following a tip given to her by Tahna's nephew, who lived in Dahkur. Tahna had returned to his family's home for a quick visit over two weeks ago, but when he had not returned to the Kohn-Ma cell's hideout, Biran put word out to his family to inquire after him. His family insisted that they didn't know where he was, but Kira was unconvinced, and contacted them again, asking if there was anything they recalled about the route he had taken that might help him to be found. After a great deal of coaxing and questioning, Tahna's teenage nephew finally confessed to Kira that the Cardassians had taken Tahna from his uncle's house in the middle of the night. The soldiers had threatened the rest of the family, telling them they were lucky they weren't all being taken—and that if they told anyone what had happened to Tahna, it was likely they would be.

Kira knew that Tahna's abduction wasn't some random security sweep, nor were the soldiers likely to take a single man from a Bajoran home if they were merely looking for workers. Tahna had been targeted specifically, most likely in connection with the resistance. He was being questioned somewhere, which meant that he was certainly still alive—and Kira knew she had to save him, not only to preserve his life, but to preserve all of their lives. Tahna was strong-willed, but he couldn't hold out against Cardassian torture without eventually spilling secrets of the Shakaar and Kohn-Ma cells' whereabouts. Nobody could.

Shakaar had managed to gather enough intelligence to suggest that Tahna would have been taken here, a makeshift interrogation center in a crumbling, abandoned section of Dahkur City, where they were questioned and decontaminated before being taken to their final destinations—usually prison camps, or in some cases, public execution. Kira could only hope that if it had been the latter, Shakaar would have heard something about it. There had been no reports of Cardassian executions since Tahna's disappearance.

Kira was supposed to be staking out this place. She was deliberately chosen for most long-range reconnaissance because it had been determined that she was just small enough not to trip the Cardassian detection grid—she didn't need a shielding device to go out, though she carried one, just the same. The others had planned on coming tomorrow, after Kira devised a plan of action for the most effective means of attack. But as she read the life sign on her handheld scanner, she knew that Tahna probably could not wait until tomorrow. She had already anticipated this possibility. Shakaar had firmly instructed her not to try anything on her own, but Kira didn't see that she had a choice.

The facility had only a single guard, the Cardassians' assumption that the detection grids would keep out unwelcome intruders acting as its own security device. Kira wasted little time in strategizing the best way to take out the guard without arousing the attention of anyone inside.

She waited, squatting on the deteriorating cobblestone street between two sagging buildings where she could not be seen. Picking up a piece of the broken road in her hands, she threw the chunk of stone somewhere off to her left. The soldier reacted immediately, drawing his phaser and looking to the place where the stone had landed.

Kira drew back into the shadows, listening carefully to the sound of the sentry's approaching footsteps, and then she sprang out noiselessly, praying that she would cast no shadows. But the soldier did not turn around when she approached. He bent down, examining the ground with his palm torch. "Voles," he mumbled to himself. Kira took a wide step forward, just before he rose to his feet. He scarcely even made a sound when she leapt upon him, twisting his neck with all her might. A crack, a thud, his palmlight clattering on the uneven ground, and it was over.

She kept her phaser at the ready, trying to keep her senses balanced as she carefully approached the entrance of the facility. The more carefully she listened, the more she was certain she could hear someone crying. The sound was faint, fainter than her own heartbeat, but Kira knew that it was Tahna. Her resolve hardened as she crept through the unblocked doors.

It was here that she finally encountered a seated guard, but she was ready for him. She swung her leg up and around to connect with his ear before he could react—best not to use her phaser until absolutely necessary. He staggered from the blow, drawing his weapon. He was shaken, but not especially hurt. With Cardassians it was necessary to strike at just the right place, where the brittle cartilage on their faces was the most vulnerable. In the instant before he brought up his weapon, Kira leaned in and drove the heel of her hand into his mouth. She felt and heard the satisfactory crunch just above his upper lip. The Cardassian lost his disruptor as he fell, but Kira did not stop to pick it up. She scurried past him and kept going into a darkened corridor, following Tahna's echoed groans and cries.

She walked as silently as she knew how, slipped around a corner—there, a Cardassian standing behind a computer console, and before he could even look up, she shot him in the chest with her phaser on its highest setting. He fell backward and seemed to take a very long time to hit the ground. Kira looked to see what he had been doing at the console and was immediately greeted with a grisly scene. Displayed across his viewscreen, Tahna Los hung from the ceiling of a dank corridor that must have been somewhere below her, judging from the sound of his screams, while two expressionless Cardassians were taking turns peeling back slices of flesh from his naked back. Tahna screamed in agony, and Kira threw her hands over her face, but not before she saw that the same Cardassians were carefully, painfully cauterizing the flesh back into place with a crude dermal regenerator, presumably so they could begin to cut once again, after his tender skin had artificially healed back into lumpy scar tissue.

Kira frantically pecked at the computer to try and assess Tahna's location, but after an agonizingly long moment with no success, she decided instead to simply follow the sound of his terrible cries. She found a spiral staircase and quickly descended, discovering a dim and sweltering underground corridor with a line of three doors. Her ears were full of the sound of it now, and the echoing sound of the questions the Cardassians were putting to the hapless Tahna:

Kira Nerys—you know her. Where is she?

Had she really heard her own name? Or was her imagination just trying to amplify her own terror? It must be the latter, for their voices were muffled, in part by Tahna's groans. He began to scream again, either determined not to tell them anything, or simply in so much pain that he couldn't speak.

Thinking with some uncertainty that she had found the right door, she took out the lock with a quick burst of her phaser and let herself inside—to find that Tahna was not in this room at all. A nearly emaciated woman was chained to the wall by her wrists. For an instant, Kira thought she was dead, and almost turned to leave her—but the woman suddenly coughed up a bilious spew of green all down the front of the rags she was dressed in, and shuddered with the resultant coughing fit that followed. Appalled, Kira rushed to her, using her weapon to burn away the chains that bound her to the wall.

"Get out of here!" she whispered, but the corpselike figure made no move, only stared at her with confused, dead-seeming eyes.

"It's too bright," the woman complained, her voice husked and raw. "Shut the door."

"You're free, you have to go," Kira insisted, but she could not afford the time it would take to help her, for Tahna's strangled cries had begun again.

At the next door, Kira found her target—but there were three Cardassians in the dark, hot room, not the two she'd expected. She aimed the line of her phaser fire at the restraints that held Tahna to the ceiling, and as he fell to the ground she wasted no time in swinging the beam around to hit one of the two Cardassians who had been administering Tahna's torture. The first one fell, but not before the other two Cardassians in the room could react. The nearest of them, the one she had not anticipated, managed to grab her, and the other relieved her of her phaser, though she kicked and screamed with all of her might.

"Tahna!" she cried. "Los!" But he lay completely still on the floor where he had fallen, apparently dead.

"You killed him," one of the soldiers said cruelly. "He

was connected to a life support system, and you put him into shock."

"No!" she screamed.

"I told you she'd come after him," the other Cardassian laughed to his companion. "You owe me twenty *lek*s." Kira could feel his groping fingers beginning to travel to places where she could not tolerate them. She screamed louder, but Tahna still did not move, and Kira bit her tongue as the Cardassians continued to hatefully explore her with their hands, tugging at her clothes. Through their sick laughter, she tasted hot salt in her mouth, unsure if it was blood or tears.

The lights flickered before they went out entirely, the Cardassians loudly expressing their angry confusion, and Kira managed to kick one of her assailants hard enough to make him lose his grip on her. The other Cardassian only held her tighter in the blind darkness—until a burst of blue light suddenly filled the chamber, and there was a loud *thunk* as the soldier who still held her fell to the floor, dragging Kira with him and pinning her to the floor. She struggled to free herself from the weight of his body while she heard some crashing and struggling, the other Cardassian shouting before more phaser fire lit up the room, and then, as suddenly as they had gone out, the lights were powered back up. They were dimmer than before, humming noisily, apparently driven by a crude backup system—but at least Kira could see again.

Breathless, Kira looked around the room to see that Tahna had weakly crawled to his knees. Near the doorway stood the emaciated woman Kira had freed just a few moments before, a crazed, haunted expression lighting up her eyes, and a smoking phaser—presumably Kira's, snatched from the table where the Cardassians had left it—clutched tightly in her hand.

"Let's get out of here," Kira said, and helped Tahna to

his feet. He leaned on her heavily, barely able to stand. The other woman reached out one terribly thin and dirty arm to steady him, and together, the two women dragged him up the spiral staircase, and outside toward freedom.

Odo could find no words. He watched his forensic analyst go over the scene of the explosion for the third time, apparently trying to find any extraneous evidence that would point to a conclusion other than what they were all thinking—that Odo had condemned the wrong men to death for the attempt on Dukat's life. Not that it would have mattered much to the Cardassians—Bajorans were all guilty of something. Odo had found this assumption to be almost universally held by his Cardassian cohorts. But the shape-shifter had always done his best to refute this prejudice, and he worried now that he had failed.

This new explosion, which had taken place on the Promenade earlier today, had missed Dukat and his entourage by such a narrow margin that the sleeve of Dukat's uniform had been singed, his hand badly burned; but his life had been spared yet again, thanks to one of his soldiers, who had managed to get the prefect out of the way just before the device was detonated. It was, curiously, the same soldier who had saved the prefect during the last assassination crisis, but Odo quickly surmised that it was because Dukat had specifically chosen this man to accompany him on an almost daily basis. At least, that was the conclusion that Odo wanted to be true.

"Can you give me a preliminary picture of what the evidence is suggesting to you, Dal Kaer?" Odo solemnly inquired of the analyst.

Kaer's mouth was an unmoving line as he faced the security chief, and then he spoke. "Whoever committed this crime was apparently in league with our three suspects from earlier in the week," he said without emotion.

Odo nodded. "A fair conclusion," he allowed, though he was thinking something very different. "It is a shame then," he added, "that our three suspects have been executed already. Otherwise they could perhaps help us with this investigation."

Kaer looked taken aback. Odo had not intended to let so much apparent bitterness show in his voice, and he modified his tone. "But there is no reason to speculate on lost opportunities," he said. "We must make the most of the evidence that we have access to."

"Indeed. I'll have Gil Letra round up a sampling of our usual troublemakers from the Bajoran sector and he can begin questioning them right away."

Odo nodded, as he normally did to such a suggestion, but an overwhelming possibility had him deeply troubled—the possibility that Dukat's current Cardassian adjutant somehow knew about the bombings, for it was simply too uncanny, in Odo's mind, that the soldier would have known to push Dukat out of the way just before the explosion erupted. Dukat would reject the hypothesis immediately; Odo knew there was little point in even suggesting such a thing. After all, several identical bombings had occurred in Musilla Province recently, and Dukat would be sure to point out that his assistant could hardly be associated with those incidents. But Odo also knew that it was not unheard of for Cardassians to occasionally assist in Bajoran mischief, for a large enough bribe, or for their own political gain.

Odo wondered if perhaps this soldier had caught wind of a terrorist plot, agreed to help carry it out in exchange for some favor or bribe, and then saved his prefect at the last moment so he would appear to be a hero. It was not beyond the realm of possibility. However, Dukat would never accept the idea. This case would likely remain open, just like that of the Bajoran chemist who had been killed.

Dukat didn't care about justice so much as he cared about making an appropriate display of punishment to keep his workers in line, and though Odo wanted to deny that truth, it was in cases such as this one that it became impossible to ignore. That he was an instrument in carrying out Dukat's draconian policies was troubling, to say the least.

The shape-shifter returned to his office to log the evidence into the security database, for all the good it would do anyone. He planned to regenerate immediately after his business with this case was completed, but as soon as he entered his office, he saw that it would be impossible. The Ferengi child was waiting for him.

"Chief," Nog implored him, rising to his feet. "My uncle says to tell you that he's dropping the charges against my father. Please—you've got to let him out."

"Then why isn't your uncle here?" Odo said, brushing past the small alien.

"He's too busy tending his bar. He tried to contact you, but you were unavailable—"

"I'm in the middle of a high-profile investigation," Odo said. "I don't have time to resolve these petty family squabbles right now. Tell your uncle that if he wants his brother released, he'll have to come to my office and fill out the paperwork himself."

"But . . . chief . . . there's nobody to tend the bar, and I thought you might—"

"Quark might have thought of that inconvenience when he had your father arrested," Odo said irritably. Of course, it was all utter foolishness. Once again, the Ferengi were having a pointless tiff, and once again, Odo had been dragged into it. This time, Quark was accusing his brother of attacking a customer, a claim Odo found to be unlikely, but the Kobheerian freight officer substantiated the claims, and Odo had no choice but to put Rom in a holding cell until he could be processed and fined.

The young Ferengi left the office, clearly upset and concerned for his father, and Odo began the process of entering the latest data into the files on the explosion from this afternoon. But something was troubling him—something more than the obvious discrepancies regarding the apparent assassination attempt. He was bothered by the false claims Quark and the Kobheerian captain were laying against Rom. Though it was the sort of thing he usually paid the very least amount of attention to, his thoughts persisted in suggesting that Quark was up to something. There was a pattern in these arrests of Rom, and while Odo might be naïve, he was not an idiot.

Odo was tired, and his body was practically quavering with the desire to liquefy, but he decided his hunch was worth a second look. He made his way back to the holding cells, where several imprisoned Bajorans called out to him from behind the force fields. He disabled the field that held the Ferengi, who was sitting silently by himself in the corner, apparently trying to avoid any interaction with the angry Bajorans in the vicinity. He did not immediately realize that the force field had been deactivated, and Odo was forced to call to him.

"Rom," Odo addressed the other man. "Come into my office, please. I have a few questions for you."

"Uh. Okay," the Ferengi replied. "But I already told you. I didn't hit anyone."

"Yes, I heard you the first time. But I'm curious to know—why are you lying for your brother again?"

Rom looked simultaneously astonished and terrified, his mouth falling open to expose his jagged teeth. "That's not true, Odo!" he cried. "I don't know anything—just ask Quark!"

"Yes, so he's told me, on more than one occasion," Odo said, folding his arms and tapping his fingers restlessly against his elbow. The urge to regenerate was becoming a need.

The Ferengi continued to jabber, but Odo already knew what the truth was, for it had happened twice before. Odo would not play along this time. "Your brother and the Kobheerian were conducting some sort of transaction."

"No!" Rom said stoutly.

"The Kobheerian is gone now. Did your brother have you arrested so you couldn't interfere? Or was it because he simply wanted to divert attention away from himself?"

"I don't know anything about any transaction," Rom insisted. "I don't know why he had me arrested. I was just—"

"Yes, how could you have known what your brother was up to, when you were locked in here?"

"That's right," Rom said hopefully, though he didn't seem to understand where Odo's logic was going. Odo knew he had hit on the correct scenario, though there wasn't any way to prove it. He wasn't sure if he was quite so concerned with proving anything anymore, at least, not today.

"It worked the first time he did it, which was shortly after you accidentally implicated him with that business that got him fined for dealing in illegal Jibetian goods. It worked the second time he did it, last month, when the Boslic freighter captain was spending so much time in the bar. But this is the last time he tries it. I want you to be sure and tell him that, Rom. I'm dismissing your case. You're free to go."

The Ferengi did not even stop to thank him; he only scurried out onto the Promenade and back to his brother's crooked establishment. It had occurred to Odo numerous times that if Quark's bar were eliminated from the station, an exceptional percentage of the petty complaints that clogged his arrest roster would simply cease to exist. But then, he considered, the station's residents would find some other means of causing trouble, and anyway, Odo did not have the authority to make such a suggestion.

In fact, how much authority did he really have here? He could release an unfairly accused Ferengi waiter, but beyond that, he was simply adhering to a rigid set of rules laid out by the prefect—rigid for anyone but Dukat himself. And within the rigidity of those laws, Odo had begun to discover that there were many curious instances in which following Cardassian policy to the letter resulted in the conviction of innocent men—as in the case of Rom's frequent incarcerations at the behest of his brother . . . or the case of the three executed Bajorans.

He pushed away the latter thought yet again, for there was nothing he could do to resolve it. It was time for him to regenerate, and he went to retrieve the vessel where he could be safely contained in his natural state. But before he could be lulled into comfortable senselessness, he recalled some of the incidents from his days on Bajor—days when he had decided that what the Cardassians were doing on this world was wrong in its entirety. Odo had believed it until he had come to Terok Nor, and had met several Cardassians whom he thought he could relate to, on some level. Their laws had seemed sensible to him at the time—comfortably well-defined, unlike the Bajorans, for whom just about anything could fall under the definition of "good." But now he was forced to rethink his assessment of the Cardassians once again, and he was revisiting his previous ideas of the so-called annexation more often than he wanted to.

If it was true that the occupation was wrong, then could any of the Cardassians' actions, their laws, their decisions—could any of it possibly be right? Or must it all be rejected as further extension of their evil? Odo had to acknowledge that he didn't know anymore, that the definition of what was right as it was given by a Bajoran terrorist, or his friend Russol, or the prefect, or the Ferengi bartender, all definitions seemed to intersect, and yet still contradict. As an outsider, Odo should have been in the perfect position, as Russol had said, from which to judge what was truly just. But it was becoming clearer to him all the time—he was not really an outsider at all.

OCCUPATION YEAR FORTY-ONE

✦   ✦   ✦

2368 (Terran Calendar)

19

Tahna Los always appreciated a good excuse to shimmy through the tunnels and speak to Nerys, though Shakaar was usually hovering over them while they talked. The cell leader was ever trying to project his "brotherly" vibe, but Tahna knew better. Edon was a notorious womanizer, and though he hadn't made any advances toward Nerys that Tahna knew about, it was only a matter of time. Anyway, Edon had been bickering with Biran and Jouvirna more than usual lately—trifling over "ethics" as always. Tahna was thankful that on this day, Edon was off in another cavern with Mobara, looking over some piece of equipment or other.

"What do you want now, Tahna?" Nerys griped. She hadn't been doing anything in particular, as far as Tahna could tell. She held a padd in one hand—she had probably been reading something. But she always had to make a show of being annoyed by him. In truth, Tahna welcomed it. After the last time he had been captured by the Cardassians, Kira had been awkward with him for a while, apparently out of guilt—or pity. But now that time had passed, Nerys's manner with him was starting to drift back toward the familiar, and Tahna couldn't have been happier that she was short with him today. "Don't tell me the grid is already back online," she said.

The cells had made numerous attempts to permanently knock out the sensor towers, but the Cardassians were always quick to repair them. Every time they went back online, Kira and Tahna began a wager to see which cell would be first to take them out again. It was unfair, since the Shakaar cell had twice the members of the Kohn-Ma, and pointless, since the two cells were practically converged at this point, but Tahna felt it was useful to have the incentive—especially since he had grown so familiar with what could happen when you got caught.

"They are," Tahna told her, "but there's more to it than that, this time. I've just gotten my hands on a schematic." He pulled an isolinear rod out of his jerkin. "Trentin Fala brought it to us, stolen from the Cardassian records office in Tempasa. Blueprints."

Kira frowned. "What's the target?"

Tahna smiled broadly. "The grind itself—at the source! We won't have to waste our time taking out the towers over and over again, waiting for the spoonheads to just reinstall them every single time. We can sabotage the telemetry processing system on Terok Nor—"

Kira interrupted him. "Terok Nor!" she exclaimed, shaking her head. "No. No, Tahna, I'm never going back to that station. Ever."

"Don't be stupid, Nerys. If we could shut down that grid for good, then we'll never have to argue about knocking out those towers ever again. Anyway, you've already been there, you know your way around—and you're the only one of us who can beat the grid long enough to figure out a way to get smuggled onto a penal transport."

Kira interrupted him again by snatching the rod from his hands.

"Watch it with that thing!" he warned her as she jammed the isolinear rod into her padd. "It's not like I can just ask Fala for another copy!"

Kira ignored him as she looked over the schematic, her lips moving slightly as she read. "I'm not going to Terok Nor," she said without looking up. Tahna started to interrupt, but Kira spoke over him. "I have another idea," she said. "I know someone on the station who can help us."

Tahna shook his head. "No, Nerys. There are only a handful of resistance people left on the station, not enough to—"

"The person I'm talking about isn't in the resistance," she said, handing him back the isolinear rod.

"Well then, how do you propose to . . . ?" Tahna stopped after seeing the look on Kira's face. She could convey her emotions with a single look better than anyone Tahna had ever encountered, and he wasn't ashamed to admit that she intimidated him a bit. She intimidated nearly everyone, even those who were older than she was, though it hadn't always been so. She was a far cry now from the skinny and eager little girl who had joined the resistance over a decade ago.

"He's not in the resistance," she said. "He's in security."

Tahna looked at her doubtfully. "In security?"

Kira finally smiled. "He's the chief, actually."

Keeve Falor did not often have reason to contact Bajor anymore. He knew that Kalem Apren and others on the surface had been trying to coerce him into helping them with their grandiose plans for a very long time, but Keeve couldn't see much point to it. It was all he could do just to keep the people on his adopted world from starvation; he had very little reason to fool around with subspace communication system anymore.

But today was different. Something had happened in the past week, and Bajor needed to know it. In Keeve's estimation, Kalem Apren *was* Bajor, being one of the very few former politicians from his homeworld that Keeve still trusted. Keeve had come to the old hangar on Valo II, the place where ships had once arrived and departed with some measure of regularity—but it was no longer like that here, or anywhere else on this world, for fuel was an import that the people of Valo II could not afford to squander without sufficient cause. The Bajorans of Valo II used the hangar for storage of salvaged parts, but it could also function as a communications center if necessary. A few of these ships still had functional communications equipment, and now that the long-range relays on Derna had been repaired, it was possible to send messages to Bajor, if the need ever arose. It seemed to Keeve Falor that the need had finally arisen.

"Apren," Keeve spoke into the pickup, adjusting for interference. He hoped the signal would be strong enough. As he tapped the interface, he could pick up bits of chatter, both Cardassian and Bajoran, coming from Jeraddo, from Valo III, from Terok Nor, from Bajor herself. He fine-tuned the connection when he recognized the Bajoran signal code on the comm's battered readout.

"Apren," Keeve spoke the name again. "Kalem Apren. This is an attempt to reach Kalem Apren, of the Kendra Valley." The channel was almost certainly wide open and traceable, but there was nothing that could be done about it—and it scarcely mattered, since the Cardassians already knew the piece of news that Keeve intended to pass along.

"*This is Jaro Essa of Kendra Valley,*" a voice finally acknowledged. "*Who calls?*"

"Jaro, it's Keeve Falor. I am trying to reach Kalem Apren, but I don't have the specific channel."

"*Keeve! I will bring Kalem here! He will be glad to hear your voice!*"

The line went silent but for a smattering of interference and a faint wavering suggestion of another conversation coming in on a similar channel. Keeve waited patiently until someone else spoke, someone out of breath.

"This is Kalem Apren," a crackling voice finally dispatched from Keeve's aged system. *"Falor, is that you?"*

"It is me, Apren."

"I am pleased to hear that you are still among the living! Tell me, how are things on Valo II?"

"Difficult," Keeve said grimly, unaccustomed to the idea of friendly small talk—but then, Apren did always have a talent for being a bit glib, a talent that was helpful in his political career. "I have contacted you, Apren, because of a recent incident in which I was put in touch with a Federation captain."

"The Federation!" Apren exclaimed. *"Was this a fruitful encounter for us?"*

"I would like to hope so," Keeve replied, but he knew he did not sound optimistic—for he wasn't. "You must know that I am not especially hopeful where they are concerned . . . however, I did feel that this encounter was relevant enough to pass the word on to you. The captain with whom I spoke was able to get a firsthand look at the colony here. He had a better idea, I think, of what we are dealing with than Jas Holza has ever given him—"

"This is very relevant!" Apren replied with enthusiasm. *"Things have changed now, Falor. Surely the Federation can see that our current Bajoran government is nothing but an ineffective figurehead. They must have enough sense to deduce what has happened here."*

"They spoke of diplomacy," Keeve said, "But we both know where that will lead us—into more of the same. You know how the Federation operates. I suppose I wish it were otherwise, but ultimately, I am skeptical."

"You always were," Apren replied. The static was getting markedly worse. *"The Fed . . . ration . . . id they leave you . . . means . . . contact . . . them?"*

"Only through Jas Holza, but he is reluctant to jeopardize his own standing with the Federation," Keeve replied.

"Any . . . ther way to reach . . . m?"

Keeve considered. "I could relay a message to the border colonies, which will eventually find its way to the Federation," Keeve said. "But . . . I am not sure what we could say to them to make them change their strategy to a proactive one. I imagine they intend to simply discuss it among themselves before choosing to do nothing—just as they did fifty years ago."

"There was protocol that . . . required to follow," Apren said.

"Federation protocol is exactly the reason we cannot rely on them," Keeve said.

"What . . . bout J . . . olza. He once sp . . . e . . . bout . . . pons."

"Your signal is getting weaker, Apren. Could you repeat that?"

"I can't . . . you're . . . could . . ."

"Too much interference," Keeve said, though it was futile.

". . . if . . . contact . . . Nechayev . . ."

Frustrated, Keeve disconnected the comm, deciding to wait until later to place another call. But he'd said all that needed to be said on the subject, and he doubted anything would come of it. It might someday prove beneficial to be on the Federation's radar, but then, it had been fifty years since the Federation was here last, and they had done nothing to help Bajor in all that time. Keeve himself had kept in touch with a few Federation people, who had tried to learn something of the Cardassians in the Valo system. The reconnaissance had eventually gone awry, thanks to a single blunder on the part of a teenager named Ro Laren, and Keeve had lost touch with those people. He shook his head, remembering the past version of Ro Laren, the little girl who had single-handedly managed to sever his

ties to the Federation. Strange, that it had been Ro to connect them once more, just these few days ago. In his wild-
est dreams, he would not have imagined that she would
have gone on to join the Federation, and yet, there she had
been, wearing the uniform of Starfleet.

It was thanks to Ro that her Captain Picard had managed to come through in an ugly situation with a resistance
fighter named Orta, an accomplishment that had surprised
Keeve not a little. Keeve had thought he'd seen the last of
that girl just before she'd run away—and there was a part of
him that wished he *had* seen the last of her. In all his life, he
had never met a more volatile teenager than she had been.
If she was going to be the person to represent Bajor to the
larger galaxy, Keeve had serious reservations that anything
useful could come of it. No, he decided, as he left the old
hangar, it would be unproductive to invest any hope in this
situation. He had not given up hope entirely—but he *had*
given up hope in any possibility of rescue from the United
Federation of Planets.

Gran Tolo walked along the Bajoran side of the Promenade,
keeping his eyes out for anyone who might pose a threat.
There were the Cardassians, of course, but there were also
the more insidious enemies: Bajoran pickpockets and collaborating snitches, and, of course, the shape-shifting chief
of security. Today, though, it was the shape-shifter that Gran
sought, for he'd received a message from a resistance cell
that insisted the so-called constable could help them.

Gran stopped in front of a shop that sold used clothing
and rags, trying to look inconspicuous while he waited for
the shape-shifter. He picked up a lone shoe from a rack of
mismatched odds and ends in front of the little store, pretending to inspect it though he had no need for a single
shoe, and even if he had, he couldn't have afforded it—very
few Bajorans could have. This shop was almost certainly

a front for something else, but whether the Cardassians endorsed it or not, Gran didn't know. It was difficult to trust anyone in this place.

He dropped the shoe as it began to shimmer in his hand, and he took a step back, realizing that he'd just been examining the chief of security.

"Hello." The shape-shifter addressed him in a slightly condescending manner. Gran swallowed.

"I'm Gran Tolo," he said uncertainly. The shape-shifter's expression suggested that Gran was about to make a terrible mistake.

"How very nice to meet you," the shape-shifter said with a trace of irritation. "I'm a very busy man, Mr. Gran, and I'd appreciate it if you'd inform me as to why you've asked to see me."

Gran dropped his voice, so nervous he couldn't remember exactly what he was supposed to say. "I'm bringing you a message from the resistance movement on the surface."

Odo looked more annoyed. "I have no interest in the goings-on of the resistance movement," he said sharply. "My job is to maintain order, not foster chaos. Is it possible you have me confused with someone else, Mr. Gran?"

Gran shook his head, though he feared that very possibility. He was beginning to panic, still unsure of what it was he was supposed to say. "I'm sorry, sir, it's just that I was told you might sometimes help . . . *certain* Bajorans."

"I could arrest you right now for that implication," Odo said, and as he spoke, his hand extended, became a tentacle that wrapped itself around Gran's wrists. Gran pulled, but he found the restraint to be impervious to his own strength.

"Kira Nerys!" Gran blurted, remembering at last. "That's the name I'm supposed to tell you! She said you—"

Odo hesitated for a brief moment, and then the tentacle unwound itself from Gran's hands, melting back into an arm. The shape-shifter spoke. "I will speak to Kira," he said, "but I will not speak to you."

"I can give you a communication code," Gran said, not sure if it was yet prudent to feel relief. "She's expecting your call."

Odo's tone was not quite so nasty now. "You will accompany me to my office."

Gran was still nervous, but he knew he mustn't falter now. The resistance movement depended on him, and if this plan could be carried out, it would strike a significant blow to the Cardassians. It was worth the risk of a few hours in the brig—or worse, really. He reminded himself of this repeatedly as he followed the constable back down the Promenade, and toward the security office, hoping hard that he wasn't about to find out what the inside of a cell looked like.

Dukat had been up all night in ops; there had been a situation down in the fusion core—an imbalance in the reaction chambers that threatened to blow out the entire ion energy network, if not for the quick thinking of the chief of engineering. *Perhaps too quick,* Dukat thought. Dalin Kedat's talent for keeping Terok Nor functioning at optimum levels seemed exceptional, but Dukat sometimes wondered if he succeeded in creating that impression merely by surrounding himself with lesser men, who, while not incompetent, were certainly far less efficient when not under Kedat's direct supervision.

But while the initial crisis was resolved with relative ease, investigation into the cause led to Kedat's discovering evidence of sabotage in the generator control system, necessitating an all-night search for more signs of tampering. Odo was of course called in immediately, and Dukat wound up virtually chained to the ops situation table as he spent the night monitoring the progress of the enineering and security teams. In the end, the cause was found to be a time-delayed software virus, one that apparently had been entered into the system months ago and remained undetected until it suddenly went active. Purging the system of the malicious code would be relatively easy, according to Kedat. Finding the saboteur after so much time and turnover would be next to impossible, according to Odo.

Dukat was thoroughly exhausted when a call came through from Legate Kell, demanding privacy. Dukat reluctantly climbed the short staircase to his office, letting the doors close behind him and experiencing the persistent ache of a restless night as he seated himself behind his desk.

"Legate," he said.

"*Gul,*" the Legate replied, seeming excited enough about something that he scarcely noticed the resigned rudeness in the prefect's tone. "*I have lately been thinking a great deal about the current treaty with the Federation. This will give us a chance to re-direct some of Cardassia's resources to the B'hava'el system. It will require careful planning on your part, to see that those resources are utilized properly.*"

Dukat was insulted; he scarcely needed the Legate to point out his job to him, and it stung him that nobody seemed to recall that he himself had suggested a Federation treaty some time ago, with this very result in mind. But he merely smiled. "Of course."

"*I strongly advise you to reorganize the Bajoran cabinet. With more troops in place on Bajor, you will have the opportunity to finally improve the situation on your host world. But unless you give the Bajorans some indication that you actually mean to change your policies—*"

"My Bajoran cabinet has been loyal and effective," Dukat interrupted. He had no desire to replace Kubus Oak or any of the others—not now, and not ever. He had always assumed that when those fools finally died off, it would be best to just leave those seats empty, or fill them with Cardassians.

Dukat had lately come to consider the bigger picture of the Bajoran venture, extending much further than the span of his life. When the older generation of Bajorans—those who actually had some memory of their world before the annexation—died out, Cardassia would begin to enjoy full-scale success on this world. In the meantime, they would have to continue to put down Bajoran revolts as they emerged, developing better weapons if they could, and occasionally accepting minor setbacks. But in the end, it would all prove worthwhile, he believed, for the next generation of Cardassians, who could expect to colonize this world permanently. The Bajorans would fall in line once they began to accept the natural superiority of Cardassian ideals. Of course, Dukat could not put voice to his prediction, for he knew that he might not live to see it come true—and it would never come true if the Detapa Council accused him of buying time to cater to his own agenda. No, the civilian government wanted immediate results, without recognizing the long-term benefits of waiting for larger returns on their Bajoran investment. Dukat believed that those returns could be tremendous, but they would require patience, something that had always been in short supply at the Detapa Council.

"Secretary Kubus is the most loyal and effective Bajoran I'll ever meet," Dukat said. "I have no desire to replace him with someone who is likely to ply me with radical ideas—or worse, stab me in the back."

"If you recall, you once told me that Basso Tromac was also loyal and effective—and he disappeared, didn't he?"

"He was likely killed by someone in ore processing with a vendetta," Dukat said, though he feared another possibility. Of course, it was true that Basso's disappearance had occurred right about the same time that Nerys had slipped from Dukat's careful grasp . . . but he preferred to think of that incident as little as possible.

"If your Bajoran adjutant could be murdered on your own space station, the crime so perfectly covered up as to provide neither body nor suspect, then you may wish to reconsider your level of control there," Kell said. *"Perhaps you need a new chief of security, as well."*

Dukat glowered in response. "The shape-shifter does a better job than Thrax Sa'kat ever did," he said. "Besides, the last thing we want is for Odo to fall sympathetic to the Bajoran cause. The best place for him is here, where I can keep an eye on him."

Kell snorted. *"Keep your shape-shifter, then. But I stand by my recommendation for a new cabinet. You would do best to simply execute the current Bajoran officials. Accuse them of disloyalty, and then make a public spectacle of it. You could then ensure full cooperation from whoever replaces them."*

Dukat straightened out his features. "I will consider it," he said, though he had no intention of doing any such thing; he was merely hoping to get rid of the old man so he could get some sleep. His wish was quickly granted, as the legate signed off, and Dukat wasted no time in alerting the duty officer in ops that he would take no more calls for the day. He had already decided against paying a call on his newest Bajoran mistress, though the relationship was very young and she had already proven a bit petulant; there were times when sleep took precedence over virtually everything else, even for the prefect.

The woman could speak to him only via voice transmission, but Odo still felt quite certain that it was really her. It had been the sound of Kira's voice that had finally brought her identity back to him those few years ago, had made him remember the incident at the Bajoran Institute of Science. It was there, in Mora's laboratory, where he had first heard the sound of her voice, from the tank where he regenerated. He had experienced a strange, unfamiliar desire to listen to her voice, to be near her. He remembered it well even now, as he spoke to her on his computer console from Terok Nor.

"So, will you help me, Constable?"

"I don't know," he said. "I still don't understand why you've come to me."

"Because!" she said, clearly exasperated. *"You helped me before, Odo. I trusted you then, and I want to trust you now. I believe that ultimately—despite your position, I mean—you are on our side."*

"I'm on nobody's side," Odo said firmly.

"If that's true, then why did you help me before? Why not just arrest me?"

"Because," he said, not immediately sure how to follow it up. "I . . . suppose I regarded you as an individual, in need of help. It wasn't your cause that provoked my sympathy, it was just . . . it was just . . ."

"What?"

"I don't know," Odo said. He really didn't know. It was true that he had helped her once, and it was therefore true that he had helped the Bajoran resistance movement once, too. But he'd been much less experienced then. He had been reacting to his immediate circumstances without thinking through the consequences.

"You're lying," the woman said. *"You knew the Cardassians were wrong then, and you know it now."*

"Do I?" Odo said, trying to sound threatening, but it fell flat.

"Yes, you do. You're not one of them, Odo. You're one of us."

"What does being one of 'them' entail, exactly?"

"It entails being . . . evil. Being a thief. A lazy, bullying thief. You're not like that."

Odo had the distinct sense that she was trying to

manipulate him with this kind of talk, but the trouble was, it was working. "No," he finally said. "I'm not like that."

"Then you'll help us?"

Odo nodded, though he knew she could not see it; the nod was more for himself than it was for her. "Yes," he said.

"Good," she said, accepting his acquiescence without ceremony. *"Your role is twofold, but most of it will not be in any way out of character for you. The primary thing we need for you to do is to distract Dukat. Do you think you can do that?"*

Odo almost laughed. In fact, it was often all he could do to get rid of Dukat, when the man sought company. "I think I can," he told her.

After the transmission had ended, Odo second-guessed the security of the line. Nobody had been listening, as far as he could tell, but he knew that if someone meant to overhear, there wasn't much he could do. He suspected that Dukat didn't really trust him, despite the man's repeated attempts to strike up confidential chats. Now that Odo had so few allies on the station—Russol was long gone, and Odo had made few friends on the Bajoran side—he had to constantly watch his back. Fortunately, for a shape-shifter, watching one's back was an easy affair.

Why *was* he helping this Bajoran woman? Was it simply because he was intrigued by her, the first Bajoran woman he had ever encountered, so long ago at the institute, or did it go deeper than that? He supposed he had never really been able to sympathize with Dukat's perspective, had never agreed with the Cardassian occupation in general, especially not since he had finally begun to understand the many facets of it. And yet, he had continued on at this station, with his job in security, sometimes staying true to his own code of ethics, and occasionally submitting to Dukat's version of things just in order to maintain simplicity and stay beneath the radar of the Cardassians here. Odo didn't want to leave Terok Nor—it came down to that. For he still hoped he would someday learn news of his own people, and he supposed this was the best place in the B'hava'el system to do that.

But now he risked it all—and why? He did not believe that it was strictly out of loyalty to whatever imagined relationship he had with Kira Nerys. No, it went deeper than that, he supposed. While he had often told himself that it had nothing to do with him, he had pretended often enough that he did not notice the disparity between Bajoran and Cardassian. Maybe now it was time to do something about it.

Cardassia City was atypically bleak and overcast. In the old times, it was said that portions of what was now the Western Hemisphere had been dotted all over with thick, lush forests, heavy with rainfall. But an atmospheric calamity of uncertain origin had let to centuries of drought, and the forests had all been shortsightedly cut down. The soil beneath the fertile canopy had, after a single generation of unsustainable farming, withdrawn from deep, silty black topsoil to the parched sands that were so well-known beyond the periphery of the cities. Desert now, where it had once been rain forest.

If only my ancestors had known better, Kutel Esad thought to himself. The dense, verdant forests that had once existed on Cardassia Prime were all but forgotten. Historians and archaeologists had an inkling of what the old landscape had looked like, and of course, the Oralians knew—because it was described in the Recitations. But most modern Cardassians were entirely unaware of the paradise their planet had once been.

Esad walked for a long time, making his way through the city's orderly sectors, navigating the tangled streets until he came to a particular residential neighborhood. Esad had been to this part of town only a few times; most of his business was conducted in the center of the city, and he lived in the area where the Paldar Sector met Tarlak, near the headquarters of the Obsidian Order.

Here in Coranum Sector, with its old, stately, and grand houses, Esad found the residence he was looking for, climbed the many steps to the front entrance, and knocked politely. He was greeted almost immediately by a servant of the Reyar family.

"I have business with Yannik Reyar," he said, and the servant, a young man, stepped aside with a deferential bow. Of course the family's staff would all have an idea of what sort of "business" was conducted by Yannik Reyar, though it would have been unheard of for an agent to actually make a showing at his own residence. Still, Esad had no doubt the servants gossiped among themselves about any unknown visitors. Little did they know that an agent of the Obsidian Order worked among them—in fact, Reyar himself did not even know it.

Esad was greeted in the foyer by Reyar after a short time. He was a tall man with carefully trimmed hair and expensive clothes. His job came with a great deal of risk, and for that, he was well paid. He scrutinized Esad with a quizzical look. Reyar and Esad had never met, at least not in person, and no doubt Yannik was trying to place him from the scattered communiqués that had been delivered from the office of Enabran Tain in decades past.

"Do I . . . know you?" Reyar finally asked.

"Sir, I am here as a friend, to give you information regarding your daughter."

Reyar's face darkened. "My daughter," he said softly. "Perhaps you had better come with me." He gestured down the hall to a darkened, windowless chamber, surrounded on all sides by stacks of isolinear rods and old-fashioned books. Esad surmised this was Reyar's personal office.

Reyar closed the door behind him, and Esad sat down, wasting no time in getting to the point. "Mr. Reyar, I know you have been looking for your daughter for some time, after she failed to make her scheduled appearance at the University of Culat . . ."

"It was Dost Abor," the man said, without hesitation. "No matter what lengths the Order has gone to to cover it up, I know it was Abor." He struggled to keep a handle on his obvious rage. "You are going to tell me that it was her lover, whoever he was, but I am no fool, sir. I know it was—"

"I am here to confirm your suspicions," Esad said. "Indeed, Dost Abor is responsible for your daughter's death."

"Her . . . death . . ." Reyar said, sinking deeper into his chair. For a terrible moment, the man could not speak, and as the shock wore away from his face, he fought tears, fought them valiantly and in vain. Esad expected this reaction, but he had not prepared himself for it. He looked away, giving the man a moment to compose himself again.

"So," Reyar said, choking on his words, "you have come to betray your colleague. Do you do this for revenge? Has the man done something to you, Mr. . . ." he stopped, realizing that Esad had not introduced himself.

"No," Esad said. "In all honesty, Mr. Reyar, I come to do what I believe is right. I acted as adjutant to Enabran Tain for many years, and I was often forced to do things that compromised my own values—for what I perceived to be good reasons. But the ultimate fate of your daughter is something with which I cannot come to peaceful terms. I felt that perhaps . . . in at least letting you know of her true fate . . ."

"You could absolve yourself?" Reyar's tone indicated that he did not think so.

Esad hesitated. "Something like that," he said. It was true

that Kalisi Reyar had tried to betray Astraea's location, but Esad himself was partially responsible for dragging Kalisi into the matter in the first place—for it was he who had brought her to the facility at Valo VI, the first time Abor had questioned her. For his role in it, Esad had always felt unsettled, that there was still a loose end that he could never hope to reweave.

There was a silence. Seeing the anger that was now replacing the other man's sorrow, Esad thought he'd perhaps do best to leave. But before he stood, he added one more thing. "You may recall that Dost Abor was stationed at Valo VI for many years," he said. "But that is no longer the case."

"No?" Reyar said, looking expectantly to Esad for the rest.

Esad wasn't sure if this was the right thing to do at all—in fact, he suspected it was not. But something within him insisted that he do it, whether to shift the blame away from himself, or whether he still had too much of the vengeful agent in him, he did not know. "You see . . . I put in a recommendation for Abor . . . that he be moved from Valo VI, and my praise has finally come to fruition for him. He is stationed right here, on Cardassia Prime," Esad said. "In fact, he lives in the Coranum sector."

"Here?" Yannik whispered. "The man who murdered my daughter is a stone's throw from my own home?"

"Yes," Esad said, keeping his own voice low. "He has assumed a new identity for his current post, per the orders of the new Obsidian Order head."

"A fool," mumbled Reyar, and Esad silently agreed with him. Not everyone could be the genius Enabran Tain had been. Tain was not a good man, that was absolutely certain, but he was a brilliant man.

"Dost Abor now calls himself Ran Lotor," Esad went on. "He is posing as an educator."

"Ran Lotor," Esad repeated. "I don't know him."

"Well," Esad said, standing up, "he will not be difficult to find, especially not for a man with military resources at his disposal. Perhaps you would like to go and . . . introduce yourself?"

Reyar stood as well. "I think it is a fine idea," he said.

Esad did not linger, not only because he wanted to leave the man in peace, but because he was still not entirely comfortable with what he had set in motion today. As an Oralian, he was committed to a certain set of beliefs, but as a Cardassian, sometimes his personal feelings overwhelmingly overrode them. Esad was no stranger to this conflict, for his entire profession put his faith in constant compromise. As the servant let him out, he had to be satisfied with remembering that he was a complicated man, as all men were, and that his own personal feelings regarding a matter might sometimes take precedence over what he knew was right—and that sometimes the things he knew to be right could directly contradict each other. Today, he had chosen to act as a Cardassian.

20

Odo was making his regular rounds on the Bajoran side of the Promenade when another man fell in step with him, somewhat more conspicuously than Odo might have liked. He told himself there was nothing suspicious about having a friendly chat with some random acquaintance, Bajoran or Cardassian—though he was sure Dukat would have preferred that he keep his friends in the latter category.

The man spoke under his breath, which Odo felt made their interaction all the more noticeable. "Kira tells me you have agreed to speak to me."

"Yes," Odo said shortly, trying to remember this man's name. He thought it was Gran. "Let's do this quickly. I have other matters to attend to this evening."

"At the start of his shift tomorrow," the man said, "The chief of engineering is going to be implicated in some black-market dealings with a Bajoran here on the Promenade."

"Dalin Kedat?"

"Yes." Gran was impatient, though he struggled to maintain detached politeness. He seemed far from comfortable with this arrangement. "You'll arrest him and somehow make the charges stick. Kedat is one of three people on the station, including yourself, who have access to the surveillance feeds from the computer core, and we need him out of the way. After you arrest him, Terok Nor is going to start feeling very cold to the Cardassians."

"You're sabotaging the environmental control system," Odo surmised.

"For starters," Gran said. "It's going to look like a malfunction. We laid the groundwork for that aspect of the plan yesterday."

"How?"

"That doesn't matter—"

"It matters to *me*," Odo growled.

"Fine!" the Bajoran hissed. "We used the environmental control interface for the Ferengi's holodecks—bribed him to look the other way for ten minutes. Satisfied?"

Odo scoffed at the revelation of Quark's involvement in the scheme, but very likely the Ferengi didn't even know what the Bajorans were up to; the better to profit while maintaining plausible deniability, as he had done with Kira. "Go on."

"The cold won't do any real damage, but it'll keep most of the Cardassians uncomfortable and busy trying to fix the problem. No one will question it if you move security personnel away from the computer core in order to guard the work crews."

"What about Dukat?" Odo asked. He was the third man with access to the core's surveillance feeds.

"Once the temperature drops, you'll need to figure out a way to get Dukat out of his office and keep him occupied long enough for my man to enter the core and take out the detection grid. Twenty minutes is all he'll need."

"That's it?"

"That's it."

"Then it's not going to work," Odo said. "Dukat won't allow me to keep Kedat in custody during a mechanical failure—not on black market charges."

"We'll kill Kedat, then."

"No, you won't," Odo said sternly. There would be no more innocent blood on his hands. This resistance member might not understand that, but fortunately there was another reason simply assassinating Kedat wouldn't help them: "You murder a senior officer, and Terok Nor immediately goes on heightened alert."

"You have a better idea?"

"Actually I do, but it means you'll need to delay the environmental malfunction."

"How long?"

"Four hours following his arrest."

Gran swallowed. Clearly the idea of waiting so long to implement the next phase of the plan made him nervous. "All right," he said finally. "We'll do it your way, Constable." The man started to move away.

"Wait," Odo said, sudden doubt overtaking him. "What if something goes wrong? Do you have a signal, some way to let me know if you intend to abort?"

Gran snorted. "Dozens of things could go wrong, Mr. Odo. We just have to take the risk, and hope that everything will fall into place. There are no fail-safes."

"But—" Odo found himself very uncomfortable with this level of uncertainty. "If we are caught, several people will be executed, and you may not get another chance to disable the grid. Dukat will take pains to ensure that no more attempts can be carried out."

The Bajoran shrugged. "True," he said wryly. "But some things are worth taking risks for."

Odo remembered someone else saying something quite similar once—it was Sito Jaxa, the little girl who had boldly wandered into the forest with the belief that she could deliver information to the resistance all on her own. She had taken a terrible risk, and almost paid dearly for it. Odo was not much of a risk-taker himself. He wondered if he should back out, even as he was agreeing to the reckless terms of the plan.

He left the Bajoran man alone on the Promenade and continued on his rounds, knowing now that if he failed to keep up his end of the agreement, several Bajorans would be guaranteed a death sentence, and it would essentially be his own fault. On the other hand, if he adhered to the rule of law, he should turn in the man and all who were involved. He didn't especially want that on his conscience, though it wouldn't be the first time he'd assisted in putting a stop to Bajoran conspiracies. He felt as though something very new and very frightening had transpired within himself these past few days—but he took some comfort in knowing that it wasn't too late to change his mind. It wouldn't be too late until fourteen hundred hours tomorrow.

Astraea knew that because of her position, Thrax Sa'kat had long ago decided not to make any "inappropriate" overtures to her, and while she supposed it was meant to be respectful, she still wished it were otherwise. He had returned to Cardassia Prime from his assignment on Cardassia III, raving about a perceived threat to the shrine—to the last remaining copies of the Recitations of Oralius, the book she had sought so many years ago, that Glinn Sa'kat's family had kept safe for generations. And to the Orb, though she knew that he did not need to worry about that now.

"Glinn Sa'kat," she interrupted him. "I have spoken to Kutel Esad, and he insists that we will be safe here. I don't wish for you to concern yourself so."

"But there is unrest fast approaching on our world," Sa'kat insisted. "The situation with Bajor is unraveling, and it is only the beginning, Astraea. The Detapa Council is gaining power, which can only mean—"

"Changes," Astraea interrupted. "Favorable changes— you said so yourself."

"Yes," he sighed. "But a shift in governmental power will also mean violence."

"Oralius will keep us safe," she insisted.

"Astraea," he said, "I have been thinking of the Orb . . ."

"The Orb of Wisdom."

"Yes." He hesitated. "Perhaps Kutel was right when he said it was dangerous for us to have it. We don't need any more reason to be targeted by the Order, or anyone else. I confess, since bringing it here, I've not felt at peace . . ."

Astraea was relieved to hear him say it. "Then you will be happy to know that I have already arranged for the Orb to be transferred elsewhere, Glinn Sa'kat."

He looked up at her, his astonishment plain. "Transferred elsewhere? What do you mean?"

"You took it with you, Glinn Sa'kat."

He was speechless, and Astraea finished quickly.

"Your business on Cardassia III," she told him. "The Orb was with you when you traveled. I employed Kutel Esad to help me with this errand. We . . . had the Orb transferred to the cargo bay of your ship, and when it was unloaded—"

"Astraea!" Sa'kat cried. "Why would you do such a thing?"

"Because," she told him promptly, "because that Orb did not belong with us. That Orb belongs to the Bajorans, and as long as we held it, Oralius did not look favorably upon us. Kutel told me he felt unsettled by the object, and I felt it too. The shrine was not a place of peace as long as it was here. I felt instant relief as soon as it was gone."

"But . . . Astraea, there is no telling what will happen to it now, the cargo of my ship was unloaded at several military ports on Cardassia III . . ."

"The Orb will go where it is needed," Astraea told him, stubborn in her certainty, "and, in time, so too will the six that are still in the Order's possession. I have seen it."

"But . . ." He stopped. Thrax Sakat had never argued with the veracity of her visions, but he appeared exasperated.

"I had to do it," she said softly. "It was what Oralius wanted, please believe me." She couldn't explain it beyond that. She could never adequately put words to the overwhelming urges and insights she sometimes experienced. Usually, Glinn Sa'kat seemed to accept her actions and recommendations without question; this time seemed different.

"I thought . . . I was doing the right thing . . ."

"You didn't do the wrong thing, Glinn Sa'kat. It doesn't matter now. Please, let's speak no more of it."

He nodded without looking up, then he stood. "I had better go," he said.

She rose to her feet also, taking a step toward him. "Glinn Sa'kat, are you angry with me?"

He said nothing for a moment, and then he changed the subject.

"Astraea, I wish you would consent to go into hiding, at least until we have a better idea of what will be the outcome of the governmental upheaval."

"No," she told him. "I cannot leave the followers, not again."

"The followers cannot afford to lose you."

"The Way will never fade into obscurity, Glinn Sa'kat. I know this—with more than just a feeling. It is a truth. I do not wish to leave this place." She said it more firmly than she had intended. "Besides," she added, lightening her tone, "you will keep me safe." She meant the last part to be affectionate, but he looked grave.

"Sometimes I miss the days that I was on Terok Nor," he told her.

She felt a stab of unhappy regret, wondering if he was truly angry with her, before he went on. "From there, I had access to information from all over the Cardassian Union and beyond—systems from the Setlik to Valeria. Here, I feel much less capable of protecting you."

She looked up, her voice trembling despite her efforts to control it. "Would you really rather be on Terok Nor, Glinn Sa'kat, than here, with . . ." She trailed off, and there was a moment of silence between them.

He gazed at her for a long moment, unblinking, before he stepped toward her. His hands came up from his sides, and he took her face in his hands. She scarcely dared to move, but after a single moment, the longest moment of her life, she felt her body go slack, seeming to melt against him, feeling the ache of long-unexpressed desire finally begin to ebb. He brushed his lips against hers, and she kissed him back willingly.

He broke away far too soon, but he did not take his hands away from her face. "I do wish you would listen to me more often," he murmured.

"I will do whatever you recommend," she told him, "but only if it means you will be with me."

He did not reply, only embraced her once again, holding on as if he never meant to let go.

Odo answered his comm with trepidation, for the moment had come. *"Odo!"* Dukat was roaring. *"Environmental control gone down, very likely due to yet another act of sabotage. You must double up your security at once."*

"Of course," Odo replied. "Anything else?"

"Find Dalin Kedat and have him report to ops at once!"

Odo feigned surprise. "But Gul Dukat . . . Dalin Kedat is gone. I put him on the penal ship following his arrest, and I believe it has already left the station."

Dukat looked quite flabbergasted. *"And exactly what are we to do without a chief of engineering? You know those fools on his staff will squabble among themselves for an hour before even getting started!"*

"Dalin Trakad has already put in for a replacement, sir, but he tells me it is standard procedure for there to be an interim period of at least three days before—"

"Three days!"

"That's what I was told. You can speak to Dalin Trakad further on the matter. I consulted fully with him, and we were simply following . . ."

"Procedure, of course you were. It didn't occur to you that we might be forced to bend the rules in the case of our chief of engineering. We can scarcely function without Kedat!"

"I . . . wasn't aware of that, sir. I only knew that procedure clearly states—"

"Just . . . be sure to double up security as I asked. Immediately!" He signed off abruptly.

Odo stood, for there was a second part to his role in this mission. He left his office without bothering to answer Dukat's call for more security, and headed to Quark's.

"Odo!" Quark exclaimed as the shape-shifter entered his establishment. "To what do I owe . . . ?"

"Save it, Quark. I need to speak with you in private."

Quark gestured to his customer, a long-faced dal. "All right. Just let me just take care of—"

"We can do it at security, if you'd prefer," Odo said sharply.

"No, no, there's no need for us to leave the premises. Come into my office." The Ferengi gestured to a room behind the bar, and Odo followed him, pretending not to notice as Quark hurriedly tried to hide a small crate under the counter. Odo had no time to address it now.

"Quark," Odo said, once they were out of reasonable earshot of anyone at the bar. "I need you to do something for me."

The Ferengi looked reluctant, but Odo went on.

"In about twenty minutes, I'm going to be bringing Dukat in here, as a way of apologizing for sending his chief of engineering on that penal ship. But I can't stay in here to watch him. It would make him very suspicious—he knows I don't eat or drink, and since I've spent so little time in here, he will certainly wonder why I'm suddenly so eager to be one of your patrons."

Quark gaped. "You need me to baby-sit the prefect?" he said.

"That's right," Odo said evenly.

Quark considered for a moment before his expression changed, a shifting wiliness flickering in his eyes. "It sounds . . . important," he observed. "Like . . . it might be worth something to you."

Odo narrowed his eyes. "What do you have in mind?"

Quark grinned, unable to conceal his delight over this newfound leverage. "Well. For starters, maybe you could re-consider the fines you were imposing on my friend from Beraina—it's made him pretty reluctant to do business with me. And speaking of fines, I'm thinking it's possible that I may have . . . a few . . . unpaid debts with your office . . . if you'd care to check your records. Maybe we could enter into some kind of negotiation . . ."

"Negotiation?"

"Sure," Quark said. "Isn't that what we're talking about? Like . . . say . . . forget about them altogether."

Odo leaned toward him menacingly. "Or, perhaps you could just do as I ask, and I'll pretend I don't know anything about that box of illegal Terran *cognac* you just stowed underneath the bar . . . not to mention the proscribed holosuite programs that are hidden in the false panel underneath the right corner of the—"

"Fine!" Quark interrupted quickly, "I'll do it!"

"Of course you will," Odo replied. He gave the Ferengi

explicit instructions before hastily leaving the bar. It was time to buy Gul Dukat a drink.

Kira had been putting out the call to the Jo'kala cell for over an hour now, with no reply. This was not the first time she had attempted to alert other cells of the possibility of a grid failure, but it was the first time anything had been attempted on such a grand scale. She'd received confirmation from Terok Nor that the plan had been set into motion, the results likely to fall in their favor, and had spent much of the last ten hours contacting everyone who would answer their comms—resistance, civilians, family and friends and neighbors of the men and women who lived in the warren. While she had met with a few skeptical voices, most of the people she'd contacted understood the necessity of action tonight, and had agreed to spread the word.

"This is a wideband alert from six-one-six, I repeat, the grid is coming down. Terok Nor wil be blind for at least one hour without sensors, starting in approximately eight minutes . . ."

"Six minutes," Lupaza corrected from behind her. "Nerys, get off the comm—it's time to go!"

"But I wasn't able to get through to anyone in Jo'kala . . ."

"Someone will have told them," Mobara said. "Get your phaser, and come on—the others are already in the tunnels."

"Someone should stay behind to monitor the comm."

"I'm staying," Gantt reminded her. He'd twisted his ankle a week before, and wouldn't travel well. "Just go! Make the best of it, and keep me informed."

Kira grabbed her phaser and her shoulder pack, following the others as they scurried quickly through the tight tunnels. She could feel a detectable shift, a change in the smell and quality of the air when they neared the entrance.

And as always, her adrenaline jumped, knowing she was to be in the uncertain world beyond the warren. Today, she could scarcely hold still.

The Shakaar cell was to approach the munitions facility in groups of three and four, everyone carrying a satchel filled with Mobara's specially designed explosive devices. This factory, just a few kellipates from the city of Dahkur, manufactured some of the components used in the phaser banks mounted to Cardassian ground vehicles. The first group to arrive would take care of any Cardassians who were guarding the facility, but the Shakaar members were counting on the building being mostly unguarded. At this time of year, few Cardassian troops would be stationed in Dahkur Province.

Shakaar checked his chrono, finally giving a sharp nod. They moved fast and silently through the shaded woods, the group excitement a palpable thing. Kira had been sure that the shape-shifter would help them again; she believed him to be a creature of integrity, and while he obviously wanted to keep himself removed from the occupation, he had no choice but to choose a side.

The ugly building came into focus, and as Shakaar and his team separated from the group, Kira prayed that their assumptions had been correct. The factory had been erected in the early days of the occupation, a dome-shaped thing, low to the ground and surrounded by razor wire with an electric current running through it. This type of fence was only slightly more difficult to deal with than an electrified force field—once the current was disabled with a shot to the control box near the back of the structure, the razor wire could easily be burned away with a phaser on a high setting. Shakaar and the others would take care of it just as soon as they ensured that any guards had been dealt with.

This close, they could hear the sounds of the machinery from inside, clanking and pounding over the hum of the fence. The facility operated around the clock, with busy Bajorans inside working to manufacture weapons that would be used against their own people. This was not a work camp, but a voluntary facility, staffed with Bajorans who had elected to collaborate with the occupiers of their world. Kira felt no remorse for their fate—she had nothing for them but contempt.

Come on, come on. . . . A beat later, she heard phaser shots over uniform humming, followed by a string of small explosions in short succession. It was her turn to go, and she ran with Lupaza and Mobara to their target.

She was passed by Tahna Los and the Kohn brothers, sprinting in the opposite direction. "Only two guards!" Tahna shouted to her, holding up two fingers as he went by. Several more explosions rocked the facility, and Kira and her companions headed toward the front as Shakaar, Furel, and Latha cut in front of them, racing ahead. Kira could hear people screaming, and she willed herself not to hear.

Kira saw an opening in the wall, a jagged hole of crumbling brick, still spilling dust. She slapped the connection panel and then heaved her entire pack inside, barely slowing. A ragged internal count of three and she sheltered her head as shrapnel and pieces of the ugly structure blew out, raining chunks of debris over them. She saw Mobara hurl his pack, and heard more explosions, from everywhere around the facility. There were no more screams coming from inside, and Kira felt sure that no one had survived.

Her package delivered, Kira was off and running back toward the caves, pushing herself until the burn in her calves subsided into a steady ache that was easier to ignore. She cherished the sensation of freedom, spelled out for her in the throbbing of her muscles, in lightheadedness and a racing heart.

"If that's all the Cardassians have for us, this will be easier than we thought," Kira called out, slowing down as she approached the men.

"I wouldn't get too cocky if I were you," Shakaar warned her. "We don't have any way of knowing how much longer the grid will be down—or how long until Dukat sends additional troops to the surface."

Kira was undeterred. "This is only the beginning, Edon."

She broke into a run again, eager to hear Gantt's reports from other cells around the planet. She was elated with the plan's success, thrilled to have played a part in such a coup against the Cardassians—

—*and the workers*, she thought, but quickly put the thought aside, as she put the memory of their screams away, in a secret place in her mind that was not likely to be revisited, except perhaps in her dreams. She increased her speed, working her muscles and joints as hard as she could, and found herself back at the mouth of the cave in almost no time at all.

Dukat shivered as he took his final sip of hot fish juice, juice that could scarcely be called hot anymore. He clutched at the cup, trying to draw the last of its heat into his hands; he felt as though his fingers were coated in ice. The failure of the environmental controls had his entire staff operating in a kind of frozen lethargy.

"Will you be having a refill, Gul Dukat?" Quark's grinning face slid in front of his own. Perhaps he'd finally tired of chattering with the Lurian freighter captain who had made such a fixture of himself at the other end of the bar.

"No," Dukat muttered to the Ferengi. "Not at what you charge. I'd have been better off going to the Replimat. At least their juice is hot."

"So hot it will sear the flesh off the inside of your mouth!" Quark said indignantly. "You can't eat food from a machine—it's unnatural. The food and beverages I serve here are made with care. I personally ensure that the ingredients are only of the finest—"

"Save it," Dukat said, and stood to go.

"Wait!" the Ferengi cried. "I'll . . . offer you another glass . . . on the house!"

Dukat waited for the inevitable second half of the offer, but Quark only continued to smile helplessly.

"*Why* would you do that?"

"Well . . . because you're Gul Dukat! It's good for business to have the prefect seen in here . . . of course!" Quark said.

Dukat supposed it made sense, but the Ferengi was obviously up to something. He sighed and gestured his acceptance. "Fine, I'll have another drink. But I do plan to mention to Odo that you're acting suspiciously."

"Gul!" Quark said, pretending to be hurt. "Is generosity really so out of character for me that you would—"

"Yes," Dukat interrupted, and changed the subject. "How can you tolerate this cold?" he asked the gruesome little man as he heated another drink. "Is it as miserable as this on your homeworld?"

Quark spread his unnervingly toothy smile as wide as it would go. "It's miserabler," he said, and laughed at his own joke. "I rather like the new temperature setting, really. But then, it's not my station."

"No, it is not," Dukat said, and accepted the hot glass. He had to admit, the juice here *was* more palatable than what could be gotten from the replicators, but he could hardly enjoy it with the persistent chill in the air.

"Remember to savor that, now," Quark advised.

"If it weren't for Odo," Dukat complained, "I wouldn't be sitting here freezing half to death, talking to you."

"Well, then, I suppose I have Odo to thank for the pleasant conversation," Quark said.

Dukat ignored him and continued to air his grievances. "Our constable put the chief of engineering on the first penal ship back to Cardassia Prime, before we'd called in for a replacement."

"Odo is nothing if not overly efficient," Quark said. "I'd say he's pretty rigid, for a shape-shifter."

"And then the environmental controls would have to go down, on the one day I'm short an engineering chief! I've just been informed that I'm not to get another one for at least forty-two hours, which means the problem's got to be attended to by an engineering team without its leader. If you had any idea what fools Kedat surrounded himself with . . ."

"You know, we have a saying on Ferenginar. 'When it rains, it rains extremely hard, reducing the entirety of your surroundings to muck.'"

Dukat made a face. "Did I ask to hear your homespun folk wisdom?" he said sourly. "At any rate," he went on, "I reprimanded him for sending away the chief of engineering without my approval, but it isn't as though he could possibly appreciate what the loss of environmental control means for the rest of us."

"Odo isn't known for his empathy," Quark agreed.

Dukat was tired of listening to the Ferengi's acquiescence, and deliberately set his gaze elsewhere until Quark moved on to ingratiate himself to someone else. It seemed to take an excruciatingly long time before the Ferengi finally lost interest in furthering the conversation. Dukat briefly remembered a time when he'd had people on the station he'd thought he could trust. There had been Damar—the young, but wise-beyond-his-years garresh—and there had been Kira Meru. Beautiful Meru, so sensible—for a Bajoran, that was—but both had betrayed him. And then Basso Tromac. The Bajoran had been such a loyal servant before he'd disappeared, never returning from his errand to collect Kira Nerys. Dukat was left to wonder if Basso hadn't betrayed him as well.

He looked up to see Quark making his usual small talk with a group of security officers in the corner, the insincerity all but dripping from his words. It was certainly indicative of Dukat's isolation that he would be forced to seek companionship from the shape-shifter—or worse, from the Ferengi. He could trust no one, he recognized now.

He hurried back to his office, warming himself slightly by the brisk walk, feeling strangely melancholy. Why was it so hard to find people he could depend upon? How could he be expected to function when there was no one to whom he could speak?

He found a message from Legate Kell waiting for him in his cold office. He reviewed it without enthusiasm, an ambiguous request for an immediate callback, and Dukat reluctantly put in a return call. Perhaps it was related to his new engineering chief . . .

"Dukat," the legate said shortly. *"I've given it much thought, and I believe my plan to reorganize the Bajoran government is best for all concerned."*

Dukat gritted his teeth. Why did Kell continue to concern himself with details of the annexation? Dukat felt smothered.

"We need to discuss the particulars of the transition, as I would like to see the alteration occur as soon as possible," Kell went on. *"But first, I feel it would be best to appoint a committee among some of your more trusted advisers, in order—"*

A red light flashed on the console to Dukat's right, accompanied by an audible alarm. Kell broke off speaking, his expression parodying surprise. *"What is that?"*

Dukat was already reacting, having swiveled to regard

the console at his right-hand side. There had been a failure of the program managing the sensor towers on the surface, guiding the sweeps and returning the data to Terok Nor.

"I must go, Legate," he said, ending the transmission without another word. He immediately alerted engineering, then called for his communications officer to start contacting surface bases for reports.

He spent a moment trying to call up more information on the nature of the failure, but the computer was giving him nothing. Frustrated, he stepped out into Ops, looking over his shivering skeleton crew as they went to task, working diagnostics and gathering information. The initial reports were bad—there was nothing coming up from the grid, no data being recorded at all, on any continent. Dukat sent them to double-check, his best hope right now was that the Bajorans on the surface would not learn of the failure.

He thought of the Ferengi, that ridiculous idiom repeating itself: *When it rains, it rains extremely hard . . .*

"Get me a diagnostic of the most vulnerable sites on the surface," he barked. "I need troops in place anywhere that is susceptible to insurgent attacks."

The dalin at communications spoke up. "There are literally hundreds of them, sir—could you be more specific?"

The female glinn working the sciences station spoke up, confirming the desolate news. "Sir. The entire detection grid has gone dark, sir."

Dukat took a breath, reminding himself that this was not yet cause for panic. If the Bajorans were not aware that the grid was off line, then unrest on the surface was unlikely—at least, for now. He made a quick mental list of the precautions that must be taken, before the same female glinn spoke with urgency in her voice.

"A report, sir, forwarded from a manufacturing facility in Dahkur—it suggests that insurgents have attacked, but the signal was only partial, they can't confirm . . ."

"Gul Dukat, there is a red alert coming in from the military base on the outskirts of Musilla Province!"

"A facility in Gerhami Province has gone offline!"

"Another report, sir, from Ilvia—"

More shouts, console lights winking and pulsing, simultaneous reports of scattered disasters, and Dukat felt his internal temperature plummeting, becoming as cold as his space station. This was not accidental, nor, likely, was the distraction of the environmental malfunction. This was sabotage, a carefully planned attack, and it had occurred on the prefect's watch—on his own station.

21

The man who now stood at the podium was proving himself to be a poor speaker. Though it had been arranged far in advance of this date that he would preside over the meeting, Natima suspected that he felt uneasy with the location she had chosen—an empty classroom at the University of Prekiv, Natima's alma mater and current place of employment.

Natima had worked very hard to get to her current position; in just under five years, she had earned a postgraduate position as an assistant professor in the political sciences department. She continued to take classes in her spare time, and expected to be a full-fledged professor within the next two years; Natima was nothing if not driven. But she was also nothing if not cautious about her own political status as a dissident, and she would not have agreed to host the meeting if she were not confident that the meeting would be private.

She knew that most of the staff here at the university were sympathetic to her causes, particularly those professors who worked in her department. Natima was confident that any members of the university staff who felt otherwise could not touch her. She had flourished within the precise hierarchy of the university system, and she knew her place in it. This classroom was by far the safest public location the group could have chosen to meet in—safer than in a private residence, for large gatherings at people's homes were often secretly monitored by the government. Universities were generally better protected from that sort of intrusion, enjoying a certain measure of lenience in the name of education. Cardassians still valued education and knowledge very highly in the great scheme of their society, for it was the Cardassians' superior knowledge that had allowed their scientific community to be one of the most advanced in the galaxy.

The soundproof room was large, with chairs arranged in semicircular rows before a podium in the center. The design of the classroom, with graduated tiers rising up to the back of the room, made amplification devices unnecessary, helping to ensure that conversation was not likely to be monitored. Natima had personally checked for listening devices, and as she had expected, there were none. But Dr. Tuken, a professor from the settlement in the Cuellar system who had been chosen to chair the meeting this afternoon, still appeared too ill at ease to speak freely. His statements were vague, his intentions unclear. Natima felt a little annoyed, for she took the man's unease as a sign of his mistrust in her. She found his overly cautious, halting manner to be distracting, as well.

She glanced across the room to Gaten Russol, now a gul in the military, and saw from his expression that he was thinking the same thing that she was. After so many years of friendship, she could read him like a book. He met her eye, and then he stood.

"Thank you, Doctor Tuken," Russol said smoothly, "for that introduction. I have a few items that I wish to address."

"Of course, Gul Russol," Tuken said, and stepped down from the podium. If he resented the interruption, he didn't show it; nearly everyone knew to defer to Gul Russol. If their unnamed movement had a leader, it was Gaten Russol, and while the membership remained only somewhere in the hundreds, the squabbling and lack of direction of days past was gone now. The small, committed groups around the Union had mostly narrowed their focus toward common goals.

"Regarding my communication with the Federation," Russol began, which brought up a faint murmur from a few people seated around the room. Talk of Federation correspondence was probably the riskiest topic anyone could have chosen to address out loud, even taking the new treaty into consideration. It was certainly an attention getter. Natima thought he may have deliberately chosen it to offset Tuken's cautious approach, and watched with mounting interest. Her friend seemed especially intense this day, his shoulders tight, his expression grim.

"The talks have been mostly fruitless," he went on. "The Federation adheres to a very strict set of rules regarding involvement in other worlds' affairs. They are reluctant to help us, especially now that they have a treaty with our government. The treaty has, unfortunately, weakened our position with our own people, for there were many who felt that the struggles over the border territories were drawing strength from the Union. Now, many of those Cardassian subjects who were beginning to lose faith in the military government have been placated by the treaty."

Natima nodded, along with many of the others. The movement had lost a few of its followers as a result of the treaty, although most of the people involved with the dissidents felt that Cardassia's social, political, and economic woes could not be solved with one insincere treaty. Natima was sure the treaty was simply a means for Central Command to buy some time while it plotted its next move. But even if it had been genuine, the treaty was no better than a sticky plaster over a terminal hemorrhage.

"We all know that Cardassia has problems that extend

far beyond the border colonies," Russol said, echoing Nati-ma's thoughts. "The violence on Bajor is worse than ever. Even more perplexing, it is said that the resources there will not last another generation—but Central Command will not admit that it is time to withdraw our presence on that annexed world. And yet—" Russol paused dramatically to look around the room at his friends and cohorts. "What if we did pull out of Bajor? What would happen then?"

More murmuring as people in the audience muttered the answers to themselves and to the people seated near them. Russol spoke again, his eyes shining passionately. "Some say our government would simply look for another world to exploit, instead of drawing on the strengths of our own world, our own people—we would look for other worlds to conquer, instead of forming alliances that could help Cardassia become self-sufficient. But I do not see that as a foregone conclusion.

"We know that the Detapa Council has relatively lit-tle power in our governmental structure. In leaner times, our world was forced to defer to the military, stripping the power away from our civilian leaders. However, a majority vote coming from that body can still make certain deci-sions for Cardassia Prime. The issue, as we all know, is that the varied interests of the council members has made it all but impossible to achieve a majority vote on anything. We know it, and Central Command knows it. But what if this were to change?"

Russol leaned forward on the podium, as if to draw his audience physically closer for what he was about to say. "We can't rely on the Federation, or anyone else, to help us anymore," he said. "It's time for more drastic measures. We have talked long enough, and now we have to act."

A hush had fallen over the room, until someone finally spoke. "What are you proposing, Gul Russol?" It was Dr. Tuken, his voice trembling slightly.

"We cannot expect any change to come about from the military—we need the Detapa Council to be on our side," he said. "In recent years, with no small thanks to the efforts of the people here, many of the civilian leaders on the council have begun to favor a position very much like our own. In fact," he added, "there is more than one member of the Detapa Council taking an active involvement in our movement."

A number of people looked surprised, others seemed to know exactly of whom he was speaking. He did not say it, but Natima assumed he meant Kotan Pa'Dar—Russol would never confirm that the man was a dissenter, but Natima had long believed it was true.

"The division of power in the Detapa Council still swings in the general direction of Central Command, however. But if one seat on the council were to go vacant—were to be filled by a sympathizer—the balance would tip in our direction. Yoriv Skyl, who is an exarch at one of the Bajoran settlements, is poised to take the next open seat. I believe that Skyl would vote in favor of withdrawal, if the issue were to come to the council. Legate Ghemor and a few other important people with influence over Central Command mean to bring the item up for decision in less than one year."

A few of the people in attendance looked poised to applaud, optimism quickly spreading from one person to the next. But Russol was quick to interrupt them.

"Our problem, of course, is how to make that position . . . vacant. How can we guarantee the dismissal of tyrannical and corrupt civilian prefects and exarchs when their terms have no limit? What can we do?"

The room fell absolutely silent, and Natima's heart sank as she recognized the rhetorical questions for what they were, what Russol was suggesting. It seemed impossible, a stretch of character she would not have imagined of him, but the gravity in his voice was unmistakable. He was so desperate to pull his world's involvement out of Bajor that he would condone assassination.

"It is for the good of Cardassia," he said calmly.

"Is there no other way?" Natima asked, before he could put voice to the details.

"There is one other alternative," he said, his tone belying no emotion at all. "But I believe that a few selected eliminations would be preferable to a coup, which may not produce the desired effect, and will almost certainly result in more deaths."

Still, no one spoke, and Russol continued to sweep his gaze across the room, making steady eye contact with each person in attendance, one at a time. "I would not propose such a thing if I did not believe that it was necessary, and that now is the optimum time to act. The only time to act."

Someone cleared his throat, and a quiet chatter began to rise once more. "But, Gul Russol," someone called out, "how can we advocate for peace and murder at the same time?"

"We can't," Russol told him. "We simply must accept that we are forced to compromise our values in order to achieve the desired result—for the greater good. But it is as I say—there is no other way."

Many questions followed, which resulted in a few short arguments, but most were quelled by Russol's blunt responses. He had examined the issue from every angle, he informed the room, and he firmly believed that the time to strike was now.

After a good hour of moderately heated discussion, a vote was taken, and though Natima was hesitant to do so, she lent her support to Russol's proposal. In the end, Natima was not the only one who chose to agree to Russol's controversial tactics. When Dr. Tuken tallied the votes, Natima was surprised to learn that a strong majority had voted for it as well.

So this is what we've come to, she thought, looking around the room at downcast eyes, faces that seemed to reflect less patriotic zeal than usual. The vote had been secret, but the looks on the faces of those present were clear enough to reveal who had voted for the advocacy of murders—the deliberate killing of Union members—and who had not. Natima knew her own expression was far from innocent. *Are we any better than that which we seek to overthrow?*

"Don't patronize me, Kubus," Dukat snapped. "I am fully aware that I look like a complete fool right now. To the Bajorans—and to my superiors in Central Command."

Kubus Oak coughed, quickly losing hope that this conversation would be brief, his placating manner seen for what it was. He disliked the prefect's office, preferring to keep his conversations with Dukat confined to the infinitely more comfortable comm system; but ever since Basso Tromac had vanished, Dukat had begun to treat Kubus more like an assistant than a political cohort. It wasn't as though their relationship had ever been on much of an even keel, but Kubus had never felt so much like a subordinate as in recent years, and it seemed to be getting worse as time went by. "As I was saying, it *was* an unfortunate incident," he said, "but there is no need to—"

"Incident?" Dukat laughed. "You speak as though this is some past event! My men have been unable to repair the detection grid on a global scale, Kubus, and we have only been able to maintain secondary systems in a few locales. Someone is going to pay for this."

Kubus was ready for him. "I have heard a great many rumors from my contacts," he offered. "They believe this is primarily the work of terrorists in Dahkur. They hide somewhere in the hills, though there has been no physical evidence of their exact location. It might be preferable to simply . . ." Kubus hesitated as he noticed that Dukat was shaking his head, but he uncertainly went on, ". . . destroy the entire region . . ."

"No," Dukat told him. "There are valuable commodities in that part of Dahkur. Minerals, timber . . . Give me someone else, Secretary."

"Someone else?" Kubus felt uncomfortably pressed, his mind going blank. He had been sure that the cell in Dahkur would be enough to satisfy Dukat, and he didn't know what to say now that his suggestion had been rejected.

There was a long pause while Kubus tried to come up with something useful. "Well, there is believed to be an especially large cell in Kendra Province. I have no hard evidence that they had any involvement, but—"

"Did I ask for hard evidence?" Dukat said coldly. "Can this cell be pinpointed?"

"I . . . believe . . . their hiding place is somewhat more definitive than some of the others, but—"

"Then why have they not been brought to my attention before now?"

Kubus suddenly realized what a terrible mistake he was making. "Well . . . sir . . . that cell . . . It's rumored that one of their members . . . is the son of our religious leader—"

"The kai's son?" Dukat said, his expression suddenly changing to reflect his apparent interest. Kubus felt his heart sink like a stone.

"Yes, sir, that's correct. No Bajoran is willing to reveal their exact location, but there is a general idea of where they might be found, near the forest just outside of the Kendra provincial seat . . ."

"Issue a statement, Kubus. If this Kendra cell does not surrender themselves, I will be forced to destroy the surrounding villages. However, if anyone from Kendra is willing to reveal their location before they surrender . . . well, the villages will be spared, of course . . ." He trailed off, a self-satisfied smile surfacing.

"Prefect," Kubus said nervously, aware that he was inching into dangerous territory, "I'm not sure you understand the gravity of what you ask. I must tell you, I think the cell from Dahkur—"

"Oak," Dukat said, and Kubus blanched. No good could come following the gul's use of his given name.

"I hesitate to bring this up at such a sensitive time," the prefect said, "But Legate Kell recently suggested to me that it would be in my best interests to appoint a new Bajoran cabinet. He believed it would be beneficial to simply execute all the current members of the Bajoran government and start anew. Of course, I assured him that I had no intention of betraying those who had been faithful to me for such a long time."

Kubus recognized the threat, but he could not be responsible for an ultimatum involving Kai Opaka's son. "Gul, respectfully—I don't believe that any Bajoran would willingly reveal the whereabouts of the kai's son."

"Well," Dukat said, "we'll see if you're right, won't we, Secretary?" He stood from his desk, turning his back on the old man, who wasn't quite sure whether he had been dismissed.

"I'll take care of your request as soon as I'm able," Kubus said miserably, rising to go.

Dukat did not turn around. "You'll take care of it now."

"This is Alynna Nechayev, Vice-Admiral of Starfleet Command, representing the United Federation of Planets. I am attempting to reach Kalem Apren of Bajor. This is Alynna Nechayev, Vice-Admiral of Starfleet Command . . ."

Apren struggled for a moment to fight his way out of the haze of sleep. He could have sworn he'd heard his name coming from another room of the house—muffled, but still distinctly a woman's voice, and something unusual about her accent . . .

Kalem Apren of Bajor . . . This is Alynna Nechayev . . .

Apren was on his feet at once, dashing for the comm system that was set up in the other room of his modest stone house. He was surprised that it hadn't woken his wife—but then, her name had not been called. He had slept like the dead, considering the excitement that had taken place in the past twenty-four hours. The people of the Kendra Valley were exhausted with hopeful anticipation. Most Bajorans were accustomed to violent outbreaks on their world, but very few of those outbreaks resulted in much measure of Bajoran victory—and never a victory as wide-scale as this one seemed to be.

He seized the transmitter device at once, and began to speak.

"Hello, hello? This is Kalem Apren, citizen of Bajor. Is . . . is this channel secure?" He hesitated before continuing, but the voice spoke again before he could say anything else.

"Mister Kalem, I must warn you, this channel is not secure. I repeat, this channel is not secure."

Did it even matter, now, if the Cardassians overheard? In fact, Apren wondered if it wasn't better that they did, considering what had been happening. The woman went on. "I have contacted you by request of Keeve Falor, who sent word to a Federation starbase that you wished to speak with a representative of my government."

"Vice-Admiral Alynna," Apren said, fumbling over the correct way to address the alien woman. He spoke quickly, frantically—for he didn't know how long this connection would hold out. "Thank you for contacting me . . . finally." He added the last word as a loaded afterthought, for he knew, from Keeve and others, that this was not the first time Alynna Nechayev had been in contact with Bajorans. Just prior to the occupation she had worked as an operative for her people, trying to learn more about the Bajoran situation in hopes that her government could help. But in the end, the Federation's political structure had barred her from interfering in the so-called annexation of Bajor to the Cardassian Union.

Apren had to admit to himself that Keeve Falor's skepticism was well-placed, but he had to maintain hope, especially now that things seemed to be taking a turn. Even as they were speaking, Cardassian targets all over Bajor were burning, and Apren expected more destruction to take place before Cardassian forces could rein in the violence.

The woman spoke. *"I have been hoping to contact someone to represent Bajor for a very long time now—someone, that is, besides Jas Holza or Kubus Oak . . ."*

"Of course," Apren said, impatient to get to the point of the conversation. "Perhaps you have heard of what is happening here today, Vice-Admiral."

"Today? Please tell me what you mean."

"Today has been a landmark in the fight for independence from our oppressors," Apren said. "Dozens, possibly even hundreds of Cardassian targets were simultaneously attacked, releasing a worldwide flood of violence. Some Bajorans are fearful, it seems, from the reports I have been getting, but most are jubilant—and angry. Even farmers from the smaller villages are taking up arms. I have been taking reports all day long from contacts on every continent—"

"A global uprising," the woman interrupted him, sounding surprised. *"This is news indeed. Perhaps the situation will warrant Federation involvement, depending on the circumstances . . ."*

Apren was disgusted. "Of course, you must discuss it with your diplomats, your politicians, and your military organizations before you can do anything. You cannot simply deduce that your assistance would be helpful here, and act accordingly. By the time you sort out whether it is prudent to become involved, it may be too late to do any-thing."

"I understand your frustration," the woman replied. *"But the Federation is not a reactionary body. We do not simply travel from world to world, putting out fires. We must make a full assessment of the conflict, and whether it is our place to interfere."*

Apren took a breath. "Vice-Admiral," he said, willing himself to sound as sincere as he could—he must put his reservations aside. "I asked you to contact me because I must humbly ask you for help. Not in driving away the Cardassians, for I firmly believe that we are capable of fighting our oppressors on our own. But once they are gone, we will need assistance to rebuild our infrastructure, our government, from the ground up. Without an established body to scaffold us, we will most likely not succeed."

Apren could not read the woman's reaction from her voice alone. *"So . . . you ask only for help once Bajor has won her independence? Forgive me for saying so, but by what logic do you believe Bajor has the capacity to drive off the Cardassians now?"*

"I don't need logic," Apren said firmly. He could not risk sharing his plans with a member of the Federation. "I have faith. I have long believed that we would be capable of triumph, but after tonight, I know it. And I know it will be soon."

"I . . . believe you are wise to make preparations to govern your world," the woman replied, *"but it would not be prudent for the Federation to sanction Bajoran violence when we have a treaty with Cardassia."*

"I repeat, I am not asking for Federation assistance in our fight for independence," Apren said firmly. "I already know I will not get it. I am only asking for assistance in the aftermath—a circumstance that I don't believe will interfere with your . . . Prime Directive."

The woman ignored the iciness in his tone. *"Very well, Mister Kalem. The Federation will monitor the state of affairs on*

*your world, and do what we deem appropriate. I will stay in touch
with you, either directly or through Keeve Falor."*

The communication concluded, Apren returned to his
bed, though he did not expect to sleep. He had been desperately trying to contact Jas Holza today, for he was certain that the former minister would finally agree to help
supply the resistance with weapons; would finally agree to
enter the B'hava'el system, once he got word of the tenu-
ous grip the Cardassians now had. Holza had proven difficult to reach, but perhaps he would learn the news for
himself now—through the Federation. Still, Kalem meant
to keep trying to contact Valo III himself.

It was only a short time before his weariness overtook
him, pulling him far from his troubles, and into a deep
slumber. It was by hope that Apren had continued to function during all these years of the occupation, and never had
his hope been more fecund than now.

Prylar Bek was only too aware of how delicate his position
was, here at the shrine on Terok Nor. Dukat had allowed
certain religious officials to practice on the Bajoran side of
the station, but it had not been so long ago that all religious activities had been banned—and there was no telling what might motivate the prefect to ban them all over
again. Bek had always done his best to stay nearly invisible where the Cardassians were concerned; any misstep
on his part could lead to his immediate dismissal from the
station—or even execution. As a spiritual adviser, he was
far more conspicuous here than any of the other ordinary
folk in ore processing—and Bek had seen plenty of them
dragged off to be put to death for virtually no reason at
all. He'd at least felt some degree of safety on the station
when the Oralian had been here, the security chief who
had seemed to genuinely want to help the Bajorans. But
now he was alone, no allies to get him out of trouble if he

needed them. He'd long had the unpleasant notion that he was only here because the Cardassians suspected he could be their conduit to Kai Opaka—for he had a rough system of communicating with her, though it was not direct. If the need ever arose, he spoke to the Vedek Assembly, who passed his word on to the kai. If the Cardassians had any ideas of torturing him to try and find her, he had often thought, they would be sorely disappointed. Even if he *had* known exactly where she was, he would never have delivered that information, not for anything.

As he lit a small *duranja,* a lamp honoring the dead, he heard the rustling of a long tunic; a Bajoran had entered his shrine. "Welcome, child of the Prophets," he began, but as he turned to see the face of his visitor, his heart went cold at the sight of the stooped old man who stood before him. Kubus Oak was less welcome here than any Cardassian soldier, for he was the most notorious of the politicians who had first fallen in league with Cardassian forces, decades ago. Every Bajoran understood that without the consent of Kubus Oak, the Cardassians would never have gained the foothold they needed to overtake this world. Kubus was a Cardassian pawn—a willing one. For that reason, his name and face were deeply reviled.

"Why do you come here?" Bek said slowly. This wasn't the first time Kubus Oak had been to the shrine. The old politician still retained some shred of his former faith and he worshiped at regularly scheduled services from time to time, but it was unprecedented for him to come here when services were not being held. Occasionally he was known to have given large sums of money toward the upkeep of certain shrines, primarily in his old district of Qui'al, a practice he no doubt expected to give him absolution for the many evils he had committed. But despite his position, he had never attempted to use his influence to protect the faith. Many believed that his attendance at services was simply a means to ingratiate himself with the very few Bajorans who still served him; even more felt that his presence at the shrines was nothing short of an affront to the Prophets themselves.

"Prylar Bek," the old man said, with his usual hardness of voice. "I have come to ask you . . . to speak to the Vedek Assembly on my behalf . . . for I seek advice."

"Advice?"

"Prylar . . . today I have been ordered to issue a statement . . . one which I fear will lead to my spiritual undoing."

Bek was confused. Here was a man whose signature on a work order meant certain death for a Bajoran—and whose signature was affixed to thousands of such work orders. The man's arrogant refusal to relinquish any fraction of his own power had caused him to land squarely in the lap of those oppressors who had taken Bajor as their own, with no regard for the fate of its people. What could Kubus Oak possibly have to fear regarding the state of his *pagh*— what could be worse than what he had already done? "What statement might that be, Secretary Kubus?"

"I am obliged . . . to inform the residents of the villages of Kendra Valley . . . that they must reveal the location of the resistance cell that hides in their region, or face total destruction."

"The resistance cell . . ." Bek trailed off in horror. "Secretary, we must warn them—the cell. We must tell them to leave the Kendra Valley before the detection grid is restored—"

"It may already be too late," Kubus told him. "The Cardassians have deployed troops to be stationed along the perimeters of the villages."

Bek could not believe what was happening. "And who informed the prefect of this cell's existence?" he asked, barely able to keep his voice under control in this holy place. "Who was responsible—"

"I had no choice!" Kubus said tightly. "You must understand my position. I have no allies left, only the Cardassians! If I fall from favor with them, then I have only the Prophets to answer to!"

"I would advise you to answer to them now," Bek said. "You had better pray, Kubus Oak."

"I have prayed!" Kubus insisted. "I have asked the Prophets to tell me what to do, which is what led me here, to you—"

"It is far too late for you to pray for guidance, Secretary," Prylar Bek told him.

"But—"

"No, Secretary, if you are to pray, it must be for forgiveness. I hope They can forgive you—because I doubt any Bajoran ever could." It was on that note that Prylar Bek turned away from Kubus, lighting another *duranja* and making clear with his posture that he had nothing more to say to the man. If Kubus Oak did not set this thing right, then all the prayers in the world would not help him.

22

Dukat resented Kell's presence on the station, but the aging legate made it a point to visit at least twice a year. This time, he had come without the courtesy of a scheduled announcement, leaving Dukat to feel as though he were victim to a surprise attack.

Dukat took his superior on the requisite tour around the station, knowing that none of it held the least bit of interest to the old man. His visits here were part of a simple effort to project the image of "involvement," and to assure the Cardassian people that Bajor was indeed safe.

"Over here is the operations center's new science station—"

"I have seen it," the Legate said brusquely.

"Ah, yes, of course, on your last visit here we had just completed it."

On the Promenade, Kell observed the opening and closing of the gates that barred the Bajoran laborers from entering the Cardassian side of the station without proper authorization. Two Bajorans were admitted as the legate looked on, accompanied by a press of Cardassian escorts.

"What business do those men have on this side of the station?" Kell demanded.

"I couldn't say without asking the sentries who admitted them," Dukat said. "I'm sure whatever the cause, it is legitimate—and trifling enough that you and I don't need to concern ourselves with it."

"Has security on this station always been so casual?" Kell asked.

Dukat bristled for a moment before forcing himself to smile. "Security on Terok Nor functions quite effectively, Legate."

Kell turned back toward the habitat ring, and Dukat relaxed slightly; the old man looked as though he planned to retire for the night. "Security was not functioning effectively when the detection grid was compromised," the legate said.

Dukat's smile remained in place. "It's true, Legate—and the situation would have spiraled out of control had I not acted promptly, with the strategic deployment of troops. I have repeatedly asked Central Command to send more troops here, and my requests have repeatedly been turned down—which I find puzzling, now that the situation with the border colonies is finally said to be diffused."

"Don't trouble yourself with the goings-on at the border," the legate said gruffly, though Dukat had made no indication of being troubled—something that immediately suggested to him that there might be more going on in the so-called demilitarized zone than he had been led to believe.

"I am only able to do so much with the resources I have been appointed," Dukat told him. "As you know, when my last chief of security left, I was not assigned a qualified replacement in sufficient time to maintain order, and I was forced to choose an alien to fill the position. Which isn't to suggest that I am unhappy with the shape-shifter's performance," he added quickly, remembering the old man's suggestion that he dismiss Odo, "but it is a fine example of the improvisational nature of my leadership. I have been—"

"Well, it isn't the sabotage of your detection grid that

compels me to warn you, Gul. You must be especially wary of assassination attempts."

"Assassination! Legate, these Bajorans plan a new attempt on my life practically every week. If you weren't aware of the danger here, then perhaps you should have stayed at home."

"I am not speaking of Bajorans," Kell told him, "I am speaking of Cardassians. Dissidents, Dukat. Perhaps you didn't know it, but a very influential member of the Detapa Council recently turned up dead. All evidence suggests he was poisoned. His seat is to be filled by Yoriv Skyl. I believe you know the man."

"Yes, the former exarch of Tozhat," Dukat acknowledged. "His position on Tozhat has not been filled yet, thanks to the hysteria that has been so long propagated by the Detapa Council."

"It is a difficult position," Kell replied. "But Skyl's resignation was not a surprise. He was given the opportunity to return home. Many men would jump at the chance."

"Of course," Dukat replied, "But I am not one of those men."

Kell eyed the prefect, and then went on. "I fear that it is only a matter of time before members of Central Command are targeted. There have been no leads as to who could be responsible for the death of Yoriv Skyl's predecessor—a colonialist, I might add—one who understood the importance of military control."

"No leads!" Dukat exclaimed. "Is a definitive lead necessary to make an example of someone? Can't you simply find a suitable scapegoat and call it done?"

"Of course we could," Kell said sourly. "But do you believe it would deter subsequent attacks, if the murderer learns that he can continue to strike and see another man pay for his crime? Tell me, Dukat, is this the method you use to keep your Bajoran subjects in line? Because I must say, it seems to me that such a tactic would only be effective in frightening children and old women, while doing nothing to discourage potential violence by those who pose the greatest threat."

Dukat had no reply, especially since random executions were a method for which Kell himself had long advocated, and he could not argue with the man without outwardly calling him a hypocrite. He escorted the legate back to his quarters in a cold fury.

"There's one last thing, Dukat," Kell said as he turned to face the gul after crossing the threshold to his stateroom. "I was contacted recently by Enabran Tain. He has asked for a favor that I have chosen to grant."

"What is that to me?" Dukat scoffed. "Tain is retired."

"Don't be naïve," Kell snapped. "Retired or not, one does not ignore personal requests from a man who was head of the Obsidian Order. That's especially true for you in this case, since it involves this station of yours."

"I see," Dukat said through his teeth. "And the nature of this request?"

"One of the Order's operatives has become something of an embarrassment to the organization. For whatever reason, sanctioning the man isn't an option Tain is willing to entertain. He wishes the operative exiled here."

Dukat fumed. "Terok Nor isn't a retirement facility."

"No," Kell agreed. "But Tain is under the impression that, for this individual, it will be a satisfactory humiliation. He's to be give the opportunity to serve the Union here in some menial capacity, without privilege or status. But—and we need to be absolutely clear about this, Dukat—he is not to be touched. Is that understood?"

Dukat's eyes narrowed with suspicion. "Who is he?"

But Kell, now wearing an unsettlingly amused expression, had already turned his back on the prefect and allowed the cabin door to close in Dukat's face.

✦   ✦   ✦

Natima's blood ran cold when Russol contacted her at home, for she knew the reason for his call. The dissident movement had been weakened as a result of what had recently been done, many of the followers dispersing to worlds outside the Union grasp, for the fear of repercussion proved to be more powerful than the hope of governmental reform.

Natima didn't know which of her comrades had actually killed the colonialist governor who had been replaced with Yoriv Skyl. She didn't know exactly how the man had died, though the comnets were all saying poison. Russol had emphasized that it was best if the dissidents knew as little as possible regarding the actual deed; in case any of them were captured, they could tell no tales of that which they did not know. But Natima felt as certain as if he had told her so, that it was Russol who had done it. While she supposed it should have made her opinion of him waver, it did not. She still admired and trusted him as much as she ever had; after all, he was a soldier, and this was not the first time he had killed. But something had changed, something she could not put name to. She would always look at him differently, somehow, if only because he had made her see exactly how driven he was to see things change.

"Natima," her friend said, the urgency in his voice unmistakable. *"It is for your own safety that I propose this."* He spoke carefully, avoiding reference to particular topics, but still his message was plain. *"The Sadera system is the safest place for us."*

"I can't leave," she told him. "Please understand. Cardassia II is my home. I . . . can do too much good here to just leave."

"You can always return when the . . . climate is more favorable."

"But I am to attain my professorship in only a few

months time," she told him. "I know you understand what a great honor and accomplishment this is for me. I did not expect to be awarded this position for another year. If I were to leave now, I could lose my seniority . . . and it would disappoint many of my students, who have come to trust me as a mentor."

Natima did not know how to explain to Russol the relationships she had with many of her students—the almost familial ties she had begun to forge with some of her younger protégés was especially powerful. It made her feel more like a mother than she ever could have imagined— something she had never expected to experience.

"I know that you can do much good in your current position, Natima . . . but I beg you . . ."

"I don't want to leave my work behind," she said firmly. "I feel that my teachings can be an inspiration to the next generation of Cardassians. It's too early for me to leave, Gaten."

He sighed. *"Very well. But I . . . will miss your friendship. I will be going to the Sadera system myself before long. I have only a few more assignments to carry out before the end of my commission, and then . . . perhaps . . . in the future, I will see you there."*

"In the future," she told him. "I will hope for that."

Natima ended the transmission, thinking how much she would miss her old friend. He had been to her like family, but within the university, she had a new family now—a new generation of thinkers, of independent-minded individuals who would help to make the Cardassia of tomorrow a better place than the Cardassia of today.

The Shikina Monastery was mostly silent, the monks of the order going about even more somberly than usual, the vedeks scarcely speaking among themselves. Prylar Bek had been putting through frantic transmissions to the vedeks of the assembly for over a week, but none had any advice for him that could allay his fears.

Since learning the news of the threat on her son's life, the kai had taken to her quarters, a secret room visited by only the most senior members of the Vedek Assembly—and Vedek Bareil. Bareil approached her there, though he knew that she had asked for solitude so that she could meditate. He was still desperately trying to work out a solution to the current danger. It was looking more and more as though it would be the villages—over a thousand people—and not the resistance cell, which would bear the brunt of Dukat's anger. Nobody in the Kendra Valley was willing to turn over the son of the kai, just as Bareil had expected.

"Your Eminence," Bareil reported. "As it currently stands, the villages are slated for destruction in less than twenty-six hours. I have contacted Kalem Apren."

"Oh?" the kai replied, but she did not look at Bareil.

"Yes, Your Eminence. I know you feel that Kalem is somehow going to be instrumental to Bajor's rebirth, in the time of the Emissary . . ."

"I have never spoken of such things with you, Bareil."

"No, but—" He stopped. She had never spoken her thoughts to him, but he knew. "I tried to convince him to save himself—that perhaps there is some means of smuggling him out of the village—but he refuses to even consider it. He says his people need him."

"They do need him," Opaka said. "Now more than ever, but they will continue to need him."

Bareil went on. "I have been considering—if I were to go to Dukat with a false location outside the Kendra Valley for your son's cell, perhaps it could buy us enough time to contact another resistance cell—someone who could help those in the rest of the villages to escape."

The kai appeared quite tired, and seemed somehow smaller than her already small size, as though she'd shrunk within her skin. "Vedek Bareil, the resistance does not have the means to evacuate the villages. Even if it were possible to convince Dukat that Fasil's cell was elsewhere, there are many people in the villages who could not tolerate evacuation—elderly people, terminally ill people, people with small children . . ."

"We could get them to the forest, somehow. The detection grid is still nonfunctional, Your Eminence—we must use this fact to our best advantage!"

"You have concerned yourself with this matter far beyond your call of obligation, Vedek. I would request that you go to the Dakeen Monastery until this incident is concluded."

"Eminence! I cannot leave at a time like this!"

"This is exactly the time for you to go, Bareil."

"Kai—Eminence—" He could not express the frustration and horror he'd felt, watching this conundrum unfold. He knew he was overstepping his bounds, but he could not help himself. "What is it that you have foreseen? Why will you not act?"

The small woman sighed, her shoulders hunched as though the weight of their world rested upon them. "All I can tell you is that this is the way it must be. Whatever happens, it is Their will."

Bareil felt frustrated by her answer. Ambiguity and pessimism were unusual for Kai Opaka. "Your Eminence . . . you have always told me that the Prophets look after those who look after themselves . . . that we show our greatest trust in the Prophets by having faith in our own abilities to solve our troubles."

"I have faith in my own abilities," Opaka said, her voice soft. "And I have faith in my own visions, as well. I have foreseen this, Vedek Bareil." Her voice dropped to a near whisper. "Your suggestions . . . will lead to an unfortunate path."

"Then we must ask the Prophets for the right answer!"

"The right answer, Vedek—or the answer that you want to hear?"

Bareil wished that for once, the steady leader would question her own beliefs. "You cannot be sure that—"

"Vedek, I am ordering you to go. I will not tell you again."

Bareil felt gripped with misery. "Yes, Your Eminence."

"But before you go, Bareil, you must put me in touch with Prylar Bek."

"Prylar Bek?" Bareil repeated. "Do you mean . . . you would like me to convey a message to him for you?"

"No, Vedek Bareil. I will speak to him myself. Please arrange it for me, and then go."

Bareil left the kai, holding out a thin ray of hope that perhaps Prylar Bek was still in contact with his Oralian, or perhaps he could somehow exercise some sort of influence over Kubus Oak—even Dukat himself. Perhaps Opaka knew something that she wasn't telling, something that could keep her son safe. Perhaps she was protecting Bareil from a greater threat that she could not reveal. He struggled with his own doubt, but he was not ready to disobey a direct order from the kai. He headed to his room to gather some things, and to contact Prylar Bek.

The streets of Vekobet were empty but for a scant bold number of Bajorans. Soldiers spilled out into the abandoned regions of towns, searching the old, ruined habitat districts for the hiding place of Opaka Fasil and his resistance cell. They would not find them—of that, Kalem Apren was sure. Theirs was one of the most carefully concealed cells on Bajor, the secret of their location fiercely guarded by the few who knew it. Most Bajorans were reluctant to give up any resistance cell, but none would turn the kai's own son over to the Cardassians.

Kalem was in his basement, the same place where he had conducted so many clandestine council meetings for the citizens of Kendra. Today, the low-ceilinged root cellar was more packed than it had been at the most hopeful of those gatherings, and Kalem still knew that it would offer them no protection from what was to come. They were here as much for the company of one another as for the false sense of security they conjured while huddling tightly together in the sweltering, sour-smelling dark. Raina had brought some chairs down from the main floor of their home, but most people were sitting together on blankets that had been laid on the hard dirt floor. Some were talking, halting amiability having begun to return to their conversation in the past few days. Others were tending to their children. Several were praying, but most were still sleeping—the best refuge they could have sought.

Kalem had made hasty arrangements with the others in his village. Anyone who requested shelter was not to be turned away, but so many had come, and how could Kalem refuse them? Despite how very futile it must be to hide under the flimsy floorboards of an ancient dwelling, at least they would not have to die alone.

Kalem continued to venture outside from time to time with a few of the others, gathering supplies as necessary and making futile attempts to communicate with the Cardassian soldiers, and with the few stubborn Bajorans who continued to go about their business, refusing to hide. Few had attempted to evacuate; it was well understood that no one could get far enough away to make any difference. There was still a hopeful current in his mind that insisted there might be a way to negotiate with the Cardassians—if the Cardassians would only answer his requests for a conference. No word from anyone about when to expect an attack, only frightened comm transmissions back and forth between the few households that had access to communications equipment.

Then all the soldiers, without exception, abruptly departed Vekobet.

It was mid-morning, or at least, Kalem thought it was, when he began to hear the sound of ships overhead. "Stay calm, everyone," he announced. "Perhaps they are coming to negotiate. We will wait to be contacted before we make any assumptions."

It did little good. People began to cry, those who were sleeping quickly awakening to slap their hands over their ears and cling to their loved ones in terror. Kalem did his best to calm them, but nobody was listening to him, only tilting their faces upward to the floor of the house. A few stumbled over one another to get to the stairs, wanting to see what was going to happen; others held them back, arguing and wailing. All the while, the terrible growling drone from overhead continued to crescendo. A single word permeated Kalem's consciousness. *Soon.* He waited for the flotilla overhead to drown out the crying all around him.

But there was no sudden press of fire and devastation, no wild screaming as bombs fell, no intense flashes of heat and light. Instead, there was a discernible shift in the direction from which the flyers seemed to be coming, and everyone else heard it too. The stillness of the air in the basement returned as everyone stopped crying to listen, even the children seeming to know that something had changed.

"They're heading for the forest," someone announced fearfully, and Kalem did not waste another moment clambering up the stairs, followed by many others who wished to confirm what they were all thinking: their lives were to be spared, but at a cost that none felt they could afford.

Kalem ventured outside to look up at the sky, and instantly he saw the small formation of attack craft in the sky—headed away from the village, passing it over for another target. There were not nearly enough ships to have taken out the entirety of the Kendra Valley, Kalem realized.

And he knew then that he was going to live, but he took no joy in that realization at all.

Many other people were standing in the streets now, looking to where the Cardassian flyers were headed. "Are we saved?" asked a small boy, standing just outside Kalem's brick home next to his sniffling mother, and the woman held her son close.

"Shhh," she said to him, leaving Kalem to wonder how much the child had known of what everyone believed was going to happen. Had his mother explained any of it to him, or simply insisted that he come along to spend the nights in a stranger's house? *How well-behaved the children have been these past days*, Kalem thought to himself, and he imagined the things these children had seen in their short lifetimes, so different from his own carefree childhood. He would do almost anything in his power to change it for this youth—for all of them.

"You'll be just fine, son," Kalem told the boy, swallowing down the lump in his throat and trying on a smile. A few others made attempts at weak reassurances to one another, more and more people coming up from the basement now and out into the glinting sunlight of a cold morning.

But those assurances quickly turned to sorrow as the flyers began to dive, at a point too far away from where they all stood now to get a proper picture of what was happening, but the resultant echoing thunder in the sky gave a clear voice to the unseen horror, and the people commenced to wailing again, even louder than when they had thought their own lives were in danger.

23

Bareil had been unable to focus on his studies at the Dakeen Monastery. The place was remote, and sequestered completely from outside influences. Bareil already knew that he had been sent to the monastery to keep him from learning the outcome of the prefect's ultimatum. For whatever reason, the kai did not want his interference in her plan, if she even had a plan.

From Dakeen, he had been summoned to Terok Nor, where Prylar Bek was in a nearly inconsolable state, where Bareil was finally informed of what had transpired. The prylar had been in almost constant contact with the Shikina Monastery for the past week or so, demanding to see Bareil, but apparently Opaka had not granted his request until now—now that it was too late.

Feeling desperately sad, Bareil traveled home to Shikina, flanked by Cardassian escorts. They dumped him off at the shuttle port just outside of Iwara, the farthest village from the monastery. He could see the peaked roofs of two of the larger structures in Ashalla, just visible over the tree canopy directly in his path: the stone house of a former member of cabinet, now occupied by some of that man's extended family, and an old building of commerce.

It had rained early this morning, and the smell of wet grasses was overpowering. He traveled on foot through two small villages and through the winding passages in the forest, used by almost no one. On Terok Nor, Prylar Bek had arranged for a religious official's permit to be issued to Bareil, so that he might travel without fear of interference by soldiers, but it mattered little now that the detection grid had been disabled.

Bareil felt half-lost for most of his journey, following a few ambiguous landmarks he relied on to help him find his way. He scarcely ever left the monastery himself, and was not familiar enough with the journey to have the route committed to memory. It was almost fully dark before he saw the lights of the monastery. The kai was waiting for him in her dayroom, the chamber where she conducted most of her daily business. He felt he had a thousand questions, but when he saw her face, saw the loss there, the resigned despair, he could find only one word. "Why?"

There was silence for a long time, and then Opaka spoke, her tone soft. "I don't know, Vedek Bareil. I don't know why. I only know that it had to be."

"But . . . Your Eminence . . ."

He saw that her eyes were shining with tears. Her voice was hoarse from weeping, but she spoke with the same coolness that she always employed. "Vedek Bareil, I realize that this is difficult. But your faith must not waver now, for things are only going to become more difficult in time."

He shook his head, not understanding. "But you keep insisting that Bajor is going to be free soon. You keep saying that peace is just within our grasp!"

"This is so," she said. "But circumstances will grow worse before they can get better. We must not falter."

"Worse than the death of your son? Kai Opaka, what more can the Prophets ask of you?"

Her face did not change, though her tone was noticeably less cool. "You must have faith."

"I have faith in the Prophets," he said. "And I have faith in you."

She nodded. "I know. But it is not what the Prophets will ask of me, Bareil. If we are ever to have peace with Cardassia, it will be because of you, not because of me."

Bareil took a moment to try and absorb what she had told him. He did not know if he liked the message he gleaned from what she was saying—that she expected him to succeed her. He was not sure if he would be up to the task, especially not if the Prophets required such costly sacrifices. He felt a new surge of anger, of incomprehension.

"Prylar Bek told me," she said softly, "that he had been in contact with an Oralian on the station, those years ago when he sent word to us to evacuate from the shrine . . ."

"So—you were the one who told Prylar Bek?" He asked her in a thin voice.

Opaka's voice was far away. "The Oralian had told him—had believed with unwavering certainty—that it was you, Bareil, who would be imperative to the future of relations between our two worlds, not me. It was you that he sought to save when we fled here from the shrine at Kendra."

"Who told Prylar Bek?" Bareil repeated.

"Prylar Bek was reluctant to tell the secretary," Opaka said. "I did my best to explain it to him, of course, but . . ." She trailed off.

Bareil struggled with her answer. "The people of Bajor . . . must never know that it was you who did this, Your Eminence."

Opaka said nothing in answer.

"And I trust you, Kai Opaka . . . but I don't know if there is any way that you could possibly explain this to make me understand your reasons."

The kai made a mournful sound, her placid resolve finally cracking. "How can I explain them when I don't fully understand them myself? I agreed to come to this monastery to be nearer to the Prophets, so that I might learn to translate the messages they send to me, but I am no better an interpreter of my visions than I was when I first encountered the Tear. I don't know why They chose this outcome. I only know that They did."

Opaka's face broke, and she let out a low, plaintive cry of unrestrained grief, turning away from him. Bareil left her alone in the vestibule, closing the door behind him, though on any normal day the door would have remained open. This was most assuredly not a normal day. All he could do was pray for her, for all of them . . . and hope that it was all somehow for the best.

Yoriv Skyl had only been a member of the Detapa Council for a few months, but apparently the young man was already making waves. Legate Tekeny Ghemor noted, as he read the latest bulletin, that Skyl and some of the Pa'Dar family had put in a proposal to bring the Bajoran issue to the table for determination yet again. Ghemor reviewed the bulletin for a third time, picturing to himself the reaction of his friend Gaten Russol, wondering if the gul had read this report yet. He decided to contact the younger man, for a casual discussion of the bulletin, nothing more. It shouldn't raise any suspicions—Ghemor felt reasonably certain of that.

But before he could put the call through to Russol, he received a startling announcement from Legate Danig Kell, a confidential transmission that was to be sent only to a handful of the highest-ranking officials in Central Command, Ghemor among them.

"My fellow legates," Kell began. The old soldier's expression was, as usual, bordering somewhere on the menacing. *"I regret to report that the subjects on our Bajoran host world are in a state of complete insurrection, because of an unfortunate*

series of decisions made by that world's prefect. I have decided to approach the situation from an entirely new angle."

Ghemor tuned in with heightened interest.

"Gul Dukat is to make an announcement to the Bajoran people regarding their government; they will be told that the current members of the Bajoran cabinet are to be dismissed. Those outgoing cabinet members will bear the brunt of Bajoran frustration, as it will be made clear to the people of Bajor that these ineffective politicians are to blame for their current complaints. A small group of Bajorans shall be chosen to lead the new government. This group will be carefully hand-picked, by the prefect and myself, although every effort will be made to establish the appearance of democratic process for the benefit of the Bajoran people."

A mock election, Ghemor mused. By Kell's logic, if the Bajorans believed they were electing their new leaders, they would be appeased enough to halt their uprisings. But Ghemor had his doubts as to the effectiveness of the plan. The Bajorans were a put-upon people, short on loyalty and long on suspicion. Cardassia could never hope to win their trust. It was the heart of the reasoning behind the Detapa Council's repeated insistence that the Bajoran situation be reassessed, and though most members of Central Command were not supposed to be in agreement with that opinion, Ghemor felt very strongly that pulling out of Bajor was the only sensible solution.

Kell's announcement continued. *"Upon taking office, the new government will declare that any member of the Bajoran resistance who is willing to turn himself or herself in to the authorities will be granted a full pardon, reliant on cooperation with the authorities."*

Ghemor could scarcely believe that Kell thought this strategy would work. If the new government made such an announcement, the Bajorans would immediately know they were dealing with mere figureheads, powerless leaders who were being controlled by Cardassians. Apparently, Kell knew what was coming from the Detapa Council—the civilian leaders were poised to vote for withdrawal, but this was Kell and Dukat's final attempt to give the appearance of putting down terrorist strikes before the issue came up for decision.

Kell went on. *"Furthermore, the Bajoran people will be told that Cardassia has plans for a full withdrawal. It is my hope that these proclamations will serve to quell the current violence on Bajor."*

Ghemor was surprised, to say the very least, but he immediately knew there had to be more. Kell was too arrogant a man to truly abandon Bajor so abruptly. With the next announcement, Kell proved him right.

"Before Cardassian personnel are redeployed, I will order the placement of several survey units to reassess the current state of Bajoran resources. The prefect assures me that there are still a great many unexploited raw materials left on that world, but that we have been long overdue for a comprehensive survey to determine the capacity of those materials. Depending on our findings, Cardassia will either make plans for a new phase of Bajoran annexation, or we will fulfill our promise to the Bajoran people and make a full withdrawal. For obvious reasons, this assessment is not to be discussed with members of the civilian government."

Ghemor was furious. Kell was an even bigger fool than Ghemor could possibly have imagined. Did he truly believe that he could effectively placate the Bajoran subjects with his false promises, and somehow avoid greater repercussions when he failed to keep those promises? For it was almost guaranteed that the Cardassian survey teams would find some useful vein of minerals or store of elemental raw materials that would convince the Detapa Council to stay. Even if the findings were meager, Ghemor knew that Kell was not likely to squander the expense of the survey units, nor cause such an indelible stain on his own pride. He would falsify his reports if he had to, for Ghemor knew it was nowhere near beneath him. This was simply a manifestation of a weak-minded man digging his heels even deeper into the Bajoran problem.

The announcement was done, and Kell had signed off. Ghemor considered his options for only a moment before he contacted Gul Russol.

"Gaten," he said, "I have news. Do you still maintain a . . . relationship with the Federation?'

Russol nodded, his eyes narrowing in curiosity.

"You will want to get in touch with them quickly. I think I finally have something that we—and they—can use."

Jas Holza had been deliberately avoiding contact with him, Kalem was sure of it by now. The former minister was uncomfortable with Kalem and Jaro's insistence that he assist in acquiring the weapons he had long ago promised to help purchase. Kalem had sent many messages to Jas by way of Keeve Falor, who insisted that Holza was getting them—but still, he refused to act.

It usually took several tries to connect with Valo II, but after dozens of futile attempts throughout the day, Kalem had finally managed to do so in the stillness of the cool night. It was late, and everyone else in Vekobet should have been asleep by now—though Kalem knew that nobody would get any real sleep for a long time to come.

A successful call meant that Kalem would reach whoever happened to be in the vicinity of one of the very few working comm systems on Valo II, and that person would either agree to fetch Keeve, or they wouldn't. This time, Kalem was lucky enough to have contacted someone who knew exactly where Keeve Falor was, and who was able to bring him quickly. Kalem hadn't waited long before the other man answered his call.

"Falor," Kalem said, his voice heavy with sorrow. "It's Kalem Apren."

"*Kalem. I have conveyed all the messages you have asked of me, but Jas Holza still says—*"

Kalem interrupted. "I have another piece of news for him. I only wish for him to know that the kai's son is dead. The Cardassians massacred Opaka Fasil's resistance cell. The people in Kendra—the people on the whole of Bajor—have sunk into a state of complete despair."

Kalem heard a sound that could have been interference, or it could have been Keeve Falor sucking a hard breath. "*I will pass on the word,*" he said gravely.

Kalem had an afterthought. "Just ask him . . . ask him if he still feels it is too great a risk for him to enter the B'hava'el system."

There was a pause, and Kalem repeated himself to be sure he had been heard, but Keeve finally answered. "*I will relay the message to him, Apren. I hope this accomplishes your objective.*"

"If it doesn't," Kalem replied, "then nothing will."

"Kubus! Come to my office at once!"

The gray-haired Bajoran on Dukat's monitor frowned, his expression grim. "*I cannot leave my quarters, Gul. Are you aware that Prylar Bek has committed suicide?*" His manner was that of a man struggling to maintain control—a sensation that Dukat was all too familiar with. Reports of more attacks on the surface were coming in by the hour, and the prefect could feel himself coming undone at the seams.

"Of course I'm aware of it," he snapped. "Do you think I don't know what goes on at my own station?"

"*You didn't know the grid was going down,*" Kubus said.

"Is that an admission?" Dukat snarled. "Did *you* know that they were going down, Secretary?"

"*Of course not!*" The Bajoran cried. "*Would you truly doubt my loyalty at a time like this? I am perhaps the most hated man in the B'hava'el system right now, Gul! I can't even leave my quarters—my throat would be slit by some scheming worker the instant I stepped into the corridor!"*

"You should have thought to shift the blame to Prylar Bek, Secretary."

"The Bajorans on the station have their own ideas about my involvement. Many of them are sure that I am entirely to blame. For the death of the kai's son! Gul, you cannot understand what it means!"

"I am sure it is difficult for you, Secretary, but this isn't why I have called. I need to know who among the Bajorans still carries influence—who is an easily reachable spokesperson—"

"I am their spokesperson," Kubus interrupted, clearly perturbed at the implication that it was otherwise.

"Kubus, this is no time for your posturing! You just said yourself the Bajorans would rather have you murdered than listen to a word you say. I need to know, in your estimation, who I can contact, whose voice might make a difference among the rebels."

"The Kai, of course," Kubus said, still sulking. *"But now that Prylar Bek is . . . gone . . . I couldn't tell you how to reach her."*

"Not a religious leader," Dukat said. "Someone with political clout, someone—"

"Don't think for a moment that the kai does not have political clout!" Kubus said.

"Shall I ask one of the other members of the cabinet?" Dukat asked, with false patience. "Perhaps Kan Nion, or Somah Trac?" The secretary's dislike of some of his Bajoran colleagues was amusingly pronounced, and Dukat often brought up his political rivals' names in order to get results from the taciturn Kubus.

"I suppose if you're looking for a secular voice . . . there is always Kalem Apren, of the Kendra Valley. Many are still quite loyal to him, or so I'm told. In fact, if you were to ask Kan Nion, he would undoubtedly tell you the same thing."

"Get me in touch with Kalem Apren immediately, then."

"But, Dukat! I can't risk going to the surface! I told you, if I so much as—"

"He can't be reached by comm?"

"I . . . don't know."

"There is no need for you to speak to him yourself," Dukat said impatiently. "Simply patch him through to me."

Kubus was still hesitant, and Dukat changed his tone.

"Get me in contact with this man—I don't care how—and I will see to it that you are relocated to Cardassia Prime, where you will be protected."

"A Bajoran, on Cardassia Prime? Do you honestly think I would be any safer there than—"

"Yes," Dukat said. "Think of it, Kubus. You would be a celebrity—an example to the Cardassian people's cause!" Dukat felt quite pleased with the image as he saw it; for if Kubus was controlled carefully enough, Dukat was sure that he could do much on his homeworld to promote Cardassia's position here. *Dukat's* position here.

But there was another reason the idea appealed to him: Kell had never cared for the secretary, and there was a pleasantly perverse symmetry to Kubus's exile to Prime. After all, Kell had forced Dukat to take in that fallen operative from the Order, who had turned out to be the very man the prefect held responsible for the death of his father, long ago. And while Dukat was powerless to exact revenge, he thought it was only fitting to burden Central Command with the responsibility for protecting a Bajoran national who symbolized the benefits of continuing the annexation.

On the screen, Kubus hesitated. *"Yes,"* he finally said. *"I'll find a way to contact him."*

Dukat's door chimed just as he said it, and he absently pressed the panel to admit his visitor. One of the officers from Ops appeared in the door, and Dukat gestured him inside as he ended the call with Kubus.

"More reports of sabotage on the surface, sir. A worker revolt at a mill in Rakantha Province—sixteen Cardassian guards killed. The facility is burning as we speak—"

Dukat let his head sink for a nearly imperceptible beat before snapping to attention again, to redeploy troops to the region—but his forces were simply spread too thin. Should he even bother to contact Central Command about this? Should he wait for the Bajorans to forget about the so-called massacre, for the unrest to die back down to manageable levels? But Dukat did not believe that they would "forget." For an instant, he was taken back, to the first time he had ever come to Bajor. A Bajoran man from his memory reminded him; permanent grudges, he'd said. They were like Dukat himself, that way. Maybe it was something Dukat had started to forget, in recent years. Maybe he'd forgotten it when he'd ordered the execution of the resistance cell in Kendra, so excited was he at the opportunity to get at the son of the kai . . .

He stopped to consider the possibility that the execution of that cell could have been as grave an error as he had ever made. It had only fueled the resistance, where Dukat had expected to deter them. It was all he could do now to contain the aftermath. But if it had been a mistake, it did no good to acknowledge it as such. No good except perhaps to learn from it, to use the lesson in a future he hoped he could secure for himself.

Vaughn had been stationed on Starbase 621 for a few months now, analyzing starship movement along the Tzenkethi border, but he had maintained his Cardassian contact sporadically over the past few years. Tonight, the man had contacted him with urgency in his voice, and now Vaughn interrupted him somewhat against his better judgment, to ask him a question that had been plaguing him for a very long time.

"Gul Russol," he said carefully, hoping against hope that he would not accidentally offend the man. He had upheld the relationship with Russol for over two years, but had never quite been able to figure out his motives. "I don't understand why you would choose to share this information with me. Why are you—"

"I told you, Commander. I oppose my world's current government. Besides the never-ending violence, the annexation of Bajor is a symptom of the disease that has infected our entire social consciousness. My world will eventually be forced to withdraw from Bajor, and when it happens, we will experience an economic depression, among other things. Cardassia has become too dependent upon Bajor and worlds like it. We will never pursue research into self-sustaining resources unless we are forced to do so. I believe that our economy will have a better chance to rebound if we withdraw sooner rather than later. Additionally—"

"So, you have no particular sympathy for the Bajoran people?"

"No," Russol said flatly. *"The Bajorans are a violent and uncivilized people. I prefer to maintain my distance from them."*

Vaughn suppressed a frown—he'd met few Cardassians who weren't dramatically xenophobic. It was a wonder this Russol had even deigned to speak to a human. But this admission seemed to at last confirm for Vaughn that the man was genuine in his pleas for help; if he had claimed to empathize with the Bajorans, Vaughn would have had much more difficulty swallowing the man's story. "I see," he said. "Go on."

"The announcements my government plans to make on Bajor are absolutely false," Russol told him. *"They are a ruse, meant to distract the Bajorans from survey teams, who are working even as we speak to determine what is left of Bajor's resources, and how best to efficiently extract them. My government wishes to*

bleed Bajor dry of all useful elements, and then abruptly leave. This would be devastating to the long-term economic situation of my world—my people are in denial regarding the current state of Bajoran exports."

"To say nothing of what it will do to Bajor," Vaughn said glibly.

Russol ignored the comment. *"Once the Bajorans realize they are being lied to—and they will realize it, no matter how shortsighted and foolish they may be—the violence on that world will only increase. But my government will refuse to abandon it, despite how bad it gets. It has become a matter of pride for them. And there will be terrible repercussions for the Union."*

"What exactly is it that you would have the Federation do about it?" Vaughn asked.

The man on the other end of the line was clearly troubled. *"I don't know the full extent of your . . . Prime Directive . . . your rules and charters,"* he admitted. *"But I imagine there are at least two feasible options. The first is for Starfleet to remove the Cardassian presence from Bajor . . . by force."* He stopped speaking, looking glum. *"That option could be quick, but it would certainly be bloody. As I see it, however, it could also have much larger consequences. My people are not likely to back down from the insult, and the conflict could easily lead to full-scale war between our two governments."*

Vaughn nodded, understanding Russol's logic. Nobody wanted more war between the Cardassian Union and the Federation. The border conflicts between those bodies had been brutal, and Vaughn suspected Russol was a veteran of at least a few of the skirmishes. "What is the second option?"

"The second option is for you to . . . somehow deliver this message to the Bajoran people. Someone in charge, I suppose, though I don't know much regarding their civilian government . . ."

"They don't have much of one," Vaughn told him. "But I do believe I can reach a few influential Bajorans who might have the means to pass the word around. Exactly what part of this message do you want to be revealed to them?"

"All of it!" Russol exclaimed. *"Tell them . . . they must not accept the offer of a new Bajoran government! Their resistance fighters must not turn themselves in! They must . . . they must continue to fight. They must fight harder than they've ever fought, because they actually have a chance of winning this time!"*

Vaughn would have been doubtful of this man's motives if it had not been for the raw sincerity that colored his voice and expression. Russol was torn. He was betraying his own people with what he was trying to do, but he had been pushed over the edge, and he knew of no other way to fight for what he believed in.

Russol spoke again, his voice lower. *"I can see that you are taken aback,"* he said, with a touch of defensiveness. *"I know I am a traitor. But I have come to see that the lives of a few more soldiers are worth the preservation of my world's integrity. This is the definition of war, and the reason that we fight. Cardassians believe deeply in the struggle for the greater good, Vaughn. I wish for peace in the long run, but . . . I have come to believe that peace must sometimes be achieved through violence."*

Vaughn was speechless for a long moment. Finally, he spoke. "You say you don't know much of the Federation's charter," he said. "I can tell you right now that there may be problems with what you have just proposed. You will recall that my government has a treaty with yours. I don't know if I can permissibly deliver this kind of information to your enemies."

Russol looked crestfallen. *"But . . . you have confirmation that my people seek to deceive the Bajorans. Is that not just cause for your government to intervene on the Bajorans' behalf?"*

Vaughn sighed. "Perhaps, but it is more likely that we would adhere to your prior option," he said. "Diplomacy failing, of course." He didn't like it, and he could see that

Russol didn't either. Vaughn had reviewed the transcript
of Nechayev's latest conversation with Kalem Apren, and
it occurred to him that even the Bajorans might not like
it. This was their fight to win, and they would probably
resent it if the Federation suddenly swooped in at the elev-
enth hour. Despite the ramifications, he promised Russol
to try his best for the latter option—to give the Bajorans
the information they needed to win the fight themselves.

Vaughn wasted no time in contacting Vice-Admiral
Nechayev once his conversation with Russol was done,
but he was immediately disappointed by Nechayev's
response. *"You cannot act on this information, Commander,"*
she informed him. *"The best we can do is to confront the Cardassian leaders and demand that they tell the Bajoran people the
truth themselves."*

"They'll never do it!" Vaughn exclaimed. "They'll pass
the word on to their puppet leaders and claim their innocence by hiding behind a cardboard panel of cowardly
Bajorans!"

"Be that as it may—"

Vaughn was beginning to lose his temper. "Vice-
Admiral, forty plus years ago, the Federation could do
nothing to prevent the Bajoran annexation from happening. Our hands were tied by bureaucracy. Right under
our noses, the Cardassians stole an entire world from the
Bajorans—and now we have the chance to give it back to
them. Let's not let that red tape tie our hands again! Alynna,
you were there! Of all people, you should be most willing
to look the other way for the sake of what's right!"

Nechayev was only shaking her head in response. She
was beginning to look angry, her usually unflappable sever-
ity coming undone, but Vaughn went on.

"If we inform the Cardassian leaders of what I learned
today, we risk putting my contact in danger, and it will do
nothing to help the Bajorans."

"The treaty—"

"Damn the treaty!" Vaughn said. "The peace we have with Cardassia is anything but genuine, and you know it!"

Nechayev's mouth tightened in annoyance. Vaughn winced, waiting for the inevitable fallout, but after a moment, the vice-admiral's expression changed, as if she had decided something.

"I'm going to pretend I didn't hear that," she said softly. *"In fact, this conversation never took place."*

Vaughn's eyes narrowed.

"I trust you will do the right thing, Commander."

"I . . . thank you, Vice-Admiral."

As the communication ended, Vaughn decided it was the closest thing he'd get to permission. There would be no safety net if the information was traced back to him. But then, he worked best without a net. Whatever consequences he faced personally, he could bear it knowing that he had at least tried to save Bajor from the fate of indefinite occupation. Before he could change his mind, he entered the approximate communication code for the post on Valo II.

24

Kalem was quick to answer the comm this time, as it awoke him from the early stages of sleep. The timing of the communication suggested a contact point from somewhere outside Kalem's own time zone—but since few people from the Kendra Valley ever sought to contact him in this manner, Kalem could have assumed as much anyway. *Holza,* he thought hopefully, though he wasn't sure he recognized the voice as Jas Holza's.

"This is Kalem Apren. State your business."

"Mister Kalem. I understand you are something of a spokesperson for your people. I have a proposition that I hope you will find interesting."

"With whom am I speaking?" he asked, still confused from sleep.

"I represent the Cardassian Union."

Kalem was taken aback, to say the least. A Cardassian representative was certainly the last person he would have expected to hear from—the last person he wanted to hear from. But his curiosity dictated that he listen. "Continue," he said.

"As I stated, my sources have informed me that you have a great deal of influence over the people on your world," the voice said silkily. *"If this truly be the case, then my people hope that you will help us to convey a message to all of Bajor."*

"What message might that be?"

"That we intend to withdraw our interests from this planet—from this system. Can I count on you to relay this message?"

Kalem felt the discernible rush of blood in his ears, the amplification of his own heart. Had he really heard what he thought he'd heard?

"Yes," he said, feeling all his hopes held hostage by the possibility that this was not really happening. "I . . . will convey the message . . ."

The voice continued. *"But I think you will agree that an abrupt withdrawal could warrant disastrous results. Your people will need an interim government, someone trustworthy to steer Bajor through the difficult storms ahead. Bajor has very little of its own infrastructure intact, and one hopes that a new Bajoran cabinet could help to reestablish some of the basic necessities that will help keep the Bajoran populace from escalating into chaos."*

Kalem thought it sounded reasonable, but the initial burst of jubilance suddenly seemed further away. The voice continued, but Kalem was losing focus, only half-hearing the offers that were being made to him.

". . . an election, of course. I look to you for advice regarding some suitable candidates for various positions . . ."

What is this?

". . . we want to represent the will of the people, but I feel we can be reasonably certain that the status you currently enjoy will translate to your being involved in the next generation of Bajoran leaders—a new generation, you understand, a generation that is for Bajor only. My people are tired of the violence, Mister Kalem, and on my homeworld, the cries for withdrawal have become too loud for us to ignore. We recognize that the best course of action . . ."

Kalem scarcely realized it when the Cardassian had stopped speaking, and grappled with the distinct sense that he had just been asked a question. He spoke, not entirely sure what he was answering to—something about Terok Nor, an invitation? "Your offer . . . sounds generous . . . sir," he began, looking for the words, and the strength, to continue. "But right now . . . I am very occupied with . . . my people . . . with—"

"Of course you are," the disembodied voice said smoothly. *"It is my understanding that Bajor still looks to you for advice and assistance. I have polled a great many of my Bajoran advisers and colleagues, and their responses led me directly to my decision to contact you first. Of course, if you don't feel you are suitable for nomination, I understand that Jaro Essa is—"*

"Jaro Essa will never accept any offers from you," Kalem laughed. "While I suppose I should be . . . flattered . . . that my name has come up in discussion with your advisers, I must respectfully decline the opportunity. I cannot leave my people at this time. You see, I am far too busy consoling the families and friends of those who were killed in the massacre here in the Kendra Valley—"

"Massacre!" the voice replied, and something in his tone confirmed to Kalem that he was speaking to the prefect. This was Gul Dukat; he knew it. *"Kubus Oak has assured me that the people executed in Kendra were part of a dangerous terrorist organization. Tell me, did Secretary Kubus misinform me? Because if that is the case, Mister Kalem, then I must point out that this is exactly why the current Bajoran government must—"*

Kalem interrupted, feeling his gorge rise at the sound of Kubus Oak's name coming from the mouth of a Cardassian. From Dukat. Was the prefect looking for a new puppet, then?

"There will be an election," he said forcefully. "But the Cardassians will have no say in it. That election will occur after your people are gone, not before." Kalem abruptly squashed his thumb against the disconnect button without waiting for the prefect's reply. His breath was coming hard. He had another call waiting for him, and whoever it was, it had to be someone whose conversation would be preferable to Gul Dukat's.

"This is Kalem Apren," he said, struggling to keep the angry breathing from overcoming his words.

"*Apren!*" cried Keeve Falor's voice, heavy with interference between Bajor and distant Valo II. "*I have news that is of the utmost importance! I have just spoken to a Federation contact who received pertinent information for us. The Cardassians—they are going to try and negotiate with us—*"

Apren was stunned. "Yes," he said quickly. "I . . . I know, I spoke to Dukat . . ."

"*Tell me you did not agree to any of his offers!*"

"Of course I didn't, Falor! You ought to know that I wouldn't have!"

"*Oh . . . oh, thank the Prophets. Yes, of course I knew, but . . .*"

Apren explained where his thoughts had been throughout his entire exchange with Dukat. Now he knew his instincts had been correct. "If the Cardassians are negotiating, Falor, it can only mean one thing—they are genuinely on the defensive now. They are frightened."

"*You're more right than you even know, old friend. You must tell the people on Bajor—they must not hold back now, no matter what happens. Now is the time to fight—and win.*"

"But the resistance cell here in Kendra—they were all massacred by the Cardassians. Jaro Essa still has a few scattered contacts, but—"

"*This message is not just for the resistance, Apren,*" Keeve said. "*Everyone must know of this. The Prophets have given us the opportunity we need, but we must show them that we are capable of defending our world ourselves—*"

Kalem interrupted as the thought entered his mind. "Weapons, Falor."

"*Weapons?*"

"We need weapons. Does Holza know of this new development?"

"*Not yet, but I will—*"

"You should have contacted him first, Falor!"

"I had to be sure that you wouldn't agree to anything!"

"Falor, you should have known that I wouldn't have. Tell Jas Holza about this immediately!"

"I will do my best to get word to him, but we can't wait for him to come through, Apren! There must be no delays in communicating this message to the people of Bajor!"

"I understand," Kalem answered, though he wasn't sure he did. He wanted to know more about the Federation contact, about the sudden change in climate that would make a full-scale victory a tangible possibility; about the true nature of the offers that Dukat was trying to make. But from Keeve's tone, it was clear that this was not the time to ask questions—this was the time to act.

"What is this place?" Tahna Los asked Biran as they crept closer to the low-lying building, several kellipates outside of Dahkur. It was old and poorly kept, with a deserted feel. "An armory?"

Kohn Biran shook his head. "I think we've managed to get all the armories around here. Between us, the Shakaar, and the Gertis cells, we've practically crippled the spoonheads in this region."

"So, what is it?"

Biran looked stern. "Don't tell anyone in the Shakaar cell. It's an orphanage."

"We're bombing an orphanage?" Tahna didn't mean for his voice to sound so incredulous, and he cleared his throat, glancing uncomfortably at Jouvirna. "I mean—"

"Baby vipers are still poisonous," Biran said. "Remember what I said about the Shakaar. Especially the women."

"Nerys probably wouldn't have a problem with it," Tahna said, though he wasn't certain. "But Lupaza . . ."

"Don't worry about them. We need to do this—to send a message."

It had been six weeks since the announcements. They had heard the news repeated from the Krim cell in Rakantha, the Carean cell from Ba'atal, the Gertis cell, and many others that Tahna couldn't even name. Jaro Essa was saying that this was the time to push harder than they had ever pushed, if they wanted to be free of the Cardassians. And they were pushing. Tahna knew that there was still heavy Cardassian presence in other parts of the world, but at least they had made headway here in Dahkur. The Kohn-Ma cell had only encountered a single Cardassian soldier tonight, angry and clearly frightened. Most of what they had encountered had been wreckage—bodies, shrapnel, burning ships and equipment. All lent an apocalyptic desolation to the once-beautiful landscape.

"So, we're going to kill them," Tahna said, laboring to avoid sounding grim as he studied the pathetic building.

Jouvirna shrugged. "We could blow them up, or we could take them hostage—use them as bargaining chips to get farther into the city, should we meet with a sizeable contingent of soldiers. But probably, the spoonheads wouldn't respond to hostages—they don't care about the orphans. We're doing them a favor by killing them, if you ask me."

Tahna wasn't so sure—and anyway, he thought it might be useful to have some leverage in case of Cardassian encounter. He hadn't forgotten the beatings he had suffered at the hands of his Cardassian captors, the horrible devices they had used in their efforts to coerce him to reveal the location of the rest of his cell. But the memory wasn't enough to dissuade him from continuing to fight. If anything, it fueled him, especially now that he believed the end was so near. Yet, there seemed to be little glory in carrying through with this particular target.

Tahna kept his views to himself as they moved in. The building was only a hecapate away, but before they could come close enough to detonate their explosives, a white sheet of blinding fire rose up from beyond the gates of the facility. Tahna threw his body backward to avoid the fallout of shrapnel, and the blast of heat washed over them. But after a moment, he saw that they had been far enough away to avoid contact with any flying debris. He sheepishly rose.

"Someone beat us to it," Jouvirna said, his voice tinged with awe.

"Someone else blew up the orphanage," Tahna said, stating the obvious, finding some measure of relief in the revelation. This wasn't the first time his cell had conspired to kill Cardassian children, or even the children of Bajoran collaborators. He found some reassurance in the discovery that other cells were capable of such an act.

Shouting had followed the explosion—shouts of Bajoran men, at least two of whom seemed to be headed in Tahna's direction. A beat later, a middle-aged man stepped out of the smoke, approaching Tahna and the others.

"Ho there," Tahna called. The man wore the garb of a farmer, dun-colored coveralls that were permanently grassy-green at the knees from kneeling for the harvest. As he came closer, Tahna saw that he was missing three teeth on the left side of his mouth, probably a result of poor nutrition. "What cell are you?"

"Cell?" The man called out. "None! We live in Petrita village, that way." He gestured to the east as a second man joined him. "We have been planning to destroy this site for over a week. It's the only place around here the spoonheads haven't abandoned."

"Are you sure?" Biran called out.

"Positive," answered the second man. He wore a stained leather vest over his tunic. "We've been scoping out all the local Cardassian sites. The only place they had anyone left was here at the orphanage. But don't worry, the children were all gone."

"Gone?" Biran said. "But the Cardassians don't claim the children of others . . . ?"

"The young ones were taken in by Bajoran families," he said. "They're too little to know any different. If they're lucky, they can just forget they were ever Cardassian."

"The young ones?" Tahna asked. "So . . . who was left?"

"There were three teenage boys in there who fancied themselves heroes," the farmer said. "They barricaded themselves inside and started taking potshots at us when we came near, though I couldn't tell you where they got their weapons—probably stolen from dead bodies around here somewhere. We figured we'd have to bomb them out—and so we did." He gestured back to the smoking rubble that had been the squat building as the other man raised his fist in victory.

Tahna felt strange as he considered the Cardassian teenagers. Abandoned here on an unfamiliar world, fighting for the very people who had left them behind. He briefly wished he hadn't asked. It was easier just to look on the remains of a building and feel triumphant.

"Are you all right, mister?" One of the farmers directed his question toward Tahna, who realized that he must be wearing his uncertainty. He forced a laugh, just before the bulky comm unit he carried alerted him with a squawk.

"This is six-one-six calling kejal-three-two . . ." It was Kira, back at the caves.

"This is *kejal* three-two, six-one-six, go ahead."

"Kejal three-two, reports of attack ships sighted in the Musilla region, headed toward Dahkur Province, estimated arrival one half-hour. Best to take cover, over."

Tahna's heart sank. "Copy that," he responded, looking to the others in his cell. Judging by their grave expressions, they had all heard it. The two farmers had heard it, as well, and did not hesitate to scurry back in the direction from which they had come.

"Helpful chaps," Biran remarked sourly.

"More spoonheads," Tahna lamented. "We had them all but wiped out in this province . . ."

"Forget it, Tahna, we've got to go," Jouvirna said, gesturing to the others as he broke into a jog. "We've got just enough time to make it back to the tunnels."

Tahna wasn't so sure that they did have time, but he sprinted alongside the others, pushing himself into the state of dogged numbness that was usually required for long-distance running. The four men crashed through brush, ambled up hills and back down them again, weaving through trees and over creeks. Tahna had once known all these routes by heart, but they had grown dimmer since the grid had gone up, every outside errand or mission turning into a carefully formulated and executed plan. It had been exhilarating to think that the grid was down for good— though a new onslaught of Cardassians in the area might mean that these days of freedom were coming to an end.

They made it back to their hideout in record time. Crawling through the tunnels gave Tahna the opportunity to catch his breath, though his mouth tasted like metal from the ragged heaving of the smoky air. He coughed as he shimmied after the Kohn brothers, and the sound echoed eerily throughout the connected caverns and passageways.

Nerys was waiting for him in the larger passageway that connected the Shakaar and Kohn-Ma burrows. She followed them into their cavern, not wasting any time with what she had to say, a bright urgency in her voice. "Jaro Essa just issued a statement over the comm."

Kohn Weir replied. "Jaro himself, or—?"

"It was Jaro," Kira confirmed. "He says that someone from the Valo system is bringing a massive shipment of weapons into Dahkur tomorrow—modern phasers, raw materials for explosives, and—"

"Who is bringing it?" Jouvirna inquired.

"What difference does it make?" Kira exclaimed. "They've already smuggled a shipment to Kendra. Prophets willing, the pilot will be here tomorrow with even more. Jaro said they'll be bringing shoulder-mounted missile launchers that can be fired from *kellipates* away, and long-range particle cannons for the raiders! We can take out heavy weapons emplacements, flyers, mechanized infantry units—all of it!"

The Kohn-Ma members looked at one another with skepticism and bewilderment.

"If what you say is true," Biran finally spoke up, "then this is really going to be the end of it."

"I know," Kira said evenly, and suddenly, Tahna knew it, too. It was really going to be over.

LIBERATED BAJOR, YEAR ONE

✦ ✦ ✦

2369 (Terran Calendar)

25

"Finally, I feel like the Prophets are listening," Shakaar said, taking a sip from his mug of *copal* cider. "I've been writing the same thing on my renewal scrolls since I learned how to write, and this time—"

"You aren't supposed to tell anyone what you write on your scroll," Kira reminded him, as she leaned up against the bare trunk of a dead nyawood tree. The sky above them was striped with a deep-cast orange, the moons beginning to rise over the farthest mountain ranges. The air was thick with smoke from burning Cardassian wreckage—and from the traditional fires of the Gratitude Festival, currently being celebrated all over the planet. It could not have come at a more opportune time in the calendar.

Shakaar laughed and took another pull at his cider. "Could there be any question what I wrote on my scroll? What we all wrote?"

"It's not my place to speculate what anyone else wrote," Kira said primly, and took the mug from Shakaar's hands to take a draught of her own.

Shakaar smiled at her, amusement shining in his eyes.

Both turned their heads to the sky as five more Cardassian troop carriers went up, bringing the day's total up to somewhere in the low hundreds. All day long, the Shakaar cell had been watching the ships leave atmosphere. All were backlit by an eerie halo in the lower portion of the sky, a clinging, stinking haze of acrid chemical smoke—not from the bonfires and braziers that had begun to smolder just after the sun dipped in the horizon, but from the remains of Cardassian factories, mining camps, and military bases. Some of the larger facilities had been burning for weeks. The Cardassians had stopped trying to put them out more than a month past, retaliating instead with fires of their own—scorching and poisoning the fields of thousands of farmers, setting the forests ablaze, ensuring that although they were finally leaving, their presence would not soon be forgotten.

The resistance had pushed as hard as they could, just as Jaro Essa had advised, following the massacre in the Kendra Valley. At first, it had not seemed that would be enough— the soldiers just kept coming, and Bajoran casualties were heavy. The targets seemed too numerous and too distant to effectively remove by people on foot. But the tide had turned two weeks ago—no small thanks to the massive distribution of contraband weapons that had found its way to Bajor from the Valo system.

Kira squinted up into the darkening sky as the winking ship lights became too distant to see, and her face split into a wide smile. Her head felt light. Though she continually warned herself not to get her hopes up, she truly believed the occupation was coming to a close.

Shakaar shook his head, as if to illustrate his own wary disbelief, and then he smiled back at her.

"This seems as good a way to celebrate the Gratitude Festival as any," Kira said.

"It's a new year," Shakaar murmured, taking the nearly empty mug away from her.

"A new era," Kira said.

"*Peldor joi*, Nerys," Shakaar said.

"*Peldor joi*." She repeated the traditional salutation of

the Gratitude Festival. It seemed funny to her now, the old Bajoran words having become nearly meaningless in these past years. Her family had still celebrated the festival when she was a child, lighting a small metal brazier and burning the renewal scrolls along with an uncharacteristically large dinner. Many friends and neighbors would come to the Kira residence to take part in the feast, and there would even be some kind of small treat afterward, for the children. But in the years since she had joined the resistance, the festival had been almost forgotten—a nod to the Prophets, but the modest indulgences of Kira's childhood seemed so far in the past as to have been imagined.

"I think they might really be leaving for good," Shakaar observed, putting voice to the thing that all Bajorans had come to believe, but had mostly been afraid to say out loud.

"Time will tell," Kira said carefully. "We need more cider."

"And I need to write my scroll," Shakaar said. "Shall we go back to camp?"

"I'll be along," Kira said, continuing to stare out at the sky, creeping over with dark. She turned for a moment to watch Shakaar amble back to the place where the cell had lit a bonfire of their own, swigging cider and gorging themselves on some makeshift approximation of *hasperat*. She admired him as he moved—she had always liked something about the way he moved—though of course there was nothing romantic about it; he was just a good-looking man, that was all. She turned away from him as the very notion of her old cell leader in amorous terms seized her, and she was overcome by a short burst of self-conscious laughter. Another carrier went up.

"Peldor joi," she told it, gazing after the transport until she couldn't see it anymore, and then turned to go back to camp; the *hasperat* was calling.

✦ ✦ ✦

"The civilian leaders' decision was nearly unanimous," Kell said. His face, almost filling the holoframe, was devoid of any expression.

Dukat cut him off with a barely suppressed snort.

"Have I amused you?"

Dukat shook his head, aware of the smile that refused to budge from his lips. There was nothing remotely amusing here, but if he stopped smiling, he was unsure of what would ultimately happen. His frustration rode so close to the surface of his bearings, he kept the reins tight as he carefully chose his words.

"I did all I could do."

"Of course you did."

"We took a few losses, naturally. Anything worth having can be expected to run into a few setbacks here and there." He extended his hand, palm up, and then, not quite knowing what else to do with it, he clenched it into a fist. "Central Command must have agreed with the civilian government to consent to this decision."

Kell opened his mouth as if to reply, but Dukat spoke over him; he did not care to hear the legate's excuses for the weakening of Central Command. The military was hemorrhaging power, and it was partly the fault of officials like Kell who were foolish enough to submit in the first place. This turn of events had been set in motion a long time ago. "It is . . . disappointing that some of my colleagues cannot envision the long-term results of their actions." His fist tightened. Someday, he would set things right—with the traitors in the civilian government, and with those in Central Command, as well. He knew exactly who was to blame for this, the loss of his legacy.

"The Cardassian people . . . have no faith in me," he went on. "They never did. Central Command had none, either. And yet, if they would only review the records of my term here, they would see that the very few times I was able to make use of my own policies, the Union enjoyed measurable success here. But when I followed the dictates of Central Command"—his voice was rising—"I failed. I failed, because I allowed others to coerce me into ignoring my own instincts."

Kell suddenly looked very tired. *"There is little sense in speaking of it now,"* he said, his tone flat. *"This is not about you, Dukat. I am contacting you merely as a formality. I anticipate the Federation will send its Starfleet soon. I assume you already know what must be done."*

"This *is* about me!" Dukat shouted. "Bajor is about me, don't you understand that? If you weren't so busy pandering to the fools in the Detapa Council— Central Command is but a shadow of its former self, can't you see that, Kell? Because of weak men like you!"

Kell scoffed and shook his head at the outburst. *"I understand how difficult it must be for you to confront your own failure,"* he said with a barely suppressed sneer. *"But there is still much for you to do, and little time to do it."*

"Yes . . . sir," Dukat said, carefully dialing back his hostility. He could not afford to make a fool of himself any more than he had already done, and Kell still had the power to ruin him completely—if the loss of Bajor hadn't already done it.

Dukat stood alone in his office for a few moments after the transmission ended. His arm had fallen to his side, but his hand was still closed into a hard fist. Slowly, he uncurled his fingers, examining his palm as if seeing it for the first time. He felt slightly dazed, but he knew he could not afford to succumb to his emotions; there was much to be done, as Kell had said, and he was the one expected to do it. There were no more Cardassians on the surface; at least, none who were authorized to be there. Now he must remove the rest of his men from Terok Nor.

He put in a call to Dalin Trakad, speaking as soon as

the dull-faced officer stepped into his office. "Get all the Bajorans out of ore processing and get them to the surface immediately," he commanded.

"Sir . . . how am I to arrange for the transport of so many people?"

"I don't care," Dukat snapped. "Put them in the cargo hold of a freighter for all I care, just get them out of here. Drop them at the closest transport hub on the surface and call it done. Get them out of here before they start rioting."

"Some of them . . . already have, sir."

"All the more reason to be swift in carrying out my instructions, Trakad."

The dalin nodded. *"Yes, sir. But . . . I don't know if you're aware that some of the soldiers . . . they have also started to destroy station property . . ."*

"Have they," Dukat mused. "Well, I advise you to keep out of their way, then. But I want you to personally ensure that all systems are permanently offline before we go. Leave nothing for the scavengers that will come after us. Purge all databases. Every system—replicators, weapons, ore-processing equipment, turbolifts—do your best to see that they are no longer functional by the time we leave. If all else fails, old-fashioned sabotage will suffice. Keep life support up, of course. For the time being."

The dalin was surprised. *"There is very little time, sir. It may not be possible to completely—"*

Dukat ignored him. "Start arranging for the transfer of first-tier military officials; all higher-echelon officers will be transported back to Cardassia Prime immediately. The rest are to follow until evacuation is complete, but I want all our people gone within three days. Understood?"

"What about . . . what about the tailor, sir?"

"He can fend for himself," Dukat snapped. Kell had made it clear enough that the disgraced operative was to be left alone; this might actually be the first time Dukat was happy to comply with the legate's order. "Carry out my intructions," he told Trakad.

"Yes, sir."

Dukat turned to go, but his thoughts quickly turned to the shape-shifter. "Contact Odo for me, Trakad."

Where Trakad had previously looked bewildered, now he looked fearful. "The . . . shape-shifter is . . . Nobody can find him. He seems to be . . . gone."

"Gone?"

"He . . . hasn't been seen since yesterday, and rumors have already sprouted that he fled . . . back to Bajor."

Dukat felt a momentary weakness in his limbs. Odo might not have gone back to Bajor; he could very well still be here, but if he was not answering station calls . . . After everything else—the treachery of the Detapa Council, the long-term flagrant disregard for his authority by the ingrates on this horrid world—the notion of Odo's disloyalty was very nearly the thing to send Dukat into a state of complete anomie.

He swept his gaze across the surfaces of his office—the eye-shaped window, framing starry blackness; the walls, his desk, the floor and ceiling. Every last fraction of it had been designed and created specifically for him, as the prefect of this world. But now—the thought of leaving Terok Nor whole and intact for Bajorans to infest like voles was repugnant to him. He doubted they would destroy it outright; without orbital facilities of their own, they might have need of such a place. Better to obliterate it himself than leave his seat of power for lo these many years to such as them.

But no, Dukat decided. Terok Nor would remain here, under the authority of whoever came along to claim the Bajoran prize for themselves, and it was looking more and more as though the Federation was going to be the unlikely victor in this comic tragedy.

Would the shape-shifter ally himself with the Bajorans? Dukat thought not; the man was a complete enigma in many ways, but the thing that defined him most was his status as an outsider. He could continue to search for his own kind . . . which meant that he would likely remain on the station, to fraternize with the democratic hypocrites of the Federation.

Dukat turned off the lights in his office. The Union had just made an enormous mistake, and Dukat had no intention of ever forgetting it. He was leaving, but this would not be the last he had seen of Bajor. His business here was far from finished. No, if he thought for an instant that he would never see Terok Nor again, he would have it destroyed with the Bajorans still aboard. But this was not over. Not nearly.

The people in the Valo system had been chattering about a possible withdrawal for a long time. Ever since the Federation ship that carried Ro Laren had come and gone, a great deal of gossip had circled around the colony world. When Jas Holza had finally agreed to purchase and deliver weapons to the people of Bajor, the residents of the Valo system had begun to speak of the coming withdrawal as fact, though Keeve had been afraid to really believe it. But as more reports poured in, and people arranged for transport back to Bajor, Keeve finally had to acknowledge to himself that it was not just a rumor, not a Cardassian trick—the occupation was over.

Those in Valo II's overcrowded settlements were speculating about what the ultimate cause of the withdrawal had been, picking up pieces of gossip as they heard them, often second-hand, or even third-hand, from Valo III. Most wanted to believe that the death of the kai's son had been the catalyst; that the massacre in the Kendra Valley was the final outrage to thrust the resistance—and the rest of

Bajor—into the frame of mind they needed to be able to summon the strength for the final push. Jas Holza was already held in high regard on this planet for keeping the citizens of Valo II alive with very little motivation. Now he was a genuine hero, for coming through with the weapons that gave the resistance the edge in the end. Keeve knew, of course, that there was more to it than that. The Federation had played a role, and Keeve imagined there was some machination of Cardassian politics that must have facilitated this unlikely outcome. Still, he was not such a pragmatist that he would not let the people have their martyr and their hero; it did much to bolster them in the uncertainty of this time. For despite the intense joy of knowing that they could return home once again, there was also unease over the consideration of what they would find when they got there.

Jas Holza had arranged for several of his transport ships to begin ferrying people to the surface of Bajor. He had already come to warn Keeve and the others that Bajor was not the same world they remembered. Jas's own ancestral home had been nearly destroyed in a recent attack, a great deal of the surrounding farmland and forest burned or permanently altered by either military strikes or the varied interests of the Cardassians over the years of the occupation. But most ignored his caution with eagerness—despite what Bajor might have become, nobody could believe that it would not be better than Valo II. A very few chose to stay behind, but most of the settlers preferred to take their chances on what was left of Bajor.

Keeve was one of the last to leave. He bundled up what few belongings he still cared to take with him, said good-bye to the handful of people who were staying, and prepared to board one of Jas Holza's outdated carriers. He waited in a slow-moving line, following a mix of people who trudged up the drop ramp and were shown into individual passenger compartments.

One of the pilot's crewmen took Keeve to a compartment with an open seat, pressing a panel so that the door would slide open, and Keeve was, for a moment, taken aback to see that the compartment appeared to already be full. But as he ducked inside, he quickly saw that he could take his place next to two silent children, close in age, though Keeve had no idea how old they might be. Twelve? Eight? Keeve had always been a poor judge of these things.

Keeve took his seat, and the man who sat opposite him spoke with enthusiasm. "We're to travel with Minister Keeve Falor?" he asked rhetorically, apparently speaking to his wife, who was seated next to him.

It took Keeve a moment to place him. "Bajin," Keeve finally said to the middle-aged man. This was the son of Darrah Mace. It was somewhat disconcerting for Keeve to acknowledge how old the man looked to him—if his friends' children were aging so much, how old must he then be? He wondered how Kalem Apren would look to him now, for he was to meet Apren and Jaro Essa at Bajor's capital as soon as he arrived.

"Hello, Keeve." Darrah Bajin greeted him with affection and respect, excitement showing through in his tone. "Have you met my wife and sons?"

"I have," Keeve said, nodding to the two politely silent boys in the seat adjacent to his. Bajin's wife, Cheren, gave him a wide smile, and then turned to her boys.

"This man was a great governor on our world when Papa and I were just small children!" she explained to them.

The children smiled shyly, and then quickly looked away, whispering to each other and looking deferentially to their mother. Keeve smiled at them. "Shy," he remarked.

Cheren's smile tightened. "Their lives have been difficult," she said.

"As have all of our lives," Bajin quickly added. "But that will come to an end, now."

"Indeed," Keeve murmured. He thought he remembered that Bajin and Cheren had lost a child, some years ago, but it was possible he had them confused with another couple. A great many babies born on Valo II had never made it to adulthood. He arranged his knees so they would not bump against Bajin's. The flyer had just jolted into takeoff mode.

The compartment began to vibrate as the thrusters took the ship quickly beyond the atmosphere. The turbulence was slight, even in the outdated ship. Jas had maintained his fleet as well as he could afford. This ship was once one of the best flyers that could be had, and she was still in fine form. She sailed out into the openness of space, and as the ship went to warp, Keeve drew back the cover on the tiny, oval porthole in the compartment, watching the stars as they streaked past.

Keeve looked to the other man. "Is your father on this transport?"

Bajin shook his head. "No, he isn't."

"He didn't stay behind, did he?"

"Oh, no," Bajin replied. "My parents were among the first to return to Bajor when Jas made the offer to transport us. Father contacted me two days ago, through a third party, to tell me that they had returned to Korto." Bajin's smile faltered. "He said to be in for a bit of shock when we land . . ."

"Yes, so too said Jas Holza."

Keeve was silent for long hours, and the Darrah family spoke among themselves in muted tones, making tentative plans for where they would stay once they arrived on Bajor. Their conversation was heavy with overtones of unspoken hesitation; they were taking a huge risk and committing themselves to the unknown.

"Look." Keeve interrupted the family's uncertain planning to gesture out the small window, for Bajor was visible. It appeared as a bright, green-blue star, but Keeve recognized it immediately from the surrounding constellations.

The two boys tried to peer around Keeve's shoulder, and he rose to his feet so that they could have a better view of the planet as it came closer into view. Gradually, the twinkling speck expanded until Bajor's swirling seas were clearly visible. Everyone in the compartment was rapt as they watched their home planet fill the tiny window.

"We're almost there," Bajin declared, his voice trembling slightly with the emotion he was trying to conceal. He turned to his wife, and she covered his hand with hers. The planet seemed to sparkle like a gem as the ship came closer still, bright with unspoken promise.

"She belongs to us, now," Keeve said, almost to himself, but the others in his compartment turned to him to smile and nod their agreement. "We will never lose her again."

The ship jolted slightly as it tore through Bajor's atmosphere, dropping back to real gravity, and one of the bundles stowed in the compartment above Bajin's head threatened to tumble into Keeve's lap. But the carrier righted itself quickly, and was setting down at Kendra, where most of the passengers were to disembark. Keeve was staying on until he made it to Ashalla. Jaro Essa and Kalem Apren had traveled there already to organize an election for the provisional government.

"Good-bye, Bajin. Good-bye, Cheren." Keeve nodded to the children, whose names he could not immediately recall. He addressed Bajin directly. "Please, tell your father—" He stopped, for he was not sure how to adequately summarize all that he wanted to say. It seemed suddenly too great a task to pass his goodwill on to another resident of the world where he had sought refuge all these years, and Keeve was nearly overcome with the emotion that he had been denying himself since the first rumors began to fly. It hit him all at once, with a stunning, undeniable blow—he was *here,* he was on Bajor. Tears threatened to spill, and Bajin reached out and took his hand.

"I will tell him," Bajin said, a moment of unspoken understanding passing through the two men like an electric current.

Keeve nodded in wordless gratitude, and then Bajin and his family disembarked for their shuttle transport to Korto. The door to the compartment closed once again, leaving Keeve alone to stare out the window, taking in the ruined scenery all around him, the world that would have to be rebuilt. The ship lurched on its thrusters again, to take Keeve Falor to Dahkur. To take him home.

EPILOGUE

The gathering crowd of Bajorans bobbed and swayed, people standing on their toes or swiveling their heads so that they might see over the heads and shoulders of the people in front of them. Their varied dress represented the myriad provinces and walks of life from which they had come, all over the planet. Though a great many were clad in shabby rags or overpatched tunics and dresses, many were wearing the very best clothes they owned for the occasion, and Odo noticed more than a few wearing matching uniforms that he supposed belonged to the newly-restored Militia.

First Minister Kalem Apren had already delivered his inaugural address, and Odo had watched curiously as the people in the crowd reacted to his announcement that the Federation was coming to help. Odo could see right away that this was a sensitive topic for the Bajorans, with many seeming to be fully in favor and others appearing to feel exactly the opposite. Odo had observed a great deal of rather heated exchanges suddenly erupting all over the crowd after the First Minister made his proclamation.

Now another official, who had the unfortunate privilege of following Kalem's volatile announcement, spoke in regard to the reformed Militia, which he had apparently helped to organize. His name was Jaro Essa, and he held a lesser seat on the new Bajoran Council of Ministers. The crowd was much thinner now, many people having moved away from the public oval—it was mostly only members of the militia and their families who had lingered behind to listen to Jaro.

Jaro Essa's voice was distinct and pleasant, but his words held traces of fire, and the portion of the crowd that was still listening responded noisily to his address.

"My Bajoran brothers and sisters—I was here fifty years ago when a group of aliens arrived on our world, with their proposals for a means to help us, to assist us in modernizing our beloved and traditional ways of life—"

Shouts of anger, the older people in the crowd crying out the fiercest.

"But we are wiser now, and never again will we allow any group of outsiders to dictate for us how we are to run our world . . ."

Odo quickly recognized that Jaro's speech was meant to do more than just address the new Militia; apparently he did not agree with his colleague's decision to bring in the Federation, either.

Which may be exactly why we need them . . . If so many Bajorans were in disagreement over how to run their world, was it unlikely that opposing factions would emerge? Could a civil war be on the horizon?

". . . the new Militia is comprised of the very best fighters currently on our world, people who fought bravely and tirelessly for Bajor's freedom . . ."

Odo was troubled at the idea of any conflict lingering behind on Bajor after the Cardassians had finally been chased away, but he laid his concerns temporarily to rest when he recognized the profile of a man in a brown Militia uniform. The Bajoran looked out of place in military clothing instead of a worn tunic, but Odo knew right away that it was Gran Tolo, the man who had been in the resistance on Terok Nor. He hesitated for a moment before deciding to approach him.

"Excuse me. Gran Tolo?" he said hesitantly, and then took an uncertain step back. How would he be remembered by the Bajorans who had been on the station?

"Odo!" Gran replied, looking immediately happy to see the shape-shifter. "Thank the Prophets you managed to get off the station!"

"You've . . . you've joined the Militia," Odo said, at a loss for anything else to say.

Gran smiled, tugging at his new uniform. "Yes, I've been awarded the rank of lieutenant already. It's a bit . . . surreal, I think, but . . . I felt it was the only thing I could do. I've always been a soldier, you see, since I was barely a teenager . . ."

"You'll be an asset to service, I'm certain," Odo said, and he meant it. He hoped Gran could see that he did, but it was often difficult for him to convey his thoughts appropriately, and he could never quite tell if people took him seriously or not.

"What will you do now that the Cardassians are gone?" Gran inquired. "You're out of a job, aren't you?"

Odo looked up at the sky without quite meaning to, for it had occurred to him often since he had smuggled himself off the station that he was now further away from finding his own people than he had been while on the station. It had, of course, occurred to him that if the Federation was coming, there might be a better opportunity to find out where he had come from, but he didn't have the first idea how to pursue that possibility. "I don't know," he finally said.

Gran scrutinized him for a moment as if he were trying to decide what to do with him, and then he said something that Odo would never have considered. "The Militia . . . is always looking for volunteers. If you tell them that you worked on the station—"

Odo scoffed. "They'll have me executed. All known collaborators are to be turned in to the government immediately."

"No, no. Odo, I can vouch for you that you helped the resistance. You did far more good than harm, and I know I'm not the only Bajoran who will say so. You remember Ficen Dobat? He joined the Militia as well, and I know he'll tell Jaro Essa how you helped us all when the detection grid came down for the last time . . ."

Odo thought he remembered Ficen Dobat, but he remembered a few other Bajorans as well—Bajorans whom he had personally committed to death. He worked to keep his face free from emotion, but it was surprisingly difficult after it had become such a habit to associate his emotions with his facial expressions. "Perhaps I *will* join the Militia," he muttered. It was like Gran had said—all he had ever known was to be a soldier. All Odo had ever known was to follow rules, although he had certainly come to question them in the end. But maybe the Militia *could* use him, and perhaps it would give him the opportunity to feel as though he could be forgiven for the sins he had committed while working for the Cardassians.

"I can take you where you need to go, if you're considering it, Odo."

"I am considering it," he said quickly, before he could change his mind, and he began to walk with Gran through the crowds.

"Where will you be stationed?" Odo asked the Bajoran.

"I don't know yet," Gran told him. "I'll be getting my assignment later today. I'm eager to find out what it will be." He let out his breath all at once. "After all, wherever I go, that will be my new home. My parents are dead—I have no one left but those I fought with in the resistance. The Militia . . . will be my new family."

Odo nodded to himself. "New family," he repeated, and saw that they had reached the recruiting office. Outside was a short line of men and women waiting to sign up and serve their world. Odo and Gran took their place in the line, but the people just ahead of them quickly spied Gran's rank designation on his uniform, and moved to allow him to pass ahead of them. He nodded gratefully, and Odo followed the Bajoran inside, suddenly overcome with what Gran had just been saying—he was about to join a new family, just like that. Of course, that all relied on the assumption that the Bajorans wouldn't turn him in as a collaborator. He looked nervously at Gran, who returned a reassuring smile as they passed the line of people outside.

Just before entering the building, Odo looked up at the sky again, thinking of Terok Nor and how it might have been as close as he would ever be to his people. But he shook off the thought as he walked through the double doors that led them inside the temporary headquarters of the Militia, an old, partially destroyed building that had once functioned as the offices of the local lawkeepers. Just as Gran had said, he was suddenly eager. To be part of a new world, and part of a new family—though he knew, on some level, that it would not be as true for him as it would be for Gran. Odo was an outsider, and a Bajoran uniform wouldn't change that fact.

He turned to Gran as he was led inside the building with towering, curved ceilings, all blackened with smoke from the fires that had destroyed the rear portion of the building. The aura of destruction was heavy in the atmosphere, but nobody seemed to be paying attention to it as the volunteers filed toward a wide table of officers. The men and women seated behind the tables tapped away at their keypads while doing retinal scans for each Bajoran as he or she approached the table. Odo suddenly felt very uncomfortable, considering that his physiology would hardly permit the sort of inspection that was likely required for a recruited soldier—until he saw something that astonished him. Kira Nerys, bearing the rank of major, was standing behind one of the tables, her once-tangled hair trimmed and smoothed neatly just beyond her chin, the rigid silhouette of her uniform lending an imposing outline to her slender shoulders.

She looked up from her computer, and recognition instantly flooded her face as she glanced in the direction of Odo and Gran. "Odo!" she cried out. "You're safe!"

"Yes," he said awkwardly, as several people looked to see what the fuss was about. Gran shifted, seeming to know that it was safe to leave Odo on his own, thumping the shape-shifter on the shoulder and backing away.

Kira gestured Odo forward to the spot at her table, and he moved through the smattering of curious onlookers. "Have you come to join the Militia?" she asked, with eagerness in her voice.

"I . . ." Odo began, uncomfortable with this very public reunion.

"I'm to be stationed on Terok Nor," she told him, and then frowned. "Starfleet has been invited to help us administrate it—they'll be renaming it to suit their own agenda, of course." Odo could see that she was not at all pleased with the impending arrival of the Federation, but her face twisted back into a smile without further elaboration. "If you'd like to serve on the station as well, I can probably see to it that you can be appointed to security—"

"Security?" Odo replied with gratitude. "You could . . . you would do that?"

"Of course!" Kira replied emphatically. "Who better to do the job than someone who already knows the station? Odo, it'll be perfect!"

"Yes," he replied with faint confidence, before his own particular brand of self-doubt crept back in. He determinedly overrode it. "Perfect." For a moment, as he watched Kira tap away at her computer console, Odo actually believed it.

Appendices

The following is a guide to many of the specific characters, places, and related material in *Dawn of the Eagles*. Where such an item was mentioned or appeared previously in a movie, episode, or other work of *Star Trek* fiction, its first appearance is cited.

APPENDIX I: BAJOR

Characters

Baj (male) resistance fighter, member of Li Nalas's cell

Bareil Antos (male) priest, a ranjen and follower of Opaka Sulan (DS9/"In the Hands of the Prophets")

Basso Tromac (male) personal aide to Skrain Dukat (DS9/"Wrongs Darker Than Death or Night")

Bek (male) priest, a prylar living aboard Terok Nor; liaison between the Cardassian occupation forces and the Vedek Assembly (DS9/"The Collaborator")

Bestram (male) resistance fighter, member of the Shakaar cell

Chavin (male) resistance fighter, member of the Shakaar cell

Darrah Bajin (male) son of Darrah Mace, resident of Valo II (*Terok Nor: Day of the Vipers*)

Darrah Cheren (female) wife of Darrah Bajin, resident of Valo II

Darrah Mace (male) resident of Valo II, formerly of Korto (*Terok Nor: Day of the Vipers*)

Daul Mirosha (male) former researcher at the Bajoran Institute of Science (*Terok Nor: Night of the Wolves*)

Dava (male) a Kai who lived several hundred years prior to the Cardassian occupation of Bajor

Ficen Dobat (male) resistance fighter on Terok Nor (*TNG/Double Helix: Vectors*)

Furel (male) resistance fighter with the Shakaar cell (DS9/"Shakaar")

Gantt (male) resistance fighter and medic with the Shakaar cell (DS9/"Ties of Blood and Water")

Gran Tolo (male) resistance fighter on Terok Nor

Jaro Essa (male) former militia officer, resident of Kendra Valley and underground political activist (DS9/"The Homecoming")

Jas Holza (male) former minister of Bajor, resident of Valo III (TNG/"Ensign Ro")

Kalem Apren (male) former minister of Bajor; an unofficial leader and underground political activist residing in the Kendra Valley (DS9/"Shakaar")

Kalem Raina (female) second wife of Kalem Apren; her family was part of the influential Lees clan of the Kendra Valley

Kan Nion (male) official of the Cardassian-sanctioned Bajoran government

Keeve Falor (male) resident of Valo II, former member of the Bajoran Chamber of Ministers (TNG/"Ensign Ro")

Kira Meru (female) former mistress of Gul Dukat, mother of Kira Nerys (DS9/"Wrongs Darker Than Death or Night")

Kira Nerys (female) resistance fighter, member of the Shakaar cell (DS9/"Emissary")

Kohn Biran (male) member and co-leader, with Ma Jouvirna, of the Kohn-Ma resistance cell (the Kohn-Ma cell was first mentioned in DS9/"Past Prologue")

Kohn Weir (male) member of the Kohn-Ma resistance cell, younger brother of Kohn Biran

Kubus Oak (male) special liaison between Gul Dukat and the Caradassian-sanctioned Bajoran government (DS9/"The Collaborator")

Latha Mabrin (male) member of the Shakaar resistance cell (DS9/"The Darkness and the Light")

Li Nalas (male) resistance fighter, famed for killing Gul Zarale (DS9/"The Homecoming")

Lupaza (female) resistance fighter, member of the Shakaar cell (DS9/"Shakaar")

Ma Jouvirna (male) member and co-leader, along with Kohn Biran, of the Kohn-Ma resistance cell

Marin (male) priest, member of the Vedek Assembly

Mart (male) resistance fighter, member of Li Nalas's cell

Mirel (female) resistance fighter, member of Li Nalas's cell

Mobara (male) resistance fighter, member of the Shakaar cell (DS9/"Shakaar")

Mora Pol (male) researcher at the Bajoran Institute of Science (DS9/"The Alternate")

Opaka Fasil (male) resistance fighter, son of Opaka Sulan (DS9/"The Collaborator"; his given name was established in *Terok Nor: Night of the Wolves*)

Opaka Sulan (female) kai of the Bajoran faith (DS9/"Emissary"; Opaka's given name was established in *DS9/Rising Son*)

Orta (male) resistance fighter operating outside the B'hava'el system (TNG/"Ensign Ro")

Orthew (male) resistance fighter, member of Li Nalas's cell

Preta (male) priest, member of the Vedek assembly

Riszen Ketauna (male) artist from the town of Yarlin, friend and follower of Opaka Sulan (*Terok Nor: Night of the Wolves*)

Ro Laren (female) former resistance fighter, later Starfleet officer assigned to the *U.S.S. Enterprise* (TNG/"Ensign Ro")

Shakaar Edon (male) resistance fighter, leader of the Shakaar cell (DS9/"Shakaar")

Sharet Ras (female) senior-most member of the Vedek Assembly

Shev (male) friend and follower of Opaka Sulan (*Terok Nor: Night of the Wolves*)

Sito Jaxa (female) daughter of Sito Keral (TNG/"The First Duty")

Sito Keral (male) farmer, resident of Ikreimi village, cousin of Mora Pol

Somah Trac (male) member of the Cardassian-sanctioned Bajoran governing cabinet

Sorash Tem (male) resident of Ikreimi village

Stassen (female) ranjen, daughter of Shev

Tahna Los (male) member of the Kohn-Ma resistance cell (DS9/"Past Prologue")

Tel (male) member of Li Nalas's resistance cell

Trentin Fala (female) informant to the Shakaar resistance cell (DS9/"The Darkness and the Light")

Vaatrik Drasa (male) Bajoran collaborator, proprietor of the chemist's shop on Terok Nor (DS9/"Necessary Evil")

Ver (male) resident of Ikreimi village

Winn Adami (female) priest, youngest member of the Vedek assembly (DS9/"In the Hands of the Prophets")

Places

Ashalla: capital city of Bajor (DS9/*Mission: Gamma, Book One—Twilight*)

Dakeen Monastery: remote religious sanctuary, isolated from outside influence (DS9/"The Collaborator")

Derna: fourth moon of Bajor, former location of a Cardassian military base (DS9/"Image in the Sand"; the base was established in *Terok Nor: Day of the Vipers*)

Elemspur: district in Hedrikspool Province, the location of a detention center run by the Cardassians (DS9/"Second Skin")

Gerhami: Bajoran province

Huvara: Bajoran province, the location of Dr. Moset's hospital

Ilvia: a city in Rakantha Province (DS9/"Babel")

Iwara: village outside Ashalla

Jalanda: population center in Hedrikspool Province (the Jalanda Forum was first mentioned in (DS9/"Sanctuary")

Jeraddo: fifth moon of Bajor; site of the Lunar V base (DS9/"Progress")

Jo'kala: population center in Musilla Province (DS9/"Starship Down")

Kendra Shrine: religious temple in Kendra Valley; the second to be built on the site after the first was destroyed in *Terok Nor: Day of the Vipers* (Kendra Valley first mentioned in DS9/ "The Collaborator"; Kendra Province first mentioned in DS9/"Penumbra")

Korto City: ruined metropolis in Kendra Valley (*Terok Nor: Day of the Vipers*)

Musilla: Bajoran province (DS9/"Things Past")

Petrita: village in Dahkur

Qui'al: city on the northern continent of Bajor, former home of Kubus Oak (the Qui'al Dam is mentioned in DS9/"Destiny")

Renday: Bajoran district

Rihjer: Bajoran district

Serpent's Ridge: high, rocky site in Dahkur Province (DS9/"Shakaar")

Shikina Monastery: religious sanctuary in Ashalla in which was hidden the Orb of Prophecy and Change (DS9/"Emissary"; the monastery's name was established in *DS9/Unity*)

Tempasa: population center in Dahkur Province; location of a Cardassian records office (DS9/"Ties of Blood and Water")

Tilar: a Bajoran peninsula, famous for its temperate climate and beautiful landscape (*DS9/Unity*)

Tozhat: Cardassian settlement on Bajor, governed by Exarch Kotran Pa'Dar, and later by his Yoriv Skyl (DS9/"Cardassians")

Valo II: habitable planet in the Valo system, home to many refugee Bajorans (TNG/"Ensign Ro")

Valo III: Class-M planet in the Valo system, home to Jas Holza (TNG/"Ensign Ro")

Valo VI: barren planetoid in the Valo system, site of a Cardassian listening post (*Terok Nor: Night of the Wolves*)

Vekobet: village in Kendra Valley

Food and Drink

copal: ciderlike alcoholic beverage (*Terok Nor: Day of the Vipers*)

deka tea: hot brewed beverage (DS9/"Wrongs Darker Than Death or Night")

hasperat: spicy Bajoran dish, wrapped in a flatbread (TNG/"Pre-emptive Strike")

jumja: tree with a sticky, sweet sap from which a popular confection is made (DS9/"A Man Alone")

katterpod: edible legume (DS9/ "Shadowplay")

kava root: edible tuber, part of the extremely versatile *kava* plant (DS9/"Starship Down")

makapa: type of bread (DS9/"For the Cause")

synthale: alcoholic beverage common on a number of worlds, including Bajor (DS9/"Emissary")

Other

B'hava'el: the star of Bajor (*Star Trek: Deep Space Nine Technical Manual*)

bell: benchmark of time, similar to "o'clock" (*Terok Nor: Day of the Vipers*)

cadge lupus: large canine predator, similar to a wolf

duranja: ceremonial lamp lit to honor the dead (DS9/"Shakaar")

Fostossa virus: source of an epidemic that swept across Bajor during the occupation (VOY/"Nothing Human")

hara cat: large feline predator (DS9/"Second Skin")

kelbonite: material known to interfere with various types of scanning equipment (TNG/"Silicon Avatar")

kellipate: unit of distance (DS9/"Progress")

kosst: swearword or curse, derived from Kosst Amojan (DS9/"The Reckoning"); however, the word's original meaning was simply "to be" (DS9/"The Assignment")

linnipate: unit of distance, roughly two or three meters (*Terok Nor: Day of the Vipers*)

nyawood: type of wood similar to mahogany (*Terok Nor: Day of the Vipers*)

Orb: also known as a "Tear of the Prophets"; one of several religious artifacts that sometimes impart visions or insights upon those who gaze into them (DS9/"Emissary")

pagh: "life force" as perceived by certain sensitive Bajorans (DS9/"Emissary")

porli **fowl:** a chickenlike food animal (*Terok Nor: Day of the Vipers*)

sinoraptor: an animal known for its fierceness and eyes that face opposite directions (DS9/"Shakaar")

spoonhead: slur used by some Bajorans when referring to a Cardassian (DS9/"Things Past")

tessipate: unit of area (DS9/"Progress")

tyrfox: wily canine predator (*Terok Nor: Day of the Vipers*)

uridium: a mineral that, in its unprocessed state, is highly unstable; uridium ore was processed on Terok Nor (DS9/"Civil Defense")

Religious Ranks

The following is a breakdown of known ranks in the Bajoran religion, in ascending order.

Prylar: a monk

Ranjen: a monk specializing in theological study

Vedek: a high-ranking priest, typically a regional spiritual leader

Kai: the world leader of the Bajoran religion

D'jarra *Caste System*

Until recent times the Bajorans had a series of castes called *D'jarra*s. This is a rough order of ranking for the ones that have been established so far.

Ih'valla: artists (above Te'nari) (DS9/"Accession")

Te'nari: unknown, but below Ih'valla (DS9/"Accession")

Mi'tino: low-ranked merchants and landowners (*Terok Nor: Day of the Vipers*)

Va'telo: pilot, sailor, driver, and similar professions (*Terok Nor: Day of the Vipers*)

Ke'lora: laborers and lawmen (*Terok Nor: Day of the Vipers*)

Sern'apa: unknown (*Terok Nor: Day of the Vipers*)

Imutta: those who deal with the dead; the "unclean" and lowest ranking *d'jarra* (DS9/"Accession")

Resistance Cells

The following is a list of the established Bajoran resistance cells and their areas of operation.

Bram: active in Jo'kala (Musilla Province)
Halpas: active in Relliketh (Hedrikspool Province)
Kintaura: active in Rakantha Province
Kohn-ma: active in Dahkur Province (DS9/"Past Prologue")
Ornathia: active in Tilar Peninsula (Hedrikspool Province)
Shakaar: active in Dahkur Province (DS9/"Duet")

APPENDIX II: CARDASSIA

Characters

Abor, Dost (male) operative of the Obsidian Order, assigned to Valo VI listening post (*Terok Nor: Night of the Wolves*)

Astraea (female) traditional name of the ceremonial "guide" or religious leader for the Oralian Way (*DS9/A Stitch in Time*)

Boheeka (male) military officer stationed on Terok Nor, frequent patron of Quark's bar (DS9/"The Wire")

Bry, Maran (male) controversial Cardassian poet (*DS9/A Stitch in Time*)

Cul (male) scientist replacing Dr. See Yopal as director of the Bajoran Institute of Science

Dalak (male) official of the Cardassian Information Service, superior of Natima Lang (*Terok Nor: Night of the Wolves*)

Damar, Corat (male) military officer formerly attached to Terok Nor (DS9/"Return to Grace")

Darhe'el (male) military officer, former overseer of the Gallitep mining facility on Bajor, political rival of Gul Dukat (DS9/"Duet")

Dukat, Athra (female) wife of Skrain Dukat (*Terok Nor: Day of the Vipers*)

Dukat, Skrain (male) military officer; prefect of Bajor and commander of Terok Nor (DS9/"Emissary"; Dukat's given name was established in the DS9 novel *A Stitch in Time*)

Esad, Kutel (male) operative of the Obsidian Order working directly under Enabran Tain (*Terok Nor: Night of the Wolves*)

Ghemor, Tekeny (male) military officer, member of Central Command and an underground political dissident (DS9/"Second Skin")

Glees, Tera (female) representative of the University of Culat

Iloja (male) exiled Cardassian poet (DS9/"Destiny")

Kaer (male) military officer, forensics analyst stationed on Terok Nor

Kedat (male) military officer, chief of engineering on Terok Nor

Kell, Danig (male) military officer and member of Central Command, direct superior of Skrain Dukat (DS9/"Civil Defense"; Kell's first name was established in *Terok Nor: Day of the Vipers*)

Lang, Natima (female) correspondent for the Cardassian Information Service (DS9/"Profit and Loss")

Letra (male) military officer stationed in security on Terok Nor

Lotor, Ran (male) an educator living on Cardassia Prime

Moset, Crell (male) civilian physician and exobiologist who worked on Bajor during the annexation (VOY/"Nothing Human")

Pa'Dar, Kotan (male) former scientist, later exarch at the Tozhat settlement on Bajor (DS9/"Cardassians")

Panh, Revel (male) faculty member of the exobiology department at the University of Culat

Reyar, Kalisi (female) civilian scientist assigned to Bajor (*Terok Nor: Night of the Wolves*)

Reyar, Yannik (male) civilian liaison between Central Command and the Obsidian Order, father of Kalisi Reyar (*Terok Nor: Night of the Wolves*)

Rike'la (male) military officer stationed on Terok Nor

Russol, Gaten (male) military officer stationed on Terok Nor from 2365–2366 (DS9/"Treachery, Faith and the Great River")

Sa'kat (male) military officer, member of the Oralian Way (*Terok Nor: Night of the Wolves*)

Skyl, Yoriv (male) politician; adjutant to Kotan Pa'Dar, later his successor as exarch of Tozhat

Tain, Enabran (male) head of the Obsidian Order (DS9/"The Wire")

Thrax (male) chief of security on Terok Nor from 2353–2365 (DS9/"Things Past")

Trakad (male) military officer stationed on Terok Nor

Trant, Seia (female) physician stationed on Bajor

Tuken (male) professor from the Cuellar region; political dissident

Vara, Miras (female) civilian scientist who went missing sometime after her exposure to a Bajoran Orb (*Terok Nor: Night of the Wolves*)

Yopal, Sree (female) director of the Bajoran Institute of Science (*Terok Nor: Night of the Wolves*)

Zarale (male) military officer stationed on Bajor, killed by Li Nalas (DS9/"The Homecoming")

Places

Cardassia II: colony, home of Natima Lang and Gaten Russol

Cardassia City: capital city of Cardassia Prime (*DS9/A Stitch in Time*)

Coranum Sector: the oldest and most prestigious district in Cardassia City (*DS9/A Stitch in Time*)

Culat: site of a prestigious university (VOY/"Nothing Human")

Hetrith: site of a station where Dr. Moset spent half of his residency

Lakarian City: population center on Cardassia Prime, site where ancient Hebetian culture was said to have flourished long ago (DS9/"Defiant")

Letau: the innermost moon of Cardassia Prime; site of a maximum-security prison facility once run by Skrain Dukat, and to which he still made periodic visits during his term as prefect of Bajor (*Terok Nor: Night of the Wolves*)

Mekisar: military base outside Cardassia City

Ministry of Science: center of learning and scientific research in Cardassia City (DS9/"Destiny")

Paldar Sector: residential district of Cardassia City (*DS9/A Stitch in Time*)

Sadera: star system that became a refuge for several Cardassian political dissidents (DS9/"Profit and Loss")

Tarlak Sector: administrative hub of Cardassia City (*DS9/A Stitch in Time*)

Terok Nor: space station orbiting Bajor; the main ore-processing facility as of 2346 and the command post for the Bajoran annexation (the station's original name was revealed in DS9/"Cardassians")

Torr Sector: most populated district of Cardassia City; a center of culture (*DS9/A Stitch in Time*)

University of Prekiv: center of learning on Cardassia II, alma mater of Natima Lang

Other

kanar: popular alcoholic beverage (TNG/"The Wounded")

kotra: board game (DS9/"Empok Nor")

lek: denomination of currency (VOY/"Caretaker")

metric: a unit of time, roughly equivalent to a minute (*Terok Nor: Day of the Vipers*)

Obsidian Order: the intelligence bureau of the Cardassian Union (DS9/"The Wire")

Oralian Way: religion dating back to the First Hebitian civilization on Cardassia Prime, forced to go underground during the era of the Bajoran annexation (the Hebitian civilization was first mentioned in TNG/"Chain of Command, Part II"; the Oralian Way was established in the DS9 novel *A Stitch in Time*)

polytrinic acid: chemical used by Dr. Moset in his various experiments (VOY/"Nothing Human")

riding hound: a large canine animal (DS9/"In Purgatory's Shadow")

rokassa **juice:** nonalcoholic beverage with a very distinctive odor (DS9/"Cardassians")

Military Ranks

The following is a list of Cardassian ranks and their Starfleet analogs. This system borrows from the work of Steven Kenson's unpublished *Iron & Ash* supplement for the *Star Trek* Roleplaying Game from Last Unicorn Games.

garresh: noncommissioned officer
gil: ensign
glinn: lieutenant
dalin: lieutenant commander
dal: commander
gul: captain
jagul: commodore/rear admiral
legate: admiral

APPENDIX III: MISCELLANEOUS

Characters

Frool (Ferengi male) waiter in Quark's bar on Terok Nor (DS9/"Bar Association")

Gaila (Ferengi male) cousin of Quark (Gaila was first mentioned in DS9/"Civil Defense" and was first seen in DS9/"Business as Usual")

Gart (Ferengi male) DaiMon, or Captain, of a freight vessel (*Terok Nor: Night of the Wolves*)

Gera (Ferengi female) sister of a district sub-nagus with whom Quark was sexually involved (this dalliance was established in DS9/"Playing God," though the name of the woman was never given)

Hagath (male, species unknown) weapons merchant; business partner of Gaila (DS9/"Business as Usual")

Ishka (Ferengi female) mother of Quark, sometimes called "moogie" by her sons (DS9/"Family Business")

Kurga (Ferengi male) member of Gart's crew

Morn (Lurian male) freighter captain; frequent customer at Quark's bar on Terok Nor (Morn first appeared in DS9/"Emissary," but was not named until DS9/"Vortex")

Nechayev, Alynna (human female) Starfleet admiral (TNG/"Chain of Command, Part I")

Nog (Ferengi male) son of Rom, nephew of Quark (DS9/"Emissary")

Odo shape-shifting being of unknown origin, recruited by Gul Dukat to replace Thrax as Terok Nor's chief of security (DS9/"Emissary")

Quark (Ferengi male) cook on Gart's freighter, later proprietor of a bar on Terok Nor (DS9/"Emissary")

Rom (Ferengi male) brother of Quark, father of Nog (DS9/"Emissary")

Vaughn, Elias (human male) Starfleet special operative (*DS9/Avatar, Book One*)

Other

Boslics: spacefaring species with which Quark has done business (Boslics were first mentioned in DS9/"Homecoming" and were first seen in DS9/"The Abandoned")

Ferengi: spacefaring species known mainly for their pursuit of profit (TNG/"The Last Outpost") *gree* **worms:** edible soft-bodied invertebrates favored by the Ferengi (DS9/"Little Green Men")

Jibetians: spacefaring species with which Quark has done business

Kobheerians: spacefaring species with which Quark has done business (DS9/"Duet")

latinum: precious metal, typically pressed with gold and used as a medium of exchange in certain parts of the Alpha Quadrant (DS9/"Past Prologue")

milcake: pan-fried cake of unspecified origin, made from rough-cut grains

plomeek: a Vulcan vegetable, best known for its use in soup (TOS/"Amok Time")

sargam: slightly bittersweet foodstuff of unspecified origin, usually cut into fillets that are easy to transport and eat

Solvok: star system near Bajoran space

Tarulians: spacefaring species with which Quark has done business

About the Authors

S. D. (Stephani Danelle) Perry writes multimedia novelizations in the fantasy/science fiction/horror realms, for love and money. S. D. lives in Portland, Oregon, with her excellent family, and is working on an original thriller in her spare time, of which she has very little.

Britta Dennison is a writer living in Portland, Oregon, with her husband and two daughters.

Printed in the United States
By Bookmasters